CHAUCER'S TRIUMPH

By the Same Author

Le Théâtre en Grande-Bretagne

French Theatre Today

Different Circumstances (play)

Dialogue Between Friends (play)

The Pursuit of Perfection: A Life of Maggie Teyte

Ralph Richardson: An Actor's Life

Darlings of the Gods: One Year in the
    Lives of Laurence Olivier and Vivien Leigh

Olivier: In Celebration (editor)

Sean O'Casey: A Life

The Mahabharata

Darlings of the Gods (novel)

William Shakespeare: A Life

Campion's Ghost: The Sacred and Profane Memories
    of John Donne, Poet (novel)

Alec Guinness: Master of Disguise

The Secret Woman: A Life of Peggy Ashcroft

William Shakespeare: A Popular Life

Paul Scofield: The Biography

Alec Guinness, The Unknown: A Life

Universal Father: A Life of Pope John Paul II

Chaucer's Triumph

*Including the case of Cecilia Chaumpaigne,
the seduction of Katherine Swynford, the murder
of her husband, the interment of John of Gaunt
and other offices of the flesh in the year 1399*

Garry O'Connor

Petrak
Press

Copyright © Garry O'Connor 2007
First published in 2007 by Petrak Press
4 Avonmore Mansions, Avonmore Road, London W14 8RN

Distributed by Gazelle Book Services Limited
Hightown, White Cross Mills, South Rd
Lancaster, England LA1 4XS

With the exception of many well-known historical figures, the other characters in this book are fictitious and any resemblance to actual people, living or dead, is purely imaginary.

British Library Cataloguing in Publication Data
A catalogue record for this book is available from
the British Library.

ISBN 978-0-9553768-0-1

Typeset by Amolibros, Milverton, Somerset
This book production has been managed by Amolibros
Printed and bound by T J International Ltd,
Padstow, Cornwall, UK

To Peter and Juliet

Cast of Characters:

Edward III, king
Philippa of Hainault, queen of Edward III
Edward of Woodstock, prince of Wales, Edward's first son (The Black
  Prince)
Lionel of Antwerp, duke of Clarence, Edward's second son
John of Gaunt, duke of Lancaster, king of Castile, Edward's third
  son (Lord John)
Edmund of Langley, earl of Cambridge, duke of York, Edward's
  fourth son
Thomas of Woodstock, earl of Buckingham, duke of Gloucester,
  Edward's fifth son
Blanche of Lancaster, John of Gaunt's first wife
Constanza of Castile, John's second wife
Katherine Payne de Roet, Lady Swynford, John's mistress and third
  wife
Henry of Bolingbroke, John's first son, earl of Derby, later Henry IV
Philippa, John's daughter, later queen of Portugal
Elizabeth, John's third child, Lady Essex, later Lady Huntingdon
Geoffrey Chaucer, the poet
Philippa Chaucer, his wife, née Payne de Roet (Katherine's sister)
Sir Hugh Swynford, first husband of Katherine Payne de Roet
Thomas Swynford, later knighted, his son from Katherine
Petronella Swynford, his daughter from Katherine
Thomas Chaucer, son of the poet
Lewis Chaucer, son of the poet
Adam Scriven, Chaucer's scrivener or copyist
John Beaufort, illegitimate son of Katherine and Lord John, later
  earl of Somerset, direct predecessor of Henry VII and the Tudor,
  Stuart, Hanover, and Stuart Houses
Henry Beaufort, as above, later Cardinal Beaufort

Thomas Beaufort, as above

Joan Beaufort, illegitimate daughter of Katherine and Lord John, wife of Sir Robert Ferrers (1), Ralph Neville, earl of Westmoreland (2)

Richard of Bordeaux, son of the Black Prince, King Richard II

William Scrope, earl of Wiltshire

Bushy, Green: followers of King Richard

Sir Walter Bagot

Brother Thomas Walsingham, abbot of St Albans

Sister Pervil, attendant of Katherine Swynford

Rachel Dempsey, Philippa Chaucer's gentlewoman

Basil, gatehouse guard at Leicester Castle

Dickie, Yole, Wade, Perkin: Cheshire archers, followers of Scrope

Alice Perrers, mistress of Edward III, sometime rumoured mother of Cecilia Chaumpaigne

Bartholomew Attechapel, the poet's stepfather

Sir Trevor Bair, Sir Jonathan Abel: followers of Swynford

England & Wales C. 1399

Estimate of Population
2-3 million

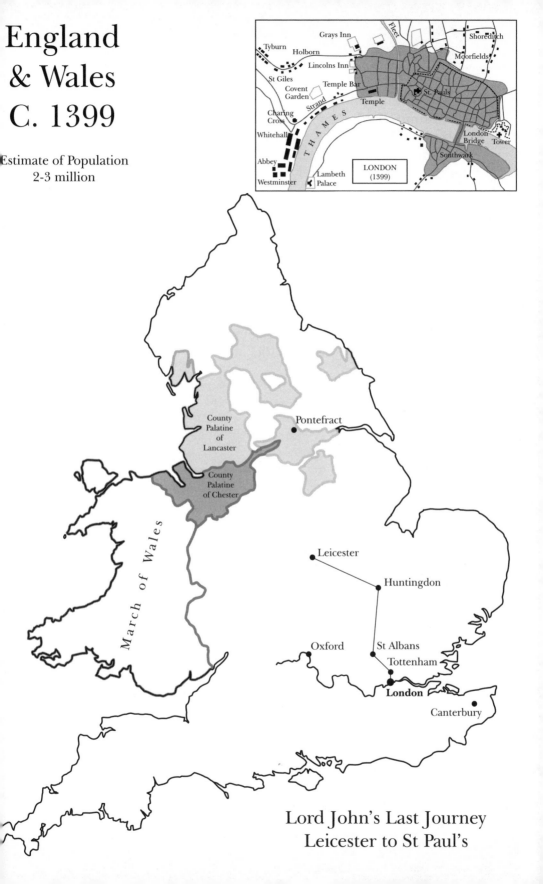

LONDON
(1399)

Tyburn
Grays Inn
Shoreditch
Holborn
Moorfields
St Giles
Lincolns Inn
Covent Garden
Temple Bar
St. Pauls
Charing Cross
Strand
Temple
London Bridge
Whitehall
THAMES
Tower
Abbey
Southwark
Lambeth Palace
Westminster

Pontefract

County Palatine of Lancaster

County Palatine of Chester

March of Wales

Leicester

Huntingdon

Oxford

St Albans

Tottenham

London

Canterbury

Lord John's Last Journey
Leicester to St Paul's

PART ONE

ONE

Adam Scriven

THE BIER OF DUKE John of Lancaster stood in the centre of the chancel, and on it lay what was left of this mighty prince from the Age of Chivalry.

Like most people I was of two minds about Lord John who, from the name of his birth place Ghent in the duchy of Brabant, was more familiarly called John of Gaunt. Most people hated him, by which I mean most of the common people, the majority, and he used to keep them at a distance, so they considered him cold, conceited, and disagreeable. But even among these Lord John knew how to take his stand, and they respected him and feared him. However, for a more active and vocal part of that majority, he was a prince of evil action, and a lifelong adulterer.

But there were many others who served him and profited from his support and patronage, who listened to him, admired him and imitated him, and with them Lord John was pleasant and natural. They still had nothing but good to say about him. There was little doubt he had some of the supreme mental, and some of the finest character, or princely, qualities. His memory was superb, he was an able administrator, he rarely forgot an opportunity to be kind or to reward a follower for services performed. He was cultured, well-spoken, attractive and so on and so forth, responsive to learning and to religious feeling, and a great discerner of talent in others, surrounding himself with the best people, and although he had little time to share for them, yet they were still drawn to him.

Lord John had the Plantagenet features, we called them 'high majestic', with piercing eyes, a long nose on a narrow face and wavy hair between red and gold in colour – darker than his older brother,

3

the Black Prince, who was fair and wore black armour to enhance that fairness. They were all vain when it came to appearance. But while no one could deny that John had the best brain of all, this was not what a woman looked for first. He cut, of all the king's sons, the most handsome figure. He was tall, he was lean, without the bulky spread of his ill-fated brother Lionel of Antwerp, who died young, or the spindly shape of the younger Edmund of Langley, who was duke of York. He looked every inch the warrior prince, yet unlike Edward of Woodstock, he could be merciful in battle.

No one in Europe rose to be his equal, and certainly not Richard II, our present monarch who had only ever ruled by virtue of Lord John's support. Fourth child of the great warrior Plantagenet Edward III, commander of the 'great chevauchee' – as they named that futile and bloody advance through all of France from Calais to Bordeaux – duke of Guyenne and earl of Richmond, brother of the Black Prince, father-in-law to the king of Portugal, king of Castile and Leon, (and as such bearer of that most mysterious appellation, 'Monsieur d'Espagne')…and all the other high-sounding ejectamenta, Lord John had everything a man could desire, while no one could ever have earned more worldly renown.

Yet here he was. Dead. And here we were. Alive. His equals. His baleful, fish-like eyes gaped at us. We had, however little, much more than he had now. What good to him were his titles as he rotted on a bier?

When I had reached the castle chapel there were already many friars in their accustomed places for vespers. I had never seen so many censers, basins, and candlesticks. By general reputation and in spite of all the masses, prayers, intercessions, and money that had been lavished from his coffers to benefit the clergy and the poor, the general consensus was that his soul still had some way to go before it reached heaven.

In anticipation of this, and to ease it from an uncomfortable lingering in purgatory, John had commanded his body should be exposed for forty days before its entombment in the cathedral of St Paul. We were due to leave here tomorrow, stopping on the way at Huntingdon and then at St Albans. Like Our Saviour in the wilderness, Lord John chose forty days to redeem his soul. Or maybe he had Noah's flood in mind, hoping at last to spy dry land. Would it work? This was the thirty-sixth day. All I could report thus far was that as yet little by way of purification had entered the air. Not even

4

a whiff, a shiver, or as the French might say, a soupçon. As he lay on his back in his resplendent robes which concealed the rotting flesh, and in the same position he put so many women (first his three duchesses, most frequently Katherine, Lady Swynford, the last of the three, and nameless others), were we supposed to cringe and wither at the degrading sight and smell of so many years spent in turbulent fornication? Were we to sing hymns of glory and celebration at his eventual redemption?

I was not sure. From the reek of decomposing fens and dead carrion carcasses which pervaded the chapel you might well say the oft-performed luxury of Lord John during his lifetime had set off the bloat and decay at a gallop. I was close to feeling sick from the smell…

Many years earlier

LORD JOHN OF LANCASTER: Over the canopy of the loge fluttered our fleur-de-lys and leopard flag. Over the loge itself, on a wooden mount, stood the statue of great Mars, in whose image my father the king had once triumphantly fashioned himself – armed, grim, full of the dark imaginings of pride and felony, as well as of chivalry and glory; cruel anger, red as a live coal – such as when he won renown at Crécy and Poitiers. But alas, this image of him had become tarnished in the eyes of his people.

My esquire Mr Chaucer, and his young scribe Adam, were there in the loge adjoining my father's: soft, well-perfumed courtiers, young both in years and appearance, although Chaucer had already served in the French wars and been taken a prisoner at the siege of Rheims before being ransomed. He worshipped me. He worshipped Blanche, my wife, even more. They stood among the court women, who were sweet and damasked in their fragrancy.

I rejoiced in the new beauties who were at the tournament field for their first tilt. Among these were Philippa de Roet, and her younger sister, Katherine, both convent-educated Lancastrian women, both in service to me and my duchess Blanche. Delightfully good-looking, both of them. Philippa was a pert, hard creature of much distinction and beauty, whose father, Sir Payne de Roet, had been a valiant knight and a master-at-arms in France. She was aged eighteen, a pretty mistress – mine, I have to confess, that is – but on the flighty and inconstant side, too sharp by half – which is why I had in mind an amusing purpose for Chaucer.

Philippa and her sister were young women whose beauty was without peer. Even Joan, my sister-in-law, married to Edward, couldn't surpass them in her attraction although her former description as this kingdom's fairest woman came also with her reputation for being the most wily and amorous, which is how – although older than Edward and twice married – she entrapped my brother.

Katherine de Roet, two years younger than Philippa, was yet unstained by ill report. Should I go on about Katherine de Roet? This day of the joust she provoked considerable trouble, although I can hardly hold her to blame for what happened.

As for Philippa, it was Chaucer who witnessed one of our secret meetings together, to his own gain or loss, which is not for me to say. This happened in the previous summer when he must have been working late in the Savoy palace, and came to refresh himself in the cool air of my garden. Chaucer was always appreciative of being able to work in my household until the small hours, drawing on the great store of candles. With stick in hand, all but invisible in his dark cloak, he was making his circuit on this hot night when he came to my secret garden which few apart from he and I ever used. I myself have observed Mr Chaucer here, looking up fondly towards the window of Blanche's chamber. No doubt he did this much while I was away, and fired the shafts of the love he felt into 'The Romaunt of the Rose', and his other ballads and poems. Ladies with golden hair, blue eyes, and rosebud mouths would always be present in Chaucer's mind, and he would breed these from his chaste and ennobling feelings of love towards my wife Blanche as he gazed upwards to her window. If she inspired his imaginative efforts to pluck the most beautiful rose of all, why should I mind?

I heard once of a jealous lord who killed his wife's favourite troubadour, and had the dead man's heart served up to her on a dish. The lady ate it without knowing what it was. When her lord told her, 'Sir,' she said, 'you have given me such a delightful dish that never will I partake of any other' – and she threw herself out of the window of the keep. In contrast to this tale I suffered no jealous feelings towards troubadours. Why should I? They depended on my patronage, and if they offended I could easily sever any connection with them. I trusted Chaucer. He knew his place, and Blanche was a faithful wife. I myself aspired towards faithfulness but could not achieve it on this particular night. This is why in my aspiration to become a faithful friend, I conceived my plan for Chaucer.

Chaucer, opening the garden gate, crept carefully and with muffled steps up the path between the rose beds. I did not hear him, nor did Philippa. But his ear must have registered, from the grass under the branches, my hot and snatched, panting breath, and the sound of kissing.

I looked up. Chaucer had stopped, utterly dumbfounded, no doubt his first impulse being to smash his stick down on these animals writhing on the lawn, defiling the sacred retreat of his poetic love. In the blackness of that night he must have glimpsed a flash of white skirt and heard a dazed voice gasping, 'Oh yes… . Oh yes…' which was that of Philippa. I have to admit that the man with the dark mane doing the pumping and sweating was none other than me. Stunned with recognition of this fact, Chaucer stole away.

From then on I could ascertain that Philippa de Roet began to haunt Chaucer's mind. Up till then, although he saw much of her by day around the Savoy, he had hardly noticed her among the other court beauties. He started to harbour desire towards her like a man, not as a poet, for she had deceived him with her separate life, one side chaste and severe, blushing with eyes downcast as they passed each other, at night different altogether, skirts up in the garden and down in the grass, saint turned to beast. It seemed that the more intensely he knew her secret, knew her and my secret, the more Philippa became attractive to him. Did he find himself drawn to her because she was mine – if only now and again – captured by the form of her limbs and hidden parts which he'd seen and heard so active?

Beggars and bear-warders selling tickets for the next baiting, mingled their trade and deceits among the shepherds, labourers, and peasants. They turned to cheer a proud young knight who trotted past up to the ladies' loge, with a token for a lady.

She wore a simple, straight-cut dress of pale blue. Her dark hair set off blue-green eyes of undersea depth and beauty. They had an unusual power, and they pierced my soul. More mundanely I considered what a tender young maidenhead she must also possess hidden away, and wanted it myself.

I pretended not to know her. Turning away I was disturbed by a new contestant storming down upon me. A thick-set knight on a large and clumsy-looking destrier jerked it up suddenly, so its hooves skidded to a halt. I saw Philippa quickly seize another bloom, as if to cover an omission, deftly place it in her sister's hand, spitting in the same moment a warning to Katherine who now, with a more assured poise, threw the flower towards the knight.

When I recognized this knight I understood the reason for Philippa's action. It was Sir Hugh de Swynford, an irritable, grumpy old Saxon of poor means, sworn to serve my house. He was, as I knew, Katherine's intended. I could see Chaucer square his shoulders with apprehension. He also was not at all enamoured of the knight. 'God help the poor girl,' I thought, for Philippa my mother had agreed that he should have her hand. Yet had the girl the name and means to do any better? With amusement I noted that her flower went astray, hitting Swynford on the breastplate, whereupon the huge Saxon caught the flower, crushing the petals, and pulled his giant war-horse away to trot up beside me, his master, like a faithful hound. He asked gruffly if he might tilt against the knight who had sought Katherine's favour. He and I wrangled some moments, and then I rebuked him for trying to make this into a personal joust, while our snorting beasts champed at the bit.

Events moved on, and distracted us. The trumpets sounded, the crowd hushed, while the marshals of the field rose up to announce that twenty knights on each side were to tilt. Swynford and I joined my side. The heralds gave the word and leapt over the barriers. At both ends of the field the forty horses started as if sparked by a flint and the jousters took in huge gulps of air, heaving upward on their lances. A pause, a suspended moment, as this rolling double cloud from each end pounded down upon the centre loge where the ladies hid their eyes and gave frightened cries. And so we met with a crushing roar and thud, lance to lance, destrier to destrier, as Chaucer described it later in my favourite tale: shafts of twenty foot shivering to pieces upon shields, hearts pricked, silver bright swords shredding and hewing helmets, mighty maces breaking bones, thick blood bursting out in red streams – except in my case and this instance I did not break a lance or even connect with my opposite number, my brother Lionel, at all. I emerged from the thrashing pandemonium of the mêlée completely untouched, trotting bewildered back to my own side. How my father, hidden in his loge behind a screen, where he could both watch, and engage in dalliance with his mistress Alice, must be laughing. I moved to the grooms for a fresh charger, raised my vizor and surveyed the scene. The fickle crowd had eyes for the thrashing spectacle of men and horses only a brief while, for they had spotted a different sport – or at least a sizeable number of them had – discovering a wanted man in their midst.

There was shouting and like a pack of hounds, with horsemen at hand uncovering a fox, the more brutal members had disclosed a religious dissenter.

One was shouting, 'I smell a Lollard', and the others straightaway stirred like an angry swarm of bees to do harm to this poor priest or dissenting clerical type, pale and underfed, dressed in a hairy and rough skirt and clogs. They now set about dragging him off from the throng, shouting questions and insults at him, such as why he preached the heresy of no confession and no penances. They pulled him over to a tree, and with a length of rope began to string him up. I wondered if I should intervene, yet on the field something then happened of even greater urgency.

The young knight, who had received the token lily from Katherine de Roet lay prostrate, a dark stain under one shoulder from which blood oozed. Swynford had sought him out, and knocked him from his mount. I kicked forward my own horse to separate that fearsome Saxon suitor from goring his rival to death.

Unsteadily the young knight regained his feet. The foil, ordered by the field marshals to blunt the killing edge of swords, had detached itself from Sir Hugh's sword as Sir Hugh now began to batter down blow upon blow on his weaker foe. Lunging and swiping he forced the younger, slighter knight to his knees, although his victim resisted to the utmost. Surely the young knight's death was imminent, and from such a one as Sir Hugh Swynford would his pride ever permit him to beg mercy? Hatred of warriors is loving. Their appetite for the death of the other has even been described as a desire for union.

I had no choice. Disobeying rules of chivalry carried the death penalty. Even I could not interfere on horseback to part them, but had to halt my horse and jump down to face Swynford on equal footing. Standing as protector before the young knight I unsheathed my sword. The crowd, swayed this way and that, looked to my father for leadership, to the heralds to blow trumpets, even for some intervention from Mars or Venus – or from the English weather, which remained benign and unruffled.

I was momentarily confused. No prince of royal blood could, according to the rules of chivalry, take on a common knight, yet man to man, face to face, we were breathing hard, our mouths dripping with saliva. I ordered Swynford to leave the field, while he, beside himself with rage, dared even to defy me. His huge, barrel-chested frame heaved like a bark about to split. I warned him sternly again not to be such a fool, and that it would be manly to withdraw out of respect for my rank. But would he? My own sword was masked in foil, but few swordsmen even in France and Spain could have bested me in combat.

At this juncture I could not resist casting a sidelong glance at the de Roet sisters. They really were gorgeous creatures, worth a death several times over. If only they could have seen that I was amused rather than mortified at this grim episode. I'd have wagered that they wished they had never been born!

The outcome was that I swiftly disarmed Sir Hugh, and two of my followers, vividly blue and white in their attire, led the sullen knight from the lists.

Chaucer waved cheerfully to me. His countenance was smiling. Having witnessed these gruesome sights without losing any of his genial air, the sunfulness of his own spirit had an alchemy of transforming all that was dark and evil to joviality and good sense. That's why I loved him so. We were partners of a kind. Accomplices.

TWO

Scriven

BUT THE SMELL OF Lord John of Lancaster's rotting corpse had no such effect on my master. Perhaps the reason was that he did not mind the odour of lust, and if so we could hazard the reason why – from his own record in that department. His face creased in a smile and I had always noted his appetite for a good funeral, although we still had four days to go for this one.

Earlier, when I entered his cell in Castle House, he was stretched on the pallet. Nothing was so sad, in my opinion, as the devastation wrought by age. My master was of the same age as Lord John, yet while Lord John had remained, even in death, thin, and as one of his titles suggested tall and gaunt, my master had spread uncomfortably from the middle outwards, and had to struggle up and down the stairs unevenly, with hoarse and broken sounds of breathing. He still acted outwardly very much his old self, reserving only his private moods and thoughts for me. He seemed more and more morbidly pre-occupied with remorse, which he temporarily assuaged with large draughts from the wine flask.

It should have been his finest hour, for his relations, close to those of John, were assembling for the journey which we were due to begin tomorrow for London, and the final entombment of his master. But perhaps he had worked too hard. Perhaps he had worn himself out with the effort of creation, for he had written one after another, over the past years, the renowned Canterbury Tales, and even now insisted on adding to them another, the Parson's Tale, which I am afraid was not so carefree, or jolly as the rest. It was not so much a tale as a sermon, and a frightening and apocalyptic one at that, full of guilt, remorse, and the profession of virtue. I'd half a mind to ask what was troubling him so after all these years (as if I didn't suspect), but I knew how secretive he was, and had ever been, in talking directly of his own life and feelings.

But now, like a bird back upon its perch, he observed and listened, keeping his eyes half closed. Clad in black robes he wore his hood well down while his left hand clutched a rosary, and the quill case, badge of his trade, hung on his chest. Mischievously, in the restrained line of his mouth, there danced a gentle temper as he nodded attentively to the relations and retainers who filed past. Could there be more than there have been already? They nodded back in deference towards my master, they bent their knees in supplication almost as fawningly as they had when Lord John was alive, for my master was now something of a power to be reckoned with; as brother-in-law to Lord John, he had been as close to him as any commoner could be.

What were they hoping for? Was it the will, to be published tomorrow, before we left for London? It was too late to do anything about this now. My master eased himself nearer to his patron and protector's corpse, perhaps sweetened to the putrefying savour by the scent of candles burning round it. Ten of these jumped and shivered, one for each of the Ten Commandments broken. There were seven more above these in honour of the seven works of charity, and seven for what his detractors would deem his favourite companions, the seven deadly sins. Above these the candles became larger and larger: five for the five wounds of Jesus, three for the blessed Trinity, and the final and crowning flame for the omnipotent reality of our life upon earth. But would they be enough to redeem Lord John? We would see, for if they were to, surely there would be some sign.

My master turned from the body, whispered to me quietly and warmly: 'And so, Adam, what did the good lady Rachel tell you about my wife that you didn't know already?'

I was not prepared to give him an account of my meeting with Rachel Dempsey, which had taken place just before we had been summoned for vespers and the vigil. 'Oh lordy, lordy,' had said my old mistress's former maid, 'is it you Adam, whom I always tried to feed up because of those tinny ribs of yours? What a man you are now, and an educated clerk at that. Come, let me give you a big kiss.'

A great wet slobbering one. I had recoiled at the musty smell of ageing female flesh. Urgh! This meeting took place in a room up at the top of one of the towers of the castle where I had found old Rachel, bent and hobbling with the ravages of time. How she mounted these stairs at her age I could not tell, for even in my mistress's service I remember she was much older than my mistress.

'Well, my master Mr Chaucer still makes good use of me. I have served him now these thirty years or more – and look.' I showed Rachel my quill fingers, all calloused and hardened with plying my pen in the furthering of his fame and glory. 'I fear sometimes I may not be able to go on doing this for ever. And yet what pension will a copyist ever receive? It is different in Italy, where such men as I have much more recognition for their calling. Here in England the written word is hardly respected.'

'But you must be well rewarded to send me money to make the journey here, Adam. And look, I have brought my finery along too, to honour our great Lord of Lancaster.' She had pointed to her dress and girdle, and red head-dress laid out on the chair, much more elaborately made than might have been expected for one of her station. 'Look here,' she winked at me. 'My lady Chaucer left me all her clothes in her will, and it is fitting I should wear them one last time in honour of the duke. Do you talk much with Mr Chaucer?'

'Of course, Rachel, I am with him always.'

'And so you are, Adam you are, so you ever were, and will always be: what would he do without you? You must know all his secrets, eh?' and she laughed, for be sure, she has kept a mischievous eye, and a rich fruity laugh.

'No, I don't know his secrets, not the important ones.'

She laughed again. 'I can tell you more than a thing or two! Thirteen years ago my mistress died, and yet I remember her sharp voice as if it is here now ringing in my ears. Oh she were a character, were my mistress...'

PHILIPPA: 'Will you ride with me?' asked Geoffrey Chaucer, a young courtier of my king's household, who as I knew had once been a page, then a soldier, then a valet, and now aspired to be an esquire of less degree, an armiger and scutifer. We stood facing one another in an outer courtyard of the Savoy Palace.

Although a mere vintner's son, his father John, as I also knew, had friends at court, and supplied the king with wine. Mr Chaucer was short, had charming bright eyes in what was still a very childish face; he was much liked by the ladies at court for his engaging and witty mind, and for the gallantry of his love poems. But how could he, with his sword scraping the ground as he walked, compare with my lord of Lancaster? In his paltock or short cloak, his red and black breeches and shining shoes, his face might glow with precocious wisdom, his tongue beguile with melodious verse. But how could this sweet, elvish servant who looked slightly ridiculous, measure up as a rival in my affections for the duke?

Even forgetting his position as a royal prince, no one could help but admire my lord of Lancaster for his qualities. In war, it is true, his reputation fell below that of Edward, his elder brother. But they say with good cause the Black Prince, for all the good queen's nurturing of him – feeding him for years on her own breast which provoked much mirth, and was contrary to the usual habit of great ladies – was a butcher, sparing neither woman nor infant.

My lord was very different; in war he was the soul of courtesy and chivalry, sparing lives, praising his enemies' courage, and conducting his campaigns with fairness and consideration. I make no claim that he did not pillage and plunder like the rest, nor take enemy mistresses to his bed, as was his right, but he stopped short of needless killing.

I stood watching Lord John take leave of his duchess, forgetting his young valet's attention. I, of all the hand-maidens and ladies-in-waiting, was inclined to weep to see him go. But I kept myself back from any public display.

The herald sounded the departure. My lord trotted away to where his troop awaited him to join the other caparisoned and armoured knights. I turned to this diminutive figure of a poet who desired my attention. Lord John's first son, Henry Derby, aged five months, lay in the nurse's arms; his little daughters, Philippa and Elizabeth, aged six and two, stood solemnly with their governess not crying, not afraid for their father's safety. No one seemed concerned that he could die, or be captured, for there clung to him a certainty, if not of victory, at least of survival. Far away as I had been in my thoughts of my lord and his favours – and he had just made me the present of silver buttons and a buckle – I had no idea that only hours before his departure he had cruelly and unscrupulously cast me off. Later I found out that he had called this esquire Chaucer to wait on him, then had had the barefaced cheek to order Mr Chaucer to marry me.

This young man must have known it was nothing for great lords such as John of Gaunt to marry off their sweethearts to commoners, yet still expect them to minister to their pleasure. To put it more callously, although perhaps a little unladylike of me, the city vintner's son, the clerk or poet with ink-stained fingers, probably had, in the calculations of John of Gaunt, his price. What made me bitter was to think that my lord might easily have offered him a knighthood in exchange for the horns of a cuckold. Bitter, on a second count, that Geoffrey should have refused the offer.

I discovered later that Geoffrey had answered, much to my incomprehension, that he would like the opportunity to woo me himself. Geoffrey informed me of this. He pointed out that I would never make a good wife unless I gave my willing consent to marriage. I cannot say. Arranged marriages, such as that of the king to Queen Philippa, my lord Lancaster to Blanche, can work satisfactorily, but I was never prepared to agree to one myself. Not to Geoffrey Chaucer anyway.

My lord could not understand. Lady Blanche, without any wooing at all, had made him such a good and obedient wife, born him six children in seven years – three had died in birth – even without anything like his consent or hers. The immense dowry of land and money she brought with her had carried some weight. Her father had simply drawn up the contract – he worshipped King Edward – consigning the richest lands in England into the duke's possession.

The terms agreed between Geoffrey and Lord John were less profitable. He was to have a year to win and woo me. That was all. He would continue his yearly retainer of ten pounds. Desirous as ever to be entertained when not engaged in leading an army, my lord was inclined to see sport in this proposal. I was to be the football.

'Yes, Mr Chaucer...' I replied distantly but politely. 'But why a ride?'

He looked so unsure of himself. He answered, 'Lord John has offered the use of Hubert.'

I laughed heartily; this was funny. I didn't intend to be cruel, but this is how it must have seemed, meaning it was beyond this poor poet's skill even to ride John of Gaunt's favourite – and, I might add, docile – saddle-horse.

'Are you sure?'

'Of course I'm sure,' he answered.

'Sure you won't slip off, I mean. Hubert's a big animal.'

I could see this hurt him. I do not know why, but something egged me on to tease and goad his temper. I knew that he had once fought for the duke of Clarence in France, where he was captured at the failed siege of Rheims. I made no comment about this.

We met next morning to ride out for Blackheath. I noticed that he had tried to do something to redress the imbalance between my lord and himself, for he sat astride Hubert with a very conscious composure and dignity. He was dressed in his finest town clothes; a doublet of slashed silk and shining hose, leaving his court clothes behind, as if deliberately not to disguise the fact that he was a commoner.

'Where is your sister Katherine?' he asked. 'I thought you meant to bring her along with you on our ride.'

We had discussed this yesterday, but my sister had been ill in the night with vomiting, and she lay in bed, unwilling to move. I told Geoffrey of this circumstance, adding that I'd sent for the monk who was the duke's own physician.

Chaucer looked pained: 'Not him,' he sighed, 'the rumour is that his principal physic consists of ministering potions to rid our gracious lord of unwanted friends. Without the duke's knowledge and consent, I hasten to add. I would not put it past Brother Finiston of having some similar design upon your sister.'

'Why do you say that?' I asked, suddenly anxious for Katherine's safety.

'Anyone is anathema to one who believes, like St Paul, the sexual instinct is troublesome and hostile to the spirit.' I must have looked confused, for Geoffrey went on:

' "Let those who have wives live as though they had none" – to which St Augustine added, "A man by his very nature is ashamed of sexual desire".'

I was not altogether sure Geoffrey sympathized with what he was saying, for he gave me a queer, ironical look, and he was smiling, as if his words also contained an invitation.

Geoffrey was very learned and had read, as I knew, a great number of books. But then so had Lord John, who was the most learned of the Plantagenet princes.

'Perhaps you should point this out to her yourself – if you know of these matters. And advise her accordingly.'

'I shall be only too happy,' he answered. And so he did later, helping to cure her not by consulting the phases of the moons, but with sensible medicine of herbs, and resting.

'Now,' I continued, 'weren't you going to tell me about the Plantagenet family – and their connection with your own…?'

This was the offer of a history lesson for which I had agreed to this ride. He cleared his throat. We were trotting gently on. I suspected that his purpose was to dislodge Lord John from the citadel of my affections, but he would have a hard job to budge him from there. Stories about how evil or disreputable a person is, often serve only to enhance their attraction.

'Ah,' he began, 'the Chaucer connection with the Plantagenets…' I should have seen that this was to become a main theme of Geoffrey's life. But I did not spot this until later.

'It started some fourteen years before my birth, when Isabella, the great French queen of this land, who was our present royal king's mother, and who was known as "The she-wolf of France", invaded this country with the earl of Mortimer, her lover, and a French army of two thousand men…'

'You mean the English queen was French?…' I gurgled. I was not the slightest bit interested.

He looked at me with a warm smile. He would not take offence, his smile told me. 'We are as French as you de Roets. My name, Chaucer – in French "chaussier" – means shoe or bootmaker. My grandfather came to England with Isabella's army: he made boots for it, and he settled in Ipswich, where the army landed. He bought an inn.'

An innkeeper! That was even lower down the social ladder than vintner. I fingered the buckle and buttons that the duke had given me as a present, dreaming of regaining that position I had enjoyed.

I yawned, then spread myself on my saddle. I sat side-saddle on my horse. I felt uncomfortable as our pace increased. I had just taken up the new fashion of wearing calçons, or panties, and if I were to take a tumble Geoffrey would be granted a sight of this new garment. Was it not better before when we wore nothing, and all that could be seen was our naked bottoms? I am not very surprised the church has condemned this garment for creating new temptation.

My escort almost unseated himself on Hubert. Every avenue he wanted to try, every tack, up reared Lord John to snatch away my attention. The poor man. What woman is interested in something other than what touches her directly?

'Oh you make me angry! You may call it what you will, it's downright stealing from others. And women, they're the worst – they refuse ever to think they're in the wrong!' Agnes Chaucer's view of women surprised me. It was two months since I rode out with Geoffrey. He had managed, very much against my better inclination, to invite me back to his father's house in Thames Street.

'Lord John is unpopular for reasons other than this,' said Geoffrey, who wanted to change the subject from the rumours of Lancaster's taste for women.

'He says right,' chirped in Geoffrey's stepfather, Bartholomew Attechapel, whom his mother had married hastily last year after his father's sudden death. He seized on this new point to use against the duke.

'Your master wants wars. We in the city of London want peace. He relishes clinking around in his coats of iron, his jambeaux, or quirboillies. It's a lot of old-fashioned nonsense!'

Mrs Chaucer turned on him: 'You ought to be grateful. War is good for business. The city flourishes.'

'Well, it is if the duke pays up: he's always raising money to pay his knights, his archers, munitions, provisions. But he falls always behind in settling up the bills. I know he has to wait himself for the crown to reimburse him. But the time will come when the crown won't pay off his debts, and then he won't pay his knights, or redeem his debts with the city!'

'Don't listen: if there's one thing our good duke does soundly, it's manage his financial affairs.'

'I am not sure. Consider that shady business he and his father the king are engaged in now. Sending out weapons smelted and forged in these very quarters to arm the infidels. It's against the holy book, and it's forbidden by law.'

'So is lending money with interest,' laughed Geoffrey, 'yet we all go on doing it!' Bartholomew was a moneylender as well as a vintner.

I shuddered: 'It is undoubtedly true our great lord has many enemies, and if they could they would murder him.'

'If he don't succeed in putting them down first!' cackled

Bartholomew. 'Many lords are after his blood – while they say that many a rich merchant would like to see him floating face upwards on the Thames tide!'

I rose to leave. I did not want to appear impolite, but I found myself disliking the talk of these London people. My family had a greater delicacy of tongue, and where I came from, Hainault, they would not, among my class, have discussed a great nobleman in such a crude way.

'Take no notice,' Geoffrey whispered to me. 'We pay no attention to the ups and downs at court.' He smiled, took my hand and patted it, which made me inclined to snatch it out of his grasp, for he had no right to be condescending. He poured more of the red Picardian wine from his father's cellar, and handed me a glass. My eyes flickered on the bottle.

'I believe Picardy is where your father campaigned with King Edward in 1355. This country's backbone, its civilization, is French – its barbarity Saxon, and its disordered soul English.'

This was certainly true. Everything good in this country came from France. Geoffrey launched into a legendary account of my father's great deeds as a herald of renown. His imagination, his embellishments, soothed and flattered me, prevailing upon me to stay, in spite of an undertow of rebellious feeling. The cup passed round freely, and the pretty Chaucer houseboy played tunes on the flute until it grew dark outside.

'I'd better take you back to the palace,' said Geoffrey.

'No, no, stay the night,' invited Bartholomew, who'd been eyeing me lecherously; the wine had unloosed a mood in him.

'We have a bed – and one for you, son.'

God forbid to put us in it together, I thought, although this is probably how commoners behaved.

Geoffrey started up. 'Philippa, we must leave at once.'

If I had been prevailed upon to stay I believe he saw his plans to trap me into marriage might be compromised. Proximity to his family would decidedly place my consent in jeopardy.

Geoffrey led me to the front door, but when he opened it, it looked so dark and unlit outside that we both stood there reflecting on the dangers. The streets around were narrow, the houses built up higgledy-piggledy almost touching each other overhead.

'I think we might be ill-advised to leave now. There are other perils, apart from killers and cutpurses,' he said, 'such as the foul-smelling river Wallbrook up at the end of Thames Street. One slip in the dark and we'll be up to our heads in shit. You'd do better to stay.' His tone was regretful.

Considering the way commoners threw slops out of their windows the city could be just like a common sewer.

'I'll see that you sleep in our lodger's room,' said Geoffrey very properly, but his mother overheard.

'Oh dear. Last Wednesday we had a flood,' she said, 'and a beam fell down. Nothing's dried out yet.'

The old decrepit man she had married for his money, although she had plenty of her own, added, 'Our big bedroom will hold us all. You, young filly, if you're feeling shy and maidenly, can be tucked away in a corner.'

Geoffrey bit his lip.

'I suppose so. Anyway, I'd rather not sleep on my own.' I volunteered graciously, 'I'm not used to it. At court I share my solar with several gentlewomen.'

A dull ache of loss hit me. I had never spent a whole night with Lord John. I blushed to think what I might have said to him first thing in the morning, so I had been spared that embarrassment.

We drank, sang songs and made merry. The Chaucer houseboy played more tunes, but I had a reluctant heart. An hour or two later the time had come for us to go to bed. The old fellow pushed a book at his stepson, 'Just the book for you,' he whispered, and Geoffrey blushed.

He handed him a tome by Don Constantine: *De Coitu*, Latin for a rude act, while I supposed the book was full of remedies to keep old men potent. He tried to wink at me and grab my leg, but he nearly passed out, and Geoffrey had to catch him, then propel him to the bedchamber. I hoped to heaven he had not laced himself up with love draughts or hot spices to inflame him, so that he might bother me during the night. We managed to clamber into beds of one kind or another with reasonable modesty, I in the one furthest away from everyone else, tucked behind a beam. The old couple was completely sozzled, but the old man fell asleep quickly before his lecherous imaginings could start him up. He began snoring like a horse, breaking wind from both mouth and arse, and in like manner his wife joined him till it became quite a concert.

Poor Geoffrey, how he must have sweated with shame. I saw the humour of it. I was modestly tucked away in the corner, but at one time during the night Geoffrey rose from his bed, I believe to further some design of his, and on the way to my bed walked straight into the beam, banging his head so hard that he fell down and gushed blood – or so I calculated by the noise and cursing. Next morning we saw the stain of blood everywhere. I don't know why he had left his bed, if not to say he was sorry.

Perhaps he wanted to keep me company, or had some other intention, but it still did not result in betrothal or a promise from me. This sorry state of affairs went on, for I reckoned Geoffrey must have been growing more and more thwarted…. At least I started to call him Geoffrey.

THREE

Scriven

'MANY-SIDED, THAT'S HOW I would describe her. Complicated. Rumour was, as I'm sure you know, she had been the mistress of the noble duke...' Rachel Dempsey had still been speaking about Philippa de Roet. 'This is thirty-three years ago, but I'll tell you a strange thing, for I reckon Mr Chaucer was more a-taken with her sister than he were with her.'

'I don't understand,' I said. 'I thought Mr Chaucer was passionately in love with Philippa.'

'Well, who would you have chosen, had you the choice?'

I thought of the two women and pictured them to myself. There was no doubt that I would have chosen Katherine, for she was softer, more amenable and much more likely to want to please a man than ever Philippa would have been. But here I could appreciate a serious difficulty: Katherine was more seductively made, she smote each man she saw with a pain to the very heart, an anguish of love wrought by her beauty, whoever they were, from the high to the low, and therefore I could see, for a cautious man such as my master, she would have ever been a risk. 'I suppose he knew where he was with Philippa.'

'Better the devil you know, eh? You see,' said the old lady, bending down as if to impart the greatest confidence of all. 'At heart I believe she never stopped loving Lord John. Often she was saying that she wanted to serve the duke more, and one day I remember Mr Chaucer became so incensed with this he retorted, with a rudeness unusual for him, "You want to share his bed !", and this at once inflamed my mistress's anger. She flew at his throat, for it was true, but she denied it with a foul curse. "Oh you know the gossip," answered Mr Chaucer, "I meet it everywhere, about Thomas's father being Lord John." '

'Yes, I reckon she was pretty brutal to him with her tongue,' I said.

'And free with her body – to others...I may tell you...'

I had left Rachel. I had rejoined my master at the vigil. He now regarded me with an earnest, inquiring expression. 'What business can you possibly have with her?' he inquired lightly, but the watchfulness was there in his smiling eyes. I stammered a reply.

'I don't know as yet. I'm talking to her tomorrow ...' Shocked as I had been at Rachel's last utterance about Mrs Chaucer – and his preference for his sister-in-law Katherine, I had been wondering if the events had something to do with that celebrated work, *Troilus and Criseyde*, finished over nineteen years ago...? The one I had copied for him, word for word, verse after verse, day after day, seven times? Or had it been eight? On good clean paper shipped in a galleon from Genoa. This new notion of mine delivered a blow in the pit of my stomach and I again felt sick. Leaning heavily against the great stone baptismal font, I tried to stop myself from throwing up into it. It was horrifying if he had, if he had gone about it so cold-bloodedly, turning the whole seduction of Katherine, with himself playing a major part in it, into the masterpiece which had become the glory of our new language...

KATHERINE: I wore a long white gown, open at the throat, and I sat by the window in my chamber, an upper solar in the Savoy Palace. It was a glorious April day. Philippa, who sat near me in a wicker chair, wore a shorter, brocaded dress mainly of blue. She was depressed, for Geoffrey was wooing her with great intensity and devotion, but all she would do was to think about our great duke.

In his absence she still pined, and after some months of writing and receiving no reply from France, she stopped writing. When she first admitted this to me I was very shocked, but also rather secretly thrilled, that my sister should be so connected to such a great personage as the duke of Lancaster.

I wondered how my mistress Blanche would have received the news of this had she known about it, but Philippa said that she never would, for now it was over. Philippa tried to convince me that it had been a very noble and chaste attraction, but I was not at all sure of this, and I abhor secrecy in love, although this was very much the fashion in the Plantagenet households.

23

I remember the verses Philippa once recited:

'When you hold her in your arms,
Welcome her and kiss her,
Secret, secret, secret, secret,
Think to hold your tongue,
For nothing good can come
Of sharing secrets.'

But Philippa's health had turned bad: instead of maintaining her usual cheerful and upright presence she drooped. Geoffrey went about the Savoy looking very forlorn, for he could no longer manage to catch her eyes in a flirtatious look, or gain her attention with one of his ballads. He became very sad too.

'They report,' began my sister, who had truly become more than obsessed, 'that our mutual master the duke is furious, for the French yet again refuse to respond to his attempts to engage in a decisive battle.' She looked inquisitively at me, knowing I did not like her to bring up this subject yet again.

'He tries to do too much,' I answered. 'I believe Lady Blanche is upset that he does not return to England to visit her.'

'He must have been busy,' said Philippa. 'I suppose that this is why he does not send word to me either…'

She followed this with a brief sigh.

'Well,' I said, 'there is this problem of the deposed king of Castile. My lady told me that King Peter the Cruel had taken refuge in Bordeaux with the Black Prince and the duke of Lancaster, and that they will shortly begin campaigning to restore his kingdom to him.'

'This means he will not even be home for the first birthday of his son and heir.'

'He will be stuck, in all probability, high in the Pyrenees,' I said, but as I said it the prospect did not seem altogether displeasing to Philippa, especially if only she could have been stuck there with him.

'Fighting to restore King Peter the Cruel on his throne!' Philippa suddenly changed her demeanour. 'What does his name tell you? You know,' she turned to me, her eyes blazing, 'I'm always defending Lord John against Mr Chaucer's slightly barbed, if veiled, remarks about his master, but sometimes I do wonder myself if the Plantagenets aren't really little more than criminals.'

I, who had just been given charge of my lord and lady Blanche's

24

two lovely daughters, answered from first-hand knowledge, 'Criminals no. But they have, without exception, appallingly bad tempers.'

My sister brightened. 'Have you heard that story of how they came to have their bad temper?'

'No,' I answered.

'Geoffrey told me. Well, Falk d'Anjou, the first Plantagenet of all, a Frenchman, was supposed to have got it in marriage from the devil himself.'

'In marriage? You mean he married a demon?'

'He did – a vampire without a soul.'

'You don't say!'

'Anger is a sin, the biggest of the seven.'

'I have never seen Geoffrey angry. Do you think he has no temper?'

'Possibly. But I don't like a man without a temper either. It is pride that kings and queens need. They need pride to be puffed up with authority. No one will obey a weak and humble prince. Or a little modest commander. Pride and anger are bedfellows.'

Further talk was cut short by feet pounding on the stairs outside. Then a rapid, shattering sound as mailed fists beat on my door. My sister went to slip back the lock and open it, and the heavy door swung open. Sir Hugh Swynford, the Saxon retainer of Lancaster, now – God help me – my betrothed knight, stood in the doorway. He wore armour and spurs and carried a sword, filling the ugly dark void with his bulky form, and blocking out the light that came up the stairs. Pride, huh!

'Good day, ladies. How lucky I am to find both of you in!'

My heart sank, and I turned my face away. What was Sir Hugh doing here in London? I had conveniently forgotten him for some months, believing that he had left the country to serve in the duke of Lancaster's army in Aquitaine. But he had been drinking, and he was here. He breathed heavily, and his thick hard neck was crimson with passion.

'When did you return, and how did you know where to find me?'

I asked the question evenly, trying to smile calmly, radiantly, as if to tame the sudden danger in his intrusion.

'I am on my way through London to join my duke in the wars,' he replied in a surly abrupt way, his eyes fixed on mine. 'Tell your sister to leave us.' There was hesitation from both of us.

'You are my intended...by the queen's signed order!'

My sister turned on him; 'Doesn't it matter to you, Sir Hugh, if she *wants* to marry you or not?'

Sir Hugh placed his hand on his sword's hilt: 'Leave us,' he ordered Philippa, 'or by heaven I'll make a ghost of you!...' he threatened.

Philippa looked at me, and I lowered my eyes. What other choice had we? He would as soon spit me on his sword as have me deny him.

'It must be,' I thought, for I had hoped to elude him, or at least gain foreknowledge of his presence, 'one of those old hags who wait as damsels on the queen. They hate youth, and any woman who's passably good-looking.' Without further words my sister turned and ran out of the chamber, as I surmised, to seek help. Sir Hugh advanced to me, and held out a gift wrapped in parchment.

'Take it,' he offered.

Trying to steady my hand as I did so, I received his present and unwrapped it. I was sorely anxious, indeed petrified. It was a four-strand necklace of pearls which glowed with a pale, unearthly light. It was a beautiful gift, which would do any girl an honour to wear.

'My mother's: she recently died. She was a widow, and I have inherited much land, whole villages in Lincolnshire that were deserted in the plague. You and I shall be married in the summer.'

'But,' I said as gently and kindly as I could, 'forgive me, Sir Hugh, but I don't want to marry you. With all respect to your generosity, I don't feel I can accept your mother's pearls!'

What could one say in such a situation? That I would petition the queen? She would not listen. Refusal counted for nothing. There was no mistaking the look Sir Hugh now gave me, for I had been given my chance to comply willingly. I had been foolish to contradict his offer and, with Philippa having fled from my room, I had to resign myself to facing up to the worst he could do, even to him stripping me naked and forcing me to obey his brutal desire.

Even so, and in vain although it was, I started shouting and screaming for help, and when that monster began to lay his hands on me to stifle the noise I made, I struggled all I could to free myself from his clutches.

I knew I would soon be overcome. One of Geoffrey's oft-repeated sentiments came to my mind: '*O che sciagura d'essere senza coglioni!*' – 'Oh what a pity to be born without balls!' Fear, horror, and despair rendered me insensate to Sir Hugh's violence, but behind his massive armoured shape – he had not removed his breastplate – I saw the door which the knight had neglected to close after him, open a little further, if only very slightly.

Who should be standing there but Geoffrey? All at once my senses returned to me, most of all my sense of humour, for I always was inclined to smile when he appeared. But fear on his behalf, no longer for myself, quickly overtook relief. What chance did he have against this metal-cased brute who was not only very drunk, but also now frothed at the mouth with uncontrollable lechery?

Geoffrey gave no hint of the terror he must have felt: 'Where's Lady Philippa?' he asked in a mild tone, although the up-grading of my sister's rank would not be lost on a man such as Sir Hugh, servile to hierarchy.

I had been pushed on my back, my white gown pulled right up around my naked thighs, even above my breasts, while the knight was trying, with his own armour open and clothing hanging down, to rip away the remains of my undersmock. My breasts were uncovered and grazed from assault. Geoffrey must have seen all this.

Sir Hugh took no notice of Geoffrey and simply carried on. Geoffrey unsheathed his sword, which I believe he had never used, and gave Sir Hugh a good hard jab, or prick, in the buttocks. He answered with an elephantine bellow, and turned on Geoffrey, unsheathing his own monstrous broadsword. I screamed and screamed, which made Sir Hugh lessen the grip of his gross hands on me. I hastened to cover my scratched and bleeding nakedness.

Sir Hugh uttered a stream of blasphemies, imputing that the little heathen knave who dared to stand up to him would be worse than roasted or castrated, which would be a great loss to poetry considering what Geoffrey one day was to write. Nostrils twitching with black hairs that bristled like a sow's, he clanked his way round to face Geoffrey.

'Disgraceful,' said Geoffrey, 'it's disgraceful! Answer my challenge, for I shall defend Katherine against such outrage!'

'You dare challenge me, a dubbed and anointed knight – you, a grovelling tradesman's son, a dirty-nailed scribbler. You shall answer for this with your life!'

'I, too, have a position in my lord's household, Sir Hugh, that of squire. I suggest we settle this before the duke himself.'

'Well,' answered Sir Hugh, 'try summoning him from where he fails to lick the pygmies of Navarre, and you won't get much help defending this little maid's honour!'

They went on thus, swapping threats and challenges. I could now hear the sound of footsteps on the stairs behind and below Geoffrey. O God, what if it was Philippa! Her appearance now would only make it worse, for there was no stopping this behemoth. Geoffrey shouted a warning.

'Is that you, Geoffrey?' answered a familiar voice, that of Philippa my sister.

'Don't come any further till I have fought with Sir Hugh Swynford.'

'Don't be foolish, Geoffrey, keep out of his way. You might as well engage a wounded boar.'

But there rose to us – piercing, authoritative, yet young – the commanding tones of my lady Blanche of Lancaster.

'Put away your swords – both of you!'

Sir Hugh recognized the voice, but would he obey? Geoffrey did so at once, leaving himself vulnerable.

'If you hesitate,' the voice came nearer, 'I shall command your immediate death.'

To my infinite relief Lady Blanche arrived and stood by Geoffrey, dwarfing him with her majestic presence, for she was tall and slim. Although feeding her young son, she wore beautiful clothes, and other rich adornments.

She had a natural authority, for she was the richest woman in England and daughter of Hugh de Grossmont, our great king's mightiest champion, although he was now dead and gone. She had her father's ruthless spirit in removing obstacles from her path, but would to God she had removed Sir Hugh for ever! At least for the moment Sir Hugh fell in with her command.

'What is this about?' she asked Geoffrey. Her eyes darted from Geoffrey to Sir Hugh, then to myself in huddled and half fainting state, and back again to Sir Hugh.

'I shall charge you for attempting to rape my governess. This is a heinous crime. By the law you should be stripped of your rank and punished.'

'Your grace,' replied Sir Hugh, who had donned an immediate mask of penitence to hide his confusion. 'I crave your understanding. Katherine de Roet is my intended bride. I lay claim to her by virtue of my right...'

Lady Blanche cut in: 'You must keep that until the wedding...'

Four

Scriven

THERE WAS A SUDDEN clamour in the chapel, a devilish harsh rattle and clank of metal at the outer door. My master, who became alarmed, turned his head in its direction. The heavy wooden and studded portal flew open with a great invading flood of cold air: the early March night chill caught me by the throat. Two burly knights, helmeted, wielding great swords and encased in cap-à-pie armour, burst in and swaggered down the central aisle.

'We've come for John of Gaunt, the murderer!' the first shouted, as the mourners of the watch cried out and fled into the confession boxes and the side benches and chapel. The flames of Lord John's candles leapt, blazed, and sent up clouds of smoke in the fresh rush of air.

'We have come with the sacred purpose: to revenge the death of Sir Hugh Swynford!'

I had scampered for a corner, darkly in shadow behind the pulpit, beside my master, who showed little sign of a limp when bolting for safety. A murderer Lord John might be, and many had accused him of this. But this charge of killing Sir Hugh Swynford was new to me. Swynford had been an ignorant, pig-headed Saxon retainer of Lord John who married Katherine Payne de Roet thirty years ago now, her first husband prior to the duke. I beseeched God I would not be found hiding here, although these intruders were more intent on the dead than the living. My master had suggested something awful might happen to the duke's corpse, pointing out that his trusted knights, John Norbury, Thomas Furnival and others would not have hastened to remove it from Ely Palace in Holborn as soon as he died to bring him back to the safety of Leicester if they had not feared some mischief might happen to it, either from the king or from some of his followers. When I had asked what might have hoped to be gained from this, my master, pursuing his morbid speculation, told me that mutilating a corpse might be seen to be an act of God to discredit a person and invalidate his will. The body could be stolen and buried elsewhere, or even thrown on a refuse dump. The mourners and followers would then have had no means to celebrate his life and bury him with honour. A body as valuable as Lord John's might have been taken by unscrupulous men and used for ransom, just as Lord John had ransomed many men himself. My master pointed out further that King Richard had to buy the body of his friend de Vere, which had been buried in Holland, then commanded that it be dug up and brought back to England for a second interment.

'He murdered the husband to lie with the wife!' thundered these knights. 'He's a whoremaster and an adulterer!' 'He bled our kingdom white with taxes!' 'He plotted against King Richard'. 'May he fester in the lowest pit of Hell!'

Well, you see, I was right from the start, but while they might agree with me I fear that in their present mood they would not be amenable to sparing me or anyone.

With other such vile, thundering accusations, the knights lowered their heads and with a mighty roar charged at Duke John's remains. I also lowered and hid my eyes, for their intention was plainly, as my master outlined, to mutilate his body in revenge, and deny his soul its resting place. I was no longer dubious about whether or not it was possible to destroy the integrity of man's physical reputation and create a grumbling and growing tide of superstition by such means, just as a man's reputation after his death could be hacked to bits by lies and slanders.

Help was at hand. The Lancastrian men-at-arms placed in the chapel shadows closed in, and swiftly, with exemplary precision, tackled the intruders. There were too many Lancastrians. Pikes and axes made quick work of the raiders: blood sprayed everywhere, and in only seconds the charging knights, heavily encumbered with armour, were weakened and overpowered, stripped of their weapons. The mess was terrible, limbs without bodies, bodies without heads, gore and viscera everywhere as the Lancastrians finished their demolition, and soon I was vomiting without control, while for some minutes or more the defilers' heads and bodies lay twitching on the polished stone floor, while the monks and mourners, myself and my master among them, were being led out, dazed and uncomprehending, into the icy night...

PHILIPPA: Though he'd been foiled, Sir Hugh's attack on my sister was the worst thing that had ever happened to her. I often wondered why Geoffrey wanted so persistently to pursue me, when he had championed my sister so bravely. In many ways she was much better suited to him than I was. She was more gentle, she took an interest in poetry, she had a sympathy and understanding of others that sometimes made me impatient.

Still, it was reluctantly concluded, in spite of further attempts made to persuade Sir Hugh to relinquish his claim on my sister, that Katherine should marry the knight later that summer in Lincolnshire. In the same period I had to trim to some degree my resistance to Geoffrey on account of his bravery.

That awful day I remarked on how, when the duchess had quelled the brute's violence, threatening him with dire punishment, Geoffrey went to Katherine's aid as she lay still bruised and crushed on the bed, scratched and bleeding from the knight's attack. He sat and took her head in his lap, and gazed lovingly into her fainted countenance. He looked as if, in her shocked and vulnerable condition, he were seeking something.

It had been the same when at an earlier time she was ill, and he had sounded her heart, uncovering her chest to listen, and she exposing to him that dazzling bosom. I recalled how he had blushed when he stretched out his hand to touch her there. I felt jealous. Why had he not taken it upon himself to challenge Sir Hugh for her hand? He had such influence with Lord John that he could have contrived such a match to fall in with his wishes, manoeuvring to avoid single combat with the Saxon, for here he wouldn't have stood much chance.

Did he have some knowledge of my sister that he would keep to himself, and if so what had been his plan?

Anyway, it was for me that he went. I who had little interest in rhyme and metric feet, but coveted fine shoes, rich cloth and solid possessions; I who wanted land and position.

He was persistent. 'Will you be my wife?' he asked again and again.

31

The time arrived when I could just about suffer him to hold me tight in his arms, and to kiss me hard. I might have allowed him to go further, but whether from timidity or design he held back. I even had a project of drawing him on, saying to him one night when we sat together a long time, hoping for once and for all to draw his fire:

'Come on, it's one o'clock. We must go to bed.'

'Well,' he answered. 'Goodnight.'

I got up quickly, left him, and entered my own bedroom. But deliberately I did not shut the door. He stepped into his own room, which was on the same floor in the Savoy Palace, so he might easily have seen that I was undressing. Nothing happened. After more time I shut my door, but left it on the latch.

I had not been in bed a minute or two when he came to the door in his gown, opened it a little way, but not enough to come in or look, and spoke softly and gently. 'Have you really gone to bed?'

'Yes, yes,' I said. 'Go away.' I took care not to sound too rough.

He came into my room, turned round and fastened the door, and straightaway was at my bedside. I had resolved that he should lie with me if he wished.

'Philippa,' he said, 'I don't mean to push this too far, but to show my intentions are honourable I have come to tell you I want to marry you. I desire you to give me an answer.'

'No, I cannot,' I said, quite upset at his sudden request.

'Why not?' he asked in a more plaintive tone. I then recognized that my idea of taking him to bed had become a bite upon myself, while I intended it as a bite for him. Once I had him in my bed I could make him jealous, and then assert my freedom over him.

'John of Gaunt will soon be home, and the year will be up,' he said.

'What year?' I asked, but he did not answer. I then suspected they might have some plot together which involved me.

'I do not understand. You suffer me to be here, in your chamber, yet you will not marry me.'

'What I do now is free, and of my own good will. If I married you I would have to give up my liberty. I would be obliged to lie with you whether I wanted to or not…!'

Geoffrey was quiet for a while. Finally he spoke.

'If I manage to guess the true reason for your refusal, and then remove the objection, will you then agree?'

I sighed. 'I suppose,' I answered slowly, 'that if you do remove the objection, then I must give in.'

'Are you secretly engaged to someone else?'

The thought of the duke fleetingly crossed my mind, for it had often occurred to me that he may have thought of seeking from me a secret pledge of love, and giving me his own. But then, and without waiting for my reply, Geoffrey went on:

'Is it because you are unwilling to share your fortune with me, and that, without me, you expect to advance yourself higher in fortune?'

I fumed at this, pulling up the covers tight about me.

'Your base thoughts make me furious. Why should I not entertain a man and gratify my sexual wishes, as a man does with his mistress?'

Geoffrey scratched his head. 'It is certainly true that when a woman is single, she has full command of what she has. And of what she does. But then,' he added, 'nothing can be more perfect than wedded bliss. Where there is mutual love there can be no bondage, and when two people are bound in one interest, one aim, one design, everything will conspire to make them both happy.'

He fixed his eyes on me. I could detect no insincerity. Oh from my heart, how I wished this had been so! But our talk was curtailed, for late as it had become a messenger arrived. He had ridden in one day the whole distance from Sandwich to London with a letter from my lord brought over from France. My composure of mind completely disappeared.

I snatched the letter from the messenger's hand. I read it, but remained dumb and silent, overcome with what I now beheld, in the hand I knew was his. I was seized with a fit of trembling. I grew so agitated that soon I began all over to shake violently.

'I wish I could relieve you of the distress you feel,' said Geoffrey quietly. His words, momentarily, made me control myself. He seemed almost as upset by the sight of my condition as I was by the letter, and he sought to protect and comfort me.

I would not let him see the letter. I fell into a crying, then a sobbing which lasted until, by signs from me – and not knowing how to stop or put a check on it – Geoffrey must have seen that all he could do was to leave me to myself.

Later, when I recovered, I fell in with the command of the duke in my letter.

I married Geoffrey.

Soon, when the time came to attend Katherine's wedding in Kettlethorpe, Lincolnshire, I was heavy with my first child. But was it Geoffrey's? Or was it Lord John's?

KATHERINE: I said all the prayers my French mother taught me, and asked the saints I could name for intercession with Jesus to stop Sir Hugh Swynford from having any desire to marry me. Yet I am now arrived here, at his draughty and ill-provided manor in Kettlethorpe, and our marriage is to be solemnized in the village church in three days time. Was it because I excited his lust enough for him to want to rape me, I asked myself, that he had to marry me? Was I myself the fault, the provocation?

I heard rumours in the court of how his Saxon blood came from a girl ravished by a fierce Dane who sailed up the Trent several centuries before. Swine's Ford in Leicestershire is where she came from, and she had even gone across the sea to look for him. Is Sir Hugh, like that Danish forerunner, expecting me to soften and civilize his brutal spirit? If so, he is sorely mistaken, for I am no Saxon and passive slave, but a French woman of the highest blood who expects courtesy and gentleness.

The queen's ladies mocked me for hanging back: Sir Hugh had a manor and serfs, they said; especially scornful was Alice Perrers, the mistress of our ageing King Edward III, who saw in me a kindred soul, although I recoiled from her admiration, based as it was upon envy of my beauty. 'You are looking a gift horse in the mouth. Consider the advantages,' she said. 'You beget him an heir, and he's off to Aquitaine with Lancaster in a month; a knight in John's retinue lives an average of two years, unless he becomes a great and famous hero like Sir Robert Knolles, and then, maybe, he is likely to live a bit longer. It's a step up the ladder,' said Alice Perrers. 'And if you do the right things in the right places and learn how to beguile and satisfy as Mr Ovid instructs us, you'll gather pensions and houses as easily as daisies and lilies in the fields.'

A step up the ladder, I thought bitterly. I was cautious about Philippa's freedom and sophistication, and hoped I could be more straight and true of heart; I would consult Geoffrey, who was now my brother-in-law. He was forever making knights, kings and royal families into something other than they were, better and more ideal people. One day, before I could do this, Alice asked, 'What does Geoffrey Chaucer think of the match?'

'Oddly enough,' I answered, 'he is very much against it, for it was he who saved me from an attempt by Sir Hugh to rape me.'

'Sir Hugh has already tried to rape you?' declared the mistress with wonder in her voice.

'It was horrible; look, I've still got the scars.' Innocent as I was I began to open my shift to show the scars on my breast, but I drew back.

Again I felt the resentment of Alice.

'Well my dear,' proceeded Alice, 'even better if he actually wants to rape you, you really can't ask better! Most men of Sir Hugh's nature will just have their way with a girl like you, and never even offer marriage!'

It made me despair even more. I prayed to the Virgin that she might help me, for I identified ever with Mary, the epitome of sincerity and truth. But could I countenance marriage to a man I would never grow to love?

I bent my head again to pray, trying to allow the divine Virgin to enter all my being, when I was cut short by the Kettlethorpe chapel door being thrown open. Across the shafted light a black shadow fell. I shuddered, drawing tight about me the light summer dress of green whose bold and simple line added, or so Philippa said, such a power of attraction to my figure. Often I cursed my body. Again Sir Hugh was on me, again dressed in full armour as if it were the outer shell of some brutal animal, an armadillo I once heard of, or a rhinoceros. His chain mail was hidden by a white silk jupon with three boars' heads on a black chevron, his coat of arms. But although he rattled and clanked, his manner this time was considerably more courteous, and while I wondered at my invocation to the Virgin, for perhaps it had worked, he sought to disarm me, his eyes losing their belligerence and lowering their focus to rest on my feet.

'I come with another offer. Of a ring.'

He held a clenched fist, then turned it and opened it; it held a betrothal ring of gold. It was a lovely ring, delicate with inlaid amethyst of bluish violet, supposed to stave off intoxication. In spite of myself my body gave a convulsive sob, and I turned away.

There were magic signs and portents before my wedding, of which the Saxon took no heed at all, such as his sword leaping from its scabbard and wounding him in the foot, and, at another time not long after, him falling down in a sudden faint.

The village had seen nothing like this feast for many years. They had been preparing for weeks before the ceremony. Kettlethorpe was a fairly grim place. It had lost half of its inhabitants in the Great Plague and had not yet recovered. When Sir Hugh first brought me back to his home, I hardly said a word to him. Yet he refrained from trying again to force me to yield to him. He had promised the duchess of Lancaster that he would wait until the wedding night. I kept and wore the pearls his mother gave him.

The night that I dreaded above all arrived. I had told my fear to my sister the day before. Geoffrey seemed blithe of heart. Although they were now married by royal warrant, she was not happy. All that Geoffrey said to her was met by a barbed or deflecting remark.

The time of year was sunny and warm, and Sir Hugh's village was decked out in flags and flowers. Sir Hugh, apart from his surly manner and his pent-up lust, had liberally spent his booty money from France in the village and among his tenants. Too often he had been an absent landlord. Largesse sat awkwardly on him, for his spirit had as little grace as his body was clumsy – except in the use of warlike weapons – but his intention was still to celebrate.

Philippa was still furious over the whole matter. 'You have had your way,' she told Geoffrey hotly within earshot, 'and we are now man and wife. Here, carry the baby. If you were a real man and had my interests truly at heart, you would stop Sir Hugh Swynford from marrying Katherine.'

Geoffrey said nothing. He took the baby, cradling him lovingly in his arms.

'You're worse than useless!'

Geoffrey sighed and looked up to heaven.

'If only the duke himself were here he would stop it! I would petition him myself. Anyway, Sir Hugh Swynford does not love my sister.'

'He does. He is besotted by her.'

'He merely wants to own her, to lock her up and keep her as a man keeps a dog.'

'Love can take many forms. Katherine is patient,' answered

Geoffrey. 'She will bear it.' He turned to me for confirmation. Baby Thomas began to cry.

Philippa walked up and down in her rage. 'It's more than I would – or ever could!' Contrary to what one might expect, the sight of her in anger did not perturb Geoffrey too much.

'Isn't there anything we can do to stop this wedding?' cried out Philippa. 'Oh God help us!'

Geoffrey replied, ignoring his son's sympathetic crescendo of misery, but rocking him fiercely, 'It's God's will that she should marry. The queen herself supports it, so does Blanche. Sir Hugh will be away much of the time. Lord John will keep him busy in Aquitaine. Since his great victory at Najera, where he commanded the vanguard of the English, our fortunes are on the turn. With any luck, and with the thought of booty to be seized, Sir Hugh will quickly make Katherine pregnant and rejoin the duke on his return to Gascony.'

Philippa grabbed Thomas, whose cries had now become howls, and stomped off. My dread of going to bed with my husband mounted by the hour, and I wanted to deny him. In advance of the expected time Sir Hugh could feel me pulling further and further away, using a thousand pretences of illness and humour to prevent him touching me. He pursued me more, trying to reassure me that he was a man of honour which, the more he drank ale, the more he insisted upon. Sir Hugh may have been a tremendous warrior in battle, none doubted this: but apart from his reassuring size and strength I found him as weak, empty-headed, and untaught as any woman could ever desire not to be coupled with.

'Oh! What am I going to do tonight?' I finally cried out in desperation to my sister. 'I shall wear my *chemise cagoule*!'

Philippa had been going to reply. She looked at me with wide, amazed eyes.

'What in heaven's name do you mean?'

'The garment that covers all, but with a little hole cut out for the insertion ...' I stared enquiringly at my sister.

'Don't be silly,' countered Philippa, raising a hand to her mouth to stop herself laughing.

'I can't bear the idea of him seeing me. Gazing on me.' I shuddered at the thought that he should find delight in seeing me naked.

So, in a gloomy and apprehensive frame of mind, myself, Philippa and even Geoffrey approached my wedding night.

The ceremonies were well and truly over. Sir Hugh was drinking more and more, but no one either was prepared to, or could, do anything about it: he forced everyone near him to drink with him, not least Geoffrey and my sister, until both he and Philippa saw the crowded hall of Kettlethorpe turning upside down.

Geoffrey became rather passive in his drunken condition.

'You better tell your sister-in-law not to behave like a French wife,' I heard Sir Hugh say to him.

'A French wife,' answered Geoffrey, slurring his words. 'What'sh thett...any diff'rence?'

'I hate a Frenchman more than I hate the devil!' shouted Sir Hugh over the din. 'They're false – the wives are even falser...I've paid a lot for Katherine – if she's dishonest I shall want my money back.'

Geoffrey made an effort. 'She might give you good advice...restrain your warlike instincts.'

'Restrain my what?' answered Sir Hugh with an uncomprehending sneer. 'Who would bring home the bacon?'

'A wife,' Geoffrey meandered on; 'listen to this –

"Peradventure she may be your purgatory;
She may be God's means, God's whip –
Then shall your soul up to heaven skip
Swifter than does the arrow of a bow..." '

Geoffrey looked around for Philippa, but the moment she heard Geoffrey quoting she had moved out of earshot to talk to a neighbour. My husband – God forbid I should call him this – was not in the mood for such verse. Fortunately the innuendoes escaped him; nor was he too keen to take me off to the bedroom. I would, so help me heaven, have had Geoffrey, even, to play the part of substitute.

'If I find her unfaithful,' went on Sir Hugh, 'I'll kill her and her lover – I'll blind his eyes and chop off his balls.'

This cheered me up no end. 'While you have her...err.. in your possession?...' murmured Geoffrey. I thought he might say something on my behalf, like 'Why don't you try to keep her by gentleness and the tenderness of your attachment?' but he fell silent. This was just as well. Sir Hugh was far away in his cups. He collared his squire Rufus, and took him down to the far end of the hall to play skittles. My sister rose unsteadily:

'I'm going to bed,' she told Geoffrey, who kept eyeing me.

'Isn't it time we all went to bed?'

I stirred uneasily. I wanted to say, 'Please, don't leave me alone with him.' This was to be my last evening of freedom, and I was very, very afraid.

'What a pity to go to bed now,' remarked Geoffrey.

'Or at any other time,' I said, looking miserably towards where Sir Hugh was casting the wooden balls and knocking down skittles. Every now and then he turned around to make sure I was still there, like a small child wanting my attention.

'He's far too old for me. He must be fifty. He says he is only forty.'

'He is in the full flower of manhood,' pronounced Geoffrey in a tone of irony. 'In France they consider a man of forty young.'

I gazed with a look of deep concern into Geoffrey's eyes.

'Why is it that all men, whether old or young, boys or beggars, dukes or doctors of physic, learned scholars or ignorant tapsters, think the highest good is intercourse with an attractive woman? Look at that…' I hesitated before the word 'husband' and changed it to 'Sir Hugh Swynford. He pretends to be occupied with something else…in reality he thinks about nothing but satisfying his desire.'

'Yes you do have – all of you women – this extraordinary power over us,' Geoffrey answered, watching me with a disarming, affectionate regard. 'When people have a need, they can be commanded. Men need women. So shall you command your husband.'

'I think the whole world is made up of men possessed by lust, who watch me on all sides, trying by every means in their power – perception, violence, purchase, cunning – to get hold of me.' I could feel myself beginning to shake with passion.

'Resist him, if that is how you feel,' said Geoffrey.

'I wish I could.'

Meanwhile Sir Hugh, swallowing more and more ale (it was with ale that he felt the greatest kinship of all) was jealously watching Geoffrey and me. He saw the frank affection exchanged between us. He turned pale and could hardly breathe. He switched his back on us, flung the ball at the skittles with greater ferocity.

'Your husband's jealousy is increasing. He is, in his own distorting fashion, construing what we say.'

'What of Lord John,' I said, trying to change the subject, 'have you heard from him?'

'He's on his way back from Castile with his brother Edward. The Black Prince is sick, unable to walk, and has to be carried everywhere on a litter. John has honoured us by writing to Philippa. You know, as it is common news, that he and Prince Edward have driven the usurping Henry of Trastamara out of Castile and restored King Peter. Last month they both attended the cathedral of Santa Maria in Burgos where Peter reaffirmed his promises to the Black Prince of lordships in Castile as the reward for recapturing his kingdom. My lord Lancaster was a witness to the affirmation. And here,' Geoffrey lowered his voice, '…here Lancaster met the fourteen-year-old daughter of King Peter, whose name is Constanza. Constanza of Castile,' he repeated, for what reason I could not construe.

'Then,' Geoffrey continued, 'events turned sour for our English princes: Edward fell ill, and Peter reneged at once on his promises, while Edward, hearing of this, swore an unrealistic vengeance on him, claiming he would seize his throne.'

Imagining these events happening in far off Spain and France, I forgot the wretched occasion of which I was the centre.

'…So this year, which began so joyfully for English arms, is now beset with troubles. John plans to return to England by the end of this year. He hungers to see his baby son Henry. At last he has a male heir.'

He turned as if to say, 'That is all you need to do – give your husband a male heir.' I felt sick again. I was wrenched from my thoughts of better circumstances by a rough hand from nowhere, which seized my shoulder.

I reddened as, propelled out of my chair, I rose to my feet.

'Tomorrow we shall hunt deer,' said Sir Hugh with a grimace. 'Are you joining us, brother?'

'Of course, of course,' rejoined Geoffrey amiably, bidding me goodnight, and kissing me with an affection that he did not try to hide from my husband.

When Sir Hugh came at last into our nuptial bedchamber his spirit was in a muddy state, yet he, having changed into a night gown, sat on a couch, waiting for me to come from the garde-robe. He tried to look at ease, but he was drunk. When I entered, attended by my maid, dressed in a gown of pale blue silk, he rose to greet me as if his moment of happiness had arrived. But his eyes flashed with danger and menace. He pressed an arm against his chest as if trying to hold himself in.

I, having summoned all my courage, dismissed my maid.

'Is it something you don't like about my brother-in-law Geoffrey?' I asked timidly.

'Yes, yes,' he tried to mask his expression of cruelty. But I detected underneath a suffering, which began to touch me as he unloaded his feelings of inferiority towards Geoffrey, and especially of his resentment, not to say unfulfilled revenge, against the time when he tried to force me, and Geoffrey stood up for me.

'I'm affronted, humiliated, not jealous. I have a knight's honour. After what happened, that you should dare to look at him with eyes like that...'

'Eyes like what?' I asked, squashing my sense that there was something between my brother-in-law and me, and that I would, above all, like at that moment to be in the safety of *his* bed, even, and I dared not think of it, although he was married to my sister.

'What attraction can I possibly have to Mr Chaucer?'

'If you knew the agony from which I suffer. I love you.'

I turned to face him, finding, to my own great surprise, that I could meet the look in his eyes on equal terms. There, instead of the dread, the disgust I felt even at the thought of him, I noticed his lips were trembling.

It was something on his mind, something I had long been making him feel, and which he had been saving up.

'Katherine,' he offered tentatively. 'We have solemnized our marriage and you are my wife. If you find me so awful, so undeserving of forgiveness...'

I could not believe it. There were tears running down his cheeks.

'Forgive me my roughness.'

My surprise so overwhelmed me, I felt so upset that tears came into my eyes.

'You cannot imagine how deeply I feel my guilt towards you,' he went on. 'You are free – free if you so wish – not to lie with me. How beautiful are your large, blue-green eyes,' he added.

FIVE

Scriven

'Have you any idea about these men?' asked my master.

'None.'

'They must have believed in their mission, or why should they want to sacrifice themselves in such a foolhardy way? How could they have hoped they would stand a chance of mutilating Lord John's body for Hugh Swynford's death?...'

There was weeping and wailing from the women. Sad funereal music permeated the hall where we gathered, a concord of sweet and melancholy sounds which endeavoured to soothe and plant harmony in our souls and lift us out of the mad slaughter-house which was much akin to the realm of England. There was appetizing food on the trestle tables in the banqueting hall but no one was inclined to eat. Most were content to sip or gulp wine to quench their shock and deaden fears. 'What a barbarous thing to want to do!'

My master spoke quickly. 'I suppose that by having made their point publicly, if they had succeeded many would have felt their revenge was justified. Before history the charge would have stuck. It certainly upset Lord John's calculation that by leaving his body on show in public expiation for forty days he would atone for his sins. If I were him I'd have got myself safely tucked under the sod as quickly as I could. Mind you, even there you're not safe these days.'

'Bah! They were just malcontents; old soldiers from France bitter at some defeat, or overlooked for promotion: they had a grudge.'

'Some grudge!' My master scratched his head and pulled at his white, forked beard. 'Yet Adam, there is this old rumour you know, that when Sir Hugh Swynford came back wounded from France...'

He stopped suddenly, sat up. 'Heavens!' he exploded, 'it must be nearly thirty years ago when he reached Kettlethorpe? Lord John had him done away with, secretly strangled or poisoned, suffocated with smoke from the chimney.'

'Do you believe the rumour was true?'

'I don't know. I never thought much about it, Adam. Too busy with other things.'

He said this off-handedly but then a wicked thought crossed my mind. Other things? What might those other things have been? But my master, who fortunately couldn't read my thoughts, although he could read everything else, was shaking his head. 'No, it wasn't Lord John's style. They were always accusing or claiming he murdered people, or made them disappear, but I firmly believe that it was never his particular trademark. He survived by sparing everyone. Look how many had a go at removing him, yet without exception he let them all off. He was the well-spring of chivalry.'

He would have to champion his old saviour, wouldn't he?

'They must be searching the wallets and pockets of those desecrators. Perhaps they will find out more.'

'I doubt it,' my master said. 'I remain intrigued. Could Lord John have plotted Swynford's death? It is a pity Katherine, my sister-in-law,' he cleared his throat rather ostentatiously as if to relegate me to my inferior rank, 'by whom I mean our gracious sister, the present duchess of Lancaster, is not here to answer the questions. She would know all about it, Adam.'

'I am sure she would. She's due to join the cortège soon, isn't she?'

My irritation at the way my master had adopted an air of condescension almost burst into bitter words, for he could be direct and confidential with me when we were on our own, and treat me as his equal, which indeed I was – and in some ways his superior. But two of Lord John's children had joined us in the hall, and they might well have overheard.

They were Elizabeth, his second daughter from Blanche of Lancaster, who was now a well-spread, jolly lady with sons of her own, and as duchess of Exeter well provided for and secure; and John Beaufort, his first illegitimate son who was, as I now recalled with a shudder, and in view of what Rachel told me (and what had now happened) born only nine months thereabouts after the death of Sir Hugh Swynford. How this young man's fortunes had been advanced since the marriage several years ago between Lord John and Katherine Swynford, and she became the third duchess, was fairly disgraceful. He was now earl of Somerset and marquess of Dorset. There were not a few who would have said this was a promiscuous litter, monstrously bumped up with titles and riches.

I said several prayers to relieve me of my distress. What a relief to see the cold, grey March morning break. I was up early. The dead knights had been unceremoniously interred in a plot behind the castle wall, the bare bones of a mass said for their salvation, while the grave-diggers, chilly and grumpy, were plied with helpings of beer and bread at the lower end of the hall, where they cursed this extra duty. Our own departure was now delayed a day. My master joined me, but I had nothing to say to him, and quickly after rose to my feet.

'Where are you going, Adam?' asked my master.

'I have some of your Parson's Tale to copy,' I answered gruffly, while I could not resist adding, 'the passage on lechery is long, and passionate – you certainly have strong feelings on this subject!'

'Such as you have on my dear departed wife,' shrewdly countered Mr Chaucer. 'I believe you are writing a memoir of her.'

'Yes I am, for Lord John's scriptorium, for which I shall be paid by the nuns in Lincoln.'

'She was often rewarded by Lord John with silver-gilt cups,' adding in case I should misconstrue his words, 'she was admitted to the fraternity of Lincoln Cathedral. On her tomb you will find the words, "Here lies the good servant of John Plantagenet". She was high in his favour.'

I refrained from coughing and even felt like choking for a moment or so. My master was in a good humour this morning, and he regarded me ironically, while returning to our previous topic. 'But you asked me about my feelings on the subject of lechery: like my Pardoner I preach against the very thing out of which I make my living.'

'Are you saying the Pardoner is you?'

'All those I write about are me.' My master's eyes were brown and merry, like a pair of ripe cherries that have gone dark from too much sweetness at the centre. But now they had a touch of red fire in them.

Oh well! I thought: Absalon seeing badly in the dark, and kissing his mistress's aperture? Or, more to the point, the rapist knight caught in the Wife of Bath's Tale? And we mustn't forget the sow-bristled, drunken Miller? All of them my master?

'None of us will be here to tell the others what punishment he receives. Anyway,' he changed the subject, 'I have more of my Parson's Tale for you to copy. Still on the subject of lechery. I know how you disapprove of some of my lecherous stories.' He struggled to his feet, taking in his soft, fat, little perfumed hand the gnarled old yew stick he used to support himself, and limped towards the door to fetch me more sheets covered in his scrawl. But I had my appointment to keep with Rachel.

(I wonder. I say no more. I have a mind to leave the castle, desert his service and take to the forest outside Leicester where the lawless bands enjoy greater freedom and excitement from heroic and charitable deeds, than ever you will find among these civilized, courtly pretenders. No doubt the brigands could use the skills of a scrivener for songs and verses, and I am sure I could make up some of my own, to add to the traditional ballads.) At the window on the narrow winding stair to her room, I found this strange man of middle age, blond, well groomed and richly dressed, lounging in the alcove before her door. I wondered what business he had there. I could not say that he was young, but he was pale and thin, about my age I supposed. He was attired neatly in the latest town fashion, and he looked at me with extraordinary fixity and attention as if to ask why I should be there. Then he jumped up, as if to make off swiftly, so I asked him, 'Good morning, brother, do I not know your face?'

'If you know you do, then you do!'

What a strange answer. He didn't exactly threaten me, but as I barred the way to his descent it was clear he wanted me to stand aside so he could pass. He now looked disconcerted, as if I had caught him committing a crime, and I understood at once he was one of those creatures who were mistrustful of their fellow men on every possible occasion.

'And you must surely know mine,' I said.

'What if I do?'

But he had slipped by me and vanished, and while I had an urge to go after him and question him further, I knew he would elude me. I knocked loudly on Rachel's door and she let me in. I was quite amazed at the transformation in Rachel since the previous night, for I had never seen her in such clothes, though I saw them hanging in her room. Years had been taken off her. How she must have wriggled into the tight-laced corset, while her face had been coated in some blending powder that made it less fat and red. She wore a glass-studded ornate belt, while her green-coloured outer gown was edged with silver fur, and her underskirt red with a white flounce.

'Well, Master Adam,' she said. 'What can I do for you now, sir?' She laughed with her rich catarrhal chuckle which revealed her age.

I was perplexed, for I was never one to see the immediate humour of situations, and found no merry response in myself. 'Who was that man?' I asked roughly, and not without fear, gesturing to the door where the man had been loitering.

'Oh him, you must know him, dearie, you always see him when his mother is about to turn up.'

'His mother, who can you mean by his mother? It suggests she's a cook, while he's a scullion or groom – is there some special feast being laid on? After last night we need it!'

She shook her head sadly. 'Sure we do. Oh men, they are for ever carving one another up in the name of justice and God,' she said. 'Why don't they leave everything to the Almighty to sort it out for himself? He's much better at it. But there's something hard and brutal inside every man.'

'Not all men,' I answered, meaning myself, for in truth I had to admit that copying my master's work on the wages and food which I received made me often feel ill and faint, so that I wondered how I would find the energy for the day ahead, let alone to stand up to another man, or argue with a woman. I never knew how men and women, such as my master and his wife, could ever meet the demands of marriage, and the bringing up of children.

'Well, that is her first child, *her* son. Come on, Adam, what's got into you this morning, for you seem dense and not yourself.'

'The shock, those two knights attacking Lord John's bier,' I blurted out '– it gave me horrific nightmares.'

She sighed. 'Adam, you missed the training in battle most young men have these days. Every man and boy in this country is skilled in the use of bows, arrows, daggers and swords, and they have special practice times for every male citizen to prove himself a soldier.'

'I know Rachel. We fear invasion by the French.' We wandered from the subject. 'What did that fellow want with you?'

She gave a flirty smile, 'Well, he came to take me out and was waiting – till you arrived, Adam, and frightened him away. For he is very strange and his chief concern is to hide himself from the whole world. Yet he was schooled with no less a personage than our great lord's first son, Henry of Derby, and he is...'

I had grasped who he was, and understood at once the subservient underdog resentment, mixed as it was with arrogant pride and murderous self-conceit. He was none other than Sir Thomas Swynford, only son of Katherine and Sir Hugh, an odd, unhappy coupling that had brought him to the light of this world. But there was much else I wanted to know, and I had to move on from Sir Thomas.

'He came to take me to Leicester fair and give me some fun, which is more than you'll ever do for me, Adam, you old killjoy, but now you're here I suppose you want me to go on with what I was a-telling you before – a fine spectacle I've made for myself... . ' She preened a little.

'I'll take you to a tavern...'

PHILIPPA: More than two years passed since the marriage of Sir Hugh Swynford to my sister Katherine. In these years, causing universal grief and mourning, died the two most illustrious women in England. First Queen Philippa of Hainault: that doom-laden prediction made of her death, and its effect on England, turned out over the next ten years to be only too true. Before her accident and the dropsy overtook her, she had shared the great King Edward's love of chivalry with him, and had presided over many tilts. But her most remarked-upon quality had been her compassion, which twenty years before she exercised with her husband for those unfortunate burghers in Calais.

In the same year, eight years after the death of her own father, Blanche of Lancaster, my own wonderful and universally beloved mistress, adored by everyone but most of all by Lord John, her husband, also died. Lady Blanche had been married to John only seven years, which perhaps explains why he was later able to claim that he had hardly been unfaithful to her during their marriage. When it came to the moment when he had to make full confession for his sins would he somehow have forgotten me – conveniently for him?

Both of us married sisters now had sons, and both these first sons were named Thomas, perhaps not surprisingly, after the disciple who doubted what he saw with his own eyes. Both were their father's heirs, while Thomas Swynford became due to inherit his father's estates in Kettlethorpe, which were falling into neglect and ruin for lack of money. They were to come to him much sooner than expected. Thomas Chaucer, as was perhaps appropriate, was Duke John's godson –proxy son might be a more suitable term.

In marriage Geoffrey had surrendered to me the modest degree of autonomy that could have been his. In these early days he always argued that men should let women have sovereignty in the home. Perhaps he believed it. I am not too sure. I soon reversed the old adage that women are angels wooing – I became the very devil, and made no secret of this. He had delivered himself to the tyranny – as well as mercy and grace – of woman. "Servant in love, and lord in marriage" was how he wrote of the ideal position of the husband. I wondered. But as far as I understood it, Geoffrey's bliss consisted in keeping it all to himself.

Could, or would, I ever belong to him? I wore him out with my distance, my evasion, my lack of logic, my 'I don't want to be pinned down to anything' philosophy. This was truly how I felt, and for me feelings were my commands. He, unable to possess me fully, turned in his spare time to making verses. And as he was also devoted in his services to the king and Duke John, he advanced himself.

'I want to serve John more,' I often said to Geoffrey. He never answered.

'You want to share his bed,' Geoffrey said one day to me with unusual rudeness, which inflamed my anger at once.

'It's not true!'

'You know the gossip. I meet it everywhere. About Thomas's father being John.'

'Geoffrey, there is no truth in that. You know very well John was out of the country.'

'No. He came back. He attended our wedding.'

'He paid for our wedding. You have no right to complain. You know very well that if I had not been attractive to John in the first place, you would never have gained such a catch.'

I sounded arrogant and haughty I know, but I put it on deliberately. Geoffrey looked crestfallen. 'John made a gift of me to you. Don't you forget this. And the preferment you've had since is due to me. Writing verses doesn't win you preferment. And don't tell me you're a warrior of the king!'

'I could have been an outlaw who'd taken to the woods. I am a brilliant archer.'

'That isn't your way, Geoffrey – you're no Robin Hood. There's no way for you to gain advancement except by guile, and by keeping a firm hold on your tongue. Don't ever tell anyone what you really think of them!'

I was going to be sure to keep my independence. I was much in the latest fashion; I liked to dress amorously so as to encourage the looks of men. I wore clothes which brought out my sex, such as shifts and dresses which clung tight to my body. I had fine breasts, such as, so the books of love tell us, women should provide as cushions and comforts to their lovers. I liked to reveal these partly, so that everyone could gaze upon them. They were of a size just right for fondling, each as large enough for a man to take in his cupped hand and fill it.

Geoffrey did very well out of me, for I had lands of my own in Hainault. Our marriage proved in a worldly sense useful to him, and contributed to his fortune rather than to mine. No sooner had he married me than favours began to shower on him, and these took the form of pensions, titles, grants, missions, official posts and sinecures which paid him well. From then on, and for the next twenty years of our married life, our prosperity was unbroken.

As a squire, one of thirty-seven attached to the king's household, he had to attend court winter and summer, and supply the lords with chronicles from history, sharpen their cunning so that they might rule better and gain more territory, or manage more astutely what they already had. With his good memory and understanding of the past he was well suited to advise the nobles what to do in planning and executing their duties and their policies, while he was also gifted in being able to pipe, harp, otherwise entertain by singing to them lays, or recounting martial deeds which would stir up their pride, and sustain their spirits.

He became skilled in the undertaking of diplomatic missions. But while the cat was away the mouse might play!

SIX

Scriven

A STRANGE SIGHT WE made of it, Dame Rachel in all her finery
for the fair, and me, black, scaly and clerklike, trooping stealthily
through the castle, past the gatehouse and over the bridge to stop at
The Fighting Cock, where we found ourselves at a table and bench
and were served with two pots of ale.

'Well, Adam, I could as well be like Mr Chaucer now, and give
you a long tale, as he does in his Canterbury stories, or so I hear,
although how all listen when they trot along the road while one
rhymes and jokes and tells of misdeeds, is a mystery. They must have
ears on stalks: the whole thing's so stupid and impossible. Better
they should be as I am now, sitting in a quiet corner, but none would
listen long as his bottom would get itchy.'

'But you,' I told her, and sure she was on good form that morning,
'are telling me the truth. Mr Chaucer's characters may have the odd
realistic detail here and there, but most of what they tell is fairy tale
or romance – apart from dirty stories of lechery and fornication –
and even worse!'

Her eyes lit up, 'Oh I missed that darling, which one is that?'

'The one told by the Summoner, when Thomas the sick rich man
in bed gives the greedy friar – instead of the gold he demands – an
unsavoury present to be equally divided among the friars.'

'Which is? Oh go on, tell me the present, Adam!'

'A great fart, Rachel.'

She clapped her hands but then seeing my expression frowned
in distaste. 'I don't find it funny at all.'

'I said you wouldn't.'

'How do they divide it up?'

I sighed with disgust and irritation. 'Exactly! How do they? Well the problem is solved by twelve friars each laying their noses at the end of one of the twelve spokes of a cartwheel. The friar, in receipt of the fart, lies in the centre and with sound and movement "departs" the fart on the other twelve!'

'Oh Adam, you are rude!'

'Reluctantly so, Rachel. Mr Chaucer's fault.'

She recovered some of her old thrust.

'Well you want me to tell you, I know, how Mr Chaucer began the seduction of Lady Swynford some three or four years after her son Thomas was born to her – and she had another child you know, a daughter, who is not right in the head. Petronella, her name is.'

I nodded. I knew her. They gave her simples to chew on, to calm and keep her quiet.

'It happened like this...' And she began to tell me the whole story, but did not get very far when...

'Shush,' I said, warning her; my master, dressed in his courtly robe as a scutifer, had entered The Fighting Cock...

LORD JOHN: Chaucer has sent me a letter. He has written a poem celebrating the life of Blanche, and called it 'The Book of the Duchess'. It is now eighteen months since Blanche died of the plague. She outlived her great father by only seven years, so I am the sole survivor of my generation of the house of Lancaster. Chaucer would like to read 'The Book of the Duchess' to my court. He has dispatched Philippa to ask for my answer, and to fix when this should be done.

I have to confess that when I saw Philippa again I became the very opposite of the virtuous knight in mourning: 'Why can't you console me at this moment? Now, now, now!' I shouted at Philippa in my grief. She (although shorter in height than Katherine) was in the full bloom of motherhood, rosy-cheeked, full-lipped and just at the point where the signs of a new and second pregnancy were not yet too visible, but promised a kind of hidden, voluptuous fruitfulness.

'I am with child,' she answered to me. 'No more games, your grace. And, besides, it isn't fair on Geoffrey, who has taken such pain to write this poem for your pleasure and consolation, and to

51

invite you to its reading.' She shifted nervously from one foot to the other.

'By God's soul...!' I was about to say something rude about Chaucer. But I checked myself, and sulked instead. I looked again at Philippa. Her healthy body excited me. I like pregnant women. They like me. They make the best sport, I have often found, their parts barricaded and insured against the production of unwanted heirs. Therefore they respond with a freedom I find exciting. Usually there is much pleasure stored up in the parts devoted to Venus.

It is good for them to fornicate, surely. It makes for lusty progeny, so long as they are not too heavy and laboured in their struggles – or too sticky.

I reached out a jewelled hand to pat Philippa on the lower part of her stomach, letting my hand rest there. It was summer. She wore only a light blue gown which enhanced her slimness, and emphasized the delicacy of her new swelling.

'We did it before,' I said.

'That was ages ago.'

'And now you're married. What's the harm? I grant Mr Chaucer a further pension. You and he will need it.'

She allowed herself to be fondled a little. I began to believe she might yield to the pressure I applied.

Her eyes started and her body jerked upright. 'Oh heaven forbid! There is my lady. Look there, my lord! Her beauty restored!' Philippa stared, transfixed, over my left shoulder, at the ghost of Blanche, which she saw. At this manifestation of my dearest Blanche I recoiled and my hand relaxed, although I smiled. Had she not contrived this ghost? Philippa eased herself away, and my hand gently withdrew.

'You'll come to the reading?' she asked softly. I could see that it had cost her dear to visit me, for she wanted more power and money for herself and her family.

How I felt virtuous. It was my own, self-generated restraint which had made me respect Philippa.

My daughters, Philippa, aged nine and Elizabeth, who was five, entered. Philippa Chaucer looked at these girls in wonder. I commanded them to greet her.

'Oh haven't they grown beautiful!' Philippa blushed at the forwardness of her observation. With the arrival of my daughters I bowed slightly to signify my respect and gratitude. 'Everyone at court

52

is enraptured by them. Just looking at them, so full of life and health, carrying their burdens so lightly, makes me feel full of life and health.'

Philippa, with a bright smile, held up a finely embroidered silk purse. 'Look, my lord, I made this for you.'

'But it's lovely!' I answered with courtly quickness and tact, taking the purse and examining it. Elizabeth rested a bare little arm upon my knee, and waited patiently for my attention. I picked her up and put her on my lap, and I felt my countenance relax, as did my shoulders and back. Blanche used to tell me that my face, when animated, revealed unexpectedly warm and pleasant wrinkles round my mouth. I hated the impression of severity I often gave people.

'Fate has provided you with two splendid daughters, my lord,' said Philippa.

'But it has taken their mother from them. And from me.'

'We all continue to love and honour our Lady Blanche. Her memory will be with us always.'

'I shall have to send Chaucer on another diplomatic mission to find me a new duchess,' I remarked ironically, adding, 'I shall be delighted to attend the reading.'

KATHERINE: I received the summons to attend the reading of 'The Book of the Duchess', a poem by my brother-in-law Geoffrey. I arrived from Kettlethorpe to stay in Thames Street with the Chaucers.

Philippa was five months pregnant with her second child. I could see from Geoffrey's face when we arrived that he was going to have to curb his feelings of desire for me, for he clearly did not find my sister, when so large with child, excited him. Although Philippa and her husband had their own room, the house was full of relations and servants, so that I had to sleep in their high bed with them, together with their son Thomas. On my first night I sensed how Geoffrey lay awake tossing and turning as he both experienced and contemplated my closeness, for my limbs were covered only in a linen shift.

I am not surprised that Geoffrey should sweat in bed when so near and yet so far: but he knew how to keep his love secret and govern his instincts, even lying as he did so close. He slept only fitfully, woke up and kept Philippa awake with his sighs, his tossings and restless efforts at self-control. 'Please forgive me,' I heard him whisper to allay her anger, while I pretended to sleep. 'I'm nervous over the reading of my poem. It touches such private matters as John's love for Blanche. What if he grows jealous of such feelings as I express in my poem?'

As he spoke he gazed, in the early light of the new day, over my sister's slowly rising and falling – and much swollen – breasts, to my inert form. I did not stir, but I was awake.

'Geoffrey, for God's sake try to sleep, or if you can't sleep, listen to the nightingale!'

Geoffrey sighed. He whispered, 'It's not to a nightingale that I listen, but to a pregnant wife snoring!'

'What?' demanded Philippa.

'To an early swallow, I mean, which has begun to twitter against the approach of dawn.' I lay half-awake listening to the bird's chatter, recalling that gruesome change wrought on the swallow Procne's sister Philomena, whom Tereus raped and then, to keep her quiet, had her tongue torn out.

LORD JOHN: Mr Chaucer's page handed Chaucer the manuscript of 'The Book of the Duchess', which it had been his duty to carry to the palace. We were in my paved council parlour, with myself enthroned, and next to me an empty chair, as if it was there for Blanche. Chaucer, whose colour came and went a little greenly, stood at a lectern. The hall was crowded with courtiers.

I felt very affable towards the occasion. 'Madam,' I said to Philippa. 'Blessings pour on your head, and on your husband's poem – and on everyone who has come here today to listen.'

Everyone rustled with satisfaction at the pleasure and warmth of my greeting. It was then that I spotted Chaucer's sister-in-law. Philippa stepped in and introduced us, placing this young woman's hand in my own.

'You remember my sister Katherine, Lady Swynford...'

I paused with her hand in mine. Yes, I recalled, she was married to that old pig of a Saxon who mortally stabbed young Philip de La Mare at my joust, one of my best knights. The brute owed us a death. The young woman, as if she read my thoughts, sought to withdraw her hand. At the lectern the poet was turning from red to green to white, and I wondered if he would be able to stand, let alone read to the company. In the reading that followed I could hardly follow the clapping, the interchanges of wit and conversation, the sighs and the laughter.

Chaucer dreams he is out hunting, and he follows a small puppy into a wood where he spies a man in black, a wandering, welfaring knight who is in great sorrow because his 'lady bright' is dead and gone from him. The knight is Sorrow – 'I am sorrow and sorrow is I' – and in a great outburst he decries the falseness of Fortune, who has taken his queen from him in a game of chess. Then he relates his lady's beauty, her virtues and their courtship.

The clever aspect of Chaucer's work was that it was personal, or so it would seem, so near the truth, and so near the quick and pain of his own life, and yet it seemed to be about everyone else, and to answer their needs. I would swear that the poem was about the young woman, Katherine, and how through her Chaucer wanted to keep Philippa away from my intemperate desire. Yet its subject was Blanche my duchess!

Chaucer has planted me and Philippa's sister in our seats in the room in such a way that – now with his eyes on me, then with his eyes on her, or with a subtle, deft and loving gesture of his soft-white, plump hands – he conducts words of praise, of courtship, descriptions of beauty and virtue, first into the heart of Katherine Swynford, then into my lonely heart. He seems to be playing a love duet between us and, uncannily, almost makes each talk to the other through his poem. After a little time nothing existed except the verses, the speaker of lines – Chaucer – myself, and Katherine. The room grew as hushed and still as the chantry by the high altar in St Paul's where Blanche herself lay, and where mass was said every day for her by my two chaplains.

Katherine's peerless eyes grew wider and wider as Chaucer read on. They seemed to fill more and more with, I hesitate to mention this, my own. Her delightfully wrought form seemed to slip and incline itself, without wishing or knowing itself to do so, more and more towards me.

The reading by Chaucer ended, and the company burst into spontaneous, heartfelt applause. Everyone looked towards me to take the initiative. To them I sat there, all knowing, all embracing. So I, in my usual habit, rose to my feet, followed by the rest of the company. Outwardly dignified and composed, I graciously thanked Chaucer, and with a cheerful flourish asked him to accompany me, then left my council hall. Inwardly my state was one of deep turmoil.

My friend the poet, terrified at what I might have to say to him, yet longing to find out, some six or more inches shorter than I, trotted after me obediently

PHILIPPA: Geoffrey's reading of 'The Book of the Duchess', and especially its passages of loving tenderness of the knight for his beautiful lady, with the descriptions of her physical charms, had left me in a state of exquisite and extreme desire. Later that night when we were in bed Geoffrey surveyed Katherine over my naked, protruding belly. My tits thrust upward with engorged blood.

'We cannot tonight – not with her lying there,' whispered Geoffrey.

'My sister will sleep through anything.'

Geoffrey shrugged, and started his gentle persuasive work on my turrets and tower work, then below on the dungeons and torture rooms. I certainly was, and very soon, in a hot state. It seemed to bring to Geoffrey a strange sensation, exciting him more than his usual habit, to be so near, and yet so far, from Katherine.

He slipped a finger, then another, into my precious purse; I was so large with the health of nourishing my womb, that he could not but wonder at this miracle of peace and fulfilment in me.

'I might almost be making love to both of you...' whispered Geoffrey. 'But I'm worried about waking Katherine.'

The idea hardly lasted a moment, for he redoubled his effort. I groaned. 'I thought you didn't like me...' I panted, 'so blown up like this?'

'But I do.' He grew bigger and bigger. I panted again. 'Quick. Inside me.'

I would not let him in. I seized his instrument and pleasured myself with it against the edge of my chose: I could hardly bear the excitement.

While this went on I guessed Geoffrey was trying to fathom out how he could separate the two of us, continue to play his seductive tune of chivalry to divert John's attention from me, quieten him down, yet at the same time provoke him into further desiring Katherine.

I let go of him, giving up resistance, and he fell headlong into the deepest of penetrations.

And that was the beginning of my husband's career as John's Pandar.

SEVEN

Geoffrey Chaucer

'AH THERE YOU ARE!' I greeted them joyfully in The Fighting Cock, but could see my scrivener, grumbling as he ever did, was none too pleased to lose the rest of his private talk with Rachel Dempsey. 'I've been looking everywhere for you, but I am thankful' – I mopped my brow and sat down, for it was hot – 'to be away and out of that castle! Lord John's will has been brought forward and is due to be read later, while the whole ant-hill is teeming with rumours, plots, high expectations, and excitement. You'd think Lord John had the earth to give away, and yet it's all absurd, for everyone knows it's the exiled Henry of Bolingbroke who'll receive the duchy of Lancaster – ' I lowered my voice with good reason, 'but then a rather nasty and sinister element, Adam, has entered this charming, family gathering.' I coughed, laughing, for I could see the humorous side of it. 'Well we can hardly call it that, can we? My Lady Rachel, you look splendid,' I turned to Rachel with infectious glee, clasped her on both shoulders. I took her hand and kissed it. My voice quivered slightly with a feigned sense of drama. 'The spies of the demon king have arrived – and they intermingle, keen to glean scandal, pick up gossip. Guard your mouth – never is the value of silence greater than now! The great pullulation within the castle has made everyone forget last night's beastly episode.'

And so I ordered tripe in cream, with a great flask of Bordeaux. 'Will you not join me?' I asked them, and as we hovered in uncertainty, added, 'The day will be long.'

I pointed to the food as it arrived so that they should not feel left out. They responded with alacrity to the suggestion. 'Of course,' I went on, 'they try to hush up the whole thing, such a profoundly sick business, those two knights, but this morning, before burying them, they found letters on the brutes who so vainly threw themselves down the aisle of the chapel. Abel and Bair they were called, Sir Jonathan Abel and Sir Trevor Bair, and they really did carry evidence that proved, so they believed, Lord John murdered their master, or rather had their master murdered on his command. It happened in the Gascon village of Le Pagenac, or some such name, where there's a fort which had changed hands between the French and English dozens of times…'

Everyone set upon the great dish of meat and onions, and the white wine, and I myself tucked in heartily. Adam sank into a daze of gluttonous delight as I, in considerable detail, continued the account of how Sir Hugh Swynford had been in charge of a small company who were ordered to capture the fort. Written in his own hand Swynford had described how two of Lord John's soldiers had set up ambush with cross-bows to kill him as he did a reconnoitre before the assault.

'So that's what they set out to do.' My mouth was deliciously full.

'Someone must have done in the poor old bastard. Even though he was forever asking for it. What do you think, Mistress Rachel?'

'Oh I remember how unhappy were my mistress's sister that day in Kettlethorpe when she were to be married to him. My mistress were furious at the whole thing. Weren't she, Mr Chaucer?'

'Indeed she was,' I sighed. 'As usual I received the brunt of it!'

'Not that you minded over-much,' Rachel turned to me. 'Poor Lady Katherine, she were so upset.' 'The what?' I asked. I looked at her amazed. 'What in heaven's name, woman, are you talking about?' She said nothing more, preferring to keep silent on this issue.

'Swynford drank like a fish,' I said. 'I wonder he didn't drown like one. And I wonder he could do anything at all.' I grew stern at the memory, feeling my brow furrow with pain. 'Except that I know that he did – Katherine told me.'

'He were drunk on the wedding night?' asked Rachel.

'He was indeed. So was I, but drinking never makes me quarrelsome – I see you raising an eyebrow, Rachel, but it's true.'

'Well, I'm not sure about that, Mr Chaucer, I've seen and heard you quite beside yourself with Mistress Philippa.'

'Yes.' I cleared my throat. 'We won't go into that now.'

'Not a happy wedding night, anyway.'

'At least he made her pregnant straight away, and then had to leave for the campaign in Gascony. Lord John called him away. Now I wonder…'

'Yes?' The wretched scrivener inquired, because I saw something had curiously crossed his mind.

'I wonder if that is not why Lord John called him away…. Plum pie, it's time now for plum pie. What do you say, Adam, to that? You know, now I come to weigh up the matter I believe they could be right, those two knights, for the circumstances surrounding Sir Hugh's death shortly after he returned were highly suspicious. I believe there was even an inquest, wasn't there, for which Thomas Walsingham travelled from St Albans to preside over. Of course no blame could be attached to Lord John, but there were many who would have removed an unwanted obstacle to his love, even without him expressly commanding it. That little Portuguese knave who served him, for one, Eça de Constanides, probably heard Lord John cursing Swynford one day and wishing him out of the way so he…'

All during this I was eyeing Rachel who listened to my discourse, and from her expression I could see she knew much about the subject, as much possibly as I did.

The time had approached for the reading of the will. Just before we left, Thomas Swynford arrived to take Rachel to Leicester fair. On her departure she gave Adam a secretive wink, which I could not, long trained as I was in observation, but pick up – as if to say they were conspirators, and they were in this together. But in what, I asked myself?

As we walked together back towards the castle I hoped I might revive the spirits of my crestfallen scrivener by insisting we stop on the way to look in a meadow where buttercups and daisies were beginning to flower. I beckoned him over. 'Adam, just take a look at these delightful fresh buttercups…'

He looked at me queerly, as if to ask what strange humour had taken hold of me now. There was nothing I loved more go than to go and lie in a meadow, or spend time watching the robin redbreasts tumbling. In the farmyard I liked watching hens and cocks – and especially a fine cock treading his paramours.

I could see him hesitating to pose a question or two. But I was not disposed to humour his inquisitiveness.

'Enough,' I said, luring him to follow, although I limped more than usual. 'Break off a stick for me, Adam.' He did so, grudgingly, from a willow tree nearby, but when I put it to use it buckled under my weight. I said no more. 'Now let's to the reading of the will, although I see it as a prelude, or beginning, of the end. Mankind has fallen from truth, for words and deeds are at odds.'

'Well, Mr Chaucer, you are for ever saying the muses should retreat before Lady Philosophy.'

'I see, Adam, you, too, have been in Boethius's cell.'

'I copied it for you, Mr Chaucer, when you made your translation. Do you not remember?'

'Yes, Adam, but it is the rarest of scriveners who reads and understands what he copies. Nothing so much destroys a work over time as bad copying. I owe you much, Adam.'

My scrivener winced at receiving the compliment.

By now, at the entrance to the great hall, we were jostling with the highest in the land who pressed against each other to enter. I turned all my efforts to smoothness and flattery, recognizing many of them, saying first to Lady Essex, Elizabeth that was, the younger daughter of the dead duke, 'How honoured your great father the duke would have been if he knew how his sons and daughters, even his old enemy Swynford's son, Thomas, have come to pay him homage on the death bed. What an inheritance!'

Thomas, singularly, was not here, not yet anyway, although Lady Essex did not check me, remarking only that her great sadness was that her brother, Prince Henry of Bolingbroke, by virtue of having been sent into exile because of his quarrel with Thomas Mowbray, duke of Norfolk, had not been able to join us, and would not be at his father's funeral, to be held in three day's time in St Paul's Cathedral. 'Can he not seek King Richard's permission to attend,' I asked, adding impishly, 'or come without it?' – I knew full well Henry would be risking his head.

'I doubt he would dare,' replied Henry's sister. 'Would he defy the king?'

'Too many spies about. They say our most noble sovereign has them everywhere. They are certainly here today.' We turned to some new arrivals. I was not sure whether they were spies or just official overseers, for this party of gentlemen had just ridden in, perfumed and caparisoned as only Richard's inner circle was, reeking of his favouritism.

'Who knows: perhaps he will be there incognito. With the speed that he can make, it will mean nothing to him to come over from

Paris.' Bolingbroke had a reputation for speed and was famed as the fastest rider in England.

'Will King Richard himself attend John's funeral mass and burial?'

'I can't believe he will risk not being seen.'

'Look, isn't that William Scrope?'

I tempered my voice in fear and deference. 'Yes. The king's most trusted counsellor. He will be asking why Katherine is not here. He has always had designs upon her.'

Scrope, the earl of Wiltshire, was a tall man, bald with bright blue eyes: because he married young, an heiress, who brought him no children and yet supported him financially, he had never found any centre or security in himself. His speech, always beginning with hesitancies and then suddenly finding fluency and direction, was like his face, put together with pieces from other people's faces, or, similar to precious reliquaries, fabricated from shards of holy objects.

'Um well met...Mr Chaucer,' he bowed low towards me. 'Respectful, reverential... . Your sister-in-law, do you expect her soon?'

'I believe she will meet us before London. It must be painful,' I replied. 'But we must pay her respect and hold her in our prayers.'

Scrope managed to smile. 'Oh erm...yes... . Writing away, are you, Mr Chaucer?'

'Not so bad, not so bad. Thank you for your inquiry.'

Acquisitive, underhand as he was, acutely and tormentedly aware of his social inferiority, Scrope was wily and felt no restraint in dealing with most people. To one person, only, he owed authority, and gave him trust. This was Richard himself.

Meanwhile more sons and daughters, and their children, arrived: the brood of the adulterous union with Katherine, Petronella the so-called mad Swynford girl, Queen Philippa and the Portuguese court, John's half-Castilian daughter and son-in-law, the king of Spain. Armed men everywhere of course, for their protection: everything had swelled to such proportions of finery and numbers, as you would have been able to see anywhere in Europe.

'Look around you, Adam, and what do you remark upon but the results of copulation, copulation, and yet more copulation. *Amor Vincit Omnia!* There is no doubt that, in this world of princes, personal affections, lust, vanity and jealousy count for much more than stratagems of stagecraft and the wisdom of good government. Even Dante Alighieri's great poem, *The Inferno*, which exhorts princes and potentates to be good or face eternal torture and damnation, has failed to influence these passion-hungry Plantagenets.' I deepened my voice. 'You can well see how my lord might have sent Swynford to his death, and, when this failed in France, arranged his poisoning in Lincolnshire. He would have wanted to remove all impediment to his seed. Yet wouldn't you feel proud if you had all these branches on your family tree?'

'Well master,' Adam replied, who was alone in the world, without father or mother as far as he knew, author of himself if of nothing else, and without issue. 'It's you who are part of all this, not me. If I was you I'd be aching to show off my new family.' He meant, of course, that Lord John had only married Katherine some three or so years ago. The eldest son John was now a bishop.

'In-laws and step-family,' I corrected him. 'Look there's Lady Philippa, whom I used to dandle on my knee and tell stories to: she's Queen of Portugal, married to King João – and has tamed him of his mistresses, quite outshining all of them, to become the most revered and disciplined queen in Europe. Their son Prince Henry, obsessed as he is with travel, wants to sail round the world. Rather him than me!'

'The poor creature, Petronella,' sighed Adam, who could not help calling attention to her, for she was so clearly apart, alone, yet crazed as she was, she had remnants of the de Roet family beauty: the high, quizzical arching of the eyes possessed by Philippa , and the unusual auburn, gingery hair. 'She's looking for her mother!'

'Who is not here, but is supposedly due to join the cortège tomorrow in Huntingdon.'

'She must have been only two when her father, Sir Hugh Swynford, died...'

'Was murdered,' I whispered back with a slight devilish chuckle, for Petronella was not far off. 'Don't forget it was murder!' When I used this special sweet tone of perfect humility people would suspect I had been employing that insidious figure of speech that rhetors call irony. Perhaps I *ought* to signal or pronounce my intention beforehand, for the world as a whole is not clever, and I had often been misinterpreted and caused anger. They all believed, in the midst of morbidity, I was cheerful, but I chose to ignore this.

'Why all this talk of Swynford!' demanded Scriven. 'Who's interested in the brutal old cuckold anyway, didn't he receive his deserts?

'Then there's Joan Beaufort,' I ignored this rude interpolation. 'Neville's second wife, the lady Katherine and the duke's only daughter. What a picture of health and beauty!' Indeed she did provide a strong contrast to the Swynford's legitimate offspring, Thomas and Petronella, as she swept by us, to take up a prominent position inside the hall.

'Her husband is intent on giving her a child every year; at the rate he goes he will end up with more than twenty, and all of them married to earls or dukes!' As I warmed to my subject I had to admit I enjoyed feeling puffed up with the conceit of my mighty relations, pointing them out as they passed. 'Look, she's the daughter of the spectacular match Lancaster made with the queen of Castile; not bad eh, Adam?' She was a tall dark Spaniard with unusually flashing white teeth, but I was quite vexed to notice she did not know me from my scrivener, for she looked right through me. 'Katherine is her name too, and she has been queen of Spain these six years. No wonder her grandfather, the head of that family, was titled Peter the Cruel. Yet he was murdered by his half-brother.'

'Didn't you include him in a list you made in one of your tales of good and illustrious rulers?' I made a rueful face at Adam's slight, although I admit I had laid myself open to this. 'You would think Lord John would have had the tact not to name his only daughter from Constanza of Castile after that of his mistress. They say that while he was married to Constanza he kept her out of the way in the convent in Hertford, surrounded by nuns, but when she came to the Savoy in London, she had special holes bored in the ceiling of his bed chamber so that she could watch how he made love to his mistress, or rather how she made love to him so that she might copy it herself.'

'And still he had more children from Katherine Swynford.'

'Oh yes, indeed. More and more. You know I'm tickled pink that Lord John might actually have got Swynford out of the way. John Beaufort, duke of Somerset, was born in the same year as the queen of Spain.'

'But these were all bastards, Mr Chaucer, and the duke was denounced from every pulpit for committing fornication and adultery! Have I said too much, gone beyond my station?'

'No. No, Adam, for indeed that is true, Lord John worshipped his second son, Henry, the one who is now bishop of Winchester. Thomas was born a few years after Henry, and last of all was Joan.

Thomas is duke of Exeter, Joan is now Lady Westmoreland. Three years ago, after Constanza died, the duke married Katherine, Lady Swynford. I tried my hardest to marry them earlier. If I'd had my way the duke would never have married Constanza.' I sighed at the very thought of the efforts I made. 'But politics, dear Adam, the vanity of kingship in this case was more important than sentiment. And anyway this happened before that great turning point in Lord John's life.'

'Turning point?'

'The bloody uprising of peasants and Londoners in the summer of 1381.'

'Ah,' Adam nodded his head in assent, but then looked away in embarrassment as if he had remembered something he did not want to mention directly in my presence. 'If you'll excuse me, master. In truth I would not miss the will for anything. But I am called to visit someone...'

'Oh there's time, Adam.'

But he took no notice and hurriedly he left the throng and made his way out. I wondered what fear and anxiety possessed him, but I knew he made his way to the room in the turret where Rachel was staying...I suspect he had secret business with her, some private preoccupation of his...

EIGHT

Scriven

I DID NOT KNOW what fear or apprehension drove me on, but I climbed the uneven steps two at a time, often stumbling and once catching my ear on a jutting stone. During my conversation with my master memories of that fateful year when he had been arrested for rape had grown and grown, and almost propelled me into blurting out some accusation. That was the charge brought against him, and he got off, didn't he? The woman released him from her rights of action against him. We don't know why, but we can guess he made a settlement on her. Conveniently for him the convulsions brought about by Wat Tyler, Jack Straw and the Kentish rebels in the year that followed eclipsed this episode. The constant allusion of my master to birds and flowers provoked me to a delayed wrath. Did he see in himself the honey-bee? Or as Chanticleer the cock? On this walk we had taken together, judging from his demeanour and his attitude to nature, it would seem he could never harm another being. Such is the delusion of appearances. He would so often say, 'Adam, I am not living on the edge of a precipice, I am in the middle of a field of solid daisies. I don't believe in extremes.' Yet he was, I believed, as we all were, on that very edge he mentioned.

I felt suddenly very anxious, inclined to run away, or be sick. When I reached the room the door was slightly open and I heard a rustle and guttural cry from within. I was reminded that I had promised to bring a flask of wine and had forgotten. But once through the door, what a sight confronted me to chill my heart and raise my gullet to the roof of my mouth! For Rachel lay flat out on the floor, her rich finery flopped around her like a deflated bladder, a promiscuous artichoke, or a sail without wind, while blood poured from her throat which had been slashed from side to side. Oh Jesus's wounds, what horrors had we heaped upon horror on this the thirty-seventh day of my Lord Lancaster's exposure to his mourners, and could this all be for Lord John's redemption? Her room had been ransacked. It could not be any ordinary cut-throat's deed. I was stricken with guilt, for what if it was I who had been the cause? I summoned Rachel here to Leicester Castle for my own reasons connected with that rape.

Nearly dead, not quite. I dragged Rachel to a couch and pulled her on to it, trying to quench the flow of her blood with a cloth. 'Who is it, was it Thomas?' I asked. She shook her head.

'He left me...someone else,' she managed hoarsely to whisper. 'Face...didn't see it. Adam, you must know more: I have been to the gatehouse...' the words came slurred and her eyes swivelled up and back, but she fought to make the effort. 'Basil...the guard...I have given to him.... He was in Moorgate that evening when Sir...plotted...' Now she strained to the utmost to tell me. 'Rachel,' I cried out, 'forgive me!...' Her mouth tried to manage a smile, while all the time blood gushed from her gaping wound. 'No, no fault...but...'

'And' – I don't know why I ask, but it must seem to me connected...'Was it Sir Hugh Swynford who plotted? – '

She seemed to be arrested as if puzzled. There was a sickening rattle and more blood swelled up. Then she was no more. I laid her back and covered her. What had she wanted to tell me? Something further about Philippa? About my master? Whatever it had been, it was now too late, except that while I arranged some drapery over her and wondered what to do next, I was assaulted by a mighty and overpowering conviction.

What seemed to me at first a question of a variable but not deadly nature, to find out more about my master and give some account of his life – with some evidence to place before the future in the way of clearing up the mysteries and telling the whole truth – had now become an absolute need for me to solve. I was bound to Rachel's death by my own responsibility for bringing her here to Leicester, just as I was obliged to find her murderer and bring him to justice. But I had little hope of the latter, given the circumstances and the great number of visitors in and around Leicester Castle, as well as the appalling laxity of the sheriffs and everyone connected with bringing felons and murderers to justice. Who could ever question, and investigate everyone who was assembled here?

Indeed I resolved that I would best serve my purpose if I remained silent about finding Rachel; to call the sheriff, and say it had been my discovery, would only prod him and others into asking questions of me, even to their raising at me the finger of suspicion. With this in mind, and carefully wiping from me every trace of Rachel's blood, I slipped out of the room and down the stairs, reflecting also that the sooner I was back by Mr Chaucer's side at the reading of the will, the better chance I had to escape any suspicion or surveillance.

But then her last words...'Basil...gatehouse...Moorgate ...plotted...' rang in my ears as I clattered noisily down the stairs. I made for the gatehouse, which was a stone's throw away, indeed only a slight diversion from the path of my return to the hall, and here I found an old soldier or sergeant-at-arms, a bulky, black-haired, unshaven giant whom God forbid I should ever meet when he was full of drink on a dark night. 'Basil?' I asked. 'No. I ain't Basil. In there – ' The guard pointed to a door to which I at once proceeded. I knocked. 'Come in,' I heard a more pleasant voice answer, and then I found myself face to face with Basil. I recognized Basil in spite of the changes brought by age; thick-set, with cheerful, regular outdoor features. Vulgar in appearance but jolly, white-haired but still strong, small but quick.

'Has an old lady been to see you?' I asked hesitantly. 'Rachel Dempsey?'

Basil answered, 'Indeed she has.'

'Did she leave anything?'

'Indeed she did.'

'May I have it?'

'Indeed. Who are you?' He was like a jackdaw with 'indeed'. I told him, and he said, 'Indeed, it's a bundle of letters, or some such matter.' He handed over a hand-sewn sack or bag which contained papers and parchment. I took this without a word, pretending I knew all about it. 'Thank you,' I said...to which he answered, incomprehensibly. 'Indeed, don't you want to know what I can tell you about the matter?' 'What matter?' I asked. 'That's not for me to say. Wait a minute. Indeed – don't I know you from some place? Yes, weren't you there that day when Sir Hugh Swynford set upon the duke with four or five men to put him out of the way for ever? Oh that were dirty work, and just as well it never succeeded, weren't it?'

Yes. Now everything seemed more and more of a puzzle. Had I been there? If I had, I could not remember. But I had to hurry away, as I had to be back by my master's side for someone sooner or later would find Rachel, and the hue and cry would be raised. My own absence from the hall would be noticed, if only by my master. So clutching the parcel I informed Basil that I would return a little later, after the reading of the will, and hold further discourse with him. He seemed disposed to agree.

'What a crush!' I whispered to my master, alongside whom I had taken up my position. 'Are you expecting something from the will?' I breathed quickly, and my heart stopped in my mouth. I berated myself all the time with Rachel's death: oh if only I had not called her to the castle. I regretted my interference, but now once in, I was stuck braving the current and there was no wading back to the safety of the bank. I just about managed to raise my eyes to look around me, to see if there was order even in this packed hall, and indeed everyone had his or her allotted place, as befitted their rank from queens and princes down, this position having been given them by the chamberlain. The royalty, lords and their ladies, knights, a mass of commoners, heralds, squires, waiting women, friars, lowlier chancery officials and their wives, all stood dressed appropriately for their ranks in deference and knowledge of their degree…

LORD JOHN: After the reading of 'The Book of the Duchess', what had gone on at that meeting between Chaucer and myself? Within minutes I had shocked my devoted and gentle poet, and felt I would have to increase his annual pension. He was amazed to find that, far from the grief towards Blanche that he expected me to feel, I had become obsessed with something else, namely how to make Katherine Swynford my mistress as soon as possible. I grew beside myself with passion for this most desirable lady.

'But don't you really feel, my lord, the deep spiritual loss of Blanche – Blanche's sensitivity, her love of poetry, and of music?' Chaucer asked me.

'Her response to you was a real response based on a solid perception of what you were trying to do,' I answered. 'But this was something quite alien to me. I am bound up with Plantagenet pride, the divine right of my family, my concern for the kingdom of England, as if it was a man-of-war entrusted to my sole guardianship.'

I loved and appreciated the lady Blanche for all she had brought to me, namely land, love, protection, fine children, unerring taste, and forthright and decent steadfastness. In fact it was really my friend Chaucer who had really loved her deepest self. He had been her twin soul.

'I shall always remember how remarkable she was,' sighed Chaucer, 'when she had died so young: only twenty-five years of age, and yet so wise, so mature in wisdom. I never heard her utter a single word of regret.'

'We create each other,' I answered. 'You, too, Chaucer, contributed to her beauty and perfection, and gave others reasons to admire her.' I changed the subject. 'Why do you wish to foster your sister-in-law's contact with me?' Chaucer did not answer.

'Ah, now you remain silent. Could it be your own lack of confidence in yourself, or your fear that you could lose Philippa?' I hardly needed such cunning, or encouragement. If anything, I needed restraint.

'But I've suffered!' I told Chaucer. 'From fearing, all these years, that I am not whom I am supposed to be.'

Chaucer asked what I further intended to say.

'As the fourth child of my father, I had very little from him, but he was astute enough to arrange for me to marry Blanche of Lancaster who became, when her father died, the richest and greatest landowner in England. I owe everything to her, wealth and position, and although she was much younger than I was, her wisdom and strength ruled me entirely. But now I am thirty, and she is dead. My father chose her for me. I did not choose her for myself. Now I can choose for myself.'

'So whom would you choose, Lord John?'

I was silent. Chaucer caught my eye. He beckoned me to draw closer to him, which I did.

'Whom would you have me choose?' I asked.

Chaucer could not but reflect that the boot was now on the other foot. But the constraint put upon him over his marriage to Philippa may still have rankled. 'I think you know.'

Upon this my temper flared up: 'Not some duchess of Milan, or princess of a palatinate? Oh no, that I can do your family an even greater honour it well suits you, doesn't it Chaucer, to make out this Swynford girl is another Blanche of Lancaster – but I tell you she's not. She's like her sister – an educated gentlewoman, but like Galatea, fashioned like a jewel. Such women Our Lord made for pleasure and joy.'

Chaucer replied: 'It was Blanche herself who chose her – to guide your children's lives, to engage them tutors, and to look after their welfare. Look carefully at your three children, Lord John. Could they have been better served – especially Elizabeth and Philippa? The girls love her, but Henry most of all will benefit. See how different he will be from Richard of Bordeaux, his cousin…'

'You mean, if my brother Edward dies, that unworthy heir to England?…' I must have looked even blacker.

'I mean the heir to England's throne, my lord, our next king.'

'Well, I should have been Richard's father…' I was silent for a moment. 'Perhaps I shall be king.'

'Perhaps you mean, my lord – and with all due respect to your great honour and position – that Katherine Swynford should no longer serve as Henry's governess.'

At this I clammed up. Of course I wanted her to remain his governess.

'If I may make a suggestion, my lord,' said Chaucer. 'Katherine Swynford has strong and inspiring qualities. She is intelligent and well-educated. Take my advice, make her your wife. After the due period for mourning and respect to Blanche has passed.'

'Wife?' I said, puzzling with a slight tone of contempt over the poet's word. 'Chaucer, you can't be serious?'

'Of course, I'm serious,' he answered. 'If you love her, marry her.'

'But she's already married.'

We looked at one another. He could only mean one thing.

KATHERINE: 'His grace sends me to command your attendance in private upon his great person at once.' This was Mr Chandler, my lord of Lancaster's servant.

'For what reason? I have no petition. His chamberlain deals with matters regarding his children. Anyway, Lord John mourns Blanche his duchess.'

'He still wishes to see you.'

'Why in private?'

'Heaven knows. He has been talking to Mr Chaucer.'

'Oh Mr Chaucer, my brother-in-law, is the poet. His mind is full of mischief, I wouldn't wonder if he doesn't want to sell me to Lord John, so he can turn me into a romance.' I bit my tongue. I had gone too far in front of Lord John's servant. 'Take no notice,' I went on, 'I don't mean this. But I feel under threat from such a command.'

'If you do not come with me I shall be punished. It is a long enough way, and we mustn't talk any more.'

We rode back to the Savoy in silence. Under the great Strand portcullis we rode, and into the outer ward. At the stables I slid off my mount, grazing myself painfully on the metal pommel of the saddle. Mr Chandler seized me by the hand, at which I gibbed and tried to pull it away. He led me by the animal pens, the kitchens, down by the ill-smelling Fleet stream, in and out of many a dank and foul passage. I began to doubt that he had any good intention.

'The duke's private lodgings are not to be found here!'

'We take a roundabout way,' said Mr Chandler. 'My lord wishes your visit to be a private one, and that no one should pass comment upon it.'

My anger as well as my suspicion was mounting. I might only be a servant of the Lancaster household, but I was not a secret courtesan, and I fretted at this undignified treatment. So when at last I was brought into his private quarters I felt my colour had mounted high. I bristled with such defiance that I had to instruct myself to keep my anger under control.

I heard this booming voice: he called out 'Enter!' Mr Chandler opened the heavy door for me, and as I passed through he slipped away into the shadows.

I swept in quickly, concealing as best I could my fear and anger.

'So what is it you wish of me, your grace?' I said when brought into his presence. He suffered me to kneel for some time in silence, to kiss his hand, extending the homage I paid him till my knee began to ache. I formed the impression that, contrary to those warm looks which had passed between us at the reading, fanned and coaxed along by my brother-in-law Geoffrey, he was not a very pleasant or courteous personality. He must have sensed that I was not going to be an easy conquest. Yet the purpose in that bristling tawny mane of his, and burning dark eyes, was plain enough to see.

'You seem to view me with suspicion, if not complete horror,' he observed. 'What have I ever done to you?'

'I can see at this moment, my lord,' I said to him, 'that you look to me for some consolation after my good mistress's death…' But here my firm words of disapproval began to take effect. He exclaimed rather bashfully. 'I only wish you to grant me your love.'

'No.' I blushed deeply and shook with a sense of my own unworthy state. 'My dear lord, I see your great worth, and I'd love to be on terms of friendliness and laughter with you. It might bring to you some ease, and it would certainly support me. You and my lady Blanche's children will need me more now than anything.'

'I look on you with complete delight,' he said, caught as he was between achieving his aim, and inspiring me with trust. 'I feel the shafts of love keenly.' Did he mean here, if I didn't obey? I took this as a threat.

'I have no wish to rouse you to anger, my lord.'

'Do you want to purchase hate, when you can stand in grace?'

'Of course not,' I answered. 'I'm not a fool. But I need time.'

His face reddened with impatience. 'I have to leave for Calais straight away. The king my father has made me lieutenant in command there. France continues to invade our south coast. I have to be hasty in everything, even in love.'

I hardly dared to challenge him. But I did. 'Pleasure and temperance lie in all endeavour.'

'Not battle,' he answered quickly. 'And I see often no difference between love and war.' He took hold of my wrist. 'I want you now.'

I looked down at my feet. 'Knowing that I am the cause of your distress,' I answered, 'I cannot despise you. But I despise what you ask of me.'

'I mean your good,' he said, letting my hand go free.

'Do not forget,' I replied, 'that you are the godfather of my daughter, my child from my marriage to Sir Hugh Swynford. I don't think my husband would look on our meeting with approval.'

He ignored this. 'I vow to you my love. How else can I shake off this grief for my wife, than by expressing my love to you in some form of action?'

Impelled by indignation at his incitement to an ordinary act of lechery, I rose to my feet. My eyes fell on Lord John's fine statue of a naked Venus, much fabled, which had come as a gift from Italy. I felt stung with reproof. While our age paid lip service to the principles of Christendom, to the pope in Avignon, to Jesus, to the ideals of chivalry, the real worship was for Venus, the naked bitch, glorious in her nakedness for all to see. She was floating in a shell on the large sea, a rose garland decking out that delectable flesh and form, which glowed and beckoned with temptation. Her endless, sinuous, binding charms and erotic power brought broken sleep, sacred tears, jealousy, vain hopes, foolhardiness and, in the end, madness.

I knew just what Lord John wanted. I was to have none of that. I abruptly took my leave.

Nine

Chaucer

'OF COURSE NOT,' I answered Adam's question. 'I am a poet and poets have no standing, while I never had land, never will. Philippa, my dear deceased wife,' I made the sign of the cross, 'while she was alive, both of us had annuities from Lancaster. She owned lands in Hainault which passed to the children.'

I felt distraught for a moment as I really did miss her. I also noticed how Scriven clutched his parcel close to him, for fear he might be separated from it. He recovered and suggested, a little mockingly, that it might not be a bad thing to be left a fine estate, indicating that I had taught him many bad tricks of speech which passed by the name of wit, such as a scathing tongue, irony, sarcasm and a host of other barbs and poison tips. I answered magisterially that the wills of great men like the duke are political documents: 'It's their final chance to influence history. I have no power to wield.' Scriven then tried to point out that I could easily have refused an estate or two, if they had been offered, which clearly they had not been. I rebutted this suggestion. 'The kind of closeness, promised by royal friendship is a mirage. I never expected it to be more than this, knowing the difference between a Plantagenet and myself.' Scriven looked disbelieving, as if I was just consoling myself. So I sighed, adding, 'I have owned something of more value than all the great estates in England.'

'Which is?' Scriven inquired.

'My solitude. One thing Lord John never had from the moment he was born up to the time of his death. Since the gentlewomen began to cosset him on their knees as an infant with golden curls and guided him to play with and suck their breasts and tickle their private parts, and while they sucked his, he never spent a minute without someone asking something of him. It's my son Thomas who'll succeed in my lord of Lancaster's world. He's already constable of Knaresborough Castle in Wallingford, and has taken my advice to marry Maud, a rich lady. He's twice been Speaker of the House of Commons...'

Of course I made no mention of Thomas's dual or dubious paternity. For maybe, just maybe, a streak of someone else had determined the grand scale of his ambition...Should I be proud of this, or angry and resentful?

My voice was drowned by the noise. The squeeze grew even greater as Lord John's numerous retinue crowded in almost to crush the speaker, Thomas, count of Worcester, the seneschal of the household of the bishop of Salisbury. Outside in the courtyard pressed the poor of every shape and description, ready to applaud or riot. As Lord John was the greatest landowner in the kingdom, through the properties of his first wife Blanche and her sister (some had condemned him for murdering her for her estates, although I believed emphatically he had not), he had had over a hundred knights and esquires in his service, and most of them were here. They showed the loyalty of those who had received larger fees and better office, as well as royal favours, through him, and altogether greater prestige, than through any other grandee. Yet, to the immediate annoyance of some, it was clear from the outset that Lord John had not intended to reward his huge band of followers except by anything more than a continuing service in the household of his heir, Lord Henry of Bolingbroke.

It was the poor of the land who for the salvation of his soul were rewarded first. Second, after the poor, the lepers, the hermits and recluses, then the friars and nuns. Several pages of gifts to the prisons and preachers were read out in a booming bittern voice by the count of Worcester. Some of the throng were now openly muttering, 'This is not what we expect to hear!' 'I've served the duke all my life.' 'This is poor thanks!' and other less reasonable and more lewd-mouthed expressions. A sense of grievance and envy began to circulate.

'I hope the beneficiaries are wise enough to take a copy,' I confided to Scriven at my elbow. 'I wonder how many of these marks of silver, these nobles, will actually reach the inmates of the lazar houses and the prisons. But Adam, it looks like we are now to come to the crux of the matter!' All chatter and discontent suddenly ceased, and faces became eager to watch the lips of the seneschal: 'Let's see to what degree he was a diplomat in death,' I observed.

'First item, I leave my dear wife and companion Katherine the two best ouches which I own, after the ouch I leave to my esteemed lord and nephew the king.'

'Well that's tactful,' I exclaimed, knowing how famous Lancaster was for his priceless pieces of jewellery, the golden clasps above all.

'I leave also my largest gold chalice…'

There was now a careful division of spoils between Lady Katherine and the king, which I noticed the hawk-eyed minions at the front of the crowd duly register. No doubt from where they stood threateningly they would report to their liege, for he had of late become unduly sensitive to any slight or deviation of flattery from his own person. Because of Lord Henry's exile over his quarrel and curtailed duel, Prince John had been intent on making sure the king would have nothing with which to reproach him or his heirs. So he bequeathed him a third of the astronomically high pension of forty thousand francs from Spain, administered by 'my very dear son' the king of Castile and Leon. While my sister-in-law Katherine had been mentioned first, the best nowche or ouch went to King Richard, also his best covered gold chalice which Katherine had given him, and his gold salt cellar with the garter, and 'Twelve cloths of gold with a red satin field, stripped with gold and which clothes I ordered for the making of a bed, which is still not begun, and the best ermine over which I have altogether with the pillow-case thereto, and the piece of arras which the duke of Burgundy gave to me the time I was in Calais.'

Only as third in the list did Lord John mention his disgraced son, Bolingbroke, leaving him two pieces of cloth of Arras, and his red and white striped bed of camocas. To Katherine went the 'great bed of black velvet embroidered with iron compasses and garters, and a turtle-dove in the middle of the compasses.' That said it all: 'What sights of adulterous passion that silent turtle-dove must have witnessed,' I confided teasingly to my secretary. 'Or chivalric, wifely tenderness,' replied that scrivener in as light a tone, but there was no mention of most of the unrelated retainers who had gathered here, for the will had turned out as essentially a family matter – apart from the poor. What began as restless muttering – 'When's something coming to us who've served him faithfully?' – had grown by the end of the endless small gifts, including one for Katherine's first son, Sir Thomas Swynford, into a stormy riot. During this the beneficiaries of the will, and the royal personages who attended, melted away, as did the followers of King Richard who, as intelligence-seekers, left with their disclosures ready to be made to their sovereign. No doubt these would include parasitical assessments of the discontented Lancastrian assembly.

I climbed to my feet. I had had sufficient of this insulting behaviour. 'Stop this!' I called out in a ringing voice to those hundreds of powerful, angry faces. 'Stop all this tongue-lashing and chiding! You should not be hostile to our late prince and lord, because he has not neglected you. His mission in life was to keep his country a whole and single nation. This land is like a family and he was more than any other its head: it is also like a human body which needs to be of one piece and whole in order to function properly, each of its parts aware of its importance and function.'

Some of the assembly groaned and some tried to shout me down, but generally these followers, picked by Lord John himself, as they reflected his qualities as faithful followers, grew quiet and became inclined to listen. They had been members of his family in all but name.

'Prince John served you all well during his lifetime, and you have been generously rewarded with the many gifts of land and advancement, and thousands of small gestures he made in his lifetime, for he never forgot an obligation, or left a good deed to pass unappreciated…'

They began to be called to order, for my assertion of Lord John's qualities rested upon the truth, their knowledge of his virtue. 'Above all,' I continued as best I could, 'he could not – such as some we might name – ' the reference became I hoped all too clear to those slimy and back-scratching sycophants of the king who bore the stamp of insincere glozers – 'buy and sell love for money or gain. But when we come to the will, I believe you were rather expecting something which was not to be, for you have been corrupted yourselves by the bribery and falseness which is rampant. Yet you are men of honour and conscience, and when you reflect further you will see that what Prince John has left you is a continuity of honour and steadfastness, and by leaving all his estates and income to his son he has ensured that this will continue, just as Henry of Bolingbroke will retain you and yours in his service. So choose,' I wound up my harangue, 'choose infamy and backsliding, or follow your conscience and walk humbly with your God…'

With such adulatory obeisance to the man to whom I owed so much did I, in the end, soothe the Lancastrian underlings and lay flattering words on their souls.

We shall never know what could have happened next, for the *posse comitatus* of Leicester, led by the sheriff himself, burst into the hall, commanding everyone to stay. The reason he gave us was that two brutal crimes had been discovered inside the castle, and that he was obliged to question everyone.

LORD JOHN SERVING HIS COUNTRY: Early this New Year I and my Lancastrian army, with mercenaries from Portugal, embarked on the command of my noble and omnipotent father to destroy Charles V of France's plans for the invasion of England.

I was sent with fewer than a thousand men, and as lieutenant of the king in the north, my mission was to destroy the French ships being built and armed. Over in France I confronted a force seven times the size of mine which inexplicably – or rather, there were dozens of reasons advanced, from bribery to treason – did not advance to attack me. After a while, and when I was reinforced by the earls of Salisbury, Warwick, March, with many more men, the main body of the French, under the command of Philippe, duke of Burgundy – a former prisoner of mine, and as such a hunting and whoring companion – mysteriously melted away. I was free to skirmish and attack the ports on the north coastline of France, looting and pillaging the villages and towns that were not sufficient in their defence to repel us. The smoke of burning villages, and of raped and looted homesteads, choked the skies. The ships returned to England laden with the spoils of war, and with valuable prisoners as hostages whose commercial value was such that our English knights would often fall out and kill each other over who should reap the ransom money. I returned to London.

This was the time I wanted to plan another meeting between myself and Katherine, although it suited me to keep us apart longer, for Katherine was sceptical of my love.

'For God's love,' Chaucer admonished me, 'if you want to write a successful love letter, have the sense not to pack it with tough arguments, or to make it scrivenish' – a reference to his scrivener no doubt – 'or too crafty. Make it light, don't write too perfectly – I mean the handwriting, my lord, don't harp obsessively on love, or even try to appear distracted by mixing your terms.'

I answered: 'I don't know if I can. I might misrepresent my innocence, while should she receive it wrongly, I don't know what I'd do.'

'Right,' said Chaucer. 'Just do as I say. I'll bring the letter to her.' I agreed.

What did I say in this letter? I called her my 'right lady', my 'heart's life', my desire, the salvation of my sorrow – Chaucer gave me the idea to use the word leech, by no means in a pejorative sense, but as a life-preserving agent to remove an excess of blood and energy, and he gave me many other terms. He suggested I paint myself as worth little, and accuse myself of all manner of unworthiness – yet implore her to forgive me of my folly and cheek in writing to her. I swore endless love, and I grew carried away with the sincerity of what I put down on paper. I bathed with my salt tears the ruby on the signet ring I wore, kissing the letter over and over again before I sent it off with Chaucer.

'What game!' Chaucer told me when he was alone with me later. 'I swear I'd never do this for anyone else but you, Lord John – although he were a thousand times my brother. I don't do it for my own gain, but to relieve my distress over Katherine. In this I am clear of conscience and so is she, although it is I who will have acted to make her – as the lady – come to the man. If this were to become known, the entire world would cry shame on me and accuse me of the worst treachery. So please, I beg you, keep the whole thing a secret…'

I was impressed, and from Chaucer I learnt how to dissimulate my desire, and go about my daily affairs with a cool, measured air. I was not at all angry at the services of a bawd that Chaucer performed for me: far from this, I implored him to undertake all that was necessary to steer me through this great enterprise. I would follow whatever he decided was best.

So I and my poet understood each other. He was after all – in the title we gave him at court – Venus's own son. But the problem that would not go away was the husband.

SIR HUGH SWYNFORD'S ACCOUNT OF TREACHERY: I looked resplendent; I rode in solitary state through the Gascon village of Le Pagenac, near the lines of the enemy forces; my spurs jingled, my breastplate shone, and my sword clanked impressively against my leg; I felt a proper fire-eater. The villagers smiled at me because they preferred English rule, as does much of this area, for it is less feudal and more bourgeois, and has given the local townsmen and ordinary people more rights, and more financial power. Under the English they are better off.

Our campaign was hard. The French were determined to drive us out of this narrow strip of land to the north of the estuary of the Gironne, and by this threaten Bordeaux, and the great wine trade with England. Already the prices were increasing. This year much of the grape harvest had been left to rot in the fields while our archers and horsemen, and the French and Genevese with their cross bolts and elaborate caparisons and armour, chased each other back and forwards over the rich vineyards and farmland.

What worried me most was the lack of good food. I and my company always need to eat well, and we had only salted meat and bad biscuits. With the weather being so bad at this time of year, it was dangerous for English boats to land provisions on the coast, while the French fleet was also harrying us.

I had been ordered by Lord John to capture a small wooden fort which the duc d'Angoulême had, over night and under cover of darkness, moved in to capture, for it commanded the road along the sand dunes north of the estuary. The morale of my company was not good, for they heard nothing else but of their comrades being driven back step by step.

Into Bordeaux, where Lord John had his headquarters, there flowed an endless stream of information, most of it false, passing to and fro; secret messengers, envoys arranging and breaking truces, bribes, agreement between the English and the French nobility, the whole place was a turmoil of bargaining. One saw sinister men in friars' capes with loose hoods, women in pages' clothes with hose which failed to hide the curves of their bodies; and churls with blackened hands but shapely legs, who had 'court-man' written all over them. There were also many other visitors to Lancaster's palace, less welcome: one heard constant rumours of attempts being made on his life.

I had billeted down my men on the outskirts of Le Pagenac, and having dismounted I was strolling back to the sizeable merchant's house I had seized for my own use, planning what I should do the following morning to ensure the capture of the fort, when I suddenly noticed, having strayed along a narrow path, the metal glint of a cross-bow behind a hedge. I quickly saw that this might be someone lying in wait for me, and I ran off. On the path back to the village I spied a further cross-bow behind a rock; this was clearly an ambush. I flung myself down and at the same moment heard the click, and the bolt fly over my head. I jumped to my feet, pulling out my sword, and the bolt from the other weapon ploughed into the sand where my head had been on the ground. I was in a trap.

'There's another; if not a fourth,' I muttered to myself. I started running in the direction of the village. My assailants had strung new bolts and fired after me, one of their bolts grazed my hand, another bounced off my leg-armour. Into my house I charged like a bull breathless and dead white in the face. I knew that it was not casual bolt-fire, but there was a remote possibility that it could be. Was it a deliberate attempt to have me put out of the way? I wondered whether my would-be murderers were French or English. That night, before the attack of the morning, I could hardly sleep.

The following morning I rose, and with my group of twenty horsemen and bowmen set out for the wooden fort. The first thing we had to discover was whether the fort was still occupied, or if the French had abandoned it in the night, and to do this we had to get up close. I left most of my men under a clump of trees several hundred yards off, and with four volunteer companions found a trench. Hidden in this we advanced upon the fort. We got to within thirty or so yards from the walls, and here we halted; two of our number had run away. The other two, my most trusted esquires Trevor Bair and Jonathan Abel, continued to go forward with me. We reached the corner of the counterscarp, and found ourselves virtually on top of the wall. We could see no one, and the fort seemed to be empty, and while I and my men were wondering what to do next, suddenly a big puff of smoke erupted from the wooden tower and a dozen bolts swooshed around our heads. We now knew: the fort was still in the hands of the French.

I decided then and there to mine the fort, and to go back for the main body of my force to collect them, and the spades and gunpowder to do this. We turned and ran back for the trench; just as we were almost back in it, and finding cover for a second time, a single bolt hissed past and sank in the chest of Jonathan Abel, wounding him badly; Trevor Bair raced back to the rest but I, not prepared to leave my trusted squire, bent down to lift him and help him back. Another whoosh from a crossbow, and my squire fell back, this time with a bolt stuck firmly in the side of his face. Another bolt narrowly missed me, and as I turned I noticed that this time the bolt could not have come from the French in the fort, but from behind me.

Where were the two retainers we had set out with, both Lord John's men, newly attached to my company? I was determined to find out, and with sudden devilish guile I fell on my friend's body, in the pretence of being dead. A moment after, I saw two heads peering over the top of an abandoned earthwork. I recognized them as the men who had run away. My guess was right: the two men had volunteered to go with me to act as scouts, but with the aim of killing me, hoping my death would be put down to enemy bolts. Now, fearing that I, their target, might be merely wounded, they were back to make sure they had finished me off. But my trick had taken them in, and imagining me incapacitated, they hadn't bothered to re-arm their cross-bows.

I had been careful not to fall on my sword, and when the pair were only feet away I leapt up suddenly and rushed at them. These traitors, aware that if they returned to the others they would be seized, had only one direction to go, towards the fort. One, taking hold of his bow like a bludgeon, aimed a heavy blow at me, but what chance did that have against my bulk? The assailant rushed past me, but the French, thinking he was attacking them, loosed on him a great hail of arrows and bolts, and even a cannon-ball. He was manifoldly struck and collapsed. While this was going on I was locked in combat with the second thug, making short work of overpowering him with my sword and swiftly wounding him in the side; he was down and I on him in seconds, the blade of my sword to his throat.

'Don't, don't kill me,' said the would-be murderer. 'Spare me and I'll confess everything.'

'What can you confess?'

'If you value your life you would do well to listen.'

'You treacherous cur!' I shouted. 'Who employs you to kill me?'

'A great duke.'

'French or English?'

'The other has the letter in his pocket.'

'How did you come to get mixed up in this?'

'He suggested I should join him, and we should do the job together.'

'How much were you offered?'

'Thirty francs.'

I laughed.

'A good price. Not a small sum for a pair such as you. Well, I'll grant you life...on one condition. Solely if...'

'What, sir?' answered the soldier, suspiciously. He believed I meant to betray him with a stratagem.

'That you go forward to the walls of the fort, and get that letter from your rogue friend's pocket. I want proof.'

'It's just another way of getting me killed!' cried the murderous slave. 'How will you be able to retrieve the letter with the French firing down on me at close quarters?'

'If you don't, I'll swear that I'll kill you myself.'

'No, sir, spare me for the sake of your dear wife. But you may think she's been stolen from you.'

As he spoke the ruffian fell on his knees, grovelling with terror, propping himself up with one arm because with loss of blood his strength was giving out.

'How do you know about my wife?' I asked.

'It's written down in the letter.'

All the more reason I must have that letter, I was thinking, 'Well now, Lord John of Lancaster, I shall arraign you before the mightiest judges. And if I do not get justice, much as I dislike the thought of smearing my sword with a ruffian like you...I swear I'll...'

I backed up my words with such a brutal look that the young ruffian sprang up: fearful dread impelled life back into his limbs...

'All right, Sir Hugh, all right, I'll go...'

I seized the man's cross-bow, stood behind him, and began prodding him forward with the point of my sword. The cur left a trail of blood behind him: I watched his pitiful progress of slinking under cover towards his accomplice.

'All right,' I said, watching him with contempt: 'Stay where you are. I'll let you see the difference between a brave man and a coward.'

Then I made my way to the second soldier, treading warily, eyes on the fort and taking advantage of every bit of cover. Having reached the man, either I could search him for the letter, or, making a shield for me with his body, carry him back to the trench. I chose the second course. I had hoisted the man on my back when the French opened fire. I felt his body jerk against mine, heard him scream. I flung him down, and began to rummage through his pockets for the letter, but there was a terrific explosion near me; 'Had the tunnels been mined?' I wondered.

Suddenly there was shouting; I saw a mass of heavily armed Frenchmen dashing out of the walls of the fort; equally there was a cry behind me, and my own followers, rallying to save me and my companions, had gathered and were advancing at the other end of the trench.

Everything began to happen in front of me in slow, fairylike motion as I wondered who was fighting whom, and whether my own soldiers would effect my rescue. I did not see how the skirmish ended, for one of the French soldiers near me hit me on the head, and the worst of it was that it prevented me seeing how the action would be resolved.

What's this? Am I falling? My legs are giving way, I thought, and fell on my back with a great crash of metal. I opened my eyes, but I saw nothing, for above there was nothing but the sky, the immeasurably wide and endless blue sky. 'How peaceful, and how infinite,' I thought. 'Yet I'll wreak vengeance on those who have done this to me!'

Ten

Scriven

TWO CRIMES THE SHERIFF'S men had said? Two? I started to shake, and the sight of Rachel as I left her menaced me more and more and prayed inwardly on my mind. What could the other crime be if not murder too, and if it was connected with Rachel, who could it be of, but Basil the guard...?

For a moment I was so confounded that I quivered and felt my blood run cold. I feared I would fall into a panic and stampede and show my confusion and alarm to everyone, so if anyone were suspected of murder it would be me. But the sense, or weight of what I carried under my arm, that package given me by the guard, held me, intimidated me with a heavier influence.

My master joined me. 'What is it, Adam?' he asked. 'You're as white as bleached cotton.'

His tales are full of guilty parties who betray themselves by their startled countenances, for their guilt has an appalling effect upon their outward demeanour.

'I've been standing too long on my feet,' I uttered feebly.

Fortunately, however, confronted with the reality my master did not notice, or if he did concealed it from me. 'You know, Adam,' he said, 'now I come to think about it, there has always been a certain knight-errantry about Lord John's actions!'

Our file approached the sheriff. Right before us stood the four Cheshire guards whose white hart badges proclaimed their loyalty to serve the king and no one else. They had not been allowed to leave with Scrope, who had left earlier, answerable as he was to no one but the king. But in the speech my master made was he not repaying Lord John from a deeper, more dark motive, namely that the duke once restored him when he lay paralysed in the gutter of his own desire, and accused of rape?

'I suppose the sheriff daren't even question Lord Scrope,' said my master, 'but he couldn't quite get away with his escort.'

From their reputation I had an exaggerated view of these Cheshire archers who were the king's personal bodyguard, and I stood back away from them as far as possible, expecting to be attacked with a knife by any one of them at any moment.

'Dickie, the short one, is their captain, and they are called Yole, Wade and Perkin.'

'Are they forenames or surnames?' I asked my master, who seemed remarkably well-informed.

'I don't know. Yole was an executioner. I knew him years ago.'

Yole was the tall one, fat and gross, well over forty, with bloated red cheeks, white teeth and a loud coarse laugh. It was evident from his face that he was the most unreasonable of men. He bowed and saluted my master with a certain ferocious disdain, which no one in their right mind would question.

'He was for a short while a friend of Mrs Chaucer's.'

'Is that why he wears a brooch with a Lancastrian device?'

'Nonsense,' said my master, who coloured. 'He can't be wearing that.'

'Seems like it to me. A tiny golden lion couchant.'

'A fake,' spoke my master sharply.

I abandoned the subject. Wade, a younger guard, closely resembled our sovereign. Probably why the king picked him: the employment of those closely resembling royal personages and even great lords was becoming common, and the beneficiaries commanded a good salary. On the battle-field they were especially useful, but even in court they could be employed with subtlety.

My master noticed how I stared at him. 'Yes I can see you wonder. The resemblance is strong.'

Wade was fair-haired, of pale complexion and a feminine and rounded face given easily to flush. He wore many marks of favour, I imagined from the king. Perkin, the other one, had an extraordinary thick lip and a big fleshy nose sprinkled with blackheads. The clothes of all four were heavily splashed with mud.

'Well, who are you?' asked the sheriff, who was a robust and loutish-looking fellow of about forty-five, with a face disfigured by smallpox, little red eyes sunk in fat, and an extremely sullen and morose expression. He seemed no match for the Cheshire men, who towered over him threateningly.

'The king's own bodyguard, your honour. I'm Captain Dickie, and these are Yole, Wade, and Perkin.'

'When did you arrive here in Leicester?'

'Just before the will was read,' answered Wade.

'King's guard. Just arrived. Only here for the will,' said the sheriff, turning round to a deputy who had been making a list of those questioned with a metal stylus on parchment. 'Dismissed.' The sheriff languidly waved a jewelled hand. Wait a minute, I thought, Rachel was killed only a short while before I was back in the hall. Yet what possible purpose could her death have served the king?

We found ourselves in front of the inquisitor...

LORD JOHN: I was back in England and I dreamt of seeing Katherine Swynford again. This evening the lovely body of Katherine is offering itself as if disrobed. I was thinking that if only she had not the conscientiousness of my friend Wyclif the priest, that thoroughness and commitment, namely, to where she would place her passion and love. It was Chaucer who had suggested she would make a perfect wife. If only she was more like Chaucer's wife Philippa: devoted wife, but a temptress and yielding distraction for others, such as myself.

If I were able to gather her fine bloom, taste and savour it to the full, would I not cast it aside? Katherine was not a woman to indulge in light diversions. Did I want a jealous passion, a stormy up-and-down affair with a woman who had two children of her own, and a husband who might well plot to murder me?

With capitulation, her capitulation, when my first curiosity was satisfied, which meant gazing on, and drinking in, her full naked form, as well as sexual satisfaction, would I not undergo the unspeakable boredom of cold pleasure? Especially without Chaucer here, who, with his poet's imagination, could make so much more out of a passion than existed in it.

Yes, I did like her for something else. But how well-formed she must be: in the end I come back to the body. In my imagination I undressed her, and went much beyond the delight of those curves that could attract the outward eye, even when concealed by a gown.

I speculated on what was secretly there, imagining it both mature and virginal. I have always loved nakedness in women, for it is such a transitional, such a volatile and much changing state, like the unstable English weather playing upon a beautiful and variable landscape, which yet takes on different shades and mysteries, then suddenly glows and blossoms. A woman is either well adorned, attired in wondrous materials, provocatively concealed, or else, in sexual intercourse, or in the act of birth, or in examination by a physician, naked not just to the surface but into the depths of her being.

So if I were to have Katherine as my mistress, would I, as much as I could find occasion, forever stop gazing on her naked part? Would I not delight, and even exult in her beauty as it was revealed to me, kissing her at my will?

And what, indeed, would she look like? While I was so engaged I lost myself in conjecture. Would she have a smallish quantity of hair, crisp and dark, with lips and prick-hole small; would she have a pretty *chose*, like a girl of fifteen, instead of a woman's of twenty who had borne two children?

While I was so engaged there was a knock on the door: Gerald, my night guard, brought me a letter. Odd, I thought. I was not expecting Chaucer at this hour, or any further message from Katherine.

Yes, I saw at once it was her hand when I took the letter from Gerald, although I noticed that she wrote with a thicker pen, and seemed to employ more compliments than usual.

'Very redoubtable and most powerful, my seignior, Lord John of Lancaster, etc etc…my most excellent, my most powerful prince, I recommend myself most humbly to the most high prince and desire to meet your noble self at Moorfields, beyond the gate of the city. If your worthy honour could possibly permit, alone without my handmaidens or ladies of waiting and you, whom the sweet seignior Jesus Christ, who in his compassion will keep free from harm, I do most entreat your most noble self also to arrive at this place not accompanied by guard, or any who may gossip of our meeting, for in my modesty I beseech you to make it a private encounter…'

I grew so excited that I could hardly read on, and at once began to prepare myself to leave. I would have gone even without my sword, had not Gerald, ever watchful of my safety, insisted that I arm myself. There were dangers in London, either within or without the city walls.

KATHERINE: The evening was falling, calm, radiant, without a rustle of sound, full of golden light, in a serenity that pierced the soul. Sir Hugh, too, would have me on such a night in some ideal world that could never become real for him, for in his dreams I was a bright goddess who was also a good mother, imbued with everlasting charm. In his dreams he loved me ever thus, extending his human tenderness through my 'marble beauty'. He imagined me in my home, in the lacework of a night shift, my hair coiled in haste, tall and white, holding our daughter in the air in my splendid Junoesque arms, talking to him with my golden laugh. He thinks me adorable, for I give Petronella my breast to suckle on, as his own mother never did. His heart flies to me. If only the right he had to be near to me, to hold me, in his intimate hours, very close, smelling my skin and smiling at our baby, were a reality! Yet how far is the reality from his imagination. His most tender and gently aspiring thoughts are so roughly set aside by his practice, his seizure of me, his ripping my clothing away from me, as if disposing of an enemy. One night he beat me when he unjustly suspected me of infidelity, then, in spite of that, I had tried to embrace him almost with tenderness – as if the beating itself had drawn from me a tiny, juicy centre of sweetness.

LORD JOHN: Deliberately not to be recognized I did not wear my colours.

I was strong, but no match for the six or so heavily armed men who set on me as soon as I met them beyond the wall in the open fields outside Moorgate; private feuds and brawls were common enough, and such passers-by as there were turned a blind eye. I, stripped of my sword unlike that earlier time on the field of honour, confronted my unknown enemy.

'I challenge you to single combat,' I said. I had, in the course of several French campaigns, challenged one after another the princes of the French royal blood, although none had answered to my call.

'Oh no, my lord. This time there is to be no match of arms, for surely you would win as you did last time.'

'Sir Hugh!' I cried out, seeing who it was. 'My trusted man, you have shown such valiant service against our enemies – what leads you to this treason? You, above all, whose loyalty I value highly.'

Swynford hesitated, then scratched his head, but I imagine some vision of his wife supplanted all reason.

'You would meet with my wife, and for this reason you are here,' said Sir Hugh.

'Who tells you of this? Did she do so herself?'

Sir Hugh pondered; I could ascertain that he had not thought this out.

'Not exactly, your grace.'

'If not her, then who is it? Who else can know?'

'It is by her command or wish that you are here.'

I looked sharply at him: I saw what had happened, yet I would play this game to the limit. 'So it is, so it is; but it is hardly reasonable to assume that I should refuse any request that she might have for a meeting. She is a servant of my household, bound to me in trust, and may have good cause to meet me in secret. What proof do you bring against me, that you act in such a manner?'

I could sense one or two of Sir Hugh's men were becoming restless. I looked from face to face, bided my time, and said nothing further.

'Are you going to deny, my lord, that my good wife Katherine is your mistress?'

Before I could reply – and I was armed in purest innocence, thanks to Chaucer's delaying stratagem – a metal-tipped shaft from a long-bow sank into the ground before Swynford's feet. Gerald and five of my bowmen, bowstrings stretched and ready to pierce Sir Hugh and five of his men before the more lightly armed group could respond or overpower them, stood well-positioned as at the points of the star.

'Lay down your swords,' shouted a commanding voice, 'else Sir Swynford is a dead man.'

Amy, one of Katherine's maids, later confessed. One of Swynford's men, cooped up with him in Southwark, had an unappeasable passion for her, dating back to the time of the marriage of Sir Hugh and Katherine. He broke the vow of silence set on him by his knight, stole off to find his girlfriend, and in the course of the pair satisfying their mutual appetite, Amy drew some inkling of the plot against me, and in particular the details of the forged letter. This became known in my household too late to stop me setting out on my own, but not too late for Gerald to collect five of my best archers and set off in pursuit.

If I pass quickly over my miraculous escapes and do not present them as if my life hung in the balance, it is because I attribute my power of survival to some angel or minister of grace who watched over me. Forewarned is forearmed, they say. Those who served me flattered me. As for my superior perception, my prescience, my skilful choice of those I chose to work for me – I put it all down to fear. Judicious fear. It was the defences of my own wit that I exercised to protect me first, before I chose others to back me up.

I spared Sir Hugh Swynford's life a second time. Once again I gambled on the freedom of one who hated me.

'Get back to France!' I ordered. 'Leave at dawn and do not, on pain of death, be found in this land for twelve months. I shall give you orders when I return.'

I retrieved my sword: 'You may rest assured,' I added, 'that I shall not take your wife from you.'

I did not add that I might take Sir Hugh from his wife, for many believed this was what I set out to do, and for this I would rot everlastingly in hell. Was I to blame if this incident fired me up even more to pursue Katherine? It was destiny. No one reported anything further of this encounter; Katherine herself was not told. But it so deepened my love-sickness that I now allowed my passion to affect my mood. I ate and drank less than I needed, and began to pine to such a degree that it was noticed that I was no longer the man I formerly was. No one knew that it was Chaucer who had given me counsel to feign as much illness as I could, to increase my chances in love, but I could reply that there was no need to tell me to put on the deceit of being ill, for I really was so.

Who knows the truth of love? The word soon travelled and it came to Katherine's ear. Soon after, Geoffrey promised he would try to arrange for her to go to my bedchamber where I lay tossing and turning in earnest pain. Before Chaucer let her through to see me he would, he said to me, abjure her by all that was sacred and holy, to think about who I was, and my extreme condition.

'Do not condemn to death this man who suffers such pain for you,' he planned to tell her. 'Try to ease the pain you have caused. Every time a straw wags, people guess at tittering, at pursuit, and at delay. Wait no longer.'

The shock, the thrill of danger when I found my throat upon the naked sword of Swynford, had left its mark.

ELEVEN

Scriven

'I AM GEOFFREY CHAUCER, scutifer or armerigus to the late duke. This is Adam Scriven, my servant.'

'Oh not another wretched esquire,' said the sheriff, in a bored and reedy voice. 'Where were you earlier today, in the afternoon, when Goodam Rachel Dempsey was murdered?'

'I was in the hall, and before the reading Mr Scriven and I were at an inn.'

I nodded.

'Did you know either of the victims?'

'No.'

'You've no idea who they were?'

I was about to tell, but my master beat me to it.

'By now we have heard that one was an ageing gentlewoman, the other an old halberdier. Why anyone should want them out of the way, heaven above knows.'

I sucked in my breath quickly, a little too quickly. The sheriff noticed. 'Dismissed,' he ordered my master, but to me, 'You stay!'

By now the pale and sinking sun had entered from the west through the few narrow windows into the hall's interior, and tinged with fire the tapestries of hunting and fishing scenes on the wall. The fine strips of vertical light fell and emblazoned the great table; the carved wooden screen and its hangings glittered with golden radiance.

'So it seems you were the last to see this good woman alive,' he said.

I staggered forwards, as if I was about to fall in a faint. 'Me?' I asked in a weak voice.

'At the inn with Mr Chaucer.'

'Yes, yes, of course,' I said, frantic to regain an outward air of composure. 'She ate a hearty meal. Tripe with cream.' I looked round for my master to confirm what I said, but he had vanished.

'Her last supper, eh?' said the sheriff grimly. 'I gather she worked for Mr Chaucer.' He paused menacingly. I waited for the next blow. 'A long time ago: perhaps this is why Mr Chaucer forgot her.'

'She did,' I agreed. 'It was the last I saw of her.'

He contemplated me for so long I wondered that my heart kept beating. 'You don't look like a murderer,' concluded the sheriff. 'Dismissed.' I jumped away from him rather too quickly. 'But come back here: you look frightened,' he called me back. 'Here,' he seized my hand and patted it. 'I don't think you could do it. But think it over.'

He bothered me, the sheriff. He appeared to know I was innocent, yet he somehow implicated me in his design. He spoke to me as if he could trap me in his guile.

'We have to unmask the man who has such an evil design on this pair,' he said next. 'Who could it be? What do they want?'

I wished he would stop frightening me. He looked the type who collected evil designs. Instead of regarding you straight in the eyes he thought about someone else as a diversionary stratagem. 'Perhaps they will strike again,' he commented very gently, speaking slowly as if it was difficult for him to find the words. 'Perhaps they will strike again.'

Thankfully I was released from the questioning and allowed to retire to my cell near my master, who was asleep when I arrived there. Nothing further had been discovered, except of course that the other man I had visited this afternoon had been found murdered too, this time more neatly than Rachel by a thrust in the heart with a sword. About my visit to see him I had as well to keep silent. I believed I might do best to entrust my secrets to my master. But not yet, for I was sorely exhausted, and had in any case first to look at what Rachel had given me.

The plan to leave tomorrow for St Paul's with Lord John's body had still not been delayed, but it had been spread about those gathered here that the sheriff would travel with us to continue his enquiries, for he believed that whoever had committed these crimes was intimately connected with Lord John and his life, and that he, or they, had further unfinished business to execute which would not only reveal more about their identity, but also if there were any ramifications of these crimes in some deeper, if not foreign, matters of state. They might well be connected with the will, with Lord John's family – and so on…. . As for me all I could feel was the direct threat to my own person, for certainly I would be the next victim.

Alone in my room I laughed aloud probably more with relief than genuine mirth when I saw how my work in copying my master's Parson's thoughts on the sin of lechery had been so completely forgotten. So I calmed my perturbed spirit for an hour or two in work. The rough, illegible hand yielded easily to my neat copy: making something fair of another's foul and untidy work (my master's).

I tidied up his sheets together with my own, and although I was keen to open my sack of Mrs Chaucer's papers, I had only just begun to unpick the thread that bound it up when I became so smitten, so completely overwhelmed with irresistible fatigue, that it was all I could do not to fall asleep in my chair and tumble as a dead heap on the stone floor. I hid Philippa's confidences under my flea-ridden pillow, but once I had arranged myself to sleep I started to quake, then shiver like a jelly, then fear for my life, for what if the murderer at once meant to turn his attention to me, and it was Mrs Chaucer's letters or her chronicle, or whatever it might turn out to contain, that he was intent on possessing? Yet my second thought was how could this be, for surely it was but a private, domestic document, and nothing much to do with important matters of state? Words and phrases that both Rachel and the sergeant-at-arms had used came back to me, turned over and over in my mind to torment me further. 'Moorgate…Sir Hugh Swynford…with four or five men to set upon the duke…'

If I had been there, why had I denied it? As my distress deepened and darkened, and I twisted and turned, I struggled to go back in my memory to that time which exceeded by far so many life-times today – it must be nearly thirty years before – and when it took some semblance of form I understood that I may have deliberately denied and plucked this from my memory, because I had no desire to be troubled further. It may also have been stimulated by the knowledge that in two nights' time we were due in St Albans, which I had not visited since that earlier occasion that Rachel and her supporter had spoken about.

It was in St Albans that I had spent my childhood, where I was a changeling, or rather a foundling, a complete orphan. I was left abandoned near to the winding lanes of Fishpool on the banks of a stream, the Ver. Here the monks of the Abbey had taken me in, fed me and looked after me as one of their own, until I did become to all intents and purposes one of them. Was there any wonder that I never did care much for marrying and starting a family, and was there any surprise that, like my mentors and guardians, I should have come to embrace the great mother, the holy church, with considerably more fervour than I saw in most people? Was it to be wondered, also, that I was what I was, and that my secret self, while intrigued by the adulteries, crimes, and confusions of these larger than life people with whom fortune had thrown me together, sometimes hungered to be just like them, and to be acting as they were acting.

As the clouds and mists departed to leave a firmer map of the past, I recalled the last time I had been summoned to that self-same Abbey where I was brought up, just after the marriage of Sir Hugh Swynford to Katherine Payne de Roet. How could I ever have forgotten?

Here the abbot had let me into the library room over his sacristy where he kept many fine specimens of his dissecting and medical skills, and where once I had studied under his tutelage before he became abbot and was only in charge of the scriptorium. After telling me to sit down, he fixed his cold, icy stare upon me. He had some inequality of feature, did Brother Thomas Walsingham, perhaps from so much writing and poring over documents in candle or lamp light, and it gave him a stare which cut through you with the force of the mythical basilisk. Yet he probably did not own his own power, for so many misjudge the force they have. He terrified me when he told me that while he admired my master beyond all other poets for his skill at making verses, he wanted to remove Lord John from his present powerful position, for he controlled the king his father, Edward, and when his father died he would even more dominate his heir, the young boy Richard of Bordeaux. The abbot regretted how all plots and policies devised to remove Lord John for ever failed, while the campaign he, Walsingham, continually waged against him in his chronicle, where John was denounced as an adulterer who supped with the devil, used artificial stimuli for his lusts, captured foreign women and so on and so forth, had little effect on him as well.

In sum the abbot wanted me to spy on Lord John, and when I responded that I did not think it was up to me or any man, and especially not up to any holy man, to try and direct the ways of God, Walsingham told me that if I did not obey his holy orders I would be excommunicated, which as far as it could affect me would be worse than death, for no one, not even Mr Chaucer, would be able to employ me. So I had no choice and there I was, commanded to watch Lord John, the first opportunity for which came when Sir Hugh Swynford arrived back in England only shortly after he had left Lady Katherine, having heard rumours of Lord John's attraction to his wife. His intention was to have his revenge and kill him.

Now at this time there was no foundation as yet to the rumours that Lord John and Katherine Swynford were having an adulterous liaison, but deducing, and perhaps adding a little memory, to what Rachel had begun to tell me of the office of bawd or pandar that my master performed with his own sister-in-law and for his own special reasons, I could see that the consummation, of which all England was to talk about and discuss, was not far away. But presumably it was my master's intention to bring off the final end by skilful degrees, for he believed in devising a plan for everything, and knew how each stage of an enterprise such as this had to be completed before moving on to the next. However, I could not help Father Walsingham with reports of Lord John's adulterous misdeeds, for I found no evidence, although others were able to do this quite fully, so that the abbot, in his scandalous chronicle, seemed remarkably well-informed.

'Ah Adam, I'm sure you're unable to sleep!' The voice invaded my memories, then a feeble lamp light, and I spied my master, wearing a cap and in his long night-gown, standing before me in the darkness. After the animation of the day he looked old and careworn. 'Neither can I. I think this taper will go out. May I light yours?'

I assented, and he did so, sitting on my chair while on the hard pallet I tossed and twisted, unable to decide if I should rise, and so offer the view of my cloth sack to his inevitable curiosity. 'I am afraid I am not progressing very fast with copying the Parson's Tale,' I told him, trying to make agreeable conversation.

'I'm not surprised. Too many distractions. On this night too, when there is a full moon, although we can see little of it behind the clouds.'

'Ah,' I said, gazing fondly out of the window into the unredeemed blackness of the night, 'so what are your suspicions over the crimes? Who can possibly have killed what apparently seem to be two harmless people?'

'As I see it,' answered my master, 'everyone in this gathering has a motive to kill. Maybe even the queen of Spain! But certainly all these legitimate and illegitimate offspring and siblings. They have motives to kill some member or other of their own, or a rival family. But not Rachel and Basil.'

'How does this come about?' I asked him.

'Too complicated to explain.'

I looked into those lustrous brown eyes which had recovered and now sparkled audaciously, so that I could not but reflect that perhaps my master had more of a motive than anyone else to rid us of Rachel, in view of the fact that she had started to reveal so many hidden aspects of his and Philippa's married life.

What he said next shocked me to the core. 'But then you, a humble scrivener, probably have more motive than most to kill Rachel.' He regarded me sternly in the silence that followed.

'Me? Why me?' I recoiled in agitation. The suggestion was so preposterous that, contrary to the guilt I felt earlier, I began to laugh – although my laugh sounded forced.

'Well you may not believe this, but Rachel was a very special person where you were concerned.'

'In what way?'

'What I am about to say may shock you even more.'

He paused and unexpectedly reached out to take my hand in his. I pulled my hand away, for I did not relish to be fingered in this way.

'She was your mother.'

'I don't believe you! I really don't believe you, master, for the whole notion is absurd! Absurd! And anyway, if she had been my mother she would have been the first to tell me, and I would have been the last to want to kill her. How can you prove it anyway?' I said all of this very quickly and with great anger.

Mr Chaucer looked at me warmly, and without pity or rancour. He was so calm, yet I could not trust him, for he was capable of any invention.

'I thought that what she gave you might have revealed this, and

97

have provoked you to take your revenge on her for her neglect of you. I cannot at this juncture go into why I believe she might have been your mother.'

'Well I don't. Most certainly I do not.'

I swelled with more dangerous anger, ready to kick my master, or something worse – harm myself, butt my head against the stones. Then the full moon appeared from behind a cloud. This sudden and awesome event, a penetration of the darkness with pure silvery light, suddenly displayed to Mr Chaucer, as I saw mirrored in the window glass, my long and fox-like features, my thick lugubrious lips, and to me my master's rotund and harmless face and form, his chubby cheeks and swift, smiling eyes. Both of us were lost in wonder and amazement.

Next day our departure from Leicester was further delayed while the sheriff continued his investigations. We became listless and I witnessed another side of my master that he allowed no one else to see. I mentioned the irritable heavy cloud which had fallen on one so richly endowed by nature with gifts of head and heart, which had from time to time caused him to drift into a life of sloth and self-indulgence. He would forget the high principles upon which he based his life. Some people worshipped him as a demi-god. But now he drank. His eyes grew lacklustre, his speech became thick and laboured, and he sat for hours in a hunched attitude, gazing either at the bottle of wine on the table beside him, or at me. Curious as I was to find out the cause, I became disturbed by the sottishly taciturn mood heavy drinking induced in him. With the drinking his moralizing grew more and more extreme. The remedy was worse than the disease…

KATHERINE: We were hardly surprised that when Lord John left for Calais earlier that year he had sent my husband on ahead, entrusting him with commands and according him the most dangerous assignments, so as to make sure that he was well out of the way.

One day Geoffrey approached me.

'So!' he began. We looked at one another. He somehow managed to peel away my defences. 'If what I'm about to say angers you, I promise you – I swear to you – I'll never trouble you further. Everyone has the opportunity for some great adventure. Should they ignore it, they will be despised and wretched.'

I started to shake, and went red. I feared what it was leading up to.

'For the love of heaven please tell me what this is all about?' I said in a shocked voice. 'I cannot stand any more. I shall go mad!' Why should I have become so extreme in my response? Later I could see that Geoffrey was giving me instructions in adultery, not a very pleasant game in which to engage, and not one you would expect to find your own brother-in-law embracing with enthusiasm. At the time I asked myself why I should have felt like this. Geoffrey knew only too well some tender souls grow alarmed at what they cannot understand, and so he found the way to serve my wit.

'Now listen,' said Geoffrey, 'the king's son – who is good, wise, worthy, fresh and free – I mean John – loves you.'

'Loves me?' I responded both with alarm and disbelief.

'If you don't help him, he will simply die. What more can I say?'

I stopped dead in my tracks and looked hard at Geoffrey. Did he mean it? I asked myself again, could he mean it? I said nothing.

'If you let him die, I'll take my own life – this is the truth. I'll cut my throat with this knife!' Geoffrey drew his dagger which was, I confess, rather rusty and not very serviceable. I wanted to laugh, as he went on with all kinds of delusion and exaggeration of John's pain and suffering in love for me.

'Woe to the gem without its own natural force,' he cried out like a declaiming mummer. 'Woe to the herb that fails to heal, woe to the beauty that is ruthless, and treads others under foot!'

And much in the same vein. It seemed to me that he was well aware that, in his mission to further Lord John's interest, he might push me deeper into rejecting him. He appealed to my virtue. 'I am not asking you to forsake any kind of honour on John's part, but simply to be a little nicer to him when he comes to see you.'

'To see me?' I replied. 'What do you mean – is he here?' I felt very agitated. He was back in England already?

'No, but he writes to me every day from France.' Geoffrey stopped. 'Do not misunderstand me, I would rather –' I blush to think that the hypocrite could have said this '– be hanged along with you and him than thought to be his bawd. I am your brother-in-law. I have your honour at heart. But I worry for him all the time, for he takes being a commander so seriously. He needs the relief of your friendship.'

'And what of the others? He doesn't find it hard to gain relief from…' I was about to say sluts, whores, slags, and other camp followers, such as I knew the generals consorted with, in spite of their professions of chivalry.

'This is so different,' Geoffrey went on with a dismissive smile. 'He asks for friendship and support. Soften the danger you hold for him. Don't be responsible for his death.'

'His death?' I gasped. 'You can't really mean this?'

The pressure he had kept up on me for so long made me burst into tears. 'Just think,' I said between my sobs, 'what you would have thought of me if I had given in. You would have shown no mercy or measure at all,' – and then I vented every fury my Gallic temperament and indignation could muster at his painted, false process, adding that I was so astounded I could die.

So it went on. We had several encounters like this, until Geoffrey did manage to convince me, against almost everything I had known and believed, that John in France was seriously pining for me. It was a most preposterous picture – when I thought about it later, but one of this great god of war beseeching Geoffrey to have pity on him in his pain, lying in his tent on his bed – a veritable picture of Mars at the mercy of Venus. Geoffrey was determined to convince me that it was only by dint of his own ingenuity that he could keep John from death. I confided in my sister, but it seemed that she was also part of the conspiracy that John loved me. Philippa, with her act of gentle persuasive words, told me that it didn't matter if a man loved a woman till his heart burst. She was under no obligation to love him back.

I had moved more permanently from Kettlethorpe Manor into a set of chambers just outside the walls of the Savoy. Here I could both tend and look after my own two children, and resume acting as governess to John and Lady Blanche's son and two daughters. One day I found a copy of the poem Geoffrey had written on Blanche's death. I read it again, this time aloud to myself.

It happened one day that I came upon a place where truly I saw the fairest company of ladies that ever my eyes had seen together in one place. I saw one that was like none of the rest… . She had so steadfast a countenance, so noble a carriage and bearing...I saw her then dance so comely, carole and sing so sweetly, laugh and play so womanly, look so graciously, I tell you in truth, never had I seen so blissful a treasure. For every hair on her head, and I tell the truth, was neither red nor yellow nor brown but looked like gold. And what eyes!

I read on and on of Blanche's beauty and virtues, so poignantly and exquisitely expressed by Geoffrey, and especially those words of her speech, and what goodly, soft speech she had – so friendly and so well grounded, that never through her tongue was man or woman greatly harmed, for from her all harm was hidden – and I could not but find myself more and more drawn to this image of perfection, of full feminine beauty, and of virtue, to which I myself aspired.

I sat and read more and more, imagining her to myself in the tones of Geoffrey's lovely soft speaking voice and so, very gradually and rousingly, changed and transferred the description from Blanche to myself.

Such fairness of neck has that sweet...white, smooth, straight, her throat, a round tower of ivory...and good fair white was rightly my lady's name; her shoulders were fair, her body long...very white hands and rosy nails...

With a shock I then recalled the hard entry of Sir Hugh into my tense and resisting loins. I had tried so hard to find an image of Sir Hugh before which I could yield and melt. What an utter failure this had turned out to be.

Round breasts and good broad hips, with a straight, flat back...I dare say she was like a bright torch from which every man may draw light without lessening the glow... . Her wit inclined her to all good, set without malice and upon gladness...

Was I doomed forever to a chilling and loveless marriage, while at the same time loving and tending for the fruits of this love that Geoffrey celebrated? Should he, could he, not celebrate some love of my own? I was deeply tempted.

The enormity of such a wish: while I drank in these lines I found a mirror. I dropped my gown, and looked at myself. If only I were free. But then, would John be in love? Probably not. And what were husbands but creatures full of jealousy, either seeking mastery, or loving novelty?

At least, with Sir Hugh away, I am my own woman.

'I am,' I was forced to admit, 'among the fairest, after my duchess, else why should such a great prince pick me out among all there are to be had? Is it my destiny,' I asked myself, 'to become successor to that woman that I loved above all the world, by gaining, in spite of myself and my wishes, her husband's love?'

I fell to thinking what might happen if the world in general, the court, and especially the children of Blanche, knew that John was in love with me. Would it dishonour me? Surely not, this was the kind of thing that so often happened. Men loved women without being loved back; would it reflect badly on me? Hardly.

As I felt better from all these cogitations the dreadful thought darkened me like an autumn cloud: 'No, no, no, keep away from the pain, the storms of love. There is always distrust and conflict in love, and even if I were free, which I am not, men are not to be trusted, the ones who love most violently least of all, they rend themselves from full sharp beginnings, into the most destructive of ends. This will surely happen to me if I answer to John's passion!'

TWELVE

Chaucer

WE WERE DELAYED FURTHER in our departure. I prayed this really was our last evening in Leicester. I invited this scurvy scourge of my servant to walk out with me. As we left the Great Hall of Leicester I could ascertain from his outwardly pale manner that he was still inwardly shaking from the fact of those deaths, although I had dropped my suspicions about him. What occupied my mind more than his maternity was my need to find an agreeable tavern. As for the murders, everyone had for a second time been questioned by the sheriff of Leicester and his followers, even the Cheshire archers of King Richard. But nothing further had been discovered, and we had been dismissed.

I stretched out a hand to him. He had followed me to where both of us resided in Castle House. 'Adam, my old friend,' I said, 'I have long neglected you. Everyone desires to live long, but no man would be old and at my age, fifty-nine, I should be counting my blessings, among which is you. I wish to make amends. I must admit I have led a selfish life.'

'Much better,' he replied somewhat ruffled by this, 'to leave it to the Almighty to sort this one out.'

'Yes,' I replied, concealing my irritation at his high moral tone, 'I should never have been the son of a London vintner – the temptations were too great.'

'Yes, well I remember when it all began,' he said, eyeing a pair of clerics whose paths at this moment crossed ours. 'Clerics?' I said aloud and both of these asses turned their heads and neighed at us. Since the Great Death of fifty years ago anyone with a grave manner and a ready smile, who could scrawl his name and stumble through a Latin prayer, could be a priest and gain an easy living that flowed in as smoothly from a sheep farm as from a populous parish. 'This pair are little more than leering apprentices – and yet, the feast of St Peter ad Vinculum – ah, what gaiety, what splendour!'

'Our noble monarch committed a capital error by turning the clergy against him – '

'Walsingham – your adoptive father, rather peevishly summed it up, didn't he, Adam? He said Robert de Vere used black magic to sway the king, and implied both men shared the same bed. Yet what splendid hospitality Lord John offered the king and queen, with their court – the archbishop of York, the dukes of York and Gloucester, the earls of Arundel and Huntingdon – and then we went hunting the boar in the forests and parks outside – '

I continued by quoting:

' "See on that mount in days of feudal pride
The towering castle frowned above the tide;
Flung wide her gates, where troops of vassals met
With awe, the brow of high Plantagenet."

But that great age has vanished, Adam – it vanished only three years later – and the death blow of all was the banishment, two years ago, in this very same month of March, of Lancaster's eldest son, Henry of Bolingbroke, because of his duel with the duke of Norfolk.'

'The past ten years have not been happy ones' – he interrupted.

'No more banquets like those. King Richard has spent all his money – unless, unless...'

'Unless what?'

'Well I have my suspicions,' I left it at that, but Scriven was not satisfied.

'What was Scrope doing here – and why are those Cheshire bodyguards still with us?'

'The king has been appointed executor of Lord John's will. That spells trouble. Trouble. The possessions of John were enormous, as great as any prince in Christendom. Do you want me to list them?'

'If you like.'

'Well, besides the castellated mansions of all sizes, the manors and towns – far surpassing in number and size the land the king owns – there are estates all over England, Scotland and Wales. Just think of the castles, Adam – I name but a few. Knaresborough,

Pontefract, Pickering in Yorkshire, Lydel and Dunstanborough in Northumberland, Cykhull in Durham; then there is Bolingbroke in Lincoln, Lancaster itself, Tutbury in Staffordshire, Hertford, Pevensey in Sussex, Monmouth Castle, Skenfrith, Blanch, Grossmont, Oken, Oggermore Caer Cynwys, Ledwell in the Welsh Marches – and more than mortal memory can recall.'

'You mean, you suspect what the king will do – '

'It is not hard to guess, Adam. I do – I dare hardly think it because – well, it spells trouble, civil war, butchery and no stop to any of it – the descent into the abyss' – I fixed him with a quizzical but friendly eye – 'besides which my or anyone's personal descent into the abyss with a few bottles of wine's but a trifle.'

'Oh I see.' He looked back at me with disbelief as if I was trying to palm him off with an excuse. 'Wine never was a path to salvation, master.'

How would I keep my temper with this Lollard? 'It does provide some answers. Or is life just a riddle that will never be solved?'

'You've set so many riddles,' he answered.

'Such as?'

'Such as what is it that women most desire, or, is forgiveness more important than revenge?'

'But none so great as myself. Who am I, Adam, I often ask.'

But I had no desire to ponder this question for more than a fleeting moment. I clapped my hands. 'Adam, thirty-eight days we have sat here in Leicester pious and sober, watching over Lord John's mortal remains. I, too, I hasten to add, have been involved in the penitence Lord John reserved for himself.'

'Well yes, you were, weren't you...very close?'

'Yes. We were. His sins were, in a sense, my sins.'

'Then it's fitting you should also be feeling remorse. Maybe in the end it will be your salvation as well as his.'

'But not quite yet. It is not my time.' I rose to my feet. Without another word I led this pious sour companion out of our bare cells in Castle House up Applegate by the River Soar into the mass of lanes, among them Dead Lane and Soaper's, that choked the centre of the squalid walled town in which they say a third of its people died, more than two thousand. Here streets were still unpaved, and swine and poultry wandered free, while dirt and refuse made some streets impassable. Inns and churches we passed, a Blue or White Boar gave way to a St Clements or St Martins till we arrived through the North gate and over Bow Bridge in the luxury suburbs, where all trades, arms making and markets flourished. Every man by law bore weapons of war and every town had its armoury. But here, too, among the mercers and bakers and wine shops you could find barbers and stews. You would be surprised to know how many houses of ill fame existed in such a provincial town as Leicester, once among the most powerful six or seven in the realm, but now sunk to fifteenth, but even so no paragon of continence and early nights. As I led on I remarked on our oddity of appearance: my clerk angular and snakelike in black, me dressed like a tropical bird in scarlet.

We sat down at the Golden Lion: the arms de Plantagenet shone in cresset light, both red and blue, and draped its upper windows. Bells were ringing all over the town, and the old town we had left within its walls blazed with light as if burning down.

'A tankard of ale,' I called out to the tapster, 'for my scribe or secretary here.' Adam stiffened, for he never touched beer. I ordered for myself a deep cup of wine.

'Like my hat-badge?' I said to Scriven. I inclined my head towards him. I was being naughty. He put his hand to my mouth in order to stifle a cry of alarm: for I wore on my cap a kind of base metal badge – so I could only describe it, of a human phallus-bird with legs and wings.

'I've never seen anything like this, Adam. I found it today in a shop in St Francis Lane. For a pilgrimage – I ask you! To bring good fortune.'

'Well,' he answered as well he might, 'many women are believed to take part in pilgrimages for amorous adventure.'

'Not in my tales, hey,' I laughed. 'They talk about the adventures, but they don't engage in them. But tonight love and wine do not counsel moderation, as Ovid wrote.'

I insisted we visit the barber. The blade of the barber's knife passed over my face but skirted the neat boundaries of my beard. Next the barber trimmed what little thatch still covered my bald, old man's scalp, patted me with scented talc and removed the unsightly hairs from my nostrils with tweezers. The Scriven's turn came. 'Sit still, please! I nicked you,' the barber hissed at him. Scriven touched his upper lip with the tip of his finger. He stared in horror at the blood. The barber shaved around the cut on his upper lip, then scythed his cheeks and jaw with rough angry haste.

'You want a hair wash?'

'No, that's all right.'

'There's a lot of dirt and grass in your hair.'

By now I was impatient to leave. I bounded ahead. Scriven followed with reluctance. He glanced into taverns and shops. Some we entered. I ordered wines and spirit and forced my companion to drink. I allowed the fumes and pure spirit of the wine to gain a hold but he did not. Feeling the chill of the evening we were back within the walls again on our crawl, in the poor broken-down sick quarters of the old town.

'Blessed Virgin, what's happening?' Scriven asked. 'I don't like this neighbourhood. Brothels are never far off death and extinction.'

'Do they have plague here, in Leicester? I've been here since January when the old duke succumbed to his final illness, and before he insisted on being taken back to London. I have heard of none.'

'There's always pockets of it here and there, master, you know as well as I.'

'So what,' I answered, 'so what, Adam?' I felt as merry and drunk as David's sow. 'You and I survived the Great Death. We're safe. It won't find us. Safe from contagion.'

We had arrived within some enclosure or garden with gaunt trees to a gloomy dark manor. At the guardroom window sat an old woman keeper.

'Keep away from here, master,' Scriven cried out. 'You might want or need some kisses, but not the kiss of the plague maiden and her red scarf and brown.'

'You need not enter the house,' I told him.

'I don't fear death,' he answered. 'Like you, master, I look upon it as the threshold to a greater bliss than ever can be found on earth.'

'Come.'

He followed. As we mounted the worn stone steps, much nearer sounds broke out from above us, a wild babble of voices, and the fluting of windpipes. I listened amazed, and in the ragged music I heard the words of a dirty song such as my miller might have bawled out merrily – 'Why does my husband beat me before shagging?'

'You know, Adam, they keep asking me for poetic favours – celebrating this or that union, this or that royal coupling – but I have no itch for favour, no chivalric ardour left. I am tired of mythology – birds yes, I see the starling, the blackbird, the falcon, the eagle – above all the vulture and the dove – these birds of the air are humans in disguise with their rapacious greed and lechery, and envy to pick the fruits of others…'

As if to echo my words there appeared a man masked as a cock with sword drawn to ask us who we were. I pretended not to know him but I suspected he was Thomas Swynford. Masks in evidence even more in the ante-room, but little else by way of clothing: amid the noise and movement nobody at first noticed us and we stood there awkwardly, transfixed in the doorway. In contrast to the raw, March wind blowing incessantly outside and chilling our bones, where our noses dripped and we had coughed and shivered, inside here the fires roared in two huge fireplaces, and the branched candlesticks lit up wall-paintings.

On a great oak table were spread venison roasts, half-eaten carcasses of peacocks and turkeys – rich claret from a barrel with half open tap splashed down on the floor, staining red the rushes sprinkled with apple and cherry blossom, and limp daffodils.

'Oh stop this flow of life blood!' I shouted with joy, and shut off the tap – after helping Adam and myself to full goblets. A human skull had been tied to the falcon perched beside the fireplace. On one great wall a mural of a king and queen. They were shown hunting and had come across three open graves; each one held a corpse. All the bodies were worm-eaten, one blackened, one covered with snakes, one with belly distended – all crowned. On one side a party of revelers, debauchees, enjoyed a debauched feast: Death, a clawed harpy, unnoticed by them prepared to swoop. On the other side lepers and the blind, the lame and the deformed pleaded to be saved from suffering.

I recognized a number of these people as noble mourners from Lord John's cortège, courtiers from the royal households of Spain, Naples, Austria, Saxony, Tuscany. Rich debauchees mainly, half naked, pranced round and disported their jerking limbs and kicking trunks on the rushes, where some already reclined and indulged in gross sport. Minstrels blew flutes and twanged strings, or clashed cymbals in rhythm, while man and woman, or man and man grabbed each other, kissing, writhing, bumping and grinding, while some cupped their hands to shout ribald comment.

One, Dame Alice I believed she was, once the widow who serviced Richard's grandfather Edward, had grown so obese that as she danced her oversize breasts flopped out from her ripped bodice, and the trinkets and ribbons that held her blanched tresses whirled and banged against her uplifted arms. There was Grace, a former Lancastrian from the Savoy, now with braided smock hitched up to show her bare behind, her face roaring as she poached with fiendish drunkenness a handsome groom on whose chest she slobbered. He sported nothing but a shirt, and his prick was visible for all to admire, drooping and limp, his fair face in a squeamish smile. Kitchen scullions fumbled members of the foreign royal train who made harlotry, a human Charybdis.

'What wantonness, master!' my poor scribe cried out. 'I fear for my life, let's go.' I put my finger to his lips.

'No, no don't be foolish,' I countered and sought to reassure him. 'Have no fear. It's not the real thing!'

'But this desperation – they *must* be ill. All must have caught the plague and live desperately to seek joy.'

'Adam, look more carefully. They purge the ill by imitating it.'

The plague fifty years ago had brought about this loosening of morals. The consciences of people had become so unstrung that they sought only to behave as immorally as they could. Leicester had been such a thriving rich town that its people – how many, I wondered, perhaps four or five thousand – had sought nothing else but oblivion.

'Don't be a Lollard, Adam, join in.'

I let fall my loosened girdle. 'The Lord of Misrule, Adam!' I called to Adam as I seized a small, pretty poppet my size, by her dress a lady who loved riot and dispense and let me slide my hand inside her rich array.

'Christ and his Blessed Mother pardon you all!' Scriven shouted. 'Have you gone mad?' He started to choke, and I could tell he still feared, in spite of it being a masquerade, he would catch the plague. I am afraid I laughed at his discomfort and while the wench held my head, or tried to, with a ribbon I kissed and softly stroked her belly.

'Sing to us of love – tell us of love! Give us a rhyme or two...' A button popped on my surcote. 'I am undone!' I cried out.

Some ribald groom placed on my head a garland of crocuses and narcissi: he whispered something in my ear. 'Is she alone, then?' I looked towards the closed door over the other side of the hall. Pipes skirled and cymbals clashed. The rest, including the naked women and men who had stopped their amorous labours in full view, took up the refrain: 'A rhyme or two, Geoffrey. Give us the old tune!'

I passed my hand before my bleared eyes. Why did they always want me to recite? I cleared my throat. 'If you must play the lover, approach her with words, use every subtle device to compel her belief. Every woman, however plain, believes she's a natural object for love. No woman there is who'd not be thrilled by her own appearance. Press on, undermine her with coaxing flatteries; so the stream will eat away the overhanging bank. And never weary of praising her face, her hair, her slim figure, her small feet. Even the chaste like having their good looks sung; even virgins bask in the praise of their own shapely figures. And don't be shy about promising delight...'

I swigged more from the goblet. 'And yes, friends, Mr Ovid says it's all right to use force, force of that sort goes down well with the girls, what in fact they love to yield they'd often rather have stolen. Rough seduction delights the ladies, the audacity of near-rape is a compliment – and the girl who could have been forced, yet somehow got away unscathed, may show relief and delight, but in fact feels badly let down...How's that, Adam?'...

KATHERINE: At first when Geoffrey trotted up hopefully with his new letter to me I shunned the missive, putting my hand to my head, and imploring my brother-in-law to place my state of mind before John's desire. 'Bear it back to him unopened,' I cried out.

Geoffrey put on some anger over this: staring and champing. Thus – 'How can you believe I'd ever bring you a letter to harm you?' Then he forced the letter on me by seizing my clothing, and thrusting it down between my breasts. 'Go on, throw it away. Rip it up!'

I smiled. 'I will not write back, that's for sure. Please yourself what you reply!'

He teased me till I fell about laughing and suggested we go through the hall to eat some dinner, yet on the way, while he went to wash his hands, I stole off on my own to read the letter. Then I came up behind Geoffrey and covered his eyes, called out, 'I've got you!'

'I give in,' he answered. We ate, and by and by when we had idled away several hours, he told me of his travels in Italy, and of his meetings with the poets and statesmen of that country so superior to ours in almost every way, but above all wonderful in the fashions with which they decked out their women. He next, subtly and with his woman's intuition, caught me on the quick by asking,

'Come on then – out with it. How does he rate in the letter?'

I blushed.

'Oh I could write, but heaven knows what I would say,' I answered.

He managed to persuade me to withdraw my disdain for John's letter – I wouldn't be tied down to love, I wanted to say, but was persuaded to thank John for his good intentions. Then I brought a letter out for Geoffrey to send, grumbling that it was all his fault. He had an answer even for this.

'You know,' he said, 'that often things loathly begun turn out best, while impressions gained easily, easily take flight.'

We argued, with Geoffrey always putting forward the case for giving John hope of joy within the form of danger. 'Don't push it too far,' he said, 'if you're too scornful, he'll answer with bitter anger.' Who strives against love had the worst of it: this was what Geoffrey would like to see implemented. We see much of these courts of love, composed of fair ladies who have nothing better to do; they would appear to thrive even more in times of plague and pestilence, as if only thoughts of something other-worldly and self-indulgent can counter the reality and omnipresence of death. The purification, the dedication of love, the mutual service engaged therein, the vows, above all the tediousness of tender ceremony and approach which I shall not list or repeat as endlessly as those stages which, with utter sincerity and delicacy, Geoffrey now led the pair of us.

There was much saving of soul, much 'pledging of myself to you', much avouching of fidelity, truth, and secrecy in service, diligence, above all the confirmation of 'honour', by which I suppose they, namely John and Geoffrey, meant my chastity and maiden modesty.

I wanted firm assurances that John really loved me. This emerged from me to him as a warning, for I told him,

'Prince as you are, king's son though you be, you shall no more have sovereignty over me in love than in this case is right; nor will I draw back from paying you what's due, if you do me wrong. While you serve me, I will cherish you according to your desserts.' I had thought this out carefully.

I then said: 'Well, now I have chosen you, you shall be happy and come alive in all your desire, for I shall truly – with all the strength I have – turn your bitterness into sweetness, while every woe you have suffered for me shall be changed into joy.'

Of course I meant one thing, but while Geoffrey did not mince words when he described similar explosions of desire between a pair, if they happened to be a town wife and her apprentice lover, or a clerk and his paramour, or a cook and his tart, he wrapped it up in the choicest, most decorated parcel he could devise when he came to treat such passion between a prince and his lady.

'So she takes him in his arms, and begins to kiss him.' That kind of thing.

Moreover, when he began to see his pair of lovers obey his will he could hardly contain his own satisfaction.

In such a fashion this matter proceeded over the next few weeks while the duke prepared for his return from Aquitaine. Transformed by Geoffrey's advice, John became so discreet, so secret, so obedient in my service, that I began to feel that he was indeed a wall of steel, and a shield from every displeasure. I started to trust. So discreet did we become that when, on his arrival in London, we began our secret and yet chaste meetings, with Geoffrey as our chaperone, and with the dozens of letters passing between us, all previous rumours of an amour between us had died down.

Yet Geoffrey, his heart set on John – and, as he believed, now his close friend and confidant – achieving his aim in love, continued with quickness and diligence. He had measured the walls and the floor, and all he had to do was to assemble the house. The timber was ready to be slotted into the frame: it only needed the right moment.

But it took time. Several months later my brother-in-law saw he had a very great problem on his hands: how to bring me quickly to bed with John before he was obliged to set off again for France, for all would now be lost, possibly for ever. Time, forever his friend, threatened to turn into his worst enemy. With this in mind, to speed things up, and bind each of us to the other everlastingly, he importuned me to leave the palace in the Strand, and to come and stay with him and Philippa in the house John had given them in Aldgate; also with a mind to draw John there at the same time, and throw us together.

We passed a merry evening, the three of us, while I, free of Sir Hugh who had been away in France for several months, was in a happier mood than I had been for some time. Although Geoffrey tried to keep me in the dark I could see he and Philippa had taken care over the drawing up of the plan, and John had been instructed to find a secret way at a certain agreed hour up to the bedroom where they were to put me. I pretended my innocence of these arrangements.

When this hour approached, Geoffrey said to me. 'Now sister, I'll show you the room where you're to sleep – I and Philippa will be in the next room, so you can dismiss your maid and send her back to the palace. Have some more wine,' he encouraged me, 'and make yourself ready for bed.'

With this I mounted the stairs to my room, and soon I was in my night-gown of finest Italian silk, such as few women could afford to wear for most still slept naked or in plain shifts. Sir Hugh on an earlier campaign had brought me back the fine garment. Geoffrey sent my woman back to court with his groom, and was now waiting for the arrival of the duke. Anxiously he stood at his house's metal gates, ears strained for the hooves of John's horse, and it was not long before he heard a horseman clattering fiercely in their direction.

Geoffrey knew well the old dance, and had his scheme in every detail exact and ready to apply. First he would bring Lord John into his parlour, set him down with some claret, and prepare him with such talk as, 'Get ready my lord, for you are about to wend your way to heaven…' Then he would steal to my closet and gently wake me, remind me of my love for John and say, diffidently, 'It has just chanced that by whatever stroke of providence completely unknown to me, or to any man, that John has called at my home. I do not want to wake Philippa to make him comfortable and do him service…'

Then he would tell told him that, quite by error, and without thinking, I 'happened' to be staying the night here. John would become 'so pained and distressed', that he feared he might suddenly fall into complete madness, for he had heard, 'You have fallen in love with a man other than him.'

Whereupon, Geoffrey hoped, I would be so struck with anguish and would grow warm and disposed to console him. Everyone knows about these little games, but I pretended not to know, and at the appointed hour I groped my way to the bed where I was to await the moment of my happiness. I pretended to fall asleep, but within a short time I actually did close my eyes. And so I remained fast asleep.

LORD JOHN: I had to ask Chaucer brusquely, on my arrival at the Aldgate house, that he hold my horse.

'She's here,' Chaucer told me, those deep-set smiling eyes of his close-lidded in complicity, 'She's inside, asleep.'

'Does she know that I am here?' I asked Chaucer.

'Come in my lord,' he insisted; 'wait just a little while, and I shall advise her of your presence. Nothing will be an impediment to your love, for I shall say that I will be all the time in the next room…'

I still refused to dismount, so Chaucer must have sensed there was something seriously amiss.

'Oh curse this day, Geoffrey!' I sighed, addressing him familiarly. 'I cannot stay here a moment. My brother Edward has been taken seriously ill and may well die! I have on several counts to be present at his castle, to make sure of his widow, and support his son and heir. You must forgive me, but on this night less than any can I afford a secret meeting with Katherine. It will have to be some other time.'

With this I rode off to Berkhampstead, leaving Chaucer with his plan in ruins. I could only hope that he had not yet mentioned anything of this to Katherine herself, and so had not inflamed her mood either of expectation or refusal. If so, little harm would come from the failed enterprise. But I worried that Chaucer would find no other occasion to bring us together.

When he came back to England my brother Edward had begun to die, although it was to take him a whole six years to complete the process. That great energy, which for the past seven years had been uninterruptedly directed into war, to keep, or pillage, or win France, had turned inwards, spreading through his wounded body, and into his no less flawed mind. In England he had withdrawn, with his wife Joan and his remaining son Richard of Bordeaux, to his favourite castle of Berkhampstead. I, left behind in Aquitaine, had to accomplish the dismal task of burying five-year-old Edward in the beautiful cathedral of Bordeaux.

The cupboard was bare. Edward of Woodstock had squandered all that remained in the kitty, and while I had been sworn in as Lieutenant of the King at the Gascon parliament in Bordeaux before he left, I had no money to continue supporting English rule. It was one thing for the barons of Aquitaine, Gascony, Poitou and Saintonage to pledge love and obedience to me, but chivalric promises could not survive the hard reality of the Valois house of

France. Charles V's policy of slowly sapping England's position was now leading to the loss of Aquitaine.

I was not a borrower like my brother, but the great desertion of French nobles to the cause of Charles V had begun. Our country, up to then mindful of its command of the sea, slackened its control of the vital routes between the south ports and Bayonne and Bordeaux, and the narrower crossings between Dover and Sandwich, Yarmouth and the Rhine and Flanders ports.

England's might ebbed away, just as the glory of the prince waned, his body and mind shackled by torturing pains. The war against the English supremacy in France gained momentum, and as it did I found myself in the role of supreme commander of a diminishing rule, while the effects of Edward's temper and waning rule (and shrinking purse) led one French noble after another to renounce his oath of fealty. My brother had summarily and foolishly executed two ambassadors, sent by Charles V expressly to inflame Edward's frustration.

Many in England knew Edward was to die, and likely to do so before our father, so they supported me as heir to the throne. My young son, Henry of Bolingbroke, was also much preferred to Richard of Bordeaux. But Edward, before he died, threw himself into ensuring the succession of his remaining son, and he succeeded both in binding our father, and indeed I myself, to the cause of his volatile and sensitive heir. He convinced Parliament that Richard was the better choice. To this end the cohorts of calumniating tongues which waged against me served well him and his son Richard.

Our second chance came a week later, this time in my palace. The great bed of black velvet embroidered with iron compasses and garters, with a turtle-dove in the middle of the compasses, fulfilled my destiny. The bed, consecrated to Venus, became the altar of our passion. It was where our courtly sacrament happened. Instead of the Eucharistic miracle, instead of the transubstantiation of the bread and wine touching those who received them with the divine, we were to commingle mortal flesh with spirit.

Since the banishment of her husband Swynford there has been no further impediment. Now we are alone. I hardly listen as Katherine talks gently of her feelings. I lay on the bed as if dead. She slowly rises from beside me. 'Let me say goodnight. I'll go.' 'No, no', I say, 'I beg you not to go. Please.'

I stroke those arms which are on the thin side, and that back which is soft and straight; then her long thighs of tender flesh, which are smooth and white. She grows still and her body opens out to me so, even more gently, do I make an attempt to touch her snowy throat, then her round and maidenly breasts.

Only then, since I now hardly dared to breathe, did I begin to find delight. I kissed her over and over again, all over her body, hardly for joy knowing how to proceed any further to cover our blushing shame and confusion. Both of us exchanged holy vows, expressing our unworthiness, adoration and complete modesty.

'Teach me how I may deserve you,' I said. I promised obedience. She thanked me with a trust I will swear was full-hearted. We held one another close. She sank down, hanging on my neck with both her arms. I slowly slid down on her naked belly and open legs, she on her back.

This was beyond any power of mine to describe. I was the contestant, as she was another, in the lists of love. I wondered if Chaucer, who in his role of go-between, was as present as a communicant as we were in our passion. If you yourself have ever been such at a feast of joy you may well appreciate this feeling, quivering between fear and security. As for any third party, what would he or she have seen? Perhaps Mars and Venus were looking down on us, for in us both of these gods were united. I wonder if sex and violence are not indissolubly married. When a man is angry, is he not lustful? Does not a woman give herself best when in her capitulation she, too, has an element of hate? No one can be sure what exactly happened and how, and what each of us did.

This magic was created alone by the female body, by Katherine's body. The female body, by its mere presence, inspires the belief that it contains supernatural power. These were the same powers that were attributed to the Holy Grail, while we know how the Grail rejuvenated those who contemplated it...

Quick, impulsive desire on the instant caught both of us. She, who had been the pursued, turned to become the pursuer; having been despoiled, she changed and quickly learned the sweetness of the spoil. With something near to fury she began to forage and, as she did so, like my own raiding parties in Aquitaine, her blood mounted and stirred up a desperate passion beating down all reason, forgetting shame's blush, and any twinges of honour, and settling in her an oblivion of all but the here and now. I too grew hot and weary, and like a wild bird tamed by excessive handling I yielded and obeyed the power of her embrace, my resistance fully overcome.

Having eaten and drunk of pain, as if in her forward love Katherine plucked the root from her sorrow, a sweetness began to manifest itself, and we melted into a profound bliss, wreathing about one another with many a twist, intermingling our limbs like the sweet woodbine and the oak.

'Let me die for you,' I said.

Swynford had upon my order served in Aquitaine, where he had been wounded, not too grievously, in the thigh. So he came down wounded from the north of Aquitaine, where he'd been in the campaigns of Champagne and Brie under the banner of Sir Robert Knolles. He had been wounded in that skirmish, and the commander told him to rest up in Bordeaux for a few days. Rumour has it that a Portuguese man-servant of mine, Eça, lent to me by João, king of Portugal, who hoped to marry my daughter Philippa, tried to do away with the wounded Swynford. His first move was to draw him into a brawl in a Bordelaise tavern. As the French were in a great state of emotional flux, it was not too difficult to provoke a man to fight, especially such a man as Swynford, who was a simple – indeed a ferocious brute.

Is provocation to anger a crime? Some say it is, and some say it isn't. The wise man will do his best not to be provoked, whatever the cause.

Eça invented quite an ingenious story; he said he got Swynford with a couple of knights who were supposed to be bound in fealty to the English throne, but were secretly conspiring with de Buescin behind my back. They began drinking heavily, then spoke of their respective wives. The French knights, whose names were Estoffe and Mouchet, and true treacherous Gascons, wanted to make a taunting wager with Swynford. Knowing the rumours of his wife's unfaithfulness with the commander-in-chief of the English army they bet, or tried to bet, Swynford that they would find out which of their three wives was the most unfaithful while they were away. Swynford, they proposed, should go and try to seduce Estoffe's wife – she lived in Biarritz, while Mouchet should try the wife of Swynford; likewise Estoffe should try Mouchet's. Sir Hugh could bear no imputation that his wife was unfaithful to him, and he misunderstood the whole drift of the wager and the game afoot, so he took offence hastily.

At the same time Eça contrived to have Swynford hear of some treasonous plan that Mouchet had been brewing up in the rear of my army, while Sir Hugh believed that the idea he should visit Estoffe's wife was a further attempt to lure him into an ambush, plotted by myself.

They swore that they were made of honour, but he accused them of being false and French – a whole spat of anti-French sentiment came off his tongue, such as they were double-dealing, treacherous cowards. They refused to believe his wife was beautiful, because he was so ugly and brutish. 'Describe her to us,' they said, but he could only say she was lovely in her looks: divine reflection had chosen to shine with the greatest brilliance in woman's body. He challenged them and they fought, but he was impaired and they wounded him more. They left him while laughing at his bleeding and feeble condition, for by now they believed he was no more than a delirious idiot.

The old knight was gory, beaten black and blue, and his wounds stank. They left him in hospital, where they gave him wine and food. Bordeaux was a hot pot of plots and plagues and no one took much notice of him there, but at last his friends found him an old carque which one of my lieutenants had loaded with spoil, and there, amid cups and tapestries, and fed by angry young French girls who were being abducted as servants or paramours, he languished while they crossed the Bay of Biscay. How that man must have suffered on the journey: from sores, from his wounds, from his cursing, irritable temper.

They carried him on a litter to Kettlethorpe. From here on Chaucer informed me of the next development: Swynford came face to face with Katherine, who had left London to look after him. Chaucer could have sworn that he would have her killed or kill her himself, for in his mind she had become all the pain he had suffered. But as pain undergoes such magical transformations, so he looked into that open, innocent face, and his heart melted. For she, tenderly, was there to gaze with compassion on him. Under her care the boils, the suppurating wounds, the lesions and twisted limbs began to heal, so she affected not to stint herself of care, for she tended not only this brute of a man who had treated her horribly, but also her husband, part of that greater union or sacrament, sanctified as being between Jesus and his church.

An old nurse was sent by my arch-enemy Walsingham to help her. Her name was Sister Pervil, and she was skilled in the arts of medicine and cure. She supported Lady Katherine, although the latter, deep in her heart, and this show of wifely obedience and tenderness apart, was – they were to say later – besieged by the devil. Fanned in her desire to further her union with me, they alleged that she was hatching the most heinous of crimes.

❧

'Is she very hideous?' I asked my father. I stood at his bedside, to which lately he had been confined, in the Palace of Westminster.

I knew why I had been summoned. There was a rumour that I was to marry Constance of Castile, the elder daughter of the usurped King Peter the Cruel, and was therefore to be promised the legitimate throne of nearly all of Spain, as the kingdoms of Castile and Leon were known. There was one drawback, however, namely that I had to win the kingdoms back from the usurper and killer, Henry of Trastamara, the murdered King Peter's stepbrother, who was the powerful ally of France in the war against England. In the meantime I had to bolster up the faltering duchy of Aquitaine. I had too much to do, and I hated this division of myself into many parts. I sent Philippa Chaucer, both to reward her and Chaucer for their devotion to me, with the duty to attend on the king my father at Westminster, and keep a watch on Alice Perrers.

'Listen.' My father read from a letter. '"I order the infant, Dona Constanza, my daughter, and he that shall marry her, shall inherit my kingdom!"'

'This was written by her father, Pedro the Cruel just before he was treacherously stabbed by Henry his half-brother – I'm not sure why he was known as cruel, because it seems he was much praised by poets – yes, oh noble, worthy Pedro, glory of Spain, is what your friend Chaucer says about him.'

'I've had enough of marriage,' I answered. 'I vowed when Blanche died that I would never marry again: I made the vow on her deathbed that I would remain true to her forever. To her I pledged my life – and to regain France for England.'

'You have a mind,' said the old man shrewdly to me, 'to keep your beautiful mistress, the lady Katherine, governess of your children. But you are too young to remain unmarried for long.' Alice Perrers was feminine enough, with her little dogs and her gloves embroidered with daisies, and she knew how to appeal to my father, in spite of the chorus of hate the chroniclers whipped up against her.

I felt perplexed. 'Please, father,' I said...

'To become king of Spain.... Doesn't this excite you?...'

'Not exactly Spain...' What I meant was that I would like to be king of England, but, as third son, I would never be adopted by my father.

'Well, Castile and Leon. There's hardly much more. And they say Dona Constanza is handsome.'

'How old is she?'

'Seventeen.'

'Father, I repeat I have no desire to marry!'

'And if it is my command?' My father looked at me appealingly. I had lovingly supported him in everything. Without condition. 'Soon I shall be dead. You know I would have liked, more than anything in the world, to have given you my crown, for you would make the best king. But this was not to be. You are my fourth child, and even before you come the heirs of dear, dead Lionel. But I want you and your heirs to have a kingdom. I know at present of no other marriage which will profit you more.'

I had to weigh the possibilities. The Castilian navy was good; our own had fallen badly behind; there were able counsellors. There was money, plenty of money. I could make two households. More self-division. There would be battles in plenty to be fought. As long as I did not have to spend any time with this Constanza. 'If I make this marriage I may be able to contain the military power of France, which on our own we will never do again. I shall have to convince the Commons that the way of Spain – *le chemin d'Espagne* – is the only way left to us to weaken the French.

'You know what they say, my lord: lucky in love, unlucky in war.'

'What can you mean by this, Chaucer?'

Philippa, on her return to London in June, had made her report. I had summoned Geoffrey to discuss the matter.

'Spanish women, I have been told, lack delicacy of feeling. Unrestrained language and the most lascivious looks are incapable of making them blush – and they speak on these subjects with the freedom of men.'

So pronounced Chaucer, adding: 'Lips, eyes, and ears are alike strangers to chastity – but pride prevents them from going further.'

The poet then said, 'Surrounded as they are with relics and scapularies, do you not wonder they bind themselves to love saints? Divided between religious duties and the pleasure of sense, a Spanish woman is in a state of continual warfare – between her passionate needs of the flesh, and her voluptuous devotion to the image of Christ, or of the Virgin.'

'They say Spanish men are disgusted by women who yield to carnal lust.'

Constanza, I noted when I met her later that year in Aquitaine, at Roquefort Castle, had a slender form, a majestic step, a sonorous voice, black and brilliant eyes, and she gesticulated vivaciously. The whole action of her person showed the temperature of her soul.

'How,' I wondered, 'am I going to resist being swept off my feet by this display of beauty and spontaneity?'

I thought of Katherine, of her delicate, passionate sense of spiritual union with me. Of those large soulful eyes, a pebbled blue and green. This one had dark hair on her upper lip, as these Spanish women do, with a special pullita, or woman servant, whose job it was to pull it out.

I married Constanza that same autumn month in 1371 at Roquefort. She was seventeen, I was thirty-one. I had now, by virtue of King Peter's will, a titular right to the kingdom, but Castile and Leon were firmly in the hands of Constanza's brother, and would not be yielded up without a hard fight.

I had gained the new and impressive title: 'Monsieur d'Espagne'.

We viewed one another with extreme suspicion. It was our wedding night. No doubt Constanza was dreaming of a child, but she knew I had three, and probably had found out that Katherine was pregnant with my fourth. Was she that bothered? She knew her duty. Women have a herding instinct like horses, and need to press close, to nudge each other as mares. They will all go for the same stallion if he is proud, well-formed, masterful and swears undying love. But then, when the child comes, and she nurtures it at her own breast, she will want the stallion transformed into a gentle husband standing by her, and gazing tenderly down.

Constanza was very devout, she would never move without addressing her prayers, and indeed her whole being, to God, and especially to her saviour Jesus, from whose image, either in her imagination, or in paintings or statues, she would never allow herself to stray.

I, to my own surprise, was oddly affected. She was not, by any means, Katherine. There was something dark and singular about her. This caught my will and attention, something that Katherine, in her breadth, even universality of being, lacked. This flashing, but dark, Castilian pride, this brooding, ever-present sense of being spawned out of darkness and conspiracy. It was royal blood.

I was limited in my capacity to betray myself to her in speech by the fact that I spoke little, or no, Spanish. We conversed in French, but her French was poor, and our conversation was limited to basic issues, such as 'Will you eat now? Will you go to bed?' But did we need to speak? I offered her the gift that I had brought, a cup of gold fashioned as a double rose, with a lid mounted by white columbine, and she accepted this with a smile and a bow of the head. Otherwise everything was arranged between the various courtiers and interpreters, for it was my efficiency and military prowess that with her title to her country she was bargaining for, and she had able courtiers, such as John Guettere, to help her.

I sent her wine, and provided for her in many other ways. I would bring her to England and establish her at Hertford Manor, making sure she was well-attended. I realized that the sooner I made her pregnant, the freer I would be to see Katherine again, and I set out to achieve this as soon as I could. I was not long in succeeding.

Constanza did not like England, but she had to live here until such time as I could mount an expedition to recapture Spain. Katherine so exceeded everyone in the court in her beauty, that all women tended to copy her manners, her hair-style, even her way of sauntering. She became the ideal beauty of England, whom everyone sought to imitate. She took cold baths and followed other methods which only penitents or self-scourgers would employ. I myself practised the inhuman method of immersion in cold water to freshen and cleanse my body; in her case daily bathing served to make her complexion radiant – Katherine never wore paint or powder…and give her a rare vitality…

Constanza grew so jealous that when she stayed the night in the Savoy she wanted to find out the bewitching love technique her rival used. She had the ceiling over Katherine's room pierced with several holes so that she could watch us making love.

She saw, or so Chaucer wrote in one of his fabliaux: 'A very beautiful, white delicate and fresh woman, half-naked, clad in a chemise, caressing her love with a wealth of charm and delicious folly, which her lover returned, until they slid from their bed to the floor, and still in their chemises pursued their gymnastics on the carpet, so avoiding the heat of the bed. It was in the middle of a very warm summer.'

Constanza must have concluded that nothing very original bound me to Katherine. The key was to be found elsewhere – in our vivid imaginations, or in our need for each other, in the feeling both of us entertained for one another. I had spent so many years in a dismal dungeon of some kind, and had read and filled myself so much with the ideals of countless romances that these had become, or gained, a lasting hold over me. Katherine was the first whom I had set my eyes upon who answered my dreams. Her soft, yet cold and slightly distant beauty was of the inaccessible type that singled her out straight away as a far-away princess – the ideal beauty for whom every prince secretly yearned. Who could not agree that

Femme est secours contre faiblesse,
Joie contre melancholie,
Sens et avis contre folie,
Courtoise contre rudesse.
Elle est terrestre paradis.

Terrestrial paradise?

PART TWO

Thirteen

Scriven

NEXT MORNING WE SET out from Leicester with the funeral cortège, to bring it to London *via* Huntingdon, the seat of Lady Elizabeth of Huntingdon, and *via* St Albans, where we are due to arrive tomorrow afternoon. The day was fine and sunny, if cold. After its long sojourn in the Collegiate Chapel the bier did not smell as badly as it did previously. I only hope the embalmers have been busy. It was a sorely welcome relief to be on the road at last and travelling south.

Last night, in that disgraceful stew, I had waited impatiently outside while Mr Chaucer, unheeding of my pleas, had passed that closed door to dally with some strumpet dressed as Helen of Troy. What he or they had done, who knows? Maybe he had, at his advanced age and with what he had drunk, merely tempted himself with the fruits of desire while the lady had whispered sweet nothings in his ear. I had repeated over to myself some of my master's more consoling and noble rhymes, in an effort to forgive, or if not, alleviate the outrage his behaviour caused in me. He had come out of this sordid palace of luxury at last, and with a broad smile on his face.... In my opinion happiness is not to be found by dancing after any heathen god of love, but by looking up to where a more terrible but more tender god of love hangs, not on Olympus but on Calvary.

Yet now it was as if the evil events of yesterday had been forgotten. The townspeople of Leicester, with whom Lord John had always been popular, turned out in force to cheer our departure. Far from a funeral and a wake, it was more and more a celebration. Our procession assembled in St Mary's Church and before the bier they carried a richly adorned image of the Virgin queen, borne aloft under a brightly coloured canopy, preceded by priests and minstrels, and followed by twelve persons representing the apostles, each with an assumed name inscribed on parchment on the front of his cap. The young Leicester girls, clad in white and carrying early spring flowers, marshalled in force under their black capes, and then the varied flags of the Lancaster domains fluttered everywhere, together with the banners, heightening the festivity of the sad occasion. Bells from the steeple above clashed, and the cortège, now joined by its notables and royal personages on horseback, proceeded up the High Street to the Leicester High Cross before turning down Swine's Market to leave the city by the East Gate.

People poured out from houses and adjoining streets, while the long and impressive train moved eastward between the rows of gabled houses whose windows were packed with townspeople. Headed by chanting priests and incense-bearing acolytes the cortège snaked in and out among the shadows of the massive trees that lined the way. In future years they would say this day marked the end of the Lancastrian rule that had Leicester as its capital, for in the following year Richard, deposed and then murdered, gave way to the rule of Lord John's son Henry. Leicester and the Lancastrian lands and possessions became, for the first and last time, merged with the lands and possessions of the king of England.

Well, be that as it may, we were on the road, and we had the sheriff and his officers trotting at the rear, still earnestly conducting their investigation into the murders. The morning passed almost silently, myself and my master riding side by side, each lost or absorbed in his own thoughts, with no need to talk, or with a sense, perhaps, that too much had already been said. Because my master had told me that Rachel had been my mother I felt subdued, tongue-tied, although I was still convinced that it was untrue. I sought often further proof or reasons from him for this avowal, but he refused to divulge more. I truly suspected that he had none. But it could have been that he bided his time, waiting for something or someone to arrive, which would confirm what he had told me.

At mid-morning, when we had travelled on Scot and Dexter about ten or fifteen miles, perhaps more, at a steady amble or brisk walking pace along the old Roman road to Corby my master pulled me closer to him, seizing my hand.

128

'Adam,' he said, 'Rachel's death has much upset me. I want you to know this. After my own wife's death, when we had been living for the most time apart – she in Hertford attending Queen Constanza, and then in Lincoln with her sister Katherine in the house Lord John provided for her – and me in London with my various occupations – Rachel, that poor old soul, did what she could to console me…'

He allowed this admission to fall in silence, its full implication to sink in, but not prepared to enlarge further. I thought of the golden lion on the brooch of the Cheshire executioner. Could it have come from Philippa, and had the sight of this prompted my master to talk? Worse, had Rachel herself told him that she was my mother?

'What I have to confess,' he went on, '…and you must listen carefully to me, for I see and fear all kinds of disaster and perturbation looming, as if a world is coming to an end – and who knows even the Day of Judgement itself…'

He stopped, as if the prospect of this became too enormous to contemplate.

'You have seen with your own eyes the size of the Lancaster family tree, and how many shoots and buds it has ready to grow, and even to graft and take new roots. What I have to confess, Adam,' and here he paused to take in a deep breath, 'is that *I* began the whole love affair with Katherine Swynford and Lord John of Lancaster – '

'But this is the self-same story Rachel started to tell me when she was killed,' I blurted out.

My master sighed with relief. 'Ah, now I know what she was telling you. You see I had good cause, for I never really found reason to trust Philippa, my wife, I am ashamed to tell you, and I sought to divert Lord John's attention from my wife onto her sister. If you will listen, I will expand.'

And so he did, proceeding to a full description. 'I felt bad enough at Katherine's wedding, but even worse next morning when we saw, after her nuptial night, how desolate Katherine was. She had nursed hopes, I believe, he would change, that because he had refrained from touching her again before that night, somehow he would be affected by her hopes for love and softness, be chastened and transformed by the solemn promises made before the priest. She was even prepared, should he show her true devotion and courtesy, to forgive him his past brutality. As for myself, I had a more realistic hope that with all the beer and skittles he would bring on the condition known as brewer's droop.

'But sadly this was not to be, for when he entered the bedchamber she saw at once he was drunk and angry. She began to weep, but this did not move him to gentleness. "Are you not a knight?" she asked. "And do not knights swear an oath to defend the fair sex?" He gave an ugly smirk, saying, "It will not hurt if you do not resist." '

'Wait a minute,' I interrupted my master. 'How do you know all this?'

'Listen. You must not be offended, Adam. This next part is shocking. I swear it is true. She sprang from the bed and tried to reach the door, but he caught hold of her linen gown. Rather than have it pulled off she did not struggle. Then he laughed: and this laugh so tormented her she turned and, feigning to give him a kiss, she sank her teeth into his neck. He roared with pain and threw her down on the floor, where she hoped he would let go of her, but he sat heavily on her, rending a piece of linen from her gown to bind up his neck.

'Then she fought back and fought very hard, for he was almost squatting on her head, and because he had nothing under his gown she could feel his naked arse against her cheek. After he had finished he rose, slid out the knife he had at his waist and with the other hand stopped her mouth. At first she thought he was going to murder her, but, with the cold steel on her naked breast, he slit her gown open to her knees. She was too frightened to move, and as soon as her breasts were bared he lowered his face and rubbed it against their lovely skin. He tore the linen from under her, so now she was quite naked. Then, dropping the knife, he began to run his hands down her sides.

'Sweat mixed in rivulets with the blood that oozed from the band he'd tied round his neck. She closed her eyes and kept utterly still since at any movement she made he seemed to grunt with pleasure. Yet when he forced a hand between her legs she struck out again. He laughed horribly. "You struggle hard for one with so soft a body." He prized her thighs apart still further. He did no more than hoist his gown above his waist, but this was enough. Soon she felt him forcing himself in and the pain was very great, so great she dug her nails deep in his neck.

'During all this she prayed and this gave her the patience to endure his cruel lust. Had she opened her eyes she would have wept piteously, not only for herself, but also for the grief she felt for the state chivalry had come to in England. He ground away, till finally with ugly, swift spasms he reached his conclusion. She murmured softly, "May God forgive you."

'Do you wonder, Adam, at my concern when she told me this in such detail to devise some means by which she could escape from this vile beast. I believed if I did not try, she, who was of all the women I have ever looked upon the most perfect (so you could with justice swear that divine reflection had chosen to shine in her woman's body above all other with the greatest brilliance) – *she* would begin to wither and close in on herself and lose that most wonderful form of beauty she possessed.'

We stopped for some moments to pick a stone from the shoe of Dexter, the bay my master rode, and there were other interruptions, such as one of our number becoming violently sick, and having to be left by the roadside. We passed two bodies of young men in spattered pourpoints fallen from disease or the savage attack of a robber band, left for crows to pick at.

Once we had to shrink from the roadway to let a column of lepers pass, each of whom had a bell tied to his or her neck. Poor monsters with fused spines, crookbacks and ulcerated skins, shunned for their contagion, doomed to a tormented seclusion from the rest of mankind. Was this God's punishment, or were they the true heretics?

Fortunately, or unfortunately, to temper my mounting fury and disgust the sheriff of Leicester rode up with two of his men. Once again I scarcely breathed. They reined in as he pointed to my master, while his companions drew swords.

'Take that one in charge – we need to question him...'

My master shrugged and put his head to one side, while a man rode up either side of him, and each seized an arm. My master's narrative had so disturbed me I had quite forgotten our inquisitors. At a fast trot we were led to an inn at Thorpe Mandeville, in advance of the main procession. The forest stretched for miles ahead, and in the far distance I spotted where our track once more joined up with the old Roman road.

We dismounted in the inn yard and were motioned to sit down at a table. The sheriff was in a brisk, business-like mood. Removing his purple roundel he revealed himself as black-haired, while his chin and upper lip were covered with two days' stubble.

He asked, 'What is your business with this man?'

'I am Mr Chaucer's scrivener or copyist,' I answered.

'Who is Mr Chaucer?' Here my master raised one of those soft white hands.

'I am here, present and correct.'

I recalled we had been through something similar to this before. The sheriff had never heard of the famous maker of verses.

'And what do you do?'

'I was a poet in the service of John of Lancaster.'

'Will you be retained by the next duke?'

My master shrugged. 'I have no idea.'

'How long have you been in service?'

'At least thirty years.'

'Mr Chaucer,' I said quietly so they would not hear. 'Can I have a word, please?' My master looked at the sheriff, who assented with a wave of the hand.

'What is it, Adam?'

'I wish to quit your service.'

'But Adam...' He had gone quite pale and I feared he might have a fit. 'You can't do that. Without you to copy I will be lost. Anyway, the tale I have been rehearsing to you is of considerable importance. There is more to come. I intend one day to write down every word.'

I turned to the sheriff. 'You shouldn't be questioning him about the murders,' I was bold enough to say, 'He didn't do them. He was all the while in the hall.'

'How do you know?'

'I was there too.'

'Two corroborating liars is the oldest trick.' I scanned my master's face, and I could see he had no intention of contradicting me. But there was something else in his eyes, a threat of disclosure about Rachel, or such I interpreted it. Did he still suspect me? 'You may ask the daughters of Lord John.'

'What have you got in that bag?'

He pointed to Scot's saddle where the leather pouch containing the de Roet girl's documents and those of Lord John seemed, from where we sat under the coping of the inn, to have taken on even greater size and importance than when I rode. Scot's grey ears pricked up and for a moment I wondered if he might not take it into his head to canter off.

'My master's work,' I answered, hoping they did not see my face

132

in which the colour rose hotly. I struggled for dear life to stop my features contorting –

'Show me!'

I jumped quickly to my feet and detached the bag from the rest of the bundle. I opened it.

'See here,' I said. 'This is the present piece of work.'

He snatched from me the papers in my master's crabbed hand. Few could read them fluently, but surprisingly he did: 'Of this cursed sin of Ire also comes manslaughter. And understand well that homicide, that is manslaughter, takes many forms. Some kind of homicide is spiritual, and some is bodily. Spiritual manslaughter is in six categories. First by hate, as Saint John says: "He that hates his brother is a homicide." Homicide is also by backbiting, about which Solomon says, "They have two swords with which backbiters kill their neighbours"...'. The sheriff swivelled round his eye to fix it on my master.

'Well, well,' he pronounced, 'you seem to be something of an authority on murder.'

My master laughed uproariously. 'No more than those reverent prophets who wrote the book that it profits us all to study.'

The sheriff was not impressed.

'Poets usually write about experiences they know at first hand. Did you hate your brother?'

'I have no brother.'

'You must have thought deeply about murder.'

'Mostly how to avoid it happening to me.'

This made the interrogator laugh. 'Let's have a drink.' He pushed towards us the great flagon a servant of the inn had brought. My master took hold of it with pleasure. Was I not to be offered some? 'Frankly,' continued the sheriff, 'if I'm honest about this I'm in the wrong business. I'm not really any good at murder, or hunting for murderers. In fact I'm an infinitely good-natured and delightful fellow, intelligent, inoffensively amusing. Mr Chaucer, I'll talk to you directly. I think you have more of an idea of what may be going on here than I have.'

I looked at my master to warn him not to say anything,

'But we have made an arrest and sent the accused back to Leicester under armed guard.'

My master did not bat an eyelid. 'So you believe you have the murderer?'

133

'Yes.'

'What makes you so sure of it?'

'She has confessed. Petronella Swynford, the duchess's first daughter, and Sir Thomas Swynford's sister.' There was a pause as I looked at my master and Mr Chaucer in turn stared at the sheriff. His shoulders moved or twitched involuntarily. 'But I am not convinced,' continued the sheriff.

'Does she give a reason?'

'Yes. She hates her mother. She believed the gentlewoman worked for her and was sent on the trip to look after her and spy on her. She believes there is a whole conspiracy against her that it is her duty to wipe out, or she will be done away with, as her father was done away with by Lord John.'

'So she knew what was in those letters carried by the men who tried to mutilate Lord John,' said my master quietly.

'I believe she has had these ideas before. She had a very confusing and unfortunate upbringing. She says Rachel carried secret plans which had been drawn up, and she passed these to the white-haired guard.'

'She must have been very strong and determined to kill both of them,' said my master.

'If she is stark mad she would have found the strength.'

'No,' said my master firmly. 'I think you should send word to have her released. She did not do it. She is muddled and confused, and will lie to anyone, Robert Wydeville, if it will alleviate her guilt.'

The sheriff looked up when my master called him by his name. I could see he was both intimidated and impressed.

'But how,' I asked, 'would anyone confess to a murder they did not commit?'

'I am afraid this is very common, Adam,' my master informed me. 'The guilt, the burden of confusion, some people carry round with them responds sometimes to anything that will lessen it. And there are those who need to be punished, or punish themselves, over and over again. For some, the burden of Original Sin is just too great.'

'She says it is all her mother's fault,' added the sheriff.

My master turned quickly to take this up. 'Yes her mother, Katherine, for her mother's sake you must free her, and let her continue the journey. Part of it is a desire to discomfit her mother, for she hated Lord John marrying her. But my sister-in-law must be

134

protected from news of this, for she lavished care and attention on this unfortunate daughter of hers, although this is spurned.'

My master's persuasiveness had found a good listener in the sheriff. He scratched his chin. 'Well, I can return her to the procession, and place an armed guard on her till someone better comes along.'

'Yes,' said my master.

'But if it wasn't her, then whom shall we suspect, Mr Chaucer?'

There was just a menacing edge in this.

'Have you considered her brother?' I said, who had suspicions the night-time intruder had been Thomas.

'Why should he want to kill the old woman? He took her to the fair.'

'So you know that.' The sheriff regarded me sharply. Oh heavens spare me, I thought, I have done it now. But my master diverted the attention of Robert Wydeville.

'Then there is the Spanish queen, the daughter of Lord John's second wife Constanza. Philippa managed the household maintained by John at Hertford. Perhaps she knew something about the Castilian family which she wrote down, and passed to her trusted servant Rachel.'

My master turned to address me: 'How does this notion appear to you, Adam?'

'Far-fetched, except that all Spaniards are murderers.'

My master opened his palms. 'If we go through a list of all Lord John's mourners I think it could be claimed every single one has a motive. My son, Thomas, for instance, could have disliked Rachel extremely; unlikely but not impossible. I could have done it myself: after my wife's death for a short while she was my mistress. The king suspects me of treason – as a close friend of Lancaster – and Rachel could have supplied charges of my misdeeds. But so might Huntingdon have been the murderer, or Elizabeth his wife, for she – '

'Well, given that it is not poor Petronella, or Thomas your son. Or you. Or Mr Scriven here – whom do you most suspect?'

My master answered slowly and in an ominous tone. 'I have my suspicions, but I fear those who committed these foul crimes will never be punished. Yes, I fear they will get away with it.'

'What a shocking thing to say,' spoke the sheriff without conviction.

135

'It's a reality of life. It happens. But there is something about this whole affair which still puzzles me. What are they, the murderers, hoping to gain?'

'You think there are more than one?'

His eyes engaged a distant point of attention.

'Look, the cortège approaches...'

The sheriff appeared irritated and he coughed noisily. 'I have questioned nearly the whole cortège, and I find no connection that convinces me between the victims and anyone who travels with the duke's body.'

'Perhaps he or they never joined us in the first place.'

Without any further comment Wydeville left. What a churlish man, yet I sensed he was not a flatterer or sycophant. Few men are honest. We collected Dexter and Scot, remounted, and waited for our place in the main procession.

'Well,' said my master, 'it looks like they've done their questioning for the day. Yet I may soon be able to tell them a further thing or two.'

I regarded him closely. 'You threatened me with a look, possibly to tell them your allegation that Rachel was my mother. How did you come to hear of this, Mr Chaucer? What is your basis for saying this? You must answer me!'

But still he does not answer, and will not. 'Just remember, Adam,' he said, 'that I know that you were with both Rachel and Basil before they died.'

I felt a surge of anger and resentment, but told myself to be calm, ever arming myself in what my master, in another part of his homily, calls 'mansuetude' or 'debornairty', or, as we might otherwise describe it, a good disposition, patience or needed sufferance...'If you will vanquish your enemy,' as he wrote.

'Well, what were the consequences of this dilly-dallying of yours between Lord John and Katherine Swynford?' I asked. 'Are you going to tell me how they finally – ?'

Scot and Dexter swerved to avoid the carriage travelling fast the other way...

Fourteen

Chaucer

I COULD SPOT HUNTINGDON Castle in the distance. A square and humdrum stone tower which showed only too well how they were skimping on the cost when they built it. The weather was turning wild, wet and windy, and we were joined by a new companion. As he rode up I whispered to Scriven, 'One hundred marks, did you hear that in the will, left to "My dear comrade-in-arms, Sir Thomas Swynford". Yes, I've got it, Adam, it's he who did it! He did the murder of Swynford. Reward enough in Lancaster's will for betraying his father! I was watching his father! I was watching his face, Adam, during the reading of the will.... Judas betrayed his master for thirty pieces of silver. What price the murder of a father?' I felt excited, and I could feel the moisture cool and glittering in my eyes.

'What's this?' demanded Sir Thomas Swynford sharply. His wet lower lip jutted arrogantly.

'Oh Mr Swynford,' I demanded in a tone just short of deliberate and overt rudeness, 'I was pointing you out to my scribe, Adam, and remarking that your dear mother is due to join the cortège, indeed ride at its head tonight or tomorrow.'

Scriven interrupted in a cringing tone. 'It must be good to be rich, Sir Thomas. Congratulations on your legacy.'

His hand went straight to his dagger, He was one of these congenitally mistrustful types, I knew this at a glance. He roped his personal demons by farming them out to others. I heard the rumour that once he had a wife and used to beat her for being unfaithful to him: he would take her into the stable, find a halter and whip her till she would drink the water he washed in. They say that in the end he killed her, but no one ever arrested him for it.

His narrow, bloodshot eyes switched quickly backwards and forwards between my scrivener and myself.

'Join us, cousin, and keep us company till we reach the house of the other Lord John.' I began trying to soften him. 'You know, Thomas, I often think of your father. You must have been four when he died. Do you remember him?" I asked Thomas more gently.

'Yes. He would beat me if I didn't do what he told me. I was afraid of him.'

'You must have heard the rumours that Lord John gave the orders for, or in some way engineered, his death, first by sending him into an arranged ambush, and then when he was back home in Kettlethorpe, having him poisoned, oh yes, and, they say, suffocated in smoke just to make sure he was really done for.'

'Later,' answered Thomas Swynford more reasonably, 'when I was older I heard the rumours, but I never believed them. Lord John was my sister's godfather. I believe my father died of wounds.'

'Yet did you know there was an inquest, held in Lincoln in the summer of 1372, and they could not come to any conclusion? These letters found on those two men who died on Monday evening...'

Swynford was not interested. But not impolite in his reply. 'Why don't you ask my mother about these matters? She knows better than I.'

'Better still,' I thought of something else, 'I'll ask Brother Thomas Walsingham, the cloister monk, when we reach St Albans tomorrow. He presided over the inquest of your father.'

Suddenly without warning the great destrier Thomas Swynford rode (no doubt snatched as booty in France) reared up and emitted a deafening whinny; clinging vertically onto his neck Thomas Swynford fought to bring the animal under control. He charged off, head down, racing over some new ploughed land, while Swynford held on to his hat.

'You know,' Scriven said to me, 'he did not kill his father, but I still have my suspicions about the deaths in Leicester.'

The look we exchanged signified that I knew what he meant. He continued.

'Is it as if, in some perverse way he is trying to serve John of Lancaster?

'Clear his name. He worshipped his stepfather, didn't he? Perhaps Rachel, and the man in the guardroom who gave away his father's plot, had some other knowledge about Lord John's involvement in Swynford's death, perhaps they knew more about it.

'And he is not sound in mind, and there is such a thing as murder without motive.'

To change the subject, 'Where do you think Lord John is now?' I asked cheerfully, shifting in my saddle. 'Heaven, hell, or purgatory? Wherever he is, I bet he is not as sore as I am. What a wearisome thing is travel.'

'If he is in hell already, we'd know about it. I believe Lord John is in purgatory.'

'Ah yes,' I said, warming to Adam's notion. 'Purgatory. Not so bad a place. I have always warmed to the idea of purgatory as Dante describes it in his *Divina Commedia*. Sinners are gratified with an unlimited amount of the sin they have practised all their lives until they are so surfeited they are unable to contemplate committing it further. Yes in Lord John's case it might not seem such a doleful thing. Quite enjoyable in fact.'

'But I have always thought that the surfeit given is unendurable. In his case it would be...I leave this to your imagination.'

'Perhaps so, perhaps so. But then you have to remember, Adam, Lord John came sincerely to repent of his sin.'

'I don't believe it. His body still stinks to high heaven,' Scriven said, 'and if this isn't a sign he is tainted by sin I don't know what is!'

To put an end to our conversation I then told Adam, 'I think I know who killed Rachel and the man-at-arms, but it would be dangerous to make it public and create fear. To discover who killed Swynford all those years ago, this is something else.'

We were wending our way into Huntingdon Castle and nothing more was said. Lord John Holland, earl of Exeter, as well of Huntingdon, flanked by stewards and servants, had ridden out and greeted us, wearing a black draped chaperon and furred gown. Huntingdon might well put on a display of unctuous and reverential homage, but he was an odious man, although he was married to Elizabeth of Lancaster, Lord John's second daughter from Blanche, who had much of the frank open character of her mother. It was forever uncertain where her allegiances lay. Taking part in our great seigneur's expedition to Castile, and having just made his wife-to-be, namely Elizabeth, pregnant before their marriage, he quite treacherously deserted his father-in-law. As the king's half-brother, he was named in one of the conspiracies to remove Lord John and his son Henry from power, even to have them murdered. But now he smiled and fawned on everyone, offering hospitality. There was rich and sumptuous provision of beer, wine, and food in his hall.

But I noticed a certain hostility in the air. It may have had something to do with the strong expectation of Lady Katherine Lancaster, who was to join us from Lincoln. Huntingdon apprised us of rumours that soon all Lancastrian lands might be confiscated from Henry Bolingbroke, and taken by King Richard himself to pay for the Irish war. Given with the authority of a great lord this news acted like a thunderbolt.

And so the war clouds gathered – on the horizon loomed an increasing sense of danger. I personally, not very different from the rest of the Lancastrian retainers, felt I was threatened because I might well lose my annual payment. 'What if,' I had wondered aloud to Scriven, 'we are met in London, or even before then on the road by the Cheshire archers who form our king's Praetorian or personal bodyguard? If they steal the body of the duke, can anyone resist them? Never. Richard is at King's Langley, near St Albans. Not very far away from where we are due to arrive tomorrow, and what if he is in his most fearsome mood? If this were to happen John would not be allowed the burial that is his due.'

For once my scrivener echoed my opinion, albeit in slightly high-flown style. 'I think we should flee for ever from this world of princes…they're such a moody lot…'

'Yes, Adam, you are right. I have always refused high office. Once the great duke offered me – this was just after my term of magistrate and Member of Parliament – the manorship of Letchbury. I refused. I'm a Londoner, a bourgeois through and through. The city is safe. Lords and kings switch from ecstatic self-adulation to abysmal self-contempt. The more the balloon of their pride grows inflated, the less of a pin-prick it takes to deflate them. Those they have rewarded become those they punish.'

In this new state of anxiety we learnt for the first time that the archbishop of Canterbury, who had, six or so weeks earlier, set out to Paris to tell Henry Bolingbroke his father had died, had been ordered by the king to inform Henry to remain in exile. Yet the true purpose of his mission had been kept secret. In the evening a letter arrived with the rumour that this same archbishop had asked Lord Henry to return to England, and had offered him the support of men and arms.

We heard that wild tribes in Ireland have killed Lord Roger Mortimer, the grandson of John's elder brother Lionel. As Mortimer had been King Richard's only heir to the throne, suddenly there was none. Anne of Bohemia, the king's first wife, had proved infertile, while the new queen was not yet old enough to menstruate. So did Henry Bolingbroke now become the legitimate heir? Not if our 'divine' steward Richard could help it.

My dearest sister Katherine, Prince John's widow and now duchess of Lancaster – our duchy that comprised more land and castles than any in England, richer by far than the sum total of the king's estates – failed to arrive in Huntingdon…Perhaps she was leaving it to the last moment for reasons known only to her…

KATHERINE: At first, I could not believe that he had married Constanza of Castile. I had opened to him like a flower. I had allowed him to that deepest and most intimate part. I had nursed and held him inside me. If this was not true love, then I did not know what was; even now, I suspected but did not know for sure, that it was at the time when I would be pregnant as a result, and bear John's child. Blood of blood, royal blood of Plantagenet kings in my womb, an honour although out of wedlock.

Then, after the briefest of visits, John had gone back to France, and within a month, a little month, he was married again and she, too, would be pregnant, cold Iberian bitch, narrow-minded – but they say beautiful – reaping the reward, the succession from her man, my sworn lover. How many times did he swear, how many times did he look pale to death, and if I had not brought to him some succour, how many times would he have died for love of me?

Then pat, without a single thought of me, he has hopped into bed with a black-haired infanta and impregnated her as if he were giving his charger a bag of oats. Up with her skirt, here you are, a royal baby. I felt sick. I vomited over the Savoy chamber that I lay in by virtue of him, I wanted to beat my head on these royal walls – and I might as well be in that dungeon where they left living bodies suspended in a metal body cage till they starved to death.

If there were one person responsible for all this, I would have it out with him. I knew who this was.

I sent for him.

'You did all you could to make me yield to John!'

I came up even closer to Geoffrey, so that he should feel the full weight of my anger.

'How much did he pay you to be his bawd? How much did you receive to deliver me up to his bed?'

'Katherine,' spoke Geoffrey quietly to me. 'I swear before God this was not so.'

He was pale, hurt, betrayed, too, like me. He began to confess:

'I am afraid,' he said, 'that I did make a fatal mistake.' He looked as if he felt like me, as if he wanted to say, 'I thought John was human, but I find out that he is not.' He too had believed in the sincerity, the truth, the complete fidelity of John's passion for me.

But he had discovered that we were different. 'They are not like us. Royal princes are a different breed.'

I was in no mood to perceive and understand such differences. I wanted only to be consoled, to have a head to lie against, a shoulder to cry on.

My brother-in-law remained silent. Was it true, what he had so often said? His family trusted and loved each other, however much they had argued. John had never argued with Lady Blanche, she had never picked on, or nagged him. They were above such ordinary squabbles, such comforting bickering as confirmed close love. All Geoffrey could say, with complete helplessness and considerable lack of conviction, was, 'I'm sure he still loves you.'

I was ready to say something very scornful to him, but he looked so bleak and smitten with grief and remorse, that I did not have the courage.

'But it's a funny way to show it, I agree,' he added.

I suppose he meant that John had a higher sense of destiny, that the fate to which he had been born precluded ordinary marriage and blissful disharmony and incompatibility, that once a king – or nearly so – was a different game, with rules which only a few were allowed to play.

'I wish I were dead,' I said, 'I really wish I were dead!'

And I went on, 'And just think what my husband is going to say when he finds out I am carrying Lord John's baby...'

I had not meant to say this, but it came out willy-nilly. Geoffrey looked agreeably surprised, not the least shocked, although he put on an expression of pain. Somewhere – and he would be careful to keep this quiet – the news made him feel good. A Chaucer-Lancastrian, a Lancastrian-Chaucer…who knew if one day there might not be kings of England with Chaucerian blood – or de Roet blood, which was near enough for him?

'John's new marriage,' said Geoffrey, 'has come as a complete shock. Also this new…aspiration of John's,' he ventured to call his potential or nominal brother-in-law by his Christian name – 'Now it may, and perhaps you can believe this, not altogether have been the wish of John to marry a second time. His children from Blanche are still young. They may not live till seniority. Young Henry is the only boy…John needs another one or two boys… . Our great king has had a hand in this.'

'Why couldn't he marry me?' I screamed out. 'I'm good enough for him. I'm as healthy and fit – and better educated – than any queen of Castile.'

'He cannot possibly love her, that's for sure,' Geoffrey added lamely, 'he merely does his duty. And you can be sure,' he emphasized, 'that she will not see him any more than you see him…' He faltered and then said, looking abashed, 'He has settled her at Hertford. He has asked for Philippa to run his household.'

Philippa had told me that she had been ordered by special messenger to go to Hertford and prepare the palace, obtain servants and wait for this new queen. Geoffrey knew very well why this was so, because Constanza of Castile surrounded herself with only few chosen women who already, it was rumoured, hated John and fed in his ears gossip of this other, the 'Swynford' woman, poisoning the queen's ears against John. He had, to establish his own presence there, chosen my sister.

'Patience, my love, patience,' was all Geoffrey could say to me. I could hardly hold back my tears, and felt more and more the whipping boy of these foul Plantagenets. I remembered John's vows, sworn unto death; I knew I was the right wife for him, that I fitted into the pattern and model of his mother Philippa, of his dead wife Blanche. Yet what if the other one had these virtues?

'Is she devout, this new wife of his?'

'Oh very devout,' answered Geoffrey. His tone was teasing.

'She goes often to mass?'

'She is always with a priest. My copyist, Adam Scriven, would love her. She is the model of obedience and chastity.'

He paused for breath: he looked this way and that, thinking best how he could phrase what to say next. Oh I knew Geoffrey so well. He did not want to encourage me too much. What if Constanza actually turned out to supplant me in John's affections? This was what I was thinking.

'Does she have strong vices – she isn't greedy, or mean, is she?'

Geoffrey then hit upon an idea, both to control my feelings and console me. He was clever. 'I'll tell you what she is: she's resentful, angry – and she has a fiery tongue. I do not think she will make John feel comfortable and at ease.'

How could he know any of this? But the Spanish – they were flagellants, one and all, and immensely proud. If they could find something to be miserable about, and feel God was going to punish them with the direst and most gruesome tortures possible, they would do it. Of course, maybe he was thinking of someone else. But in that moment Geoffrey created a new model for me, perhaps it is not correct to say 'created a new model for Katherine' but he named it, gave it identity and credibility. I must have decided that, wife although I was not, I would become the model of a patient mistress: I would suffer all John could put on me. I would – out of proving that I was better than this painfully named Constanza – show myself to be the more constant, the more sweet-tongued, the model of suffering love. I would achieve this without being a mere, unthinking vegetable, and determined it should not be out of some cold and sterile notion of duty and obedience towards God.

I tell you, my brother-in-law was a genius.

The model did not last. I wanted very much to return and give vent to my passion for John; and let anyone judge what must be the anguish of my mind. I cannot but reflect that I have two children of Hugh, and am big with another, this time one of John's.

I am the most unhappy woman in the world. I have such a load on my mind it keeps me perpetually awake; to whom shall I reveal my monstrosity? To conceal it is also near an impossibility. Hugh is dead, and they believe I was the cause. And while I did not plot it myself, I fear I might well talk in my sleep, and tell my own children, who kept my bed chamber with me, that I wanted him dead. If that is discovered I fear, although innocent, that I would lose my children. I would be placed under arrest, and they would take my children from me and put me in prison, or cut off my head, or expose me naked in the streets as they do prostitutes or adulterers, or tie ropes to my legs and private parts to make an example of me.

And now I feel I shall be undone I have no mind at all to see John, although I am convinced that I still love him. For I live in open complicity of crime and whoredom, and yet have the appearance of an honest widow; I believe my action has something shocking to nature, and it makes the duke even more nauseous to me. Yet when I consider it sensibly, and with a degree of calm and sedation, I resolve it is absolutely necessary to keep a secret, and not in any way to reveal to John what one holy friar has told me, lest they blackmail me with regard to my lover. During this time Philippa has come and told me of her amorous encounters, how to both court and keep her lovers, while Geoffrey – well I suspect he too has had his escapades.

I live in the worst sort of whoredom, for as I can expect no good, no good issue will come, and all my seeming prosperity has worn off and ended in misery and destruction. It was some time indeed before it came to this, but everything now seems to go wrong between me and John, and which is worse John himself becomes strangely altered, forward, jealous and unkind. I grow as impatient of bearing his marriage as his own disposition towards me is unreasonable and unjust. We have come to be on ill terms with each other, and I claim a promise of him that I can, when he wills it, break off our love and fidelity, and leave his palace here to return to Kettlethorpe.

Then John left again for France to defend Gascony against the inroads of the French.

'Philippa tells me I had to come at once to see you.'

I had shut every door and window in my chambers, and I had banged my head on the wall, thrown my body on the ground; abusing myself I cried out as if someone was there, 'What shall I do? Shall I, while I still live, go on in torment and cruel pain? Shall I end my darkness like Oedipus, and put out my eyes?'

Hearing this from outside Geoffrey had rushed in; a knight had opened my door. I could see how my brother-in-law was affected with tender pity, and in the dark chamber, which was as still as stone, he came towards the bed where I lay. 'I am so confused I do not know what to say,' he told me, 'and for very grief my wits have nearly left me. Like a dark shaft entering my very being, the sight of your beauty rends me with heaviness and makes my life-blood run cold.'

I burst out, 'Look, brother, now I am dead! There's nothing more for me!'

'But the Savoy is full of fine gallants,' Geoffrey answered, 'a dozen or more who can, and will, make you happy. I will search them out and there will be new love for you; pleasures mustn't all come from one source. If you lose one quality in one person, you find another in another. One man can smile; another fight; each has his own special grace, both heroner and falconer have their quality. New love often chases out the old. Just as night comes after day; love is but casual pleasure, and after such pleasure self-preservation comes first... . Absence of him will drive away the bitter pain.' So went on my brother at length, able to turn every thought and feeling to the advantage of his case, not minding what untruth he spoke. I took little notice. I could have sworn at him, until finally I was provoked to answer:

'Geoffrey, your leechcraft might suit me if I was a fiend, but I pray to God to let no such cynical counsel prevail. You might as well have me killed before your eyes. I will die *his* woman, and if he can find as good and fair a creature, let him!'

My brother-in-law looked chastened. I went on:

'Honestly, Geoffrey, the way you talk to me is like someone who sees a man or woman suffering and casually strolls up to them – "Just put the pain out of your mind and it will go!" You'd have to transmute me first to a stone, and rive me of every passion before enabling me to cure myself so lightly!'

My brother-in-law said nothing.

'Do you think I should go and see him; fight it out with Constanza?'

I could no longer restrain the tears which welled up and gave a signal of bitter pain; my servants ran in distress around me wondering what they could do, and to stop themselves falling into despair they told me I ought not to grieve and to bite back my tears: as if you could cure a headache by clawing someone by the heel. I threw myself down on my bed, purposing never to rise once again from it, when the children of Gaunt came running in to see me, and my own Thomas Swynford, and my little girl, Petronella.

So all I could say was, 'Out of his region I – wretched and unfortunate – born under a cursed constellation, compelled to leave my love, must go!' And with my children there I was at last able to cry, tears starting from my eyes like an April shower, streaming down my naked breast.

Fifteen

Scriven

WE SETTLED IN FOR the night. My master and I had been placed
in two narrow little rooms or shelves above the chapel, reached by a
winding stair next to the second altar. I was so impatient for my
master to snuff out his lamp and bed down, first of all because my
own candle burnt apace and I had reading to do, and so needed his
lamp, and also because I had to be on my own.

The appearance of Thomas Swynford had again made me
shudder. As for other matters, the name of my adoptive father had
sent a shiver down my spine. If I had known then, or found out,
what my master had confessed about Lord John, Katherine Swynford,
and Swynford's murder, I would probably now be an abbot myself,
employing my own scrivener to copy for me.

I would have given a brooch to know his meaning about the other
deaths.

But he even insisted on speculating when I could see he was about
to fall asleep.

'You know, Adam, I don't think ultimately it could have been
Lord John who murdered Swynford. "He that has a broken and
contrite heart..." runs the psalm of King David (and certainly Lord
John had this in mind and in his last years echoed David even more,
with "my sin is ever before me"). And if he had been so guilty God
would have punished his family more. Look what happened to King
David's: his family was shattered, his sister raped by her brother,
another son killed in rebellion against his father, and so on. What a
contrast this was to John's family. He repented before it was too
late.'

'Yes,' I answered, 'but we don't exactly know what will happen

147

next...' It was too late to continue the conversation, for my master was asleep. The church bell struck midnight.

I quickly started to work, feverishly thinking I had the solution: my master, with that confessional tale of his own seduction of Katherine, was unburdening himself of a lesser crime, one that he now felt quite confident in, and comfortable with, in order to conceal a greater crime. I mean the alleged rape of that young woman which he so successfully covered up. For years I had carried round my neck the legal release from this charge that my master wangled through the courts. For years until now I've carried in the pilgrim's scrip hung from a cord round my neck the scrolls I covered in a tiny hand from those Latin writs: '*Noverint universi me, Ceciliam Chaumpaigne, filiam quondam Willelmi Chaumpaigne et Agnetis uxoris euis, remisisse, relaxasse, et omnino pro me et heredibus meis, imperpetuum quietum clamasse Galfrido Chaucer, armigero, omnimodas acciones, tam de raptu meo, tam de aliqua re vel causa...*'And so on. It says she lets him off the '*raptu meo*', and three knights of the realm, among them the king's chamberlain and a future mayor of London, witnessed the legal deed so it wasn't some obscure, hushed up piece of business. If he had been found guilty the obligation placed upon the victim was to tear out his eyes and cut off his testicles. Before history and for the future there needed to be a truer record. I was determined to find out the truth.

Enough. Now to my much delayed purpose. Fingers shaking with excitement I unstrapped my saddle-bag, and feverishly seized the unbound sheets in Philippa Chaucer's clear, bold hand, which was so much in contrast to my master's when he was in a hurry. I was amazed to find my former mistress dated everything so carefully, following the practice of the venerable Bede.

As I began to read the moon came out and lent force to my candlelight. After the full moon of last night it was only slightly pared. What did I find but such lewdness, such smut that I would never have expected from one so ladylike, so haughty and dignified, and one who ended so pious and honoured in her grave in Lincoln Cathedral. From what she wrote she sounded much more like my master's good wife ('Good' I ask you?) of Bath, who had five husbands at the church door and relished her immodest pride in explaining how she wielded her carnality to win power over each. I never for a moment could have imagined that Philippa Chaucer had been like that herself, or worse.

To be strict about it the Wife of Bath, according to my master, did not abuse her marriage vow, and she performed her duty in bed, although always with a manipulative, self-interested motive. But I always believed my master had invented such an old trollop who played Jezebel in bed with her husbands to have something of an extra jibe at the opposite sex. This was ever his theme. Eve corrupted Adam. '*Mulier est hominis confusio*' – 'Woman brought about the downfall of man', but he translated this with the joke, 'Woman is man's joy and all his bliss.'

Well I was certainly surprised to read of his wedded bliss, and what a titillating dame his wife had been. Did I really have to go on reading?...

PHILIPPA: 'These fur-lined garments due to me before last Christmas have only just been delivered!' I raged.

Geoffrey nodded. He had not been fully paid for the recent trip he had made to Italy, although the clothes were part of his payment. The house to which he, I, and our children had been moved was in the city gate of Aldgate, once the guardhouse of the sergeant-at-arms who occupied the city wall, but in these less military times the residence of a court official. It was but half an hour's walk from Geoffrey's place of work, the custom-house of the Thames.

Lord John had advanced him swiftly, giving him the permanent salaried position of comptroller of the customs and subsidy of wools, skins, and hides in London port.

'At least they are in time for the cold weather.' He smiled. He had every reason to be contented. Raw wool is the mainstay of the realm, moving in a heavy stream from the Cotswolds, from Yorkshire, from Kent, where the pastures are rich in sheep, to the looms of Flanders and Italy. London is the chief of all the English ports where customs officials are stationed to levy a tariff on this golden fleece as it passed through. Wool is the chief jewel of England, the sovereign merchandise: Edward has used it all his reign to finance his armies and bribe his allies into compliance; a little rhyme which a wool merchant had engraved on the windows of his new house sums it up:

'I praise God and ever shall.
It is the sheep has paid for all!'

No tax levied itself is a great sum but what it adds up to, with the volume of trade being so huge, is formidable. The city lent the king money, the king repays with revenue from the wool trade; this is how the king is always in the city's debt: he is good at bankrupting both individuals and banking houses, but in the city of London he has met his match.

So Geoffrey had begun his life of dual allegiance, a Lancastrian esquire raising money from wool in the name of the king, so as to be in a position to repay the merchants who financed the king. This being able to face two directions at once suited him by nature.

We had the house to ourselves, which was rare in London, each floor of a three tiered house generally being occupied by a different family who used a staircase outside the house; in the morning we heard the rumble of carts under the arches beneath our house, where at the portcullis, open for the day, the carts were charged a small tax to keep the city's streets paved.

The house was made of stone and Flanders' tiles: it was an airy and comfortable dwelling, looking west to the roofs and spires of London, with the gilt cross of St Paul's rising in the distance. The other way we could view green fields and woods. I could walk to shop in Cheap.

I was proud of this position. Geoffrey's office was a building rented by the government on Wool Wharf between London Bridge and the Tower; the ground floor had the weights and balances for weighing the wool, the second the counting house for staff and customers, the third and top floor the private offices. Geoffrey had searchers, packers, weighers, clerks working for him, for it was his job to present the Exchequer with the statement annually to check on the collectors; the authority had a boat of its own and a boatman, and if any boat tried to slip through the customs without paying the tariff his goods were forfeit to the government, and the full price of wool was paid to the officer who apprehended him.

Geoffrey forestalled one evader trying to ship wool to Dordrecht without paying the duty, and was rewarded with the value of the wool – over seventy pounds; he had a large salary, with a bonus according to how many evaders were caught. In a year there were over twelve hundred and twenty wool merchants passing through

Wool Wharf to have their goods weighted, and it was hard to keep such accounts, especially as they had to deal in all kinds of currency: there was no common one, although the Italian florin was the strongest.

As such Geoffrey was now known and much respected among the powers in the city, the substantial burghers and men of wealth who controlled its affairs. But I was not happy. Some weeks I could hardly speak to him because he had so many faults, and each time I told them to him he put up such a barrage of defence, that I saw red and could not discharge my duties properly as a wife and a mother.

First of all he dressed slovenly, and we were expected in Lord John's service not to disport ourselves like a pair of impoverished clerks. He looked worse than his Mr Scriven, who was a poor, red-headed fellow without any mother or father or home, and who inhabited our loft and smelt and itched abominably (although he can write in a much better hand than I).

I could not pardon it when Geoffrey came home, and just stood and stared at me. Then, when he lost his temper, he clutched with his hand as if his wits had left him. He paced up and down muttering sayings out of books, and exhorting me to behave like Jesus, or at least some of the disciples. I wished that he would give me a bit of that Jesus behaviour himself.

If I found him neglecting me, unaware of my problems with the children, he would hit back so hard at me that he had been woken six times in the night, and how he had fetched and carried wine, and made medicines. True, he did physic them well and understood their ailments, and therefore saved on the payments to the physician, but when I needed him for some urgent problem like as not his head was in the clouds. He hardly ever gave me money, expected me to take it from my own retainer from John, while I argued these sums were for clothes and perfumes, such as a woman in my position needed if she is to keep her allure and not become an old hag.

And when I had come to the end of my complaints maybe he would be contrite and he would give me sympathy, but I knew he was but feigning, for if I switched my complaint to another as a test, back he would jump with his bitchy tongue, as waspish as that of any corrupt churchman, pardoner, or seller of relics. I had the knack of overflowing with outrage, but I needed sympathy. Geoffrey would extend his pitying looks and words to me, but woe betide if I did not accept them: as far as I was concerned they needed to be deep.

He was of too easy and happy a disposition. I needed to see him suffering before I'd ease up a little. If I could but bring him down to where I wanted him, then I would feel secure; and if I could not, then I'd be angry with him, and believe me nothing gave me force and definiteness of intent as a good rich fury. I knew where I was, and had the confidence of my passion.

Geoffrey tried to undermine it: anger he told me, was a great pleasure to the devil; it was his furnace, hotted up with the fire of hell; chiding and wicked words came from pride. He liked to make a whole list of the woes brought on men by their wives, such as that of Hercules being driven mad by his Dianyre; poor Socrates who after a bellyful of insult had piss cast on his head by Xantippa: he sat as if dead and then reflected, 'The moment thunder leaves off, down comes the rain!' And many others who poisoned their husbands, either for love or hate (both are strong emotions, say I, and what is the difference?). Geoffrey cannot abide my angry tongue. And my finding fault with him, always quoting the proverb, 'Better it is to live high up in the roof, than have an angry wife down in the kitchen.'

Most of all I caught him on the quick when I belittled what he did. This would make him mad with anger himself, and then he would be turning on his own spit! I scorned every effort he might make to be nice to me. He tried his slippery tricks to turn the tables on me by saying that if I annoyed him it was because I am annoyed with myself, and that I would never turn on him if I had not need of a goatskin into which to escape. I could outwit him in this: I'd say, 'Geoffrey, if you wish to have power over me – and that is what you want – you must adopt the virtue you preach, namely patience. If you want to defeat me, your enemy, learn to suffer and you will conquer me.'

That fixed him, for he knew not what to reply. His decent nature saw the wisdom of what I said.

'Why don't you practice what you preach yourself?' he demanded in one last feeble attempt to turn the tables. 'There is but one golden rule – Do unto others as you would be done unto.'

'For men, but not women,' I said under my breath, but not out loud. I knew truly that each woman is a rule unto herself, and God made each of us in our nature unique, and to be valued for what we are. He made men more roughly and fitting a general pattern.

'Obedience is perfect: men must learn obedience.'

'You dictate a law for me,' he went on, 'but you don't abide by it.'

Then he tailed off, for he knew he better be silent or he would not receive what he really wanted, which was the gift of myself, my body and the precious quality I would reveal to him later, when I took off my smock. When I get him dreaming on this he would become as docile and sweet as a new lover.

Thus, he would say, I was the only woman he had ever been to bed with, and wondered at , as if always it was the first time. And he never knew if I would surrender. Until the last moment I kept him in suspense. Well, wasn't it right that I should behave like this? Like Tantalus, son of Zeus and Pluto, who stole the food of the Gods, Geoffrey had stolen my food many times over and given it to the court in rhyme. It was just that I should make him forever hungry and thirsty for me; make him stand in ditch water up to his chin, with the fruit over his head, and just out of his reach, while unable to bend over to reach the water. I would lie in bed spruced and smelling sweet, my dainties well in view – knowing he was expecting me. At the crucial moment, when he reached out his hand to touch my thigh, I would tell him I was much too tired, 'Not tonight.' Thus the water disappeared, the wind blew the fruit away. He knew that big stone – that I was unhappy and could leave him –hung over his head, always threatening to fall. The penalty of life with me was everlasting fear.

Constanza of Castile was alone, for now she was pregnant John had left her. She had moved from Hertford to Guyenne, a village near Bordeaux, with her sister Isabel, when she was visited by me and four knights sent by Lord John to work out the terms of a further marriage, that of Lord John's younger brother Edmund, duke of Cambridge, to Constanza's sister Isabel. When the marriage proposal was explained to Isabel by our knights she did not believe for a moment she would become duchess of Cambridge, and have any English role in life.

Constanza was very pale, raven-haired, with large, very dark eyes; her carriage, the bearing of her shoulders, was queenly, stately, her figure strong yet straight and even thin. She was by no means ungainly, while about her mouth there was more than a hint of flesh, of sensuality. But her mind was ungiving. She was haughty; she had her purpose fixed on one thing, and one thing only: family honour.

This was even more important than the immense power and wealth she had lost.

The honour was of her lost kingdom of Castile and Leon: she had had her hereditary right stolen from her by her uncle, or half-uncle. Worse than this, and in order to achieve the crown that should have come to her, he had murdered her father, Peter the Cruel. She sought only one thing: revenge, and she sought this through marriage with John, for he seemed to her the way that she might achieve this. France, with a force led by the legendary Bertrand de Guesclin, had helped her wicked uncle to take her throne, and France it was above all which the duke and the English crown wanted to check and reduce in power.

There was no love between them. This was purely a contract. But she had her pride, her feeling, and she had to go to bed with him. They hoped their child and heir would unite their two countries, and one day become the king of Spain; he would be acceptable, in his legitimate claim, even to Constanza's enemies, while the heirs of the usurper Henry of Trastamanta could be discarded.

She was young, she was palatable, she was clean and washed much. She dressed with a taste to match her haughtiness and arrogance. She was prepared to do her duty to her country, and she had made her body available to John in order that she should give him an heir.

Having discharged John's commission I had returned to Aldgate, and gone straight to bed. Geoffrey, who had worked late, came up to our bedchamber. As I lay there I could tell he was listening to my breathing, and wanted to lie with me. Anyway, I had allowed Geoffrey to get down to all the usual preparatory work when the messenger came knocking on the door from John to collect my report on Constanza. He had to suspend action. He knew that he had to be very careful not to offend me, or I would assuredly say no to any love; it was easy for me to say no, and to be frank I enjoyed it. So he sat by me till the messenger had left, and sent out these loving looks and soft sensual regards, as if these could influence me. I kept myself aloof from him so that sometimes he was afraid to touch me, or give me any affection, because he knew I'd remove myself further off.

If he managed to touch me without my taking against him, or even perhaps persuaded me to pull up my gown a little bit – it would make him feel he had reached the starting point of the game. He was careful not to alarm me – he didn't suspect that if I wanted to I could be quite devastatingly lustful myself, and not care what I uncovered and when. All he knew was how oblique I liked to go at things of the flesh.

This is the way, I avouch. Make them anticipate what is going to be the right mood to carry us through to the bedroom. What is love, but to seek change? And if there was something he neglected to do, like prepare the children's clothes and books for school tomorrow, or empty the slops, he'd have to use all his diplomatic wit to escape from my refusal. Otherwise he could observe me slipping out of my clothes while my maid untied my hair, knowing it would be but moments before his nails would be lodged in my buttocks.

But now he had to wait; wait while I filed my nails and put a salve on the sore on my ankle. I could see his stiff member ready for action under the front of his gown like a clothes peg. There was nothing to do while we waited for my maid to finish, except he would sit behind me and recite a love poem while fondling my breasts, while I continued to pretend nothing like this was happening; after a while, if he was tender enough with my shoulders and neck, and didn't hurt me too much by pressing tightly, I might be persuaded to become completely naked. But not without a great shiver or two to show him the demand on me he was making: and maybe a yawn or two when he was becoming carried away too much with his idea, and not going on fast enough from place to place.

The end of love alters my temperature, so sometimes I am too hot, sometime too cold. Just when he feels he is really having his way with me I'll find a criticism or two to pull him up short, so for a moment or two I feel his enjoyment drop, his member slacken, and his intention become grimly purposeful. With luck he'll panic and try harder. And then as soon as he has performed his husband's duty, and I may have been carried away, I'll jump up and go to the water butt. No lingering on sweetness. Ah, those are the moments of mummery for me: the unpredictable moments. Otherwise what is sex in marriage but a drudge and a bore? At first it was different: my love was like an invasion, a charge in full armour, that of my vulnerable, hot and open body which would do all he would and more; he had to fight sometimes to keep me off him, for no man likes a woman too forward, too like the Venus to grab what she desires, it makes him shrink and draw back. Who could resist a woman fully roused? Be it in anger or lust, she would carry all before her, and even have ten men or more to service her, and not feel raped or all that nonsense but herself the conqueror?

Sixteen

Scriven

THE GREAT CANDLE IN its holder on the wall began to burn low as I grew weary of these sordid confessions. But I was looking for something more. I tried to speed up my search. There must have been something else, a change in their marriage, a shift in time, a cooling of passion, of her exacerbated moods. But when? True, the marriage had received a terrible shock when Lord John married Constanza of Castile. Philippa had been sent to convince Constanza to accept John's proposal. Philippa was over thirty and you could sense how she flagged in her hopes of ever regaining a hold over Lord John. More and more she accused Geoffrey of becoming jealous and possessive of her and then…and then…the next section I came to appeared, in my tired bloodshot eyes, to glow with an unearthly light, a nimbus such as might surround some godlike presence! My master might well have invested moments of vile sexual gratification between a pair of forked and fornicating lovers with idolatrous sanctimony, but for me it was truth which shed lustre on all life, truth which illuminated the soul and re-established God's presence in this all too fallen world.

So it was with the mention of the word 'RAPE', which occurred at the beginning of Philippa Chaucer's entry for 6 May 1380. With a thrill of satisfaction and fulfllment I confirmed that the date tallied with those legal documents of release in the chancery rolls. At last I had something…

LORD JOHN : A wretched, ginger-haired, scaly scrivener has arrived from Chaucer with an urgent message. I question the boy, who is patently resentful and full of hate towards me. All Londoners are, but I think he meant me no harm, while he loves his master much, that he would come and see me, of all people, to plead on his behalf.

'Mr Chaucer sends me,' says this lad, barely able to look into my eyes as if he feared I had some power to strike him dead on the spot. 'For he has been flung into the Fleet Prison, and wants you to petition for him and get him released.'

'What is the charge?' I ask.

'The charge of rape. He has been caught with a young woman half his age, who has brought a suit against him.'

'The charge of rape!' When I hear this I burst out laughing. 'This is not possible,' I declare. 'My dear friend Chaucer, with his wisdom and understanding of human nature? A rapist? Never, surely.' But then perhaps, to myself, I think, he may have been smitten, as we all are sometimes, with uncontrollable desire.

'They will punish him with death unless we do something,' says this villein, who is well-spoken but cringes with fear.

'Indeed they might, we must act quickly.'

My head shaking with disbelief, I call for my esquire, and scribble a note requesting that Chaucer be at once released, that I vouch for his innocence, and that he should be dispatched straight away to me for questioning.

'But the charge is written to be brought against him in trial,' says this lad. I look at him. There are so many ways round this, from quashing the charge for lack of proper evidence, to the common practice of summoning one's own jury to try it.

'First let's see if this will work.' I give the letter, duly sealed, to Butler esquire. 'Take the boy with you,' I tell him, 'and bring Chaucer back here.'

While I wait, I dispatch much business of state. I have been gifted to work quickly, and brook no delay in managing my estates and the various courts under my jurisdiction. If this matter with Chaucer is serious it would be no great matter to have him moved to a Lancastrian jail, and convene my own court to have him tried. But what if he really has raped a woman, and there are witnesses besides the woman concerned? Could Chaucer's lust or rage of the body have got the better of him? He is now forty years old, or thereabouts.

157

But Chaucer is about as good-natured and agreeable as it is possible for any man to be. It might be said that this whole realm could not supply a man who in every respect is more of a gentleman. I have heard rumours, too, that Philippa is not the most exemplary of wives.

This may go back to my original plan to marry off Philippa to Chaucer. You cannot force love. Like truth it must come of its own time, and in its own way.

The scrivener is now returned with Chaucer, who, while dressed in his usual sober habit, is much torn about in his attire, spattered all over with mud and filth, and scratched about the face. He is much distressed.

'My good lord,' he says, falling to his knees and stretching forward his hands in supplication.

'Now what is this they say about you, Chaucer? Rape is a brutal crime and it implies a degree of depravity of which I should not have thought you capable.'

'Too true, too true,' replies Chaucer, hanging his head.

'Then tell me what has happened.'

'Even to be accused of such a heinous action brings shame upon me and my family,' says Chaucer.

'Well are you guilty, or are you not?' I ask curtly. 'I have little time.'

'My seigneur,' he begins, 'I shall come straight to the point. May I speak to you in private?'

'This has been made the subject of open complaint, so it cannot now, I fear, be kept quiet.'

But with a gesture of hand I dismiss the measly scrivener and my esquire.

'Ah,' sighs Chaucer when we are alone, climbing to his feet and growing sure of his words, 'I fear the good offices I performed on your behalf have won me a bad name, worse, made me susceptible to undertake such work for others. For such it was, saddled with a request from your noble armourer, John Grove, who supplies much of your weaponry, and supported by Richard Goodchild, the cutler and purveyor of your short swords and stabbing knives, I fear I undertook some evil business...'

I relax. I can see the pattern. Chaucer has been sent to procure some lady. When you gain a reputation for one thing, people expect you to live up to it. I will have to make sure it did not go badly for him, for I am sure he acted in the best possible faith. 'And so,' I interrupt, 'you were to be the go-between?– '

'There was a fine-looking young widow just come to court, very young, name of Cecilia Chaumpaigne, whose husband, hardly older than her, died on the battlefield in Artois. Mr Grove fell much in love with her, and desired her to become his wife. He asked simply that I should arrange it for him. Unfortunately it was not as simple as that...'

'So what happened to you then?'

'The sight of this young woman at first quite turned my head, my lord,' says Chaucer, 'and although I acted with tact and restraint, it well might be that I transferred on to her my own hunger...'

'Are you saying that you did something to encourage her?'

'Quite the opposite. I pressed Mr Grove's suit, and we – he and Mr Goodchild – resolved in the end that we might be impelled by her resistance to carry her off to marry her to Mr Grove – and settle on her a good sum of money, of course. But before this could happen, it was she who delayed the matter, asking me again to come and see her on my own and press what suit I liked.' And here he gives me a wink so I am reassured he has come back to himself. 'To confide in you, my lord...I believe she fell suddenly and secretly in love with me.'

I laugh. 'Well here, Geoffrey, was your chance, and with Philippa away...'

'But I was sworn to perform my duty to Mr Grove.'

And you liked it that way, I could have added, knowing how zealous to press another's love Chaucer could be.

'Anyway she came to believe that her desire would be met only if she could overcome this obstruction of my shame in discovering to myself this desire. So this is what she does. One day she sends for me, feigning some matter or other. I have no idea what is in her mind, except perhaps a final answer to Mr Grove's suit. My mind is far from this, and we sit down together upon a couch, and I ask her why she has sent for me.

'She is long silent, but incited finally by her passion, and trembling all over, she declares herself in broken and confused words something like this my lord. "My dear friend and esquire, your acute judgement must have noticed how great the frailty is of both the sexes, for diverse reasons, and one more than the other. Therefore the same offence, before a fair judge, is likely to be of different quality, depending on its circumstances." '

159

'Wait a moment,' I interrupt Chaucer. 'What by Jesus' wounds was she aiming at?'

'Well she went on thus for some time making excuses for herself, on account of her youth, the death of her husband, but all leading, my lord, to the inescapable conclusion that she, a lady, not a poor woman who daily had to labour, had found me a worthy object of her love. And that I should vouchsafe to show the same towards her, and take pity on her youth, that was consuming itself for my sake even as ice melted before fire.'

I was struck speechless. I could say nothing to Chaucer. He was a man of forty, cosy and round as an acorn, no double chins or bags under his eyes, for he always smiled.

'I see you don't believe me, my lord, but even as she said this the tears poured down from her cheeks so fast that she couldn't manage to speak further, and then so full of lamentation was she that she laid her head on my chest.'

'Are you telling me you refused her, Chaucer?'

'I reflected that this was not right; I could not say my honour was of the strictest kind, but I gently took hold of her hands and arms which were enfolding me, untwined them and eased myself away proclaiming to her that I could not suffer such advances, and would rather cut myself to pieces than wrong my own wife, or allow others to do so.'

'Well what is to come next, Chaucer? Unless I am badly mistaken I think I know.'

'Yes, well Cecilia Chaumpaigne, hearing what I said to her, at once forgot the deep love that she was feeling for me...'

'It being in a most conditional form.'

'And in the most vehement rage screamed at me, "Vile, vile man, so you think my request can in this sudden way be refused? As you want to make me suffer, know that I will either cause your death, or force you to leave this country!" and with these words, my lord – and I can hardly believe what happened next – she started to tear out her hair in handfuls, to rend her clothes, ripping off all her garments so that her naked skin became visible for everyone to see. All the time she was crying out most violently, "Help, Help! Mr Chaucer is about to offer me violence!"

'At the piteous sight she made of herself – and before I could do anything to defend myself or run away – I was seized and bound by half a dozen men-at-arms, and brought before the sheriff who ordered me into a dungeon...'

I look at Chaucer and can hardly restrain myself from uproarious laughter at the treatment he has suffered.

'My good esquire,' I say to him, 'I shall make sure you experience no more pain for this. I shall see the wench, and arrange matters with her.'

Chaucer returns my glance, as if I intend a further twist upon the matter. 'But take good care of yourself, my lord, for she has formidable charms.'

'Let us now attend to more important matters.'

'They claim,' says Chaucer, 'that a woman taken with lechery should be beaten with staves – and that he's a great fool that will kiss the mouth of a burning oven or a furnace. Adultery is like murder, my lord. It breaks and carves in two those that were made of one flesh.'

'If you are talking of your sister-in-law,' I answer with a hint of steel in my voice, 'I have sent her a gift of wine, and with my agreement she has proceeded to Lincoln where I have granted her a house. I also want to honour your wife, Chaucer, who has served me most faithfully with Constanza.'

At this Chaucer changes the subject: 'How is your new consort, sire?'

I answer: 'It is a most painful and piteous affair, Chaucer. She is so proud and so Catholic that she is not interested in sport. She is bent only on one thing: that I should revenge King Pedro her father, and set her upon the throne of Spain.'

'But she is beautiful,' Chaucer then observes.

'I am glad you think so,' I reply, 'but not as fine-looking as your sister-in-law. They have such pride, these Spaniards, with stern father-confessors at each elbow, and the Inquisition in the background. They take literally that exhortation for no sex that we find in the Bible. I am merely to give her children.'

'I am sure the new duchess – or do we call her queen? – will continue to make you a devoted wife.'

'As long as I live up to my reputation for making war. But my army is weak, we have let the navy slide, nor am I as young as I used to be. I have…I am…'

Chaucer now asks with a frown: 'What, my lord?…'

I change the subject. I repeat my request: 'Will Philippa continue to serve the queen of Spain?'

I can see Chaucer's heart miss a beat. Is he thinking of Ulysses caught between Scylla and Charybdis? If she avoids the court, then there are lusty city apprentices to contend with. I can see how Chaucer has failed to live up to Philippa's ideal of what a man should be, and the kind of figure he should cut. A lover of wine and good British beef, Chaucer likes to sit at home by the fire in the evening, read his books, and then start some of his writing. Philippa is no companion in this. Headstrong, self-willed, she needs the life of my court, which went on even when darkness fell.

This is how, as I heard tell, that Philippa started, possibly out of revenge, to take a secret lover or two, some of them closely under Chaucer's nose, too close for comfort. Chaucer, polite and well-meaning and thoughtful as he was, did not want to make a fuss, or in any way cause any argument or violence between them, so he turned a blind eye to all of this – as in his tale of old January which I read and laughed heartily over, especially when the old lecher tries to tread his mate like a swan.

'Do you still love Lady Swynford, my lord?'

I look at him: 'You must be mad, Chaucer. After all the scandal that I murdered Sir Hugh – that I plotted to send him to his death at the siege of Le Pagenac. Of course I do.'

'Well my advice, my lord, is to see her again. When can I arrange this?'

'Always harping on Katherine. Why?'

'Because, my lord, she is as true to you as any woman could be true to her lord or love.'

I turn away to hide my pain. Is it true that I don't want the responsibility of loving any one? Is there a core of difficulty, of loneliness in my heart, which obstinately refuses to open up?

'Well, you are an unusual man, Chaucer,' I tell him. I smile with affection because I value him above all others. 'I shall make you a justice of the peace, and a Member of Parliament.'

PHILIPPA: Of course, when I heard from John through his secretary what excuses my husband made for the rape of Cecilia Chaumpaigne, I could only laugh. He was lying from start to finish.

All that farce about him acting as bawd for a cutler and an armourer – as if they couldn't take on themselves the cutting and armouring of their own love life. This was but the ruse, wasn't it, to allow my husband to escape the consequences of his crime, and keep his reputation clean before history? After all John would hardly have liked his favourite poet, his double almost, his other self, the celebrator of his dead wife, the man who would perpetuate his name for ever in the annals of time, brought down to the level of a common felon, would he? And yet Geoffrey would say, who was to decide between rape and willing submission, or even bringing a man on? A woman can always decide afterwards she didn't want it, can't she?

Thus it was between my husband and I. Ever at odds. I was like a cat; if you singe a cat's skin, then the cat will abide with you and keep within your house. But if your skin's slick and shiny and ready to go, who'd dwell half a day in the house? I'll be out before the dawn, to show off my hindquarters and go caterwauling.

I suppose Geoffrey couldn't stand it. But what point in being a woman, and meek and mild and submissive to any bidding? Even men don't really want you in the end, because they want game and adventure, and what's freely given, and with a willing heart – or they come to despise it, for it's too easily won.

So I let him have my tongue. I caught him well and truly the other night when he came home from his confession. I know he did the girl, but Lord John was good to him and gave him an extra ten pounds and I said, 'Well, I don't want to go to that filthy Lombard down the road to raise another loan to buy me some fine clothes, I'll ask to borrow it from my husband.'

'But it's what we need to live on, and pay the wages,' he said.

'I'll pay you back by Christmas,' I said.

He was so grateful for the extra money he didn't notice how quickly I took it off him, for he wanted to make amends.

I reckon he was also that relieved not to be strung up by the neck, for such is the penalty for rape, that he would have agreed with anything I said. Well anyway, and seeing how he lent me the money, I decided he should have my belle chose that evening and play with me at his will, and he was that aggravated and fed up with solitude from his night or two spent in jail that he let fly at me with a lust quickened and sharpened by terror.

While Geoffrey could always be relied on to start things off gently by undoing my bows and ribbons and easing me enticingly from my gown and touching, oh so gently and flutteringly, my breast or its nipples, or lower down to make several or more advances against my privety, this night he was more than usually forward, and who then wouldn't blush to tell what he did to me, except to say that I used his instrument right full and well.

I could take no more, and pulled him in straight as far as he would go to deliver his penance. Ah, this way rapes do us all well!

Seventeen

Scriven

OH WONDER OF WONDERS. What glory! I read over the entry for that date a second time. '6 May 1380. Of course when I heard from John through his secretary what excuses my husband made for the rape of Cecilia Chaumpaigne, I could only laugh. He was lying from start to finish.'

Then again a third. Rape, rape, and forever rape! Here it was at last. What joy! The glorious four-letter word which gave me identity, proclaimed my right to set the record straight for posterity.

This was all I had time to read. The sheets of parchment were seized, held fast, about to be ripped from my hand before I could read on. I thought at first it must have been my master who had stolen up behind me unseen, but it was not. It was a tall man with a black hood drawn over his head and most of his face, so that in my candlelight only his yellow pupils danced. I still held on to the sheets of parchment, and he did not snatch it. But then I felt the sharp point of a sword pressed into my adam's apple.

'Give me these sheets!' he spoke in a low, what seemed assumed, voice and while I hesitated I heard a rustling and stirring as my master, the other side of the open casement between our narrow chambers, woke up.

'What's that? Who is it, Adam?' I heard him call in a slurred voice, and the intruder was momentarily thrown off balance so I and the sheets slipped from his grasp, knocking the candle in the wall recess which fell to the floor and went out. But I had to suck my hand, for I had scratched it on a metal fastener, or something the ruffian wore.

The deaths and uncertainty of our journey had put my master on his mettle, rejuvenated him, for old and white-haired as he was he showed he was no carpet-knight. He seized his sword and scraped it on the stone ledge to make a loud and terrifying sound. The prolonged loudness of this metal on stone was spine-chilling and backed as it was by my master's powerful shouts of, 'I'm coming, seize the villain!' and so on, it unnerved the thief. He now backed away, dithered a moment or two, for so much I could see in the moon's full glare, then ran off.

In a moment or two my master, who wore his night-cap and had thrown a silk-gown over his night-shirt, came charging through the door.

'What did he want, Adam? Not to kill you, or if so you've had a narrow escape.' He removed his cap from his head and swabbed his brow.

Oh, how I faltered, then recovered. 'No, no,' I gasped out, 'I believe it was not to murder me, master. But thank you for your swift response. It saved...' Thank God, fortunately I stopped. By now I had dropped the sheets and they were out of sight.

'...The copy of your last Canterbury tale, the Parson on anger, lechery and pride.'

'Ah yes,' said my master, knowingly. 'The physician of the soul. You or me, Adam?'

'Perhaps,' I answered him, attempting a joke, 'the would-be thief would ride off with it to France or Italy, and sell this latest work of the famed English poet Geoffrey Chaucer for a great sum of money!'

'Perhaps.'

My master laughed long and gently, in waves like the sea breaking on a shallow beach. 'But you cannot be serious, Adam.'

'Then see here.' I snatched up some of his own prose sermon which I was copying and gave it to him. He held the sheets to the candle, which he had now relit from his lamp, and used a finger to guide his eye.

'This is very odd, Adam.' I blushed with anger and confusion. For he devoted none of his attention to what he had written, but only to my comments in the margins about the pains and torments of copying his work.

While he did this, which he performed with leisure, I remained defiantly silent. Think what eight hours of writing at a desk was like, the fingers were seized by the fiendish scribe's cramp, while the thumb ached as if it had been crushed under a horse's hoof. My impatience and misery often exploded: 'I'm praying for the end of the day.' 'Give me a glass of good burgundy.' 'It's freezing, the light is dim, this vellum has hairs sticking out everywhere, it's not been properly scraped…'

My master read all these. 'I think your marginal comments are more deserving of immortality than my prosaic ramblings on the nature of sin.' He handed the sheets back. 'Adam, I had no idea of your fondness for burgundy. We shall share a bottle when we reach London.' He went to the door to return to his own cubicle. 'Do you know the ancient proverb, Adam? It runs thus: three fingers hold the pen, but it is the whole body that works and aches.'

Out he went, and through the decorated casement which joined us I could hear almost at once, through the door he had left open, that he was asleep and snoring loudly. Because he had forgotten to replace his cap his white hair was spread over his feather pillow like a halo. I regarded him a moment or two, seething with frustration. 'Of course when I heard from John through his secretary what excuses my husband made for the rape of Cecilia Chaumpaigne, I could only laugh. He was lying from start to finish.'

Dawn was now streaking the sky with red and white. The sheets I had dropped from Philippa's day books had gone from the floor, but I still had the main bundle with me. A horse neighed, and I heard the furious clatter of shod hooves over courtyard stone of someone riding out fast…

KATHERINE: Then my sister died. Without warning and quite suddenly. Of the sweating sickness. Geoffrey was nowhere to be seen. He had gone travelling. He had left to seek relics in Canterbury, and many reproached him for not returning to be at his wife's bedside during her last moments.

This was so many years ago. At least ten. I often wonder if Geoffrey did not, even as far back as that day of the joust in Windsor, see something in me which would make John my future prisoner: a look that passed only between himself and our gracious lord. Some unspoken affinity, like Gaunt's grandfather Edward falling for Gaveston the French boy, which would, or could, awaken great love, desperate forbidden love, but productive of the best in a man?

Was Geoffrey's service to his lord, his obeisance, a recognition in him that what was more important than love, or even service, was inspiration, to fight or love for something other and greater than oneself? Did this idea of honour and nobility which, so far from the city's selfish and materialist aim of every man and woman for themselves – lead ultimately to virtue? Thus Geoffrey avoided me for himself, keeping me for something greater.

As for my predilection that if he were to receive it and find wedded bliss with me, this would have been the end of him as a poet.

The irritation of one such as my sister was his castle to be surrounded and stormed, the suffering and torture such as he was to experience with her would yield up its own treasure or pearl. What otherwise could those words of his have meant?

> A man loves most tenderly,
> The thing that he has bought most dear.

The years passed. King Richard, on assuming full powers as king, murdered his uncle and protector the duke of Gloucester. My ward Elizabeth came to maturity and married. Wounds have healed, as they always do. I have come to understand much. It is better to have loved one person, and given of that love. I have always been the one with the ability to give my love steadfastly.

One day when I was quietly attending to my life in Lincoln, where John had established me in a fine and spacious house, the strangest of events came to pass. Two visitors were announced. Both were covered in mud, for they had ridden hard, and as they climbed the open stairs their features were impossible to distinguish under the cloth hoods. One was short, the other tall, although the tall one climbed stiffly. He did not stop for breath at the corner of the stairs, while when the other was still for a moment or two his chest heaved. Heaven forbid that they should be…

Yes. They stood before me, their hoods were lowered. They said nothing, but in turn each advanced, took both my hands, knelt and kissed them.

John appeared worn and grey. He seemed nearer sixty than fifty, although he was not that age. I didn't know why, but just at this moment, when no words between us were spoken, I recalled a conversation I had with him over twenty-five years ago. 'Why did you decide to marry her?' I had asked him of his forthcoming marriage to Constanza.

'To keep France,' he had answered. He had turned his eyes upon me sadly. 'I marry this woman to keep the land I see in *your* eyes. For you, for me, are the land I love so much. Your eyes, your body, our fascination, all come from France.'

But now he said to me, and it chilled me as if any icy hand was laid on my heart; yet he also spoke as if across the space of so many years he could read my thoughts:

'Constanza is dead.'

I made the sign of the cross. 'God rest her soul,' I replied.

We then, all three of us, became tongue-tied and none spoke. 'What brings you here, my lord?' I asked after some time had elapsed. 'And with Geoffrey?'

John ignored this.

'We are at peace. I have taken steps, and asked the pope for a dispensation to marry you.'

'To marry *me?* But my lord...' I found the words were out of my mouth before I could stop them. 'I am your former concubine. Other ladies such as the duchess of Gloucester, the duchess of Aumerle, consider that you have disgraced yourself. I am of coarse extraction. They will never enter any place where I am to be found.'

'Nonsense,' replied John. 'They will do as I tell them. You will be my wife and that's that!'

His eyes had all this while been holding mine steadily, tenderly, with a most gentle, even humble, gaze which seemed to hold a promise of that different man whom I knew formerly.

'Do I agree?' I answered foolishly.

'And John, Henry, Thomas and our beloved Joan shall be our legitimate children.'

I recalled how I lay in the enfolding arms of John, in a state of nakedness, trembling all over, shaking like an open leaf. 'I looked on him and saw glory in his face: "Thus," had said he, "it is ever so that we arrive at paradise through suffering."'

'And because,' I went on to my brother-in-law, 'I felt how fully I became released through his love from all care, or feeling trapped, my trust in him became total. I opened not only my heart to him, but everything. He took me, he had all of me, as one who sees his death taking shape, and as if then there is no possible way out from

169

certain death – then of a sudden he comes back from death, and more than is released from it, he finds ecstasy and a new security – such I believe it was for the prince.'

'So he had said to me, "Chaucer tells me this: I owe you," yes, he said to me, "a death I can never repay. I owe you my life." '

'To which I said: "Well I owe you mine, my lord, for had you not ordered Philippa to marry Geoffrey…" '

'But he stopped me…"Anyway I bless you for your kind office…" '

And then I added from Geoffrey's poem, which he later showed me, that the reader must not expect any one on earth to be as virtuous as the wife in his tale, whose name was Griselda.

Part Three

EIGHTEEN

Chaucer

THE NEXT STAGE OF our journey was from Huntingdon to St Albans. A thief had stolen Lord John's wedding finger as he lay on the hearse, cutting it off to take his ruby ring. There was more fury and outrage over this, while still we suffered fear and uncertainty over the future.

About an hour after we had started out to St Albans, there was one further unsettling incident.

A messenger arrived with news that when the duke of Northumberland, father of Henry Percy, had informed King Richard weeks ago in Chester that Lancaster had died, King Richard, who was planning to set out shortly for Ireland with an army, had ordered all of Lancaster's plates and movables to be seized, and at once left Chester. So it was firmly believed he was going to overthrow Lancaster's will, and take everything – palace, land, castles, coin revenues and rents, to finance his army. The atmosphere had become one of danger and distrust. Richard had remained at King's Langley and from here we received report of a terrible row between Edmund of York, Richard's uncle and Lord John's brother, and Richard, referring back to the wrongs Richard had done to the rest of the family, especially the recent murder of his other uncle, Thomas of Woodstock, duke of Gloucester.

York, who was usually deprecatory and irresolute, knew that he was now the last of Edward's sons and he tried to bring back to Richard the image of his own father, Edward the Black Prince, and make him see reason. Most of all York rebuked Richard for his action of banishing Henry Bolingbroke and said that, with Lord John dead, if he did not revoke his banishment of Henry it would be hard to keep his popularity. 'You are inviting great danger, and you will lose thousands of well-disposed hearts.' Words to that effect.

Richard had descended into tyranny and would not listen to reason. York left King's Langley. We grew more and more agitated at these reports.

At this juncture my sister-in-law Lady Katherine joined us with her son Henry Beaufort, now legitimized and bishop of Winchester. She had ridden hard from Lincoln. She was a fine, upright woman of nearly fifty years. Her presence stilled and calmed the assembly. Unlike Joan of Woodstock, King Richard's mother who died long ago, she had preserved her slim and attractive figure. She was dressed in black and she came over at once to me, kissing me on both cheeks and holding me close to her for a moment or two. She seemed pleased and took my hand, gently voicing a greeting. She introduced her travelling companion, a nun, a strange old biddy who had often accompanied Katherine in the past.

'Sister Pervil.'

I bowed and took her hand. My scrivener embraced her too.

'Sister Pervil has been in the service of Lady Katherine since the days she was the wife of Swynford,' I confided to him.

With her puckered skin, faded and scaly locks the colour of parched and sunbaked earth, I found something about her appearance familiar to that of Adam Scriven. Could they have been related? Certainly she gave him a queer look or two, as if they might have met before.

I noticed that Lady Katherine's eyes, as they meet mine, had deepened and darkened with time and suffering. We said little, but our silence spoke volumes. I was very content to gaze upon her again. Her beauty still resided at the mean, or perfect middle, a balance between excess and deficiency. Could she ever have been a murderess – an accomplice of Lord John in the murder of her husband? As the cortège resumed its solemn progress south, she turned to ride alongside the bier. Sister Pervil accompanied her.

Deprived of her momentarily I felt a pang of grief, and said to Scriven, 'You've no idea what a lovely creature she was at seventeen. I don't mind telling you I completely lost my heart to her.' I exhaled with a sweet mixture of regret and the desire to instruct my follower and admirer.

'You see, Adam,' I went on, 'that after all, my honourable intention with "The Book of the Duchess" was fulfilled...'

'In *Troilus and Criseyde*?' he answered. I had miscalculated his response yet again. 'Is that what you're saying? Queen Anne objected strongly to your Criseyde, Mr Chaucer, may I remind you?…'

I could not stand for this distortion of the truth. 'The queen was angry, and complained that I implied women were more faithless than men in matters of love. It's a matter for debate.'

'You lost your job as comptroller of wool.'

'I sat down and wrote a sequel to calm the angry queen.'

'The legend of the servants of Cupid.'

'The legend of Good Women…'

'Which you abandoned…'

'I was hard put to find enough good women. My disciple Lydgate told me it encumbered my wits.'

'It needed Lord John to restore you to your former favour…'

'No. I began to write the *Canterbury Tales*. The Clerk's tale of patient Griselda restored me in the eyes of the queen. It became her favourite.'

He had nothing to say to this.

New orders had gone out, and there was a noticeable tightening up of discipline in the Lancastrian entourage. But would Richard have dared to interfere with the funeral of his uncle John? We assessed that these rumours could possibly turn into reality at any moment, but that Richard's more probable plan, before revoking the will, would be to wait until the day *after* the funeral, which would be a grand affair, with royal emissaries from France, Spain, the Low Countries, and Italy all in attendance.

Observing Katherine, who had taken up a position at the head of the cortège, I started once again to find myself unduly captivated by her beauty and majesty. I began to believe that, if anyone could, she might be able to tame the weak-minded king. But had she, I wondered, heard from her stepson Bolingbroke, who was deeply fond of her too, and now treated her, who was formerly his governess, as if she were his mother?

This was the present situation, as we established it from our spies. Our 'great king', who was now thirty-three years old, sat in his palace of King's Langley. For those whose picture of him has remained shadowy, we can say that he was in the prime of his manhood; he had an elegant but slightly feminine appearance, but he had worn well, this flower of boys, and, six foot tall, he was vigorous and active.

He was so recognizably a Plantagenet: long straight nose, flared nostrils, large eyelids and a short goatee beard.

He was constantly on the move. That year alone he had visited Coventry, Wolverhampton, Shrawardine, Chester, Newcastle under Lyme, and now, at King's Langley, his most evil councillors and fosterers of his malice attended him: Bushy, Green and Sir Walter Bagot, upstarts whose divisive counsels he had too often followed, disgracing his queen and imposing tyranny and extortion on his subjects.

The king was rich and had never been richer. He was joyful in the greedy expectation of his plans; he was unsuspecting of any opposition. With him also were his 'brains', Scrope of Bolton, earl of Wiltshire, who, a few days earlier in Leicester, had been with us. Richard had no great power of thought, but Scrope was a very clever man and indispensable to him. There, too, was the duke of Aumerle, a gadfly, with honours heaped upon him by Richard, but a lazy, idle man.

From a Lancastrian spy, the same who had brought news of the row between York and the king, we heard that Scrope, who gathered and spread intelligence with the assiduity of Brother Walsingham, had argued with Aumerle, who suggested that they should stop Lancaster's cortège at once, as it might pose a threat to Richard's authority and provoke an uprising.

'Lancaster is popular,' he had said, 'the people will take it very badly.'

'It is I who am popular,' answered the sun-king.

'Of course my liege,' said Bushy, and he and Green had bowed low. 'Never have you been so tumultuously received by your subjects.'

'D-d-damn him, d-d-damn, damn my uncle for dying on me when I still needed him so much!' had exploded Richard petulantly. 'Who would have thought he would go now? Only four months ago I visited him in Leicester. He was well. But he told me that his grief over not seeing his beloved Henry would shorten his life. For his peace of mind, and only for that, I promised him that Henry Derby would inherit his castles.'

'I think it would be unwise to stop the process of his funeral, or go against his final wishes,' said Scrope, 'he has been generous to you in his will, your grace, leaving you a third of the revenue from Spain – '

'What of Bolingbroke's estates and income? You're not going to allow the scoundrel to inherit, are you?' interrupted Aumerle.

Scrope had continued. 'We cannot confiscate Lancaster's lands, even though Bolingbroke is in exile. The repercussions will be dangerous.'

'Not with Henry,' said the king, 'I hear he plans a pilgrimage. Besides he loves Paris too much. His son serves me faithfully in my army.'

'I don't agree,' interrupted the ruffian Bagot, whose time as sheriff of Warwickshire had been tainted with murder, thuggery and extortion. 'Henry of Bolingbroke is a plotter. If we hold Katherine we have a hostage. Bolingbroke plans to take the throne. We should abduct Katherine of Lancaster.'

Richard laughed. 'Bolingbroke cannot do that. We are too well defended. By my uncle York, and you Scrope. My Cheshire brethren guard me night and day. Besides Henry has sworn his oath to me. Like his father he will never break an oath.'

'I have a plan, my liege,' suggested Scrope. 'Let us leave Langley tomorrow and ride to London, meet the procession and take note of those who are taking part, mingle with them and learn from the Lancastrian family of Henry's intentions. We can judge by the procession's size and mood whether it means harm to your majesty. But if we honour Lancaster, we too will reap the reward. He has been much loved by everyone and is even more popular now.'

'Is this enough?' asked Richard, his brow darkening.

'For the moment, yes,' answered Scrope. 'But when the time is ripe, and the common people with their short memories forget Lord John, we can act.'

'A-a-act?' questioned Richard as the others turned towards Scrope to look at him. Richard laughed loudly but not easily. 'Come, come my noble lord Wiltshire, what devilish and underhand plan are you hatching?'

Scrope smiled. 'One that will benefit us all, but especially you, my most gracious sovereign.' Taking the king's hand and kissing it, he bowed low.

Richard withdrew his hand, bit his lip and turned his head away. To Green he said, 'Go and tell the captain of my guard that we leave first thing tomorrow morning.'

Scrope interceded: 'No, no, your majesty, please. Halve your Cheshire guard; don't make a mighty show of force. Be subtle.'

'I t-trust no one except my Cheshire guard,' Richard blurted out in an especially painful stammer. 'I'll h-h-have it all or n-n-nothing!'

All this and more we learned from our intelligent and well-placed spy.

With such and other preoccupations we rode the whole morning in silence. It was warm and sunny for March, with the young sun running high in the Ram, but I was sorely fatigued with the journey. 'Master, may I speak alone with you?' my scrivener importuned me along the way.

'Why, what is it Adam, you look out of sorts today.'

'Don't tell me you slept soundly after that episode, master?'

'I feel less funereal than usual.' Plump and easy in disposition as I had become his hostility put me on my mettle, and I adopted a robust manner to deal with him. Why was he so suspicious all the time, forever questioning and probing the past? 'You are marked, Adam. I am marked. We are probably all marked. Who could it be? Look how' – here I pointed forward to a figure at the front of the procession, 'I believe that, after all, you could be right about Thomas Swynford. You say last night's intruder was about his height?'

Adam nodded with due respect and subservience.

'Look how proudly he rides with his mother at the front of the procession, and with that odd-looking nun. She was with Swynford and Lady Katherine. How his wounds stank. Now if it was Katherine herself who wanted Sir Hugh out of the way, and the boy already hated his father because he beat him, then it follows that Philippa knew, and the old servant Rachel knew, for she knew all the…secrets. Did Rachel, or perhaps – what was his name? – Basil, give you anything, Adam?'

He looked away, pretending that he had not heard, and I could see he was concealing something he knew.

'Well perhaps you know more than you are prepared to say,' I added with more than a slight petulance of tone.

'Master,' he answered me now urgently. 'I have to talk to you. I want no interruption. I suggest we gallop ahead, reach St Albans before Lord John and the rest of the company, and here we may talk at leisure until they arrive.'

'An excellent notion,' I said, determined to listen to whatever he felt impelled to say. 'I feel the exercise will do me good.'

Toward late afternoon we had spurred on Scot and Dexter to the western hill outside St Albans where in the distance we could see the long and spacious nave of the cathedral, raised out of Roman stone and brick in the reign of William the Conqueror in the place where once the occupying Romans built their flourishing town of Verulamium. Here in this prosperous settlement a dissolute young Roman nobleman had sacrificed himself to save a practising Christian, an old man whose life was nearly at its end. Descending the hills we came to several cheerful and well-appointed inns, and at one, The Six Bells, we stopped to refresh ourselves.

'Are you not relieved to be away from the throng? I have to admit that I have found it most upsetting to know we may have a murderer or murderers in our midst.'

'Do you, master?'

'Come now, you look for a moment as if you still believe it could be me.' And I still had my suspicions of Scriven. Why had he been away from the hall before the will was read out?

'Well, you could always have slipped out from the hall while I was not there!'

'I have very nimble legs.'

The sun was out, and the sudden warmth of this early spring day had quickened the sap. With the general warmth and sense of well-being I felt towards all human kind I even felt, for a moment or two, like embracing this scaly clerk.

'Master,' he now said in a strangled voice, as if aware that his throat was tight and he had to speak slowly and deliberately to avoid sounding strange. 'I may be mad, but I believe there is a connection between these two terrible murders and that incident, you must remember, the "rape" of Cecilia Chaumpaigne years ago.'

I believe my mouth fell open. I looked at him aghast. I felt devastated. 'You can't mean it, Adam,' I said, with a breathless croak as my heart beat violently. All this had happened twenty years ago.

'I do. Everyone believes you committed the rape. Your wife believed it. Lord John believed it. The young woman herself believed it, else she would not have filed the release in the first place. You bribed her, didn't you, to withdraw her charges.'

I slumped sluggishly on my chair and reached for my ale. I looked at this wretched creature for a long time. Should I even bother to answer his charge? 'Adam, you do not know why she brought the release in the first place.'

'Because you were about to be formerly charged in the king's name! What other reason?'

'No, no,' I said. 'It wasn't like that at all.' Suddenly, as if the receiver of some form of grace, I felt more disposed to open up and tell him, but I could see from the twisted expression on Scriven's face that he was not going to believe me. 'You remember, Adam. You were there with me when I was arrested and thrown into the Fleet. You came to the prison with me!'

'I do, master, and then you sent me off to plead with Lord John for your release. He questioned me, and I felt patently resentful towards him, so it took me some time to convince him that I loved you, and that you wanted him to petition on your behalf and get you released.'

'Surely he pointed out at once that I was not capable of rape?'

'When I told him you'd been caught *in flagrante delicto* with a young woman less than half your age he burst out laughing.'

I was ashamed to hear this, and indignant too, but I could see I needed all the dignity and restraint I could muster. Adam had thrown caution and restraint of tone to the winds. 'Our good poet Geoffrey Chaucer with his wisdom and understanding of human nature,' Scriven reported Lord John saying about me, 'surely never a rapist? Ho-ho-ho!' And other sentiments of a similar kind.

I could not believe my patron had been capable of such betrayal. I had brought to him so much, not least my sister-in-law. His much-loved wife and mother of his gifted children. 'So in the end anyway, at least, he didn't believe the charge was true?'

'I don't think it bothered him much one way or the other. "Perhaps he was smitten," the duke told me, "as all of us are at one time or another with uncontrollable desire." What did rape mean to one such as him?'

The contempt in Adam's tone suggested he was deliberately testing me. I have to say that hearing how the duke described me, believing, that is, my secretary was not inventing it, I felt so much relief at being out of the cortège, away from the remains of my patron: could it be that in that body, in the remains of that princely presence which had so dominated our lives, there persisted a contagion even in death?

'I think he would have taken it seriously. He upheld the law.'

'What about his own adultery? It was also against the law.'

'These days this is primarily a moral law, no longer a civil one. He wrote a letter requesting my release, although he must have found out that the charge against me was written down, and would have to be brought against me in trial.'

'He could just as easily have had you moved to a Lancastrian jail, and convened his own court to have you tried.'

'Perhaps. But if I really had raped this girl, Adam, and if there were witnesses to it besides the victim concerned, it wouldn't have shown him up, if he had defended me, in a good light. Remember at this time he was not very popular. He'd had a few, very bad years. He defended Wyclif who attacked the pope, and fighting had broken out in the streets outside St Paul's. He was accused of plotting to kill the new king, his nephew Richard. He fell out with the city of London and a mob stormed his palace, beating a priest and others to death, then pursuing him till he had to take flight by water and seek his sister-in-law, Joan's protection. This was long before the Great Revolt when the rioters sacked and burnt the Savoy, murdering anyone they could lay their hands on. They even spread rumours that his mother had lied and was not his true mother, that she had by chance lain on her child at birth, and was so frightened of his father's anger that she bribed the wife of a Flemish butcher to deliver up her son in place of the dead child.'

But Scriven, like a dog digging out a buried hedgehog, persisted, 'Then I, having secured your release from prison, came back with you to Lord John…'

'Yes. He questioned me severely, while I told him that such an accusation, untrue as it was, brought great shame on me and my family.'

At this point Scriven frowned with disbelief.

'So what actually did happen?'

'Well, as I told the duke…' here some flea itched horribly and I shifted uncomfortably, while a constriction of the throat made me swallow more of the excellent St Albans ale. I thirsted for some different relief. 'I feared the good offices I had performed on his behalf, such as I told you, Adam, had won for me a bad name, and made me susceptible, or vulnerable, if hard pressed upon to do it, to undertake such work for others. And so it came about that John Grove, the duke's armourer, approached me, with this other man, Richard Goodchild, who supplied the duke with short swords and stabbing knives; I became involved in this business…'

Scriven smiled with some kind of triumph as if he knew something that I did not. 'And you were to be the go-between this John Grove and Cecilia Chaumpaigne?'

'I'm afraid, Adam, that when you gain a reputation for one thing in this life, people expect you to go on repeating it.'

I clasped my chest with one hand, for I could feel my heart knocking the inside of my ribs. I paused to catch my breath, but then gave the account I believe I had given to John all those years ago.

This discharge of a distant memory did not only have its bad side, for suddenly I remembered just how I had felt at what had happened next, a mixture of confusion and gratification. I smacked my lips. 'You know me, you know how helpful I like to be. To confide in you, Adam, and you must swear not to tell a soul – .' Adam remained impassive, as unmoved as a stone…I coughed and cleared my throat again. 'She fell suddenly and secretly in love with me.'

He laughed out loud, and I waved my open hands in order to deflect this unfeeling response. Scriven, uncared for as he had been in childhood, did not care much for others. Nor even for himself, which was much the same thing, except for fits of envy and resentment, or sudden surges of feeling that he must assert himself.

'It's true, Adam, she did…'

'Well with my mistress, your wife, away so much, what stopped you, master?…'

I looked at him grimly: 'I had sworn to perform my duty to Grove, even though when I came to meet Cecilia I felt reluctant to do so.'

I could see he did not fully understand. But had he ever experienced for himself a similar situation? Copying the work of others hardly engenders much understanding of life, except at second hand.

'Anyway,' I went on, explaining and lengthening my response and still with cheerful optimism hoping to win his belief. 'She came to believe that her desire would only be met if she could overcome this obstruction of my shame in discovering this desire of hers to myself. This is what she did. One day she sent for me…'

But while I was telling him this, another thought pursued me like a fury. Hell and damnation! The inmates in that place of eternal punishment when Our Lord was harrowing it, couldn't have had a worse time than we were having, with threats of Richard's Cheshire archers, his murderous angels, pouring in on us every hour.

Here Scriven interrupted. 'I think we should come straight to the point, master. The others will catch up soon.'

My mood changed. For some moments I could say nothing, genuinely tongue-tied.

'Well what, by heaven, was she aiming at?' asked Adam Scriven in a more kindly tone.

'She went on for some time making excuses for herself, because of her youth, the death of her husband, all leading up to the conclusion that she, a lady, with her father a reputable saddler, by no means a poor woman who daily had to labour, had found me, Geoffrey Chaucer, an object worthy of her love. She went on further to say that I should be ready and willing to show the same towards her, take pity on her youth.'

I grinned. I could see I was finally winning over his doubts.

'The tears were pouring down her cheeks so fast she could hardly manage to speak further. Then she laid her head on my chest.'

'You're not telling me you refused her love, master?'

'I'm afraid so, Adam. I eased myself away, saying that I would rather cut myself to pieces than wrong my own wife, or allow others to do so. Cecilia, hearing my words, at once forgot that deep feeling she had professed to me. She...'

Adam had pursed his lips and become grim, hostile. 'But were you, at this stage, really trying to abduct her? If so, what better way than...?' In spite of this I continued.

'She screamed at me that I was just a vile man to think that her request could be spurned. She began tearing out her hair in handfuls, rending her garments, shouting and screaming for help. "Geoffrey Chaucer is raping me..."over and over again. I was seized and bound by a dozen men-at-arms, and brought before the sheriff...'

I looked Adam squarely in the eye as my shaking hand reached for my jug of ale.

The only response I received from Scriven was him saying, in the coldest possible way, 'Why don't you just admit it was rape? Rape pure and simple?'

I thought I might have hit him. I was beside myself with anger. It was the nearest I ever felt to responding to another person with extreme violence.

But a bent and venerable figure stood before us, and before anything further happened I found myself on my feet, thankfully smiling again and bowing low in deference to this august presence.

NINETEEN

Scriven

I HAD BEEN STRUCK dumb by Mr Chaucer. I could say nothing to him. I had tried hard to imagine this ageing poet with bags under his eyes, double chins and gammy leg as a man of just forty, as he had been then, making up to this Cecilia. Yet even so, how could I ever believe that she, a girl not yet twenty years of age, had fallen for him? What could she have possibly seen in him? My mistress Philippa had, in the sheets of her confession, much advice for this Cecilia: 'Unless you make a man run after you, there's nothing in it for either. No dutiful unbuttoning, it needs a bit of venom to bring the man on.' And more in a similar vein.

Yet while he had been telling me all this his report had been shrewd and glowing and not – yes, undoubtedly – softened with the emotion of memory.

For a shocking moment or two I had believed he meant to embrace me.

Wait a minute, I had thought, this was decidedly not what Philippa reported. She had written, 'All that farce about him acting as bawd for a cutler and an armourer – as if they couldn't take on themselves the cutting and armouring of their own love life! This was but the ruse, wasn't it, to allow my dear husband to escape the consequences of his crime and keep his reputation clean before history.'

On the tavern table at which we sat, my master's hands met in front and close together with fingers interlaced. It often seemed as if he wanted to protect himself from intrusion. And then, when my confidence returned that he was not telling the truth but losing me in a fog of romantic imagery, for lying was so much of my master's personal style on occasions, I wondered if he himself knew whether he was living in this world or that of his poetry.

His lips were moistened, his brow glistened, his face was flushed – and he would try, from time to time, to give me a feeble wink. Such a show of tender sincerity might well have convinced someone weaker and more prone to the passion of others. Surely he had been, for most of the time, lying, even if there had been some participation of a cutler and armourer in the whole affair. Remember how he used his hands in a defensive gesture, as people do who are desperate to convince an unbelieving audience.

Yet I could see that pressing the suit of others could have had grave complications; but even then, I might have deduced, knowing how zealous and skilled to press the love of another my master could be, he liked it that way.

Thomas Walsingham was not a tall man, less even now that he was old. His build was stocky – chunky was a better way to put it – and it suggested he was someone who knew how to endure a hard life. His hair, neatly cut, was thin, fine and now very white. He had a square face, a flattish nose, a cleft chin, a wide, full-lipped yet sensitive mouth and – his most famous feature – steely blue eyes which conveyed an impression of endless memory and intelligence. It was still hard to look into those eyes, and if I did, it was even harder to avoid their power. Yet he could be very warm, and when he was, his otherwise cold, hard eyes expanded to spread geniality and kindness everywhere.

My master, when he recovered from the ardour of his fruitless endeavour to convince me of his innocence, embraced the monk, and having apparently forgotten about my upbringing here in this very place, tried to introduce us. He was severely flustered by what had just passed between us. I gave my spiritual and foster parent a short, sharp embrace. I was surprised that my master was so affectionate towards him, for Brother Walsingham had campaigned so fiercely against Lord John for twelve or more years before the time of the Great Revolt. But on that day Mr Chaucer and he were friends. Tomorrow, who knows? The monk led on foot, talking affectionately to us, and we made our way up Fishpool Street hill towards the abbey. The mixture of emotions that I felt back there, half love, half repulsion, was curious. Time had served my spiritual father well for, as I remembered him, he had no warmth of humour at all, but, with the passing of the years, he had mellowed. He used to be so reserved and cold at heart, and when he had talked to me he seldom looked me in the eye, but would stare down at his feet or let his eyes dart around the room. This must have been because he had so many plots on his mind. I recalled a story that once when he tried to sit down on a non-existent chair, not realizing that it had been moved from where it was supposed to be, and that he fell to the ground. When he came out from behind the table, after taking a terrible tumble, he showed no reaction. His nickname had been the man with eyes of ice. His great enemy had been no less than Lord John, and with all the power of the church behind him he had waged war on the duke's reputation.

I always felt shy in his company and invariably fell silent, for he was so superior in learning, so many-sided and supreme in memory and understanding. Yet now I noticed a change, for he demonstrated an unmistakably genuine interest in my master. 'Rough and bitter words the late duke too often said,' I heard Walsingham say, 'but his death will have deep repercussions for all of this kingdom.' And then to me he said, in quieter tones, 'Adam, you must come and see me later, for not only do I have something I want you to copy for me – and copy twice – but I have some important information for you.'

Ah, I thought at once, I would take up with him the possibility, which my master had raised, of my connection with Rachel Dempsey. He would know the truth. I also formed the resolution that, as well as sounding out his opinion on the matter of whether that poor soul could ever have been my mother, I would pursue my inquiries about my master with the monk. But I was aware that as we neared London and the day, delayed as it now had been, of Lord John's funeral, I had little or no time left for the completion of my self-imposed task.

But when we reached the abbey itself, and the great cathedral of St Albans, I was dismissed to the kitchens where I was told I would find old Alison who once had been my wet-nurse, and now passed her years preparing food and herbs for the Benedictines.

'Well now, Adam,' she addressed me upon our meeting again, 'you are such a big fellow these days, how often I dandled you on my knees...' and she offered other such coarse familiarities as to make me blush with shame, for I did not like to be reminded of such origins, nor to be told I was a handsome-looking, strong man, for I was no such thing. While we were employed in cloying pleasantries, with me grateful for food and drink as the exertion had been long and wearisome – but not knowing which way to put my glance – two of the sheriff of Leicester's men found their way into the kitchen.

One was a balding young man with a very sallow complexion who kept pursing his lips and wetting them with his tongue. The other was tall, with a jutting chin, and a forelock of straight black hair. They were accompanied by a young woman whom, having seen her two days ago at the assembly in Leicester, I recognized as Petronella Swynford.

As Robert Wydeville had indicated to us as his intention, she had been brought back to rejoin the procession and travel on with her mother. My master would be pleased, for he had been worried the effect her arrest might have had upon the grieving widow.

I offered a sign of recognition to Petronella. Under her fox fur coat she wore a simple, a straight-cut dress of pale blue. Her eyes avoided mine. But she did not look mad at all, and I wondered why she should have felt a need to confess to those violent crimes. Perhaps Wydeville had not been telling the truth either, and he had forced her to confess.

She was not as fine-looking as her mother, but still a comely, slim young woman upon whose virtue men might well have entertained designs. I had heard that she leant towards incontinence. Those eyes of hers were unlike her mother's, dark and watchful, and I suspected they hid much.

'Here's another murder where we fail to see justice done!' declared the sallow-faced one.

'There's so many like it,' said the other.

'Since the plague they say the land is lawless...'

I asked them, agreeably enough, 'Mistress Petronella is released, I see. Do you not have any further suspicions?'

She smiled at me with a hesitant yet impulsive recognition.

'Oh that we do,' answered the balding one. 'Except we can't do nothing about them. And then there's our leader, Sheriff Wydeville. He's been bribed, why everyone knows that, by the king.'

Really? This was a new consideration. But they would not be drawn further. Alison came to sit down with me and I asked after her daughter Susanna, who had been a young girl when I left the Abbey.

Petronella excused herself and left, turning at the door and casting a backward glance at me.

'And you,' Dame Alison repeated over and over, 'you look such a fine gentleman now, with your court clothes and kept hair! And I had such a crush on you all these years ago.'

'Why are you back in the abbey?' I asked. 'I'd heard you'd left the monks and moved out.'

'I was a difficult wife. I bore my husband five children. I pursued my own trade, that of brewer in the town, and also miller. But then my businesses failed, and I decided to devote myself to God. You see, Adam, my husband didn't come up to much, and I had plenty of moods and fits, wounding myself and once I tried to kill myself. Now I fast and mortify my flesh. Oh I once wore gaudy and fashionable clothes. Now I wear white and the ring of Christ.'

'So you are inspired by God?'

'Yes, but I aren't no ordinary Christian, and I'll boil bacon in Lent, and defend meat-eating on a Friday.'

She lowered her voice to a whisper. 'There was a time not long ago I used to go about preaching against stocks and stones and dead men's bones, saying the holy communion bread could not be the true body of Christ, for if it were, a thousand priests made gods a thousand times, ate them, and excreted them, and these gods were therefore to be found in their excrement.'

She laughed: 'Especially the abbot here, of St Alban's. But then I abjured. I stripped to wear only a short kirtle, and bearing my wax taper I was flogged in the market place four times.'

I recalled her desire to be a priest, and commit the heresy of ministering the sacrament, but now I wondered at her conversion.

'I will send my daughter to you,' she said and left.

The hard riding, the food and drink, had lulled me into an aching desire for sleep, but a solemn mass was to be held for Blanche in the cathedral, which I was obliged to attend. And I was called in later to talk with Brother Thomas. But while I hovered there, sitting at a table, with the voices of the sheriff's men not far away, inclined to doze, I pondered yet again upon Philippa's chronicle. I had it so searingly engraved on my memory that it presented itself to my mind with greater authority: following on from that tally of my master's rape, how she and he were at odds with one another, and how Mrs Chaucer kept saying that she was like a cat, and if you singed a cat's skin then the cat would abide and keep within your house. But if the skin were slick and shiny and ready to go, she'd be out of the house before dawn to show off her hindquarters and go caterwauling. 'I know he did the girl, but Lord John was kind to him, got him off and gave him an extra ten pounds.'

When my master came back that night from prison she reckoned that he was so relieved not to be strung up by the neck, that he gave her the money John advanced him. So she, that very same evening, decided she would let him have her 'belle chose', while he was so aggravated and fed up from his nights in jail that he let fly at her with a lust quickened and sharpened by fear.

I lapsed more and more into dreaming: my master gently undoing her bows and ribbons, easing her enticingly from her gown and touching, oh so gently and flutteringly, her breast or its nipple, and lower down, 'Then who wouldn't blush to tell what he did to me, except to say that I used his instrument right full and well? Ah, this way rapes do us all well!' God forbid, but why am I becoming like one of them? Then there was Philippa's coarse confession of her amatory exploits, one with a giant mason's apprentice named Yole. Yole. Funny name. Christian or surname? It struck a bell. Yes, I remembered, the tall, gross Cheshire archer. Must be some mistake. Impossible.

' "Nice," he had said, his breath coming in little bursts. "Nice, nice, nice…" I shut him out by closing my eyes. I concentrated on my rhythm, impaling myself on him, rising and sliding slowly down, listening to his breathing to decide when to move faster when to go slow…'

So wrapped up as I was in thoughts like these I had been unable to notice someone else had entered the kitchen of the abbey, and come over to stand by me.

'Susanna,' I said, 'is it really you? How like you are to Petronella Swynford.' They could have been sisters. But Susanna's face was more gentle by far.

'My mother told me you were here. It's late, and I had already gone to bed. I was up at four this morning. I couldn't sleep. Do you want a drink?'

'No. Do you mind sitting with me?' By now the others had left.

I could see her hair, uncoiled, reached almost to her waist. It was dark and silky, and I had an uncontrollable impulse to touch it, but I did not move. She looked at the cup near me, picked it up and filled it from a pitcher. As she held the cup under the running water

I became transfixed by her movement, her hands with their long delicate fingers like a lady's, and their almost white nails. They were perfect ovals, with large half moons at the cuticle.

She returned with the cup and as she reached out to place it by me on the table her satin night- gown parted, opening to the thigh, and I was excited to think that she was otherwise naked. As she smoothed it back she inclined shyly towards me, but the top of her gown opened just a fraction and I looked away. I could not see but I knew that the crease between her breasts that were bare would be showing. I wanted so much to turn and look, but I did not.

'What was my mother telling you about herself?'

She wanted to know. She twisted her long hair around her finger.

'She told me of her reformed Lollardry – how she abjured her difference.' My legs shook, and I squeezed together my buttocks, feeling myself harden. I dropped my hands into my lap beneath the table. My whole body tingled with heat, and I knew my cheeks were turning red.

'She has become very conventional and dogmatic. She hates it when I swear; "Beware of the bee," she says, for every bee will sting and therefore look that you swear neither by God nor by Our Lady, nor by none other saint, and if you do the contrary the bee will sting your tongue and venom your soul.'

We both laughed. There was such quality in a laugh and hers was the best I had ever heard, open, honest and free, truly joyful. My legs were still shaking, and I had to change my position on the hard chair. 'Does it...' I pressed my *membrum virilis* between my hands...'Does it stop you?'

She bit her lower lip and unconsciously ran her hands down the satin of her gown, outlining her breasts, and tightening the sash. 'Mother says I should talk only a little while.' She was completely relaxed. As she left the room I came, soaking my under-drawers.

The relief of this caused me to sigh, with a quiet moan of pleasure. As I got up from the table I was wet and sticky, and I tripped and fell to the floor. I felt angry at my clumsiness and absence of control, but I was summoned and had to obey. Reeling as I was from my encounter with Susanna after all this while, but above all from her response to me, for this was the most unexpected part that I, an ink-stained scrivener, should awaken some light of recognition – could it be called desire? – in the spirit of one so young and tender, I staggered to the cavernous and empty dark space of the cathedral.

Help. Help. I said this silently to myself, for I felt Cecilia's rape slipping away into oblivion, and as the introit began so did solemnity come to possess me wholeheartedly. Suddenly twenty-four men dressed in Lancastrian blue and white gowns, and with black hoods, appeared in the humbling and spacious gloom, which was dripping with the savour of incense. Now there began this awesome requiem mass sung for Blanche of Lancaster, deceased these thirty years. And here, piously worshipping her former mistress whom even I have to admit she never wronged or betrayed, attended Lady Katherine, newly widowed duchess of the great lands and power of Lancaster. The suggestions made by the messenger from King's Langley, and recently by those sheriff's men in the kitchen, put her very life at risk. Could she have been so rapidly transformed from whore, to protectress of the kingdom?

❦

'Sit down, Adam,' said Brother Walsingham after the mass was over, gesturing towards the table in his library room over the sacristy where he kept, or used to keep, many fine specimens of his dissecting and medical skills.

I feared that I stank of gluey semen. How I longed to strip myself of my clothes, and climb naked into my own bed.

'Why have you summoned me?' I asked. I looked over to the polished pale yellow table where my master sat. He was pinched and white, not at all expansive in his gesture, or at his ease. Usually he was so still and tranquil, but not on that evening.

'Tell him, brother monk,' he said gruffly. 'Tell my scrivener. He is so obsessed with the truth.' He looked suddenly womanish, vulnerable, about to fold up in misery.

Brother Walsingham was, on the other hand, soothing; his eyes expanded and warmly reassured me. 'Come come,' he said. 'We must put our faith and trust in the Lord, but this is the problem, Adam. Your master has described to me the events of your journey, and especially the two murders, and far from believing this is the work of one individual – both he and I know who you have in mind, I am afraid the whole chain of actions suggests to me something more sinister – and with no doubt further consequences to come. I am afraid, or rather I suspect, that not only is King Richard plotting to seize the Lancastrian inheritance, but he is also using Lord John's death as a pretext for ridding himself, or perhaps it would be true to say, revenging himself on those who have offended his vanity.'

My master butted in: 'To put it bluntly, I fear for our lives, Adam. Perhaps it would be better for us to leave now, turn back, embrace what safety we can in Leicester and Lancaster.'

'How and why does this affect you, master?' I asked.

Mr Chaucer said nothing further, but Walsingham explained: 'Two years ago the king began to tyrannise his people, in other words misuse his subjects' property by sending out agents with letters for forced loans under his privy seal. The sums which were to be lent were specified, but not the names of the lenders, for these were to be filled in when the agents found out who had the money, and who could be forced. Then as we all know we next had the despicable arrest and trials of Lord Arundel, Lord Warwick, and the duke of Gloucester. The last was brutally done to death in Calais on the order of the king.'

At the fearless mention of this we all looked around in fear, in case the king had spies in the abbey.

'– Warwick was sentenced to life imprisonment, while Arundel was executed. But this is not all.'

My master interrupted:

'You mean the death of Lord John.' Walsingham's eyes lit up: 'Exactly, Geoffrey. Anne of Bohemia's death had a strong effect on King Richard, and it wasn't a particularly rational response of his to burn down Sheen Palace, where he had lived with her. At first the duke was always at his back, strengthening his crown and lending mature and experienced management to the realm. But then the king's confidence declined. It began when the envoys from Germany who came to offer him the imperial crown suggested he was not fit to wear it if he could not control his subjects at home. This was followed with mounting criticism, and then the quarrel which broke out between Mowbray and Henry of Bolingbroke, which the king stepped in to curtail, didn't help his weakening position. The whole country felt deprived of a great heraldic spectacle of arms. So criticism, which began as a trickle, rose to a flood.'

'And now it seems, to descend from the sublime to the ridiculous, according to brother monk,' my master took over and regained some of his usual smiling composure, 'that the king still nurses deep offence at my poem addressed to him as laureate – unofficial of course on "steadfastness". The very poem which Lord John asked me to write to stop the king from sliding into tyranny! You see the weakness of my position – and yours, Adam, for the copyist is implicated. We no longer have Lord John to hide behind, and what once was condoned as paternal reproof now appears to the king as slander and calumny.'

I felt roused. 'Among the best lines you have written, master' – In my quavering, rough voice I quoted

'Truth is put down, reason is held feeble,
Virtue now has no domination,
Pity exiled, no man shows mercy
Through covetise discretion is blinded…'

'Yes, yes, Adam…'

I stopped, seeing my master's sour expression. He said impatiently, 'Humdrum work, cheap moralizing …'

Walsingham continued, 'The king never forgives an insult or a criticism. It's not hard to start up old plots and revive old injuries. Your poem…'

My mouth fell open. I interrupted Walsingham.

'Surely he cannot feel such a burning desire for vengeance simply because his narcissism has been wounded?'

'I'm afraid so. To attack his image, his own idea of his own self-perfection, is as bad as attacking his body.'

'If this is so, things can only get worse. What will happen now?'

'This,' replied Brother Thomas Walsingham, 'is anyone's conjecture. Come here, Adam.' He beckoned me over, and took my right hand in both of his. I felt prickly and inclined to speak out, but I kept my mouth shut. 'You are going to have to be very strong, for towards you I have a special commission which I have sworn, after the death of Lord John, to undertake in person.'

'What is it?' I asked anxiously, seeking to withdraw my hand, but aware that this could give offence. My hand was cold, those of Walsingham firm and warm, and they imbued me with a hope and confidence which divided my spirit.

'I have to tell you,' and here he paused so that the full impact could sink in, 'that Sir Hugh Swynford was your father. I was enjoined and sworn by Swynford himself not to tell you until Lord John was dead. I have no further reason to remain silent.'

It hit me square between the eyes.

Katherine Payne de Roet, duchess of Lancaster, entered the library. She stood just inside the door. She really was so beautiful. Could I belong to these people? I looked at Lady Katherine. She averted her eyes from mine. That time at the joust years ago, it flashed into my memory, when she had stood in the loge and threw the token of a lily to her devoted young knight. Then the old bastard rode up…. Her sister quickly seized another bloom, placed it in her hand and Katherine tossed it to Swynford. The flower hit the knight on the breastplate, whereupon the Saxon caught the flower, crushed the petals like a fly in his iron gauntlet.

I changed my position and stared out of the window: I remembered how in daytime the jackdaws wheeled before and around the circular abbey tower which had lain untouched these four hundred years. I had nothing I could say or could do, nothing – except glare back again at my benefactor and now destroyer.

I began to reel as the truth of the disclosure bit more and more into me. That swine my father? I simply could not believe it. I swayed round and toppled over backwards. I found myself fighting for air as my beloved room in St Alban's Abbey, where I had devoured the contents of so many great books, swam and pirouetted before my very eyes.

All three of them were staring at me. 'Adam,' gently spoke the good monk. 'I have some urgent work for you. Part of my chronicle. Two copies please, one for Lady Katherine, to whom it was promised, the other for posterity.'

He pushed over towards me a neatly tied score of pages.

I could say no more. With a mighty effort of will I seized hold of the copying chore. My thoughts pounded on, unstoppable. Sir Hugh had been – since I knew him or had known of him – and even now was an influence on me, hadn't he, an act or example *not* to be followed? Yet buried in him must also have been the good in me that could never have found the way to express itself. For as I knew I myself was good, so must he have been – and if good, so much of that must have been recognized – able to see the good that was in Katherine, and wanted to make it live for both of them, so that they could have shared a happy life together.

They continued to stare at me. They must have thought I had lost my wits. I had to cling to something, if only to go on calling the brother 'father', as I used to as a child.

'Can you tell me, father, for so I shall go on calling you…who my mother is?'

I saw the curiosity light up in my master's eyes. Perhaps at last we could give his speculation the conclusive lie.

'Was,' answered Walsingham coldly. 'She is dead.'

I had my old room in the Abbey, and that was a comfort. It reminded me of the former days of Thomas de la Mare who was abbot when I grew up. St Albans had been then, and still was, the premier religious house in England. Because of our abbot's strict rule, we did not live like most monks in personal luxury, hunting and hawking. But he was not as remote as he looked either, but human and understanding. I benefited from the daily cycle of services, for Abbot de la Mare perfected these by more chanting, slower recitation and fewer prayers. I fasted often which explained how, although my appearance counted against me, my health remained good and I would possibly live long. I knew as a child, like the monks, the rigours of a rough bed, a hair shirt, regular flogging, early rising and constant attendance at services, but also to perform the most menial tasks with grace and a good heart.

There were many of us now crowded into the great abbey gateway, which the abbot had done much to beautify. As I ascended the winding stone stair I tiptoed past many sleeping forms, and many tossing or snoring bodies. I was relieved for once on this journey to be away from my master, and not to know for once where he slept.

This had been my home. How could they do this to me, tell me I was not who I believed myself to be, I who had always embraced virtue, chastity, abstinence, rigorous intellectual pursuit, all the holy aspirations, such as peacefulness, wishing no ill to any man…. . How could I be put in a box, associated by blood, with that beast, that raging boar, that ferocious wild animal…?

Yet I was his bastard son…and now Katherine of Lancaster was demoted to being my stepmother; so wouldn't I deserve the fortune or harm that might accrue to her in her future life? Although we had no inkling of what it might mean in the future, I was now part of her family, tied in even more closely to her fortune and fate, and those of my master, who, monstrously, had become some kind of relation. The conflict was terrible: how to deal with this surge of anger, yet also a surge of something else, the forever squashed energy

I always had, perhaps instinctively knowing it was this which I had always been obliged to keep down, stifle at all costs, because of the harm it could have brought me. Yet what if the evil in him had brought out so much the worst in Katherine, that she had conspired to do away with him, because the ill he put on her was so suffocating that she might have, heaven forbid, have been justified before God even in her desire to plan or plot his death? Was this what my master had seen? Did I not have to find out for myself, just as I was on this journey with Katherine herself? The inner and outer dangers seemed unspeakable and without limit, not least having to face the monster of my father in myself…

Alone at last I pulled off my belt and sat down on my bed to remove my shoes. I suddenly realized how tired I was. I pulled off my doublet, then peeled down my hose and threw them on the prie-dieu. I lay on my back, and thought I would take off my chemise. It felt sweaty and grimy on my body. I closed my eyes for a moment and let my head sink back on to the feather pillow. Then I felt a pinching, and something tugging at my eyelids. I heard a chirping sound and thought in the moment of horror that jackdaws were pecking at my eyes.

I heard an urgent sweet voice, saying, 'Open your eyes, Adam. Open your eyes!' And I realized it was Susanna, my old cook's daughter, gently trying to prise my eyelids open.

'Help,' I said. I glimpsed moonlight, a further waning moon. I rolled away, buried my face in the pillow.

The tormenting voice paid no attention. 'Adam, open your eyes.' Gentle though she was I knew she would continue saying this, over and over again, until I lost my mind and I had this image of this same Susanna, as a tiny little girl of four or five, doing exactly this, which of course she knew, while those many years ago I would plead tiredness not to be awoken. I rolled onto my back.

'Adam is still tired.'

'Adam open your eyes. Open your eyes.'

I had no choice but to obey. She had slipped out of what she was wearing, and she became outlined against the moon, and I saw the kind of phantom glow around her as if the moon's nimbus had become her own, softly tracing the gently round shape of thighs, breasts, shoulders. As she turned the silver light washed her like a lake of luminous water. Her lustrous eyes, for the moment paler in hue than the black, for they had been paler than the shadows of the stone garret, reached me where I lay on my back, and I was stricken with excitement and fright.

I did not want to take my eyes off her. I had never felt such appetite excercized by one person on another in such a soft and piteous way. It was one thing to squeeze out influence – either gently or crushingly as circumstances guided – of another such as my master, quite another to find oneself in the suction or jaws of such a dancing swell. And then she smiled, so light innocence and health left me breathless, denying all slights and subtleties of woman. In a gesture so innocent it startled me she knelt and put her head back so that I was able to see as an unbroken line the soft underside of her jaw, the moulding of her throat, the abrupt thrust of her breasts.

It was a sign fraught with naked privacy, a gesture that was primitive, a kind of unmasking, revealing an intent that was a confession that went beyond lovemaking. It was the kind of show one wild cat or dog made to another, the surrender of an uncovered spot, an obedience that said, without use of words, I will starve to death to do your will.

And in the breathless second I knew my desire for this girl surpassed all that I had ever wanted before.

Later, alone, I could not sleep.

It had been awful, foul, rotten, detestable and loathsome. I was benumbed, spineless, shattered, unhinged. How could I have been so caponized and gelded? Was it the punishment for rape, and my master's rape at that? Oh how the shame burnt!

I felt for the skin of my legs. Bare skin. I felt higher. Bare skin…I had nothing on… . A delicate neck and throat was above me. Two light hands touched the underside of the arms and down to the armpits, then down my sides; stopped at the hip-bones, pushed in slightly on them… . Then, then she picked up… . Oh horror, horror, I felt an overwhelming desire to be inviolable… . Here, she said, guiding my hands to her breasts. They were warm and firm. But even with my anger, I was slipping towards disaster…I closed my eyes while my entire moral being continued to protest against the abject surrender to animality, this blatant pandering to the basest instincts… . She teased my face with her exuberant young breasts…this suddenly erect girl… . I opened my eyes but I was beyond words, could only answer with a baleful stare, unbelieving of what was happening, as Susanna – or was it Susanna, or was it someone else? – suspended on her arms, lowered her loins, cambered, arched, adjusted… . Boing! I was sunk, buried deep, cased.

Rape, this is rape, I thought…

This is rape.

But I'm not half your strength…

From the gateway I wandered out into the grassy March freshness of Romeland, as it used to be called it when it was my playground. Here was slippery mud too, peppered with tiny holes, covered with little earthpits of excreting worms. I was confused, light-minded, released yet scratchy, jittery and deeply unquiet. What had I done but tasted the delights of the flesh which I imagined unimaginable and forever beyond me, finding them real, pure and innocent delectation? With no shame or blame attached.

I wandered on and on, down towards the river, and here, unable to make sense of it, from behind an old decaying wall I heard two voices. Were they real? Yes – they were those of my master and the duchess of Lancaster. Katherine. No less than Katherine. My new stepmother. Earlier she had determinedly avoided my eyes. Had this been because of my father? Had she killed him? If so she must have been as confused as I was.

I crouched and listened to what they were saying.

'My bitterness over those years has never left me, Geoffrey. This is why I am so distant from you. When Lord John left me and married Constanza of Castile, and just as soon, after making me pregnant with John, made her pregnant, my anger with you knew no bounds.'

'Katherine, I swear to God I didn't want it to turn out like that,' answered my master.

'You did all you could to make me yield to John.'

'I reasoned with him all I could that he should marry you.'

'Both you and Philippa, who was promoted by John to manage Constanza's household, ignored and denied me. I am sure you remembered how I felt sick to death.'

'I made a mistake,' conceded my master. 'But John had so many royal duties to perform. The marriage with Castile was ordered by his dying father to save France. He had no pleasure in lying with her.'

'These excuses didn't convince me then, and don't now! I had to suffer, don't you see that Geoffrey? Suffer all the time. I suffered the poison of gossip which Constanza fed with tales of how John used me as his whore – '

'You became the model of suffering...'

'Yes, Geoffrey, in your dreams or pictures I was this. No doubt you used me as a model. But you didn't see *into* me.'

I bit my lip as I listened, for my master had always told me that his example for Griselda, that pattern of patient suffering in the Clerk's Tale, had been his sister-in-law: how false to the reality of what she had been through!

'Well,' said my master: 'You were determined to remain his woman and die so.'

'Yes, this was so.'

'I proposed others.'

'Thank heaven I did not let such cynical counsel prevail.'

'Well,' said my master. He quoted '...."Or can we arrive at paradise through suffering?" ' The gentle tone was my master's special irony, in which he encased so many of his thoughts. This subtlety of humour was lost on women, who take everything at its face value, so I feared my master should have given prior warning of his jocular shadow.

'Oh Geoffrey,' exploded Katherine as I expected. 'I hate you! My trust in him was total. He took me, he had all of me. I gave him my complete love and fidelity!' She raged on. I had to admit it endowed her with awesome majesty, enhancing no end the power of her beauty.

'I know, I know,' my master said again, attempting to soothe her. 'So why did he withdraw from me even more, why and how did he come to renounce me so that I was then deprived even of his visits?... Then he sent a man of law with a document to sign: he would provide for my children, but neither of us could make any legal claim upon the other...'

Her thoughts tumbled out without order or design: who would not want to feel chastened in this turbulent stream?

'It was the peasants' revolt. That great upheaval of hatred and murder which was solely directed at him.' My master vainly tried to muster more excuses.

'...When word came to me of his confession, and that he would never see me again I threw myself down on my bed, proposing never again to rise from it...'

'You are going to read John's confession, Katherine. When my scribe has copied it... . It will explain.' My master tried again to bring her to a halt.

'Your scribe, your scribe, Geoffrey!' she regained, or rather sustained more, her violent recriminating tone. 'And what am I to make of what the brother said? – your scribe indeed! My stepson! What do you think this brings back to me? That violent, bestial monster's misbegotten little chiseller...'

Enough. I had heard enough. Sick, my ears buzzing, tears starting from my eyes at these sad and awful recriminations, I returned to my room. But the shock made me determined more than ever not to wallow in self-misery. By insult I was braced up. To my task and my duty.

Dawn was streaking the sky as I began to read and copy the document of confession. I had no need of a lamp, but suddenly I could not but wonder at the awesome importance of the pages that my spiritual father had placed in my hands.

TWENTY

Brother Thomas Walsingham

1st Confession of Lord John of Gaunt to Brother Thomas Walsingham, St Albans' Scriptorium, 16 October 1381

Walsingham: You seem, my lord, to have a poor opinion of women, and never talk to any of them much, or listen to them, except to further your own designs upon them.

Lord John: I flatter all women. I never engage in challenging them or arguing with them. It is only men who cannot satisfy their desire who seek to subjugate them by argument or other means of making them comply. As in battle, so in love. I am never prepared to sacrifice my pride by conceding victory to another.

Walsingham: When did you first indulge in carnal intercourse?

Lord John: The first woman I loved was Marie de St Hilaire, a tall and voluptuous Flemish lady who was married. She instructed me, and I did as I was commanded. I was sixteen. She taught me courtesy towards her sex, and I began by being respectful towards the wishes of those ladies who lusted after me.

Walsingham: You were a very young man! Did it not change?

Lord John: It changed when I was married. At first I was faithful and held Blanche in the highest regard and warmest affection. Then in time I did not believe any corporeal connection with others could interfere with my love for my wife.

Walsingham: Did she know of your attachment to other women? Such as...Philippa Payne de Roet?

Lord John: Secrecy was essential.

Walsingham: So you gave her up as soon as someone else, Geoffrey Chaucer for example, found out about her?

Lord John: That is so, brother.

Walsingham: Why did you not stop seeing other women?

Lord John: It was about this time, 1366 or 1367, after the birth of my son and heir Henry, and having left once more for France, that I grew impatient and full of desire. I could not bear these absences from Blanche and resented them; perhaps it was campaigning which inflamed my constant itch. Who could refuse delicious intrigues with free-hearted women of beauty, sentiment, and spirit?

Walsingham: I find it hard to trust your spirit of penitence. You do not seem very contrite.

Lord John: To be honest I could never satisfy these strong instincts basely, although in France they have desirable and skilled courtesans. But how could I refuse with an amiable woman of good standing, who would grant genuine reciprocal affection and pleasure?

Walsingham: Are you saying it depended on the lady's class?

Lord John: I have to maintain my rank.

Walsingham: I do not understand why you could not say no.

Lord John: It was expected of me. It went with my position.

Walsingham: So why do you now think it fit to make your confession? Perhaps you should return when you feel better disposed.

Lord John's 2nd Confession to Brother Thomas Walsingham, 1381

Walsingham: We come to the time, twelve years ago, when Geoffrey Chaucer read you his poem, 'The Book of the Duchess'. It sounds to me as if you and Chaucer began a conspiracy to keep chivalry as an ideal alive, while serving your and his ends to seduce and bed the lady of your desire.

Lord John: Chaucer convinced me that it was an allegory for divine love, that in serving my mistress sexually I was serving God...in a way (Here the duke paused and reflected). But I was muddled.

Walsingham: I am not surprised. Wasn't the physical possession of a woman, wasn't this considered in the courtly ideal the profanation of true love? Sir Lancelot betrays love in the Arthurian tale by his sin against it – he commits carnal intercourse with Guinevere. This is why he fails to find the Holy Grail, this is why countless times he is humiliated. He has chosen the earthly road. He has consummated his love.

Lord John: I think this is meant, Brother Thomas, rather in the nature of a paradox: if to love with a pure passion is the supreme virtue, then how can yielding to physical sensuality be the supreme sin? The ideal of courtly love is to be plunged into a secret, even an adulterous passion for some seemingly unattainable lady who has been placed on a pedestal.

Walsingham: Man has always adapted spiritual aims to earthly ends. Turning adulterous love into an ideal – even if never consummated – is heresy. Passionate love is a heresy. The court of your father never recognized this. The heresy of passionate love is called Catharism, and it began in Florence. The Catharist idealized the Gospels and treated love in all its forms as a leap out of the created world. The craving for this flight into the divine – this 'enthusiasm' – and its ultimately impracticable transgression of human limitations was bound to find expression, and so to betray itself, through the magnification in divine terms of human love. The rhetoric of courtly love developed from this love's 'arrow that wounds but does not kill' into the way passion sets you apart, rendering every other kind of love colourless; into how love is a 'purifying' emotion, and the substitution of this will of love for the real will; into the 'stolen' heart; and, above all, into love treated as the ultimate 'understanding'. To any rational being this is nonsense.

Lord John: I confess, brother, I went through all this. With Chaucer as my guide.

Walsingham: Please have no illusions, Lord John, about your being just an ordinary fornicator. Your fornication was a deliberate, willed, and malicious sin. Backed by an ideal, a false ideal.

Lord John: I came to the point, father, where no one trusted me. Large numbers of my people wished to see me dead. I believed this was mainly due to my arrogance, my aloofness. But can it really be that it was my sin, my adultery, which has torn the country apart?

Walsingham: As a figure-head you are an example to your kingdom. This is why I conducted in my so-called 'scurrilous' chronicle a campaign against you. Not for your incontinent, mindless, or promiscuous lechery – not being able to help oneself is the weakness of an unrestrained drunkard. But yours is a true sin of the flesh. You have the highest ideal, love for your country, a fine intellect, a controlling will, and still you dedicated yourself to sin in a full awareness of what you were doing. Do you wonder why knightly standards are in decline!

Lord John: Do you not think, brother, this has come about because marriages are arranged, my own included, and no one makes a free choice of their partner? (The duke laughed.) Except for Chaucer, who married the woman he wanted. Poor fellow!

Walsingham: No. Like all passionate people you revel – revel foolhardily – in the sense of power which comes over you when you are in deadly peril. Man commits most adultery to create excitement. But *you* have to accept the limits of your terrestrial vocation. Man has the obligation to place himself, as St John of the Cross said, at the centre of his humility. Are you prepared once and for all to renounce your long habit of adultery and fornication, and to become a true prince? (Here Duke John became silent.)

Lord John's third confession to Brother Thomas Walsingham, 1381

Walsingham: So now you argue that your love-making to Lady Swynford was chaste?

Lord John: It was, Brother Thomas, a chaste desire. I revere Katherine. We are told lust has no part in love. I wonder whether it is not an essential part, just as remorse or penitence can be a prelude to danger.

Walsingham: This is sophistry, my good lord. You are not married to Katherine Swynford. As I understand it, you have had with your mistress some seven or eight years of consummated passion. She has borne you four children out of wedlock. You have paraded her everywhere, mingled your legitimate seed with her unlawful children. She is measured by the frailty of her sex, her dependence, and her motherhood. But you cannot be. Ever.

Lord John: I still fail to see the connection between my country and my private conduct.

Walsingham: Your pride prevents you from submitting to that part of your nature that is good. You seek to defend, to justify this love. Why do you obstinately refuse to own up to your fault? What is stopping you?

Lord John: Chaucer. I am loyal to him. He is a great man, a true philosopher and an original and fine poet. He defends my love and my honour. To renounce my love would be to reject him.

Walsingham: You say that Chaucer wanted you to marry Lady Swynford?

Lord John: He did.

Walsingham: But you married Constanza of Castile instead.

Lord John: This was my duty. My father who was on his sickbed summoned me. His mistress, Alice Perrers, sat out of sight behind a screen. 'You have a mind to keep Lady Swynford, your beautiful mistress,' he said. 'You are too young to remain unmarried. The duchy of Aquitaine is faltering and soon we shall lose it. Constanza, the elder daughter of the usurped King Peter is promised to you, and by these means, with the Castilian navy and the money to support us, we have a powerful ally with which to hold on to France.'

Walsingham: Wouldn't it have been more sensible to let Aquitaine go?

Lord John: My father had a stronger argument. He would have liked me, he told me, more than any of his other sons to have his crown, for I would have made the best king. He insisted that this marriage would be solely a contract, and that I could amuse myself elsewhere as I pleased.

Walsingham: You took his advice?

Lord John: I had but one aim in mind with Constanza, to make her pregnant and then be free again to visit Katherine.

Walsingham: So you and Constanza were hardly man and wife?

Lord John: Yes.

Walsingham: In this world there is only one way to enjoy carnal knowledge without hindrance to the honour and dignity of a Christian prince – which is to marry where you desire. If your burden is tied to your back you can do something with it. If you drag about you such a burden without marriage your hands will always be so full you can do nothing. Besides, in getting to know one wife, if he truly loves her, a man gets to know all women better than if he knew thousands of them.

Fourth Confession of John of Gaunt to Brother Walsingham, 1381

Walsingham: At last you have made your full confession. Sin is an offence against God. It is not necessarily an offence against man. Your sin comes first in the list Paul makes in his letter to the Galatians: 'Fornication, impurity, licentiousness.'

Lord John: I have denied the connection I know. These disorders, this uprising of the common folk against their masters, have much to do with my adultery.

Walsingham: These disorders have *everything* to do with your adultery. One sin makes an accomplice of another and together they spread through the structure of a land into its noblest and most holy institutions.

Lord John: Our Lord Jesus, whose kingship I admit over my own, for he was the mightiest prince of us all, came down in the very hour of our darkness to sacrifice himself. This secretly, I hope, will be the source from which will come the forgiveness of my sins.

Walsingham: Can you give up Lady Swynford? (Here Lord John sighed.) There is nothing to stop you loving Lady Swynford chastely. You are a married man. It would be continued disobedience to God to go on fulfilling your passion with her. You have lost your palace, and some of your most faithful servants, murdered because of the outrage you have committed against the laws of God. Your concupiscence encourages in others the concupiscence of violence. All these sins are interchangeable, and one leads to another. Victims of sin in turn become contagious carriers of evil, and repeat on others the sins committed on them. Adultery is as spreading as the plague.

Lord John: I have wounded myself enough, Father. I truly and deeply repent.

Walsingham: It will mean a re-orientation of your whole life, a return and a conversion to God. You must give yourself a new heart. You must cherish and bring those children up in the light of your repentance, and in God's mercy with hope in the help of His Grace. You must adopt a salutary pain and sadness, the *animi cruciatus* and *compunctio cordis* that will free from your sin those children of yours.

Lord John: Oh God! How my heart is heavy and burdened.

Walsingham: Fix your eyes on Christ's blood, and understand how precious it is to his Father, for, poured out for our salvation, it has brought repentance to the whole world.

Twenty-one

Scriven

READING THESE CONFESSIONS TURNED my head beyond endurance. With the arrival of daylight I spun with contradiction and confusion. I decided to rise, dress, and go to early service. I hungered for the salving comfort of communion when the sweet body of Jesus would enter my own body and strengthen me, and I could pray to my name saint who through so much danger and vicissitude had kept me alive. So murder had been the end result. The murder of Swynford, my father, by Lancaster.

Was this what Geoffrey in Leicester had seen and remarked on, the night before we began our journey? I had to find this out for myself, and my source would be Katherine.

I had started copying the fifth confession when I fell instantly asleep on my straw mattress. When I awoke I called out violently.

'What is the matter?' asked a quiet, calm voice.

'I had a dream,' I answered with a choking sound from deep within my throat, then coughed and spluttered till I regained my breath. 'Two bears and two bulls were in an arena let loose to destroy each other in a frenzy of claws, horns and teeth, and thrashing hooves!!'

'Easy, easy.' My master stretched out his hand and placed it on my forehead, which was cold and wet as a cellar stone. 'Just a nightmare, Adam.'

I groaned. 'Oh Christ forgive me, but what a pain I have in my head!'

'Let's hope it's not the bloody flux.'

I moaned and writhed. On my lips there was discoloured slime, and in a glass I saw my glistening face was greenish. I began to vomit and purge all over the place.

'I'll fetch a draft of physic and water,' said my master. He was swiftly gone. My heart beat thunderously fast, and I wiped the sweat from my brow, trying to lull myself with calming words and thoughts. Too much had happened, too much had gone on. There was a smell, and I wondered if it was not Death come to find me. I doubled over with spasm, and began to vomit again, this time into a basin. My master returned. He gave me water from a washing pitcher in a cup and with it mixed powder to swallow.

'The bloody struggle, the bear and the bull – the bear has you by the throat, Adam!'

His eyes widened with compassion and he looked down at me. He bent and kissed my forehead. I subsided into silence. I crossed myself. My breathing steadied. A calm descended on me. I was saved. I was going to live.

I looked around my bed. My leather pouch, with Philippa's bundle of disclosures in it, had gone. Someone had taken it. Now who could that be?

Prime was so soothing, the singing of the psalms gave me time to reflect on my sin of concupiscence (and the disgust and despair) with Susanna. At least I had been reluctant, at least I had held back, pushed the girl into…increasing her provocation. But then, how she tickled me, how she fought, how she had used every guile of advance and retreat to trigger me into arousal. I had wanted to stand back, to the very last moment I had wanted to refuse.

But then, when it happened, when at last I could hold myself back no longer, but shouted with joy or pain, I could not tell which – often had I heard, just like my master, that there was joy in heaven and pain in hell, but as I had not been in either place I could not vouch for the truth of it – the moment of great release, of spiritual ecstasy, as well as of physical pleasure, had overwhelmed me.

Here was something quite odd. The confessions of King David the psalmist had become linked in my mind with John of Gaunt, and with my father. Had Katherine Payne de Roet been Bathsheba?

They were all here.

Afterwards as we left the dark cathedral for the rain-washed bright March air my master asked: 'You haven't noticed, have you? I'm surprised, Adam. It's so unlike you not to.'

Noticed what? His words hit me like a hammer.

'What in heaven do you mean now?' I lashed out in anger. Everyone was attacking me.

He stood here, grinning: 'Stop, Adam,' he said. 'Breathe in deeply. Reflect. You are exhausted. Overwrought.'

I obeyed. 'Well?'

'I ask if you have noticed anything different.'

So caught up as I had been in contrary currents of guilt and satisfaction, physical and emotional release, so preoccupied with my own sin, that I had even failed to recognize the subject he brought up.

'No, nothing different. Should I have noticed anything?'

'Well, just now you walked past the hearse of Lord John. So did I.'

'Yes?'

'And you noticed nothing? Not even when the coffin was opened for holy water and incense to be sprinkled from the censer?'

I was deeply puzzled. What on earth was the devious, playful mind of my master up to now? 'Not in particular.'

'Not the smell?'

'No.'

'Adam, I simply don't believe it!' My master stared at me in dismay. 'It's you who've been going on endlessly about the taint of sin, and the effect it has on the body of a dead man!' He spoke gently, as if to a simple child. 'I tell you, Adam, the corpse no longer smells of decaying mortality. Go and find out for yourself.'

I hesitated. Who was I to care any more? I grudgingly went back into the cathedral and sniffed indifferently at John's body. What had he ever been to me? What was he to me now?

It was true. Something had happened which might only be described as a miracle. Was it a holy one, a true miracle, or was it an evil deception of the enemy? John's corpse no longer stank of rotting and decaying flesh like a bloated and putrescent whale. Smitten as I was with remorse over my own lechery and uncleanliness, I instantly fell prostrate on my face in awe at the wondrous purification.

And I was not the only one, for there were dozens who did as I did, in lines, heads bowed, fervently praying. Staring upwards from his royal cart John's face in its repose had been transformed into something other than it was before, and it appeared handsome and brave, with an expression of peace, and even joy.

Outside the cathedral I rejoined my master.

'Well, Adam,' he said with an affectionate glance. 'Are you convinced that he has been freed from the shackles of his great sin?'

'Not altogether. It seems too sudden. How has it come about? What is your explanation?' I was lost for further words on the subject. Perhaps, I thought in a mad moment, it had something to do with my copying of his confessions, that they were now published for the world. 'But Mr Chaucer,' I heard myself say, 'I cannot really believe in this manifestation of God's will that Lord John's soul is no longer tainted with perdition and crime.'

'Well, for a start, he no longer can have had anything to do with the death of Swynford, can he? That's cleared up one suspect.'

'But Katherine, what about her? – '

His tone became resolute. 'Believe me, Adam, she is innocent.'

'Then who killed the old knight?'

'You mean who killed your father...'

I looked at him angrily. 'If you do not mind, master. I don't see much in Swynford to address myself to his memory with any intimacy.'

'Yet unfortunately, Adam, he was your father. This is exactly what he was.' He stopped. He regarded me a long time in silence, peering into my face with deep and menacing curiosity. 'What has happened to you, Adam? Is it just this news? What did you do last night?'

I turned away. My master was about to find out my secret. I could not face this. I would refuse to own up.

'There are rumours...' he continued gently, 'that in the kitchen, Adam, well you know...'

'No,' I wriggled to escape. I cleared my throat noisily. 'Mr Chaucer, it has always been your contention that power and strategy are complicated forms of self-delusion, that they corrupt, just as the magician is engulfed by his own magical powers, and the madman's self-protective manias destroy him. And most of all the politician, such as Lord John had been all his life, the power he built around him eats away and corrodes him until he is dust. How then, in heaven's name,' I paused for a moment and looked at him directly in the eye. 'How has it come to pass that God has forgiven Lord John?'

Confronting my master with such a thick and knotty problem made him forget his amusement for a moment or two over the rumours maliciously spread about me. I had put him off balance.

'Well, Adam,' he said. 'What is better than wisdom? Answer: woman. And what is better than a good woman? Nothing.'

'I've heard this somewhere before.'

'You copied it. Chaucer's Tale of Melibee.'

'The dullest of the lot.' My master appeared stung to the quick. His vanity was wounded.

'An evasive reply, master.' I continued trying to be conciliatory. 'Is it a sign that in a short while Lord John's soul will be received into heaven?'

'We hope and pray. But I fear you falter, Adam, while you should rejoice at another's salvation.'

'Another's salvation, another's salvation? Why should I rejoice at that? We have travelled here with two unsolved murders. And now I find I am the bastard of a brute. Not to mention the son of my master's cast-off mistress.'

'Forget the last. Brother Walsingham has dismissed the idea. Come, come, Adam. You torment yourself unnecessarily.'

'Well, shall I die with the mystery of who my mother was unsolved, and of who killed my father?' He said nothing. 'As usual I suppose Brother Walsingham will say no more. It's all very well for you, master,' I continued, 'You can lose yourself in an abstract argument on the nature of the soul's immortality, or disappear with Plato into his cave of the real and the ideal. You know where you come from.'

I stung him again with the truth, for he shuddered a little and drew his scarlet robe tight about him.

But he remained silent. I tried something different to provoke him into making a reply.

'You'll be telling me next I ought to go on a pilgrimage!'

This goaded him into a sharper reply. 'Why, Adam, have you sinned, or are you ill?' he asked quickly, although not losing his tone of concern.

'No, master,' I answered. 'With all due respect it's you who are sick. You want Lord John to go to heaven before you because you think he is going to clear the path ahead, just as he cleared it for you on earth. You won't accept responsibility for yourself, master. You've hidden behind your double, Lord John, just as you've hidden behind the characters you've created. Then when you had enough of them you creep out from them, leaving them behind as worn-out husks. Finally you paint your confession in subtle colours, and this serves the more to conceal your sins.'

Silence. At this point my master sought to inject a humorous vein into the conversation as a way out. He took advantage of the silence to lead it in another direction.

'Adam, what actually did happen to you last night?'

I ignored this, for my indignation was mounting fast. 'You sold your sister-in-law to the richest man in England! You exploited for your verses all those around you ...'

'Adam, you are going too far! I'll have to call Robert Wydeville...'

'It's no good thinking of him, he's gone back to Leicester. No, master, you know very well what's at the bottom of all this.'

'I know...? What, Adam? I do not understand.'

I could contain myself no longer. I burst out. I howled. 'It's you!!! You, master!! YOU WILL NOT OWN UP TO RAPING CECILIA CHAUMPAIGNE!!!'

My master stared at me. He instantly looked exhausted and ill. His jaw sagged and the skin of his usually rosy and pouchy cheeks drooped. My charge had affected him. At last. Deep lines of weariness and fatigue ate into his face. Yet even here a very faint smile crept over the bluish-tinged lips. He murmured, 'How and why, has this paltry affair become so important to you, Adam? I do not understand. Moreover you are building a whole castle of superstition on one word...'

'Me, me,' I answered, 'It's important not only to me. But to the world, to everyone!'

'You flatter me. I should be surprised if anyone is interested. But no, Adam, this allegation of rape happened nineteen years ago. Then, as now, there are lots of incentives for crying rape, as did that young woman. Revenge, attention, sympathy, money. She withdrew the allegation, remember, on payment of ten pounds. The price of my whole yearly stipend from Lord John. I had to sell my family home in Thames Street. Anyway, you exaggerate the importance of rape. All women suffer some sexual indecency from men during their lifetime. The reverence once enjoyed by women has been eroded.'

'I thought you supported and defended women.'

He drew his hand over his mouth as if to conceal a smile. 'I do. But it is as much up to women to restore this reverence, as it is up to men to observe it. Look how you...' he pulled up short. He could not stop himself. He gave himself away. He smiled. 'We won't go into that.'

I was irritated. 'It is you, master, who devalues sex by treating it as a bodily function, or an animal need for mere pleasure.'

'One can be mistaken.' I must have looked confused, so he continued patiently to explain. 'Often saying "no" can be part of the game.'

I bit my lip. Could this be true of me too? No, I could not face in myself the possibility of this. At all costs I must not. By my insistent shrinking had I not been raped by Susanna, as Adonis was by Venus? How I missed Rachel, and the clear-sighted wisdom she could have given me at this moment.

My master seized the opportunity of my evident doubts to continue, 'Rape, I'm afraid Adam, is an ever-expanding definition. Any woman allowing herself to be alone with a man runs the risk of rape.'

He paused a moment then continued.

'And are you saying, Adam, that I took advantage of Cecilia Chaumpaigne? If so, I am afraid the answer is no. My friend, I would not lie to you. As I told you before Cecilia was naked, and if voluntary nakedness occurs there can't be rape… . She…'

He was still secretive. He was still hiding something. Yet I had reached my limit. I saw red. I had been pushed too far by my master. By his evasiveness. By the slippery, many-sidedness of his soul. But also by everything else. 'Mr Chaucer,' I shouted, 'You lie. You are no more than a murderous rapist and brute! You procure for your muse, you make mankind vulnerable, expose them in their failings, most of all in love. But it's you who have the gravest fault of all!'

I could not stop. I began to hurl obscenities at him. Soon I turned to shouting blasphemies. I felt an increasing horrible surge of violence in me, the energy blazed with a terrible force through me as I felt myself about to be overcome by the black ecstasy of destruction. My master took no notice of this ominous change. Or if he did see, he chose to ignore it. He adopted a brisk, matter-of-fact tone as he sought to soothe and dominate me with his argument.

'No adultery, Adam! No adultery without penetration. Law of England. Technically nothing happened. You can close the curtains and forget it. A man, if he knows what is good for him, wants a soft, mild, biddable woman to look after him, not a clever, hot-headed siren… . Carnality is a funny thing, Adam.'

He drew himself up, as if possessed of a noble and disinterested emotion.

'Master, stop it,' I heard myself saying, 'stop it, or I don't know!!...'

He turned. And here he tipped me over the rim. Into the pit of violence and dark despair. 'You attack me because of one obvious reason. Here is your cause of this so-called, pure search for the truth! It is self-interest, pure self-interest, as is all your harsh and severe strutting and intellectual insistence on the right to truth, all your prying subservience to fact and circumstance... . Nothing is more violent than to pass judgment on others. Adam, you're saying all this because you are yourself the issue of a rape.'

To suggest I am the issue of rape is to hit below the belt in the genitals, which my master identifies as the centre of man. He always insisted that this organ of generation was the physical centre of the body. Dante placed the bond between potential and act in the centre of creation. There lies the difference. My master had pushed me beyond endurance. I could stand no more insult or teasing.

Uncontrollable rage seized me. I found my hands at his throat.

Twenty-two

Chaucer

COULD MY SCRIVENER HAVE throttled his master? I am sure his intention was not so murderous, but he gripped me with a strength I could not believe he owned, then shook me like a cur. I shouted for help and then he threw me down on the ground. It was monstrous behaviour, yet he was so angry he could not stop himself. No one came to my help. He stood menacingly over me, breathing heavily, trying to hold himself back from doing me more harm, such as kicking in my head. I rose slowly to my feet, brushing the dust off my clothes, groggy and with aching head.

'Adam,' I tried to say as mildly as I could. 'Come with me. I have pushed you into such anger and rage, so it is I who must take the blame for your violence.'

'But I could have killed you, master! You don't understand.'

I nodded sorrowfully. 'I said too much of a wounding nature. I lacerated your own deep division. I wanted the power to silence you. This was because you wanted to know too much, and I simply did not want to tell you the whole truth...'

'I am frightened of my own rage.'

I could see this only too well as he was still shaking with fury.

'All of us have the wish some time or other to murder someone. But the will to carry it out is rarely there. The truth is indeed very different from what you imagine...'

I beckoned and he followed me meekly to a stone recess just out of sight behind the main porch of the cathedral. His rage had chastened me, but he was still beside himself with the enormity of his own violence.

'Truth can certainly kill,' I said to Adam, rubbing my neck ruefully, but the irony was lost on him. 'I shall let you into a deep secret. You must swear never to repeat this to a soul. Most of what I said about Cecilia Chaumpaigne is true. Most of it, but by no means all…'

I shifted my position, and contrary to the manner in which I had talked to him on previous occasions, I could feel that my pose and demeanour had become assured and confident, my voice low, discreet, and direct. From where had this power come, if not from the shock of Adam's assault?

'It is true that I was first asked to approach Cecilia because of my connection with Lord John, who was, I agree with you, in many ways my double – living out for me the life which I, a retiring writer and royal servant, could not live out in action myself. You may draw from this whatever conclusion you like with regard to Katherine.

'But where I glossed over the truth was when it came to Cecilia's rending of her clothes, and her claims that I raped her. I am afraid the whole business was considerably more contrived than this.' Here the confidence vanished and I could feel my voice become grounded, like a boat upon the rocky shore. I desperately needed a drink. 'But, Adam, I am parched. Will you go and fetch me a drink from the sacristy? In there is a tap from the well where the water is cool and crystal clear.'

Scriven was most reluctant to leave, but he could, at least, see that I could not say much more without a reviving drink. One thing more I managed to say to him before he left in search of this. For as I walked away the residuum or deeper implication of his reaction sank in: 'Please don't forget, Adam, not the worst of rape, but worse by far in my view, is that for every rape committed there are a hundred avid ears who mentally and emotionally take part in its report. Are those who swallow filth any worse than those who commit it? Yet they can, while feeding this evil side, absolve themselves. They can pat themselves on the back for their virtue and superiority. It is not they who will be strung up for the crime.'

Twenty-three

Scriven

I WAS STILL MORE than eager to boot him in his 'moon', or 'centre of creation'.

But what about those last words of his, still ringing in my ears: was my obsession with this rape something to do with my own repressed nature, and had my master hit upon the truth about me by implying that I had suffered all this, unknowing, because of a stigma of nature, having been brought into this world by an obscene, ungodly act? I myself was the testament of impurity.

While I made my way around to the sacristy as hurriedly as I could, for I could not wait to hear the rest, I came across, suddenly and unexpectedly, Susanna. She was balancing a full pitcher on her head, such as we imagine the women in the Old Testament to carry. Her carriage was so noble, so upright, her legs in their short servant's tunic so firm and well-formed, that I was just as suddenly ashamed and humbled in spirit, wondering how with this angelic creature I could have played the two-backed beast.

In spite of myself I stopped and greeted her. She gave me the most radiant and open – dare I call it loving? – of smiles.

'Why?' I cried out in pain. 'Why, Susanna?'

She stopped. Her softly moulded arms and finely tapered hands, which had been so intimate with me, lifted down the pitcher tenderly and placed it at her feet.

'Why, what's gone on with you, Adam?' There was no rancour or reproof in her soft, country tone.

Then something in her stoop, in her gesture, the innocent posture of her straight young back, I could not say exactly what it was, caused me to realize it had not been her who had come to me in the night.

It had to have been someone else.

I backed away from her. Then who was it? A phantom, a devil incarnate in woman's delectable form? The shock, the horror, was indescribable. It must have been that I had transferred my feeling for her, from earlier yesterday evening when we were alone in the kitchen, on to another, more skilled and whorish body, one who could so easily sell herself to men as in my master's unfinished Cook's tale of Perkin, and the apprentice whose wife swived for her sustenance.

'Oh no!' I tried to stifle a tortured shout. 'Oh no!' I beat my forehead with my fists.

'Are you ill? Come with me.' She reached out a hand to comfort me.

As Aristotle says, acts of the sensitive appetite are named as passions only and entirely from the effect of change they cause in the body.

Suddenly we heard a posse of horsemen arrive at the gateway, some hundred or so yards off, and there was a great flurry of activity. A boy came running over: he was one of the kitchen servants. 'Mr Adam,' he said, 'you are to join up and ride at once.'

I inquired why.

'The king!' he shouted in a voice of shrill panic. 'He plans to snatch the duke of Lancaster's body, and hurry it off to bury somewhere else!'

There was no time. I made a dash for the horses and mounted Scot. On the way out I trotted past the porch of the cathedral to retrieve my master, expecting to find him where I had left him. But, horror of horrors, he had disappeared. I could make no further search for him but was swept along in the tide of horsemen and ladies, with the cortège in their midst, hastening in a final dash for the sanctuary of the City of London. Oh, what pace we set ourselves to make for the last twenty miles or so, avoiding on our way Barnett and Mill Hill, for there it was rumoured the king had set up an ambush. You should have seen the pandemonium as the crowned heads, the dukes and duchesses, the earls and their ladies, knights and humbler retinue, came pouring past the abbey, some still not fully dressed, clutching their robes, coronets and insignia, clinging for dear life to their saddles. Such was the way to the London road filled, down steep Holywell Hill and out of the city of St Albans.

So madly intent not to lose the procession were we, and not miss the final interment, that I even became caught up helping Lady Katherine and her companion, Sister Pervil, control their palominos, and for a while I completely forgot my master. It was only some hour or so later, when there had been no ambush by the Cheshire guards, and the long procession had been swelled by a host of ordinary Hertfordshire squires and village people (Hertford had been Lord John's favourite castle near London, so his name was well regarded) that I detached myself from Lady Katherine and went again through our ranks, in search of my master. I was shattered and dismayed, for I could not find him anywhere, and believed he must have been left behind, perhaps through the effects of my own anger upon him, or weakness, or some other ill health. It probably had become all too much for him.

I rode back to Lady Katherine and conveyed my fears. Although no word on that other subject passed between us, I could see she was well aware of our changed relationship. Unless I was mistaken she would seem mindful and tender-looking towards me, as if she might become disposed to seek some exchange of mutual comfort.

We rode side by side in silence for a good four or five miles. While I had to admit that once I felt like the rest of the kingdom ready to have abandoned her as the celebrated adulteress to fate, or whatever God might have had in store for her, now Brother Walsingham had told me of my parentage I began to have some creeping feeling, if not quite an affection, towards her.

Even now, and she was near fifty, she looked remarkable in so many ways, while her proportions, as any man might see or desire, were still quite unusually perfect. But more than her beauty, she had this extraordinary quality which she had tried most of all to keep hidden from the world.

But the question remained: did she kill my father? Did she give him the sleeping draught, or, so they rumoured, block up his chimney with stone so that he became starved of air and choked to death? In her love for John she had shown nothing but selfless devotion, goodness and true humility. These were not qualities that ordinarily could be linked with murder and betrayal.

It was with such reasoning, if with caution, that I came to support her, and began to do her bidding, riding beside her as an ally and a companion. Like Aeneas, who in the ruins of burning Troy came upon the defenceless Helen, the cause of all that needless slaughter, I might once have raised my hand to cut down the guilty centre of the terror. But now I had my own moderating vision of goodness which appeared to ride beside me, and convinced me to hold my hand. In the case of Aeneas, wasn't it his own mother, gentle, placating and soothing, who had told him that to punish the beautiful, seductive Helen would be useless revenge? It would only inflame more bloody conflict between the gods, which would be passed onto mankind, so that more men and women would be hurt. While I had no such vision of my mother (indeed, who was she? – still this question had found no resolution) and had no source of gentle kindness in my heart, it was something else which restrained me. A look, possibly, from that old bent supplicant with grey hair who trotted along beside her, alert and jerky as a little old mother wren fluttering with nine babies hidden in a bush. To think of further revenge was not the way.

At sext, around midday, we could not be far off the villages near London, while the fear of ambush had receded. Later we came to halt at a chapel of Our Lady. This must have been near Tottenham, or so my neighbour advised me. We dismounted and entered the chapel, and as Lady Katherine passed the threshold of this last Benedictine outpost before the city, the congregation of monks and nuns solemnly erupted into divine sound and music with chanted psalms, and a further mass for the preparation of Lord John's soul. It was the penultimate day of mourning.

I sat down at the back of the chapel, head and arms folded over my stomach, for I was starving. Continually they went on singing, praying, these sombre and chaste Benedictines. I followed them, unaware of the words my lips were mouthing, while my head nodded mesmerically, and my heavy lids kept closing involuntarily. The long morning had been so exciting, so full of incident that, with the sudden calm, the smell of incense, the air close and constricting and if not exactly warm somehow rarified by the banks of flaring candles I nodded again, then woke, then nodded. This happened over and over again. During the Gloria I suddenly fell asleep; the chanting and regular lulling responses acted on me like a mandragora root. I slipped into a blackout so profound, a sheer dog-tiredness which was like falling over a cliff. My head was bent double over my knees, like a baby still in its mother's womb. Then, in this miasma of the soul, I left for a nether-region somewhere beyond this world, and not of any recognizable dimension, for I had a vision or dream.

SCRIVEN'S DREAM: *First of all I am travelling very fast down some narrow slope or passage-way, as one might find in deep snow upon a mountain. Up above I see an illuminated chapel, far away, perpendicular, out of reach, perfect.*

The dark region to which I descend glows with warmth and heat, and then I hear hammerers and forgers preparing instruments of war, siege engines and battering rams, catapults and cannons, halberds, shields and swords. I see sparks flying everywhere and I can hear the clamour of noisy, industrious voices shouting orders to one another.

Armed men, almost naked, wearing sandals and short skirts, carrying broadswords, greet me as I come into a wider area, and then into an opening where I behold – this takes my breath away in its devastating effect – the ancient walled city of Troy. Here are the high, fabled towers such as are described in Homer and Virgil, opulent and of unsurpassable grace and proportion, richly ornamented with gold and silver.

These Myrmidons, for such they must be, sweep me along to the tents of the invaders, those who surrounded the city and wait, or fight for its fall. I am, for so I believe, being taken to the council of the mighty warriors, such as Achilles and Ulysses, and even mighty King Agamemnon? But no, instead I find myself amongst a strange host of derelict, and quite disappointing, misfits.

There is Dame Alice, the Wife of Bath, nattering on that she has been on three pilgrimages to the Holy Land, as well as to Rome, Boulogne-sur-Mer and Galicia where she saw the shrine of St James of Compostella, and the shrine of the Three Kings in Cologne. Boisterous, adventurous and dominating is her drivel, and she boasts fulsomely how Venus brought her lust to the surface, while Mars stiffened her resolution to exploit her assets.

There is the foul-mouthed Cook, Hodge of Ware, a dry-scabbed ulcer on his shin, drinking away and shouting; there is the Miller, a quarrelsome knave, thickly built with short shoulders, a wart on his nose, flared nostrils and large, ugly mouth: he shouts at the Host, Harry Bailey, who tries to remain serene and smiling, while Godelief, his shrewish wife, tries to interrupt. There is fat Hubert the Friar, hypocritical and cynical, smarmily making a pitch for his confessions to the Franklyn, who easy-tempered and well-to-do, pats his well-nourished belly. There is the thoughtful and considerate Squire, the courtly lover, fresh as the month of May, who sings scales for choir practice and carves for his father at table.

There is both teller and tale; Palamon and Arcite, valorous yet pitiful knights of chivalry, the Shipman who steals wine from Bordeaux, the Sergeant of Law, the Summoner with his fire-red, carbuncular face, narrow eyes and black scabby eyebrows which frighten children. He is full of Latin tags such as 'Questionis quid juris', and he eats and drinks ferociously, as if his life depended on it. There is Phebus the great warrior who is jealous and kills his wife; there is the Pardoner with his yellow hair which hangs like a hank of flax, with glaring eyes and the bag he carries stuffed with fake relics: he pretends pigs' bones are the bones of saints and the pillowcase, he says, is Our Lady's veil…. All these are here, gabbling at once, stirring a fearful and mounting clamour to affright the ears. There are many others too, everyone of them from my master's tales, the poor pretty little chorister boy murdered by Jews, the Clerk of Oxford with his impossible yarn of female virtue, and then last, but not least, for he is worth more than a mention, the young knight of King Arthur's court who ravishes the innocent maid, then saves his life by answering correctly within a year what it is that women most desire, only to be condemned to marry the foul old hag who fed him the answer. She asks if he will have her foul and old but faithful, or young, fair, and maybe free with her sexual favours…. Whereupon perfect joy…she is restored to youth and beauty. Here in the fields outside Troy the knight doesn't look much of a rapist, for he has Nicholas, the carpenter's lodger, haranguing him, and Absolon on his other side, tuning his two-stringed fiddle…

Into this mixed throng, or rather rabble, for there are few fighters (I leave out Arveragus and Aurelius, the Brittany knight and squire who are honourable husband and lover of the same woman Dorigen), there struts imposingly in their midst my master, who is dressed in all manner of dilapidated and complicated armour as Sir Thopas, the lover of the elf-queen; next to him he leads Sir Oliphant, the giant.

'Gentlemen – and Dame Alice,' he calls out, rubbing his hands in glee, 'to arms, to arms! Tonight is the night we are due to capture Troy and rape her!' They raise a great ragged or rousing cheer, and those that have instruments blow them, such as the Miller his bagpipes, the Squire his flute, the Knight his trumpet, the Host his horn, the bible-clerks their violins; Walter the cruel marquess of Saluzzo beats a drum, Phebus holds up his white crow which warbles with joy, the Pardoner raspberries a counter-tenor squawk, twelve friars fart on a cartwheel, while January scrapes a pear-tree with a branding iron as if it were a cello profundo.

My master leads the great rabble out of the billowing tent and here, lo and behold, is the giant deception with which they are to capture Troy. It is not the wooden horse as famed of old; it is a great long and hollow male member, a giant priapus on which carpenters have lavished all manner of correct and well-chiselled detail, even on its accompanying testicles in their scrotal sac, with every crinkle of skin sharply crafted. Everyone crowds wonderingly and admiringly about it.

'Who's inside there –?' demands the peevish Reeve, and some surge forward as if to tap on the wooden case.

'Stand back, I command you by heaven! Stand back!' shouts my master who then waves his sword and lets rip a whole string of colourful and threatening obscenities. 'Stand back, for the one who is inside is, and must remain, for ever a mystery. Or the plan will fail, and Troy will never fall. History will be cheated. I myself will make sure that, under cover of darkness, this engine of peace shall slip between the gateposts of Troy and enter the very citadel itself!'

They cheer. And so my brave master is left behind, while his miserable rout of followers depart for the boats and sail out to sea where they sit on the tide and wait.

Meantime the Trojans, heavily armed, leave their city and come to this deserted and extended machina, surround it and my master admonishes them to worship and cherish it as an offering to the gods and bring it into Troy. 'My army of people,' he says, 'has gone for ever. They were an unworthy lot – most if not all of them – and I retract them. Each and every one I spit out!'

So cunningly, and with snide and insulting comments about his followers, does he put over his case – and with such flattering signs and a convincing tone of voice – that they fall for his line and instruct men with ropes and wheels to bring the engine into the centre of Troy that very night. He tells me to go with him and the deadly offering.

'Look Adam, we have arrived,' he says to me as we approach the battlements. On the stately proportioned towers we spy many beautiful women. Most are naked, but bashful and modest in demeanour, with downcast eyes. There is Virginia, the exquisite virtuous daughter who chooses death rather than the shame of surrender to a crooked judge. There is Prudence, wife of Melibee, and Sophia, beaten by thieves; their wounds are healed. There is Lucia, wife of the Roman poet Lucretius. There is Emilie, sister-in-law of Duke Theseus of Athens, chaste beauty but something of a bore, prepared to switch her allegiance at the drop of a pin, when one promised lover dies, to the other. There is no end of virtuous women, Stymphais, Lucrece, Alcestis, Penelope, Ladomia, Portia, and so on, but all without a stitch. My master rubs his hands with glee.

Night falls, and at the appointed hour my master drugs the guards who watch over the offering, and they fall asleep. He gives the signal, three taps on the tip of the foreskin and with a fearful rumble of machinery the member opens. Inside, there is only one warrior. Can he take Troy all by himself?

Advancing slowly from the cavernous interior it is Lord John, helmeted, blazing with heraldic colours, fully armed with breastplate and every knightly accoutrement, confidently gripping his sword. With a rumble and clank of armour he leaves the deceitful offering. 'Show me where I shall find her,' he calls out majestically to my master, and my master has in the meantime been coaxing the buildings and paving stones of Troy with a recital of his verses. This works well for they crack, on all sides open up, and from them drunkenly waving makeshift weapons, in some cases unbuttoning makeshift weapons of another kind, in a few other cases convincingly armed, is the motley company which deserted the tents and sailed out to sea.

'After them, they're yours!' shouts my master and they speed off after the virtuous maidens, after death, song, wine and pleasure. There is no fight, for those who defended Troy seem to have fled. 'What is the matter, where's the enemy gone?' asks Lord John, brandishing his weapon, 'Don't say I've been cheated yet again?' 'Ah ah,' says my master, 'Well might you ask.' He points. 'But Helen is that way, my lord.'

I follow John who strides off towards the inner citadel. But here the resistance is fierce, and the duke is in the middle of the affray where men are falling on all sides. He fights at length one great knight, then topples him over: I bend over the face of the dead warrior and recognize him as my father.

With fire and sword John and his followers mount the marble steps and penetrate to the inner chambers of the palace: everywhere conflagrations have started. For a short time there is resistance from King Richard and some of his baggy-eyed, flaccid-fleshed vassals who appear nearly naked, clutching their clothes to them as they fight to withstand the duke's advance. They are quickly overcome and killed. Next we pass through the temple of Venus, goddess of the sky and earth and of course you know what. Here are paintings and statues of the harm done by love: Callisto, the Arcadian nymph, whom Zeus seduced then changed into a bear, later killed by Achilles; Atalanta, turned into a lion by Cybele; Semiramis, changed at death into a dove; Candace, the Indian queen of the Alexander romances; Hercules who died in agony wearing a poisoned shirt; Byblis, a nymph; Dido, who to escape marriage with Iarbas, sacrificed herself on a funeral pyre; Tristan, who died in despair – Isolde found her lover dead and died also; Cleopatra who, to escape being carried a prisoner to Rome, took her own life; Scylla, turned into a monster by her rival in love, Amphitrite, Rhea Silvia, mother of Romulus, thrown into the Tiber by order of her uncle Amulius.

At last Lord John arrives at the inner chamber of the temple harlots where, at the window, beautiful naked Alison is leaning her naked bottom out, and parting her legs along the sill, while May, the young wife of January, equally attired in sweet all, offers herself to her lover in a pear tree, while Dorigen *prepares to bare herself before the rocks on the Brittany coast. There is the Merchant's wife lying down for the corrupt Friar, and the wife and daughter of the Trumpington miller tussling under the bedclothes with students from Solar Hall.*

Right in the centre of the room, reclining on a sumptuous bed furnished with every rich cloth and trapping reclines Lady Katherine, attired in transparent veils as Helen. John comes over, kneels before her, but seeing him she utters a shriek, breaks into convulsions and gives birth quickly, one after another, to a succession of kings and queens, babies for sure, but with regal faces, small crowns on their heads, royal robes and orbs and sceptres. They totter off to join one another in a line, clutching to their bosoms their emblems of blood and regality.

Her vulva and womb open further and I am invited to enter, and here I find myself in a sweet-smelling cave, fed by Virgilian streams and dripping with gentle murmuring springs, quick with the flashing plumage of finches and doves, the soothing susurration of insects, and the intricate harmonies of leaves and flowers. The walls shine with gentle, amethystic radiance and in them and in the roof is every kind of softly muted stone where gems are set. Jasper for faith, sapphire for hope and contemplation, onyx and beryl for the powers and virtues, and the rest of heavenly gems such as sardonyx for martyrdom and emerald for angels. In the very centre of the cave grows the tree of life itself, fragrant with fruit, copious in leaf, the shelter which itself needs protection.

I awoke from my dream to pain and misery.

Until now I had pushed away an awareness of what my meeting, earlier, with Susanna had revealed. It was my squashing of this knowledge which brought unusual weariness down on me. Closeness to Lady Katherine, to the contours of her beauty, had produced ripples or echoes of intimacy.

I now understood fully, and for the first time, it had not been Susanna last night, but Petronella, my stepmother's mad daughter, who had visited me.

I staggered incoherently from the chapel into the sharp March air, blinded by the brightness.

TWENTY-FOUR

Katherine, Duchess of Lancaster

'WHERE IS YOUR DAUGHTER? I didn't see her this morning, your Grace.'

'I am relieved, Mr Scriven. She said she had no wish to carry on with this ride, but to return to Leicester. For one so sensitive to crowds and indifferent impressions which overwhelm her, I trust this is what is best. The journey has been too upsetting and eventful. So, by the grace of God, we are freed from her for the rest of our sad wake.'

Why should this newly acquired stepson be so interested in my first daughter? I supposed he was trying to show some concern about his family. I would have to keep up my politeness in this morbid encounter. I wished it could have been at another time or somewhere else. He was such a miserable, scruffy-looking fellow who took so little care of himself and there was something coarse and unfinished, certainly gruff about him, that reminded me of…and that voice of his, so loud and unmusical.

'If I may be so bold, my lady, what happened with er…' Mr Scriven cleared his throat, 'Sir Swynford on your wedding night?'

'With your father? Has Mr Chaucer been talking to you?' I caught my breath. What an impertinence of such a social inferior to pose this question to me. How could I keep my distance? He had no right to inquire into such an intimate matter. I said nothing, but he looked at me and he was biting his lip, and nervously fidgeting with his reins.

'No.'

Yet he deserved a proper reply. After all he only wanted to find out, and what harm could it do now? Tomorrow we might well be dead . I could not blame him for the circumstances of his birth. 'I was terrified. I have to admit, Mr Scriven, that when on my wedding night he entered the nuptial chamber – I am telling you because he was your father long before Petronella came along – that I was frightened. Very frightened indeed. His eyes flashed with danger and menace. But, surprisingly and with unexpected consideration, he told me that if I so wished I was free not to lie with him. I could not understand why he had so suddenly changed.'

'You gave in to his needs?'

'As best I could. Not altogether with good grace.' There seemed no more to say on the subject. I longed for him not to question me any more.

Mr Scriven steered the subject back to the present. 'I am worried about Mr Chaucer. Where is he?'

'Oh Geoffrey,' I answered with relief and a smile, 'is always able to take care of himself. Perhaps he has some business on the way, who knows? Let him be, Adam. He'll be at St Paul's tomorrow.'

'If there is a funeral...'

'I do not fear the king. There are too many of us. Do you fear him?'

His anxieties tumbled out. 'This is all very well. But will you, madam, be able to stand up to him? Will there be a civil battle and butchery if our people insist on forcing their way through his archers, while they are bent to obey the king. He was brave when he met the rebel Wat Tyler, Jack Straw and his company.'

'He had right on his side. But when it really comes to the sticking point he has no strength of will. It was my husband who gave him his strength. John of Gaunt ruled England, not he. I believe he will not dare to usurp him now, it will be like rebelling against and abusing his own father.'

'But with all due respect, Lady Katherine, I do not trust his followers. William Scrope...'

I stopped him. 'King Richard is a peaceful man at heart. His father, the Black Prince, had too much of murderous hate and the noble qualities of the warrior, and little of this was passed on. His son was in this respect wasted.'

'Well, Richard is the second son. If the older, Edward, had only lived...'

'Ah yes,' I sighed, 'the duke watched him die in Bordeaux, where they buried him in the cathedral. Edward was direly wounded and enfeebled, and John stood in his place, watched the poor child die, then buried him. Do you think King Richard would ever repay my husband for the endless succession of good deeds he has performed for him by denying his last wishes?'

'It is not the king,' my brother's scrivener answered, 'it is those who counsel him...' His continual anxieties were beginning to unnerve me and I spent the rest of the journey fretting, even though as we proceeded the gathering of mourners for my husband swelled more and more into festivities, with musicians playing flutes and tambourines. As the numbers increased, a profusion of early spring flowers, daffodils, tulips, broom and early fruit blossoms, showered upon the carriages, the chariots and the bier of my dear departed. We passed the northern gate into the city.

Some say London was but an oasis in this great uncleared forest of England. By the standards of ancient Rome, twelve or fourteen centuries earlier, London was a tiny centre, but in the person of the duke it had controlled much of France as well as England. Under the peaceful policies of Richard it had never been so rich, but the riches were of its citizens for, as John instructed me, the king distrusted it and distrusted Parliament. Indeed he told me that the king had more treasures stored away in Chester than were in the Tower, which as a last bastion of the king against rebellious nobles and subjects was still moated and heavily defended.

Mr Scriven continually bewailed the absence of his master. There continued to be no sign of Geoffrey.

'Dear Adam,' I said and, seeing how disquietened he had remained, put much, and as I believed unexpected, warmth into my expression. 'Do not agitate yourself on account of Mr Chaucer. He has ever been thus: he probably felt he had had enough of our company.'

He frowned, giving me the feeling that all, perhaps, had not been in perfect harmony between himself and Geoffrey. 'Yes, your grace, in quieter circumstances than these he would hurry home without speaking to a soul, shut himself up like a hermit with his books. He loves and reveres them, giving them such lust and credence that no game or distraction can draw him away from them unless he is on holiday – or during the month of May when the flowers open in all their glory, and the sweet birds sing to their heart's content.'

I smiled with affectionate memory. I had much to censure Geoffrey with, but overall my love and loyalty to him won – just about. 'Yes, but with his vacant eyes, reserved manner and meditative tastes, my brother-in-law has been every bit the clever, supple and adaptable court poet. He can bend in every wind, and he will never break.'

'Madam, you are right, and we may well inquire how he has managed to survive, to side-step – as it were – the murderer's sword, escape the executioner's axe, avoid the poisoned chalice, or even the calumniators' evil words, the lawyers' snares, the disfavour of princes, the exile and neglect that have been the fate of so many of his fellow poets in Italy, and above all…'

'One trait explains all,' I answered, for I believed this had ever been the truth. 'Geoffrey has been the master of turning his own wit against himself. In so doing he forestalls disdain and mockery from others. He embraces and gives to the world an image of himself as a small, insignificant, and even ridiculous man. Because he is modest in his pretensions, complete in his self-effacement, he claims that he upsets no one.'

The sudden appearance of the sun warmed our faces. This did not deter Mr Scriven.

'But the penetrating observer can spot the subtle mockery, my lady, behind all this defence that my master wields. This is the shield that reflects those who look on him back on themselves, in a softened and enhanced light. Sometimes this is aimed at the person to whom he is speaking, sometimes in general at the whole monstrosity of human conceit, and the disorder and folly of mankind in general.'

'Well, I always told him he should stand up for himself more.'
I could sense that Mr Scriven had a very different idea of his master as he tried to contradict me with 'I rather think he is not like that,' while I began to grow a little impatient of his need to question everything I said. It drove me more and more to defend Geoffrey. 'Perhaps the foremost poet of love has to be numbered among the most abused and unsuccessful, not to say pathetically bashful of lovers. Wooing Cupid, he is treated with disdain, dismissing himself for his failure to wait on the god as too old and heavy. Neglected, all he does is plead for more forward and favoured lovers…

'He has been married, but he has, alas, suffered so much that he will never be caught again. His poems are the acts of penance of a small, truly insignificant talent…'

My last words were drowned in noise. I felt relief that this painful conversation was at an end. We had passed through the meadows of North London, and were in the arms and munitions streets where they forged cruel instruments of siege, spears, bassinets and helmets, hachetons and reinforced jackets. As the armourers burned sea-coal in their iron works, there was a thick pall of blackness in the sky which made us cough and choke. The blows of the great hammers in the forges made such racket as to silence more talk: they said that here even the wine and ale in the cellars were spoiled, and lawyers claimed damages for them.

A little further on we came down through great parks and were near the rich burghers' houses of the city. There were near three hundred aldermen, and control of the commercial life of the city rested with them. Many in this quarter had rich and splendid houses. Dotted all about, with their enclosed and cultivated graves, were the churches of London, over a hundred in all, with attendant monasteries, priories and abbeys, centres of learning, of charity, hospitals for the sick, refuges for those seeking asylum, protection from the law or from violence, or from enemies. Priests, however much they may have been defied, derided or even executed or murdered by the king, were the ultimate authority. However corrupt and venial they were, however much they acted for the indulgence of their own appetites, they wielded control over the fate of men and women, most crucially of all, over where we would go when we died. But John would say that this golden age of priestly authority was in its death throes.

We rode into the heart of the city, the fashionable quarter for buying and selling. This part we now entered was crowded to the point of suffocation. Here, just to be near the money and the foreigners who flooded into the markets, in the days when I was a poor governess to my lord, I knew families that lived in a single room, or above a shop. Because the countryside was so near – there were farms in plenty within the city walls – pigs rooted in the open garbage, butchers slaughtered their beasts even in Fleet Street itself, leaving mounds of offal for crows and kites to pick over. Liquid refuse ran through streams and ditches into the great river Thames, where bustling trade was carried in broad-beamed 'logs' and great galleons, flat-bottomed barges, carracks and carosells with their four masts, and every kind of fishing vessel with sails.

Lepers and foreign businessmen intermingled. Jewellers' shops glittered in the raw March air and sunshine as we trudged past on our horses. As I had so recently been the beneficiary I knew how London was the world's most famous jewel market. And as we approached nearer to our destination, fashions appeared more wild and louche, more flesh of female bosom was revealed, while young men wore clothing so short it showed their buttocks like the backsides of she-apes at full moon. Nothing stopped the flow of people: not the city dwellers' notorious hatred of foreigners, not the dread of crime and disease, not the ever-present 'gong' farmers and 'dung' agents who emptied the cesspits at night, and the myriad scavengers and criminals, could stem the tide of humanity.

And then we were winding our way through the very centre to the Carmelite monastery in Fleet Street. There must have been, the stewards told us, upwards of sixteen or seventeen hundred. London had not seen its like for many a year, not since the death of King Edward. Since we set out people had gathered to line the roads, falling on their knees before my husband's hearse, which was sable-draped and drawn by eight great black horses in silver harness, with black ostrich plumes strutting forward from their heads with each step they take. Everywhere a deep sense of unease set in with the afternoon sunset, as if a dark shadow had crossed the land, for its great protector, who was also my love, was no longer here, his reliable support to his nephew no longer existed.

Where was the king? The complete Narcissus who could brook no criticism, and never much listened to anyone, had to fend for himself. 'How long will he last?' everyone must have been asking. And where, also, was my brother-in-law? Did he still worry over those critical verses which had so offended his monarch? 'One time this world was so steadfast and stable that man's word was obligation... . Oh prince, desire to be honourable and wed your folk again to steadfastness.' As we passed the ruins of the Savoy Palace, where so much had happened to me, but which now was decayed and neglected, overgrown with weeds and shrubs, our numbers were greatly swelled. Had London ever seen such an awe-inspiring, black-garbed procession which was surrounded on all sides by colour and gaudiness, so no one could fathom if it was a celebration, or a wake? My husband would have been so proud of his popularity. We turned into the Strand itself. The Strand was filled to overflowing with great lords and ladies, chanting monks, the citizenry from all walks of life, the poor, oh yes the poor everywhere who loved my husband for his generosity to them. My Lancastrian household flowed out on all sides.

Here, attended by my nun Pervil, I rode behind the coffin – as upright as I knew how to appear, dignified, unsmiling – then behind me came, in order of precedence, the kings and queens, many lords and ladies.

And then. There they were. A wall as solid as Cotswold stone. No need to hide behind anything. Here was the ambush we were promised. The forward riders pulled up their horses, which neighed and whinnied as our peaceful rhythm was jerked to a halt.

At the far end of the Strand, just before we were due to wend our way into Fleet Street, we now faced the solid phalanx of brown-coated archers. They did not brandish arms, but stood side by side blocking the road. These were the Cheshire men, Richard's private army that protected him day and night, consisting of a dozen or so knights with their pennants and shields, scores of esquires, and several hundred heavily armed archers. Look at any one, John would often say, and you see a hired killer. Our main body of Lancaster's funeral procession quietly slowed to a dignified halt.

The king's favourite, Green, dressed extravagantly, rode out before the archers. There was a flourish of trumpets and a muffled roll of drums.

'My lords and ladies,' shouted this upstart Green, 'the king of England desires to greet and pay his personal obsequies to the great duke.'

How could they do it to us? The thick rank of surly, half-savage archers parted with precision into a passageway, and along it rode King Richard. I had to agree that he cut a magnificent, imposing figure. His pale face was deeply furrowed, his blue eyes red-rimmed. He was richly dressed, mostly but not all in black. On his head he wore the silver mourning crown.

'God rest the soul of my dear uncle,' he called out loudly and cheerfully. The king was enjoying, as usual, the huge spectacle of himself that he was making. The man would dramatise every event, including that of his own death.

Mr Scriven and I exchanged looks, and I could see we were in accord over this. We spoke quiet words to each other. 'I fear he is going to cancel the funeral. Or re-organize it. He likes to change events so that he can project his own power, and show his command over people. He should have been a mummer.'

'I suspect he will divert the burial of Lord John from St Paul's to Westminster Abbey. He's done this kind of thing before. He wishes to humiliate Lancaster.'

'I don't know. I don't know.' I shook my head in consternation.

Richard dismounted in front of the hearse, came over to me, so that as best I could I curtsied deeply before him. Graciously, I have to say, he lifted me from my knees by the hand, and conferred seriously with me for a moment. But instead of offering his consolations he had something else in mind. In spite of my respect I stepped back and away from him, concealing or trying hard to conceal my dismay or amazement.

He had presented me with a parchment which commanded me, and my company, including Mr Scriven and my brother-in-law, to dine with him this evening in the great hall of Westminster, then to attend a celebration or pageant of my husband's life mounted by mummers. I was not happy with the invitation but I was powerless to refuse.

But then, to add insult to my bewilderment, 'Open the coffin,' he commanded to the attendants who stood behind him. What? He dared to order this without so much as a by-your-leave?

My entourage, deeply shocked as I was, moved with alacrity to obey his order. The great oak lid was slowly raised, creaking on its hinges.

'I wish to touch my uncle's finger, and g-g-gaze one last time on his face.'

And so his bowed head passed from my view, as he picked up one of my husband's decomposing hands in his. He was sobbing loudly.

Twenty-five

Scriven

WE WERE OFFERED THE same choice of courses for dinner: first course, boar's head, pheasant stew, red deer, cygnets, capons, pike and so on, and custard apple fritters and other sweets. There was a 'subtlety' of jelly and candied sugar representing a king. Second course roe deer, peacocks, larded rabbits, grilled eel, brawn, capon in sharp sauce, then sweets and a further 'subtlety'. I could see what killed the first wife Queen Anne.

Then a rather lighter course; selected from cranes, plovers, sturgeon, quails, pheasant in his royalty, larks, cold red deer and so on. Water was brought to everyone to wash hands.

Then the play –

All the time I could hear whispering, see stares and signs that signified Katherine was a marked woman...

This in the new hall of Westminster Palace, designed by my master's friend Henry Yevele. Mr Hoccleve, the master of ceremonies, had been taken into service by King Richard and given ten pounds a year, much more than the pay of most parsons, but he was well-known for self-indulgence and vanity. He refused to wear glasses, and bending and concentration had so strained his back, stomach, and eyes that he looked like a crooked gnome as he stood before us dressed like a gentleman, for he was ostentatious in the extreme.

Hoccleve spoke the prologue in his cracked voice, although the accent was good and clear, easy to follow and not at all like the myriad regional abortions of our tongue, each of which vied for prominence.

'Your grace, my lords and ladies, I now bring you some scenes from the great lovers of the past as recounted by the illustrious poet of Italy, Dante Alighieri. The musicians will make some music to represent the dark underworld where the play is set – '

The strings and wind instruments struck up a medley of lamentations, shrieks, moans and cries of damnation which delighted with their humour and their outlandishness.

'You must imagine these are spirits whirled and swept by an unceasing storm. When the poet asks of his guide and mentor, Virgil, what these are, he is told they are the spirits doomed to eternal damnation by carnal lust – '

King Richard reposed on his throne. Next to him, in the position of honour, sat Katherine. I reflected on how her version of her wedding night with my father differed from that of my master. So which of them was lying? The only way I could solve this was by raising the matter once more with my master.

Queen Isabella, who was eleven years old, was absent. It was well past her bedtime. The king believed that the display bore visible witness to his wisdom, and his extravagant show of wealth was to appropriate and belittle the Lancastrian household which he entertained. In his robe lined with precious stones which they said cost twenty thousand pounds he projected a rich and splendid image. He wanted to dwarf his dead uncle. Before dinner there had been a show of dancing from a hundred mummers and dancers with blazing torches. Now there was the short dramatic entertainment.

There was a deeper purpose behind all this which made me uneasy. To the east, near the great spire of St Paul's, safely, or so we hoped, protected in the Carmelite monastery, the body of Lord John awaited its final rest tomorrow morning. But King Richard's design had soon become evident. The king's purpose was to draw as many of the Lancastrian retainers and knights as possible to his palace, make them drink and loosen up, then – who knows? – capture and steal away the body. But the sensible heads, while agreeing that Katherine and a few score should attend the king's function, had not allowed the main body to go, but ordered them to stay and guard the duke.

So there was great fear and expectation among the Lancastrian supporters. There appeared to be, in the city, two great rival armies, the king's and Lord John's. Some of the Percies were here from the Scottish borders and they were angry at King Richard's recent attempt by purges and killings to curtail their power. There were loyal Lancastrians, armed to the teeth – such as John Norbury, the famous mercenary captain, who followed the duke in his campaigns against the Portuguese and had been rewarded at Aljubarrota. He had married his daughter to the treasurer of the ducal household. He often, like my master, had refused knighthoods and remained an esquire, a rich one at that, trusted, like my master, in royal service more than mighty lords.

There was also Thomas Chaucer here, another of Lord John's retainers, and as we know a possible illegitimate son, destined one day to be a great and powerful landowner; he also, like Norbury, had served abroad with Henry of Bolingbroke. He, too, was armed and ready.

But Mr Chaucer was singularly not here, which was a worry and a vexation.

The lovers, Paulo and Francesca, from Dante, played a scene together:

> **Paulo:** I thank the poet for his poetry and wish him peace.
> **Francesca:** Let us tell our story.
> **Paulo:** I can do no more than weep.
> **Francesca:** I was the wife of Gianciotta, the deformed older brother of Paulo. He was a beautiful youth. For ten years I have been married to Gianciotto but one day I read of the love of Lancelot for Guinevere, the queen of King Arthur. I and Paulo, who was my friend, read it aloud to one another, and as we read on so many parts of the story seemed to tell of our love for each other. I am afraid that this story was what encouraged us to cross the boundary of chastity and to kiss for the first time, and then thereafter to lie down together. (Paulo weeps).
> **Thomas Hoccleve:** Your sin is not all that great compared to that of your husband who murdered you.
> **Francesca:** I now find only hell in the love I bear for Paulo, for once this was my whole heaven and being, for I am passionate and I committed adultery over and over again.

The drama proceeded thus, and truth to say, although its choice displayed the sanctimonious king at his worst, it was, after the journey and trials we have been through, soothing. But as the number of unanswered questions paraded in front of my mind, with all the forwardness of some of the more wanton-looking of Richard's courtiers, I became restless. The play ended with the murder of Paulo by his brother Gianciotta in the very act of adultery with Francesca.

There followed some short diversions on the theme of Lord John's heroic deeds, such as his victory at Najera, and his later Aljubarrota, and his investiture as duke of Aquitaine. With two queens, those of Spain and Portugal, there to celebrate their father it was fitting King Richard should flatter his uncle. He needed these allies for they provided much of his income, although less now that he had an eleven year old queen who was the daughter of the king of France. Not only was this century due shortly to come to its own end, but also there were signs and portents everywhere of impending catastrophe!

Katherine was visibly tired. The queens and their followers retired. Katherine sought to excuse herself before the king. I had to say that, if only in a figure of speech, I could have raped her myself. But in the same moment I see also how my beastly father could have come to her with love and contrition in his heart.

'You are welcome to remain here in my palace,' said the king.

'No your grace. I have preparations made for me in Fleet Street, at the monastery.' Katherine knew but did not say that she was to lie that night at Ely Palace, which Lord John had used as his own, and not at the Carmelite monastery – we had been instructed to return by a back route.

The touchy king grew immediately suspicious.

'What, do you fear something ill might happen if you stay with me?'

Katherine forced a smile: 'Of course not, your majesty.'

I was seated behind Katherine. The king spotted me.

'Who is that languid, reddish-haired, mean-looking thing, with the blotchy complexion?' he asked no one in particular.

'My brother-in-law's secretary.'

'I thought as much. And where is Mr Chaucer?' he asked me, and without waiting for any reply went on, 'My great poet. My Anne's favourite. Mr Chaucer has such a beautiful speaking voice.'

'He was with us until St Albans. We have lost him,' I answered in my rough-throated tone. My master was ever telling me to speak more softly. The king mockingly placed his hands over his ears. 'What a loud racket for one so insignificant,' he remarked loudly, while his courtiers and sycophants near him laughed cruelly. 'With us till St Albans!' he mocked.

'And just as well for Chaucer that he *is* lost! His verses have much offended me,' he added.

'I thought, your majesty, you have praised him greatly for his Clerk's Tale, the story of Griselda, and his Knight's Tale,' interceded Katherine softly.

'Not bad, not bad, but why does he not flatter me as he flatters others? He finds *them* models of virtue? I am one myself you know, and even if I were not, he has no right to criticize me, for he and everyone should know my right is divine.'

'Everyone respects this, your grace,' replied Katherine compliantly.

'Yes, they do,' repeated Richard petulantly. 'I am successful. I hold England in my two hands as I hold this cup. Never has England been so rich, or its king so free to exercise his will. Peace with France has lasted and Mowbray, duke of Norfolk, after ridding me of Arundel and Gloucester, has died in Venice – so good riddance to him. And now to Ireland, for which, as the crowning triumph, my uncle from his great estates will provide the funds. In life he served me by supporting my policies and ridding me of my enemies, who were his enemies too. In death he shall serve me even better, for I shall use his estates to subdue the Irish. It shall be not so much a disinheriting of Henry Derby, as a levelling of the score.'

He looked around him. No one dared to contradict or answer him. He went on, 'What a little show-off as a child Henry was; he thought he was such a great horseman, such a powerful warrior. Well I denied him his triumphs, didn't I? – I made peace with the French. I thwarted them, all those bloodthirsty knights and earls! Thomas of Woodstock, earl of Gloucester, perpetually angry and about to explode; stupid Arundel; Norfolk; my "earl marshal" Mortimer, who would have taken my kingdom from me if I'd turned my back; De La Pole; I quietened Edmund, my other uncle, poor sap that he was. Your relations, Katherine!'

'Yes, your majesty,' agreed Katherine deferentially.

The king collapsed with laughter. 'We'll feast the Irish and knight the traitors. Last time I was there two of the kings didn't know what forks were for and…a third tried to eat his plate! I like their manners. Now Katherine, I have to make the funeral address about my uncle. What shall I say?'

'Say what you like, your majesty. I beg to be excused.'

She rose from her throne.

'Oh dear, oh dear,' said the king aside to me, quietly, so she could not overhear. 'Temper, temper. I've offended the lady. Well she never liked Anne much, and Anne never liked her. Anne was so clever, she read three languages, German, Latin and Czech. Besides English. Much more civilized than M'moiselle Payne de Roet. She knew how to settle my disputes for me, how to calm, how to intercede... . I'll lock her up, keep her out of the way. There'll be trouble.' He shouted out as loud as he could: 'Where's W-W-W-Wiltshire gone? Pass me more porcupine seethed in almond milk: I prefer the milk to the meat.'

'Come Adam, we must leave.'

'No,' ordered the king, pointing at me. 'You, thing, shall stay. That is an order.'

Katherine curtsied and left the hall. She was in no position to defend me. I feared for her safety, for the king felt no constraint towards her as he did towards the queens of Spain and Portugal. As soon as Katherine and her gentlewoman had gone, and with them most of the noble guests, the atmosphere changed.

'I am sad there's no more Chaucer,' the king confided in me with a crocodile smile. 'But if there was, perhaps *Chaucer* would be no more!' He laughed at his menacing joke. 'I've heard a rumour that when I was eleven your master committed rape. Do you know anything about it?'

I bent my head towards King Richard, trying to hide my eyes. He took no notice. 'I wanted proof. I won't stand further dissent or criticism. I sent my men to find out.' He clapped his hands. So now the king was implicated. I should have seen this all along.

Richard had tired of the entertainment he had provided for his important guests. He commanded another diversion. I could not catch the name of it, except that it was in the Cheshire tongue – for he seemed more to want to please his archers than anyone else: there lay his safety.

There was not the slightest reason or logic about the whole of this, but the action happened in an inn, and a well-dressed, elderly knight and his servant came in from the cold, and were led into a room by the inn-keeper. The knight disarmed and took off his surcoat, while the servant, Robin, carried a trunk and a chicken wrapped in red paper. Robin was a great glutton. The inn-keeper warned them the room was haunted by devils and went off. The knight, who was bad-tempered and morose, said he has known it for a long time and he ordered Robin to unpack and make supper.

But Robin, a coward and glutton, hearing about the devils turns pale and trembles like a leaf. He would run away but he fears his master, and also he is hungry. The knight is weary of his wanderings and hopes the present evening will see the end of them. Robin listens, grimaces, mutters asides and makes the audience of Cheshire archers laugh with every word. The knight explains about the devils to answer Robin's fears by saying he once turned to them for help when he was in a tight corner and tonight perhaps his time is up and they will come for his soul in accordance with the bargain he made. Robin grows terrified again, but when his master cheers him up and tells him to prepare supper he takes out the chicken and wine, and in a twinkling nips off a piece of meat and eats it. The audience guffaws. The doors creak, the wind rattles the shutters. Robin crams a huge piece of chicken too big to swallow into his mouth. 'Is it ready yet?' calls the knight, walking about the room.

So the knight was made more and more of a fool while the audience was more and more delighted. With Robin's deception of his master continuing as he ate and hid the chicken he soon realized there was nothing left of the dish but a leg. The knight, too gloomy and preoccupied to notice, sat down to his feast while Robin stood behind him grimacing and mimicking him, every word, every gesture being greeted with uncontrollable laughter. But now, as soon as the knight began to eat, the devils appeared.

Here everything became quite incomprehensible, and the devils were fantastically impossible. A door at the side opens and there enters something in white and in place of its head there is a lantern containing a candle; another apparition, also with lantern on its head, holds a scythe in his hand.... The knight boldly confronts the devils, and says he is ready. But Robin, timid as a hare, creeps under the table, not forgetting in his flight to seize the bottle as he goes. The knight addresses himself once more to the chicken but three devils burst in and seize him. 'Save me,' calls the knight as they carry him off. Robin hides under the table, but when they are gone he comes out and celebrates: 'Now I am alone...without a master...'

Everybody laughed because he had lost his master. He is so comically triumphant: 'The devils have taken my master...' But next, in the moment of his triumph, it was his turn. He raised his cup to his lips, but the devils reappeared, stole up behind him on tiptoe, and pounced on him from each side. Finally he is lifted and carried off screaming and screaming...

There followed a dance in which everyone joined.

'Do you like our country play?' the king asked above the din.

'Oh yes, sire,' I answered; yet I had hardly understood a word, on account of the Cheshire dialect.

The music increased in tempo and the dancing grew more and more wild.

The clapping and cheering king's archers who lined the hall were ugly: most were young, smooth-shaven and had cropped heads, shaved half-way up the back, close-cut in front of the ears, lying cape-like on top of the head. They carried daggers hung round their necks, in the ornamental manner, although these were sharp kidney-weapons or misericords, to give the coup-de-grace. Observing around me I witnessed how extreme fashions had become: while some women still wore veils, and men trinkets such as bells in the old manner, mostly necks, revealing bare breasts, were very low. In most cases the V's went down as low as the tummy button. The court favourites sported whaleboned-fur right up the napes of their necks, while beneath their short jacket skirts of six inches and less their abbreviated underdrawers showed. The scantiness here was more than made up by the voluminousness of the sleeves, the idea being a mixture of luxury and nakedness.

Bonnets were whipped off. Circlets untangled from locks, and how over satin and fur the women's hair did flow! Women were more oftener than not plucking their locks in the Italian style to make their foreheads high.

I noticed many were attended by smoothly dressed losengers and male demoiseaus.

'Here you, come with us,' some guards beckoned with threatening gestures.

'What do you want?'

'We've orders to fetch the Lady Katherine, take her to Woodstock, to keep her out of trouble. You shall be our guide.'

'Trouble? What trouble?' I said, knowing that the trouble would be of the king's making. His mood was one of risk, danger. Pessimism was fashionable, all enthusiasm and joy was considered old-fashioned and childish. France should take the blame, for the poet Deschamps wrote popular ballads whose shallow gloom appealed to everyone. The king's pleasure-seeking court displayed the same unsatisfied weariness.

They danced with skulls and death-heads, and attendants

circulated with sweets and pies shaped in the figures of the plague-smitten, Death, and the Great Reaper. I suspected that those who remained behind were about to sink into ribald songs, with squealing pipes and slack gaining the upper hand. The women would tear open their bodices and gowns, transforming themselves into bacchantes. None of this was for me, for I was hauled out by a pack of these bloodthirsty mercenaries who professed great loyalty for Richard, but in reality their loyalty was more towards the generous rewards, both of gold coin and licence to eat, drink, and kill whoever they liked or whatever they liked.

They laughed, intimidatingly. 'Come with us,' the big one clenched a fist and hectored me, 'or we'll do to you what we did to that old woman and Basil the guard!'

I shuddered at the mention of these forgotten names. How quickly, in times of extreme new peril, past horrors and terrible events recede or are forgotten. So that was it. They had committed those heinous crimes. My master had been right. I recognised them at once only too well. Yole, Wade, and Perkin. There was a fourth. And their captain was Dickie.

Twenty-six

Scriven

IT WAS NOW AN hour or so later on that forty-first night after the death of the duke. I was being frog-marched to the east. I tried my best to decoy them away from the Ely Palace in Holborn, but it was for this they aimed: an informer had come back to Westminster and told them Lady Katherine had retired here for the night. Otherwise they were on a rampage and woe betide any who fell out with them or tried to impede their progress. Most fled on hearing their raucous laughter and shouts, and the clatter of their boots on the stone streets. They seemed in particular to fear or vow vengeance upon one prince.

'Death to Henry of Bolingbroke,' shouted Perkin.

'Death, death!' repeated his Cheshire companions, joined by another called Tervet or Trevers, while waving their weapons of death. They stamped their boots and roared as they pushed aside the passers-by.

'Dickon say no plundering, no ravishing. Don't offend him lads. Look else on all the pardons, grants of land, offices he do heap on us.'

'Aye, we are his invincible guard. Vigilia number five. One day we'll be knights. The king always tells us, don't he, "London is an enemy country, I must be watched night and day".'

'Who are you?' one of the guards demanded of a foreign merchant in long, Hanseatic robes. 'Off with his head!' They laughed.

'Do you support the people's king?' asked another.

These were not angry, deprived countrymen, I thought, like Wat Tyler, Jack Straw, John Ball and his followers of the Peasants' Revolt. They were the spoiled, the bored, the reckless who had everything and wanted more and more.

The Hanseatic merchant on the way to his steelyard home where there was a private enclave of foreigners who had their own aldermen and guilds, and even printed their own currency, mumbled in fear, 'I am just a poor merchant! Let me pass.'

'Hear that,' spoke a guard. 'Poor? – in all that silk and trimmings! Come on, give him a shave.' They raised their swords to hack at him.

'Hold on, brothers,' called Wade. 'Let the bloodsucker go – he fills the king's coffers. He brings in money. If you want to punish the wicked, aim for the Flemings in the Vintry – they take money *out* of the kingdom.'

We passed into the Strand, twinkling on both sides with lights from great houses and the enclosed courts of noblemen. Two of the men had wanted to cross the river to Southwark and promenade with the Winchester geese, the painted whores that lived there, but the leader kept them in order.

Several times I had a mind to escape this enforced march, but ever behind me or in front or beside walked Yole, the suspicious great mountain of an archer, who watched over me to make sure I didn't run off.

Once I tried, when the Cheshire men passed some bear-baiting and taunted the cooped cocks that were to fight with one another for sport – to dodge away down a side street. This Atlas came storming after, asking me what I was doing. I lied that I had gone to relieve myself, and then was forced to simulate doing so, opening my hose and under-drawers to summon forth some water.

So I was sucked along, witnessing brutal sights, for when a crowd of men such as these was loose there was no stopping mischief. They claimed to be seeking Henry of Bolingbroke or his followers, who were rumoured to have landed to overthrow the king. They forced those they met to declare allegiance to their 'Dickon'.

We came to the bishop of Ely's Palace in Holborn, a vast mansion with a gatehouse where I hoped to find Lancastrian guards. There were none, for upon receiving news of our impending arrival they had fled. The rows of lodgings occupied by household officials of the bishop were also deserted.

Upon entering the great carpeted hall we found this almost empty. The archers wanted to pull down the Lancastrian coats of arms hanging on the wall. They began to un-nail them. An archer fetched great blows at one of Lord John's French trophies. Outside in the palace yard the archers yelled obscenities and instilled terror.

Suddenly Dickie the knight, who had knocked the trophy off the wall, turned round. He was covered in sweat. He hurled his sword at one of the mirrors. The others followed suit. They began to smash everything. Their faces were furious. They were intoxicated, and to themselves they were beautiful, they were holy. They smashed the glass of the chapel, and bore all the gold down to the stream outside to throw it in. Smoke was already appearing. And fire followed. Would they drink deep in the bishop's cellars, and forget their quarry? If only to heaven the walls would fall in and they roast for ever. Rage towards everything, despair towards everything: this fury said no to the whole world. It became the senseless revenge of men who had lost their reason.

Could I ever restrain even a single one, or show the cut-throats I did not feel the same as them? I would be eaten, devoured. Yet they did it in the name of the king and to him, and to him only, would they bend their will. Their violence had an aim, to instil obedience to a man whose practice was to sit enthroned from dinner till vespers, who expected everyone when his gaze fell on them to bend the knee. An upper crust of fawners and cronies, and his duketti – courtiers who could be counted on to agree with him: and then below, this naked force! The largest private army of thugs a king had ever commanded.

I ran up three flights of stairs to the highest and most secret rooms of Ely Palace where I knew Katherine was likely to be. I wished to be first. My mouth was sucked dry with fear, my heart beat violently, and I prayed she had left the place long before. But Pervil, the timid shabbily dressed nun, sat in the ante-room, her back bent as she pored over her holy book.

'Shall we take this one?' bawled the rough brute Perkin, who had chased me up here.

'She serves the Lancastrians. We've just seen to a father confessor and a physician. Their heads are swimming in blood down there in the courtyard gutter.'

'Wait,' I called out. 'You'll bring certain punishment if, before carrying out any sentence, you do not proceed to a proper court.'

Dickie, still puffing with the climb, turned to me. 'A proper court of law? What's that?'

Perkin, the grimy one with hands blackened from charcoal burning, and a very seared complexion, said, 'We are such a court!'

I raised my eyes to heaven, thinking in my terror that if they saw fit to do something dreadful to this harmless old nun, what would they be up to doing to harm Katherine?

'Sentence passed. She shall die for being a Lancastrian!'

'Yes, yes, hang her for being a Lancastrian witch!'

'Probably John o'Gaunt's strumpet...'

'Satan in Eden as a snake had such a woman's face as hers! Wily and treacherous.'

These five Cheshire archers had no respect for anyone in church garb, even if they had beads and coral trinkets about them, and relics of holy persons. All was the same to them, as if nuns were thieves and adulterers like the rest of mankind.

'Tear off her cloths, rip 'em away. Let's see what her real wimple's like – ' the jibe was met with raucous laughter.

Suddenly I caught a look in the old nun's eyes. They were clear blue-green, they stared directly at me, calm and quite resigned. They continued to hold me in their gaze. She was not a nun, not the nun I had briefly talked with on the journey. It was Katherine. For that brief moment I had her in my power for the death of my father. All that remained was to finish off here what I had begun. I could reveal to her tormentors who she was, and she would be carted off to Woodstock, or worse. I would never again have such a chance.

A voice inside me spoke before I could restrain it: with a horrible lewd accent, a jaunty, sardonic coarseness.

'Wait a minute, wait a minute there, mates! Who wants tough old game when fresh young rabbit meat awaits a sharp appetite. In there!!??'

I stabbed my finger towards the inner bed-chamber, where I knew the tapestries hung bedecked with naked nymphs, and other representations of gods and goddesses, praying to myself the other, the true nun, had been able to bolt out to safety through a back way.

I prepared myself to flee or jump into the night through the high window. Anything to avoid the deadly jaws of this rout, which was now so out of hand.

'Yes, I say he's right,' shouted Yole, suddenly surprised, even shocked, by my sudden change from one so full of peace and restraint to bellicose fury.

The others rushed to the inner chamber...'Out! Out!' I hissed at Katherine, and she picked up her long skirts and without a word scuttled down the staircase and out of sight.

246

My heart sank to worse than despair when, only moments later, they brought the nun into the room, for so I remarked it was she after a moment's hesitation. She had been carmined and berouged, with lipstick making a great cupid's bow out of her mouth. Dressed in all the finery and allure of a great lady balanced on the latest chopines, her head was topped by a blonde wig.

She looked every inch a queen, at least to these yokels' eyes – or a decidedly ageing great duke's mistress. The gang was not able to notice any cracks in her paint, or the stoop in her vertebrae, because her performance proclaimed her so proud and regal.

'John o'Gaunt's strumpet herself. What a prize!'

They laughed gloatingly, jumped up and down, and rubbed their hands and some of them their privy parts.

'Easy, men,' said Wade, 'better not let Sir Henry Green see what we have. He order us that we weren't to harm the woman but to take her into safe keeping, then transport her to Woodstock.'

'Hide her then,' said my giant keeper. 'We know what to do with her!'

My tormentor came up right behind me, and having recovered some of his former, probing suspicion, asked, 'What happened to the old nun?'

'Jumped.' I nodded towards the open window. 'Threw herself out – before I could stop her. Didn't you hear her scream?'

He moved to look out of the window, but one of the others grabbed the sleeve of his tunic. 'Come on. Don't hang about.' They were half tugging, half carrying, half-pushing the painted Helen they imagined was the cause of all this threat to the king, and whom the king had doomed to sacrifice. 'Don't want to miss the fun with John o'Gaunt's whore!'

I avoided meeting the old saint's eyes as they swept her out. I could well imagine what they were going to do, but I did not hear any more, nor ask anyone, but even, to my relief, my persecutor left me there so I would be able to make my own escape. They had their prize. Without appearing a fugitive I intended to hurry away as fast as I could.

Then Wade, posted on guard, came running up to the others, 'Lancastrians,' he shouted. 'Look alert. Take her down.'

'How many are they?'

'A mere handful.' They drew their swords and dragged out their prisoner. They had forgotten me, but I followed them down. I

247

thought there had been some mistake when I reached the court below, for there were only three men, that was all the 'Lancastrians' numbered. My heart sank. They were but three.

And one of them was my master. What a shock to see him again. After his bewildering disappearance he had, I could only suppose, one of those sudden inspirations peculiar to people of genius in great crises. This was to arrive here now. Accompanying him was a strong, healthy and handsome young man of about twenty who was, in spite of his youthful look, well-armed. An even bigger surprise was Sir Thomas Swynford, now freed from any suspicion of murder, and also heavily armed. The unknown boy's face was tanned and even though his hair had been cut almost to the scalp, it seemed like a golden halo round his head. He drew his sword from its scabbard in the most elegant manner possible, like a courtier born and bred.

'The king forbids duels of honour,' Dickie told them. 'Put up your swords please, and come with us.'

'Captain,' my master said, 'we would be only too happy to accept your kind offer if we were our own masters. Unfortunately we have to take our orders from the duchess – now Lord John is dead. She has commanded us to defend her.' The disguised nun regally nodded in assent.

My master's challenging tone stung Dickie to a sudden and mad fury.

'If you don't come along with us we'll force you!' he shouted at them. 'You're under arrest.'

Thomas Swynford said softly, so that only my master, this astonishingly beautiful youth, and myself could hear:

'They are five, and we are three. If they win here they will win elsewhere, and our chances will be even less.'

They closed ranks. At this moment I, coward and non-combatant although I had always been; cringer, whiner and creeper away from confrontation; avoider of rage and fighting – came to a swift and untypical decision. It was one of these occasions which determine a man's whole future life, for better or worse. I had to choose between remaining on the watching, full barriers, the sidelines of life, as I had always done up to then, or becoming a participant, master of my own fate. I had to abandon my conviction that life was predestined, that faith alone counted (and this, among other weaknesses, often masked cowardice), and risk disobeying the law, risk losing my head, making a lifelong enemy of favourites of the king, who in many ways were more powerful than the king himself. Yet I found I did not hesitate.

'I think, good fellow men, there's some mistake. Mr Chaucer says there are only three of us. I make it four.'

'But Adam, you have no skill at arms!' protested my master in a tone of horror. 'You will assuredly be slaughtered!'

'I have the blood of a warrior – if I have never had cause to acquire the skill. Moreover, I am against tyrants.'

Dickie had more than guessed my intentions. 'Out of the way, old fool,' he shouted. 'I won't stop you leaving. Save your bacon while the going's good.' Yole smirked.

I made no move.

'Take this sword,' said Swynford, pressing the hilt into my open hand. At this moment the young man who accompanied them drew himself up to his full height. The leaping flames of the torches shone on him, and brought out the bold, clear-cut features of his face. His slanting eyes were green with the grass beneath his feet. Who was this showing such readiness for death, to risk himself on our behalf?

'At least give him a trial, gentlemen,' he said. 'I swear that if we're beaten I will not leave this place alive.'

'This is not quite what I had in mind,' I said, but I was unable to add anything further.

The court of Ely House was enclosed, but spacious and it had grass, which was used as pasturage for goats: these were shied away by the fifth Cheshireman, Trevers.

'Well, friends, we are ready,' said my master in a voice which carried over the whole quadrangle. Everyone, including the enemy, answered yes and our swords now flashed bright in the flaming light of the torches while the fierce battle started up. The nine of us here, both sides, were fighting a double cause. The Cheshire thugs, for all their loutishness, were sworn defenders of the king and felt intense pride over their honour.

As for us, well my master was fighting for his life, while surely I could not believe the transformation in his old fat carcass, although I knew that, for all his short stature, he had fought bravely in his youth. But he seemed to grow in inches, and like all of us needed to save his own skin.

Our young champion that stood by Mr Chaucer's side picked the biggest brute, the giant Yole, and would seem to have the most transcendent, self-sacrificing nature of us four. Thomas Swynford fought for the honour of the Lancastrian house and for his mother, and surely, as with his father (and my father) he was such a warrior that I was profoundly grateful he was on our side.

Sir Thomas fought Wade, who had the likeness of the king, and the fifth Cheshireman; the fifth held back a shade as if he was fearful of contact, which gave Sir Thomas some advantage, and he swung and plied his sword coolly and warily, playing a cautious game, for he was mindful that in wielding his great weapon he had better not leave himself undefended.

I was face to face with Perkin. At once our two swords engaged right up to the hilts, and when we were pushed close to face one another I experienced a surge of great joy. Tears streamed into my eyes, but joyous tears as I felt such honest and true loyalty to those others who stood by me, even to my half-brother, Sir Thomas, who was ready to die alongside me, and alongside my master. This brought such delight, for I was not afraid of death in the slightest, and so strengthened me that I hardly knew where or who I was. Perkin, who seemed to me if not the mightiest swordsman on earth yet a glutton for fighting, joined combat like a demon, encircling me ten times and more, constantly changing his stance and ground until I was dizzy. I had my work cut out to defend myself against a nimble enemy of such extraordinary speed who kept bounding about, but did not know how to thrust good and straight to end the contest. I was just about able to hold him at bay. Out of the corner of my eye I saw Dickie swing at my master who passed quickly, and who, before his opponent could regain his balance, glided like a snake under his guard and drove his sword right into his body. Dickie collapsed on the ground in a lifeless heap.

At this my own opponent lost courage and turned to the two unarmed guards who stood with the woman. The young man and Yole still lunged and slashed at one another and both had landed blows, although none serious or fatal. But seeing how the fight went against them the Cheshire man who resembled the king called: 'Stop fighting. I order you to stop fighting.' His assailant might have taken advantage of this, but he spared him, so the remaining Cheshires ran off with their prisoner.

They did not go far, however, for while we stood there panting with pride an avalanche of a dozen horsemen fell on them. They were led by the distinct figure of Scrope, Earl of Wiltshire, who singled out Yole for himself.

The fight was fierce and sudden, and all the more inexplicable, but over quickly for Scrope and his esquires, although lesser of muscle, were far more skilled. In spite of his huge size and strength Yole was outmatched by the bald adept counsellor and soon was at his mercy, lying on the ground. I expected to see him spared, for I believed they were both of the same inclination and loyal supporters of Richard. I was starkly amazed when Scrope, apparently without stopping to consider the matter further, thrust his sharp sword straight into the archer's heart.

My master painfully walked over to the dead man, his limp more pronounced than ever, for the exertion of the sword fight had tired him in the extreme.

'Help me roll him over,' he called to me.

Could a more onerous and despicable task be imagined than to touch this dead brute? However this was not a time for questions, although I could not imagine why my master should want him on his back, if not for a final time to look upon his face, or perhaps to give the crows a chance to peck out his eyes?

'Come on, Adam, heave.' We both had our shoulders to the mighty hulk of the murderer and former lover of Philippa, but lingered a moment, for Scrope had been leading away from us the nun disguised as Katherine, and we turned to go to her rescue. Her disguise had all but vanished; before we could do anything he ripped off the wimple and exposed her for who she was. He doubled over howling with disappointment and rage.

I heard later that Scrope had a lifelong unsatisfied desire to possess Katherine, and even to marry her, for he was widowed and childless.

Apparently he tried one night, some years before, to seize her and carry her off (shades of my master here?). So overcome with passion had he been, that he had burst into her private lodgings in Lincoln, fallen on his knees in front of her, and clasped her in both arms. 'Get out of here, at once, or I'll tell Lord John!' she, faint with rage and terror, had tried to warn him. 'Please, please, have a heart,' he uttered, pressing his lips to her knees. She, with both her hands, seized the huge bald pate of Wiltshire to stave off more of his kisses.

'Please, please,' he repeated. 'Have pity. If you did but know – I'm on my knees, beside myself with love for you' – on and on he had raved while she cried distractedly for him to loose her, or she would have to spit in his face. Finally, while invoking her worse indignities upon him, she managed to persuade him to leave off pressing her further with kisses, although she was palpitating, exhausted and nearly vanquished. I guessed, in the end, that Scrope was too careful, too mindful of his position to resort to other measures, and of course Lancaster was still alive at the time, although estranged from his love.

Now I had become at one with my father. I knew what it was like to feel the clash of steel on steel, how to be the winner on the battlefield, to bathe in the flood of frenzy juice, personal outrage, the delights of danger, the joy of noble death.

Scrope, having dispatched the rest, remounted and breezed over to my master.

'Well Mr Chaucer,' he said, 'it must seem as if it is your lucky day. The king in his infinite wisdom and mercy has changed his mind about you. He had hoped to find evidence of a crime but this idiot here bungled it.'

With this, and without waiting for a reply, he cantered off, followed by his troop. My master shrugged. He went over to Wade's body. He called me.

'Look here,' he said. He pointed down at the shallow, rash face of this young man. 'A mere lad,' he commented, 'a green capering fool.'

I met the eyes of the dead boy. They were those of my sovereign king. I turned back to Yole. He wore the Lancastrian brooch which earlier I had pointed out to my master, and which had scratched me when Yole stole the dossier I was reading. What had Scrope meant by 'bungled it'? But my master avoided looking at the one-time mason's apprentice, and gave his attention to Pervil who had been left with us and who had collapsed. He felt her wrist, then lowered it gently onto her lap.

'I fear it has been too much for her,' he said. 'She has passed on.'

Thomas Swynford and the unnamed young man had, in the meantime, left for the Fleet in search of Lady Katherine. I asked who the stranger was, but my master told me that I would see him again at a later time, at the entombment.

'Oh, I expect you noticed, Adam,' he added. 'The brooch.'

I was tongue-tied with embarrassment. I knew about Yole 'Yes well, it was he, wasn't it?' I stuttered at last, 'who killed Rachel and Basil. Not Sir Thomas Swynford as we suspected. This was why the king wanted him out of the way.'

'How did you solve the crime?' asked my master.

'Very simple. The murderer told me himself. He did it on orders from the king.'

'The king?' My master whistled quietly to himself.

'The king wanted Philippa's confessions. Why master,' I added, seeing the look of bewilderment on his face as he remained silent, 'aren't you interested?'

'No, Adam. Remember what I wrote:

"One shouldn't be the inquisitor in life,
Either about God's secrets or one's wife." '

Then I understood. My master had taken them, first the sheets and then the main bundle. Reading what was in them must have had a chastening effect.

'Well anyway, thank you,' I said to him a little while later, 'you saved my life. But I still must warn you that, in spite of what Scrope said, the king has empowered the duke of Aumerle to arrest you and hear your case, one of slander and disparagement, in the Court of Chivalry.'

I observed that my master had remained hot and breathless. His passion was now doubly inflamed. 'The Court of Chivalry? What a joke! He is trying to create a strong and lofty monarchy, but it's too late!'

'Sit down, master. Rest a while. You need to. A man of your age needs rest after such exertion. Then you must give me your final explanation. You know what about. Where we left off in St Albans.'

'Oh yes,' answered my master with reluctance. 'You are persistent, Adam. You will not give up. The "rape".' He sighed and gave me a melancholy smile. 'Are you not weary from the fight?'

'No longer.'

'You surprised me with your valour. But you look odd, as if something unusual has happened.'

'It has. I will tell you. I have lain with a young woman.'

'Good heavens, Adam. And was it a satisfactory experience?' This acted on my master like a cordial. He regained his cheerfulness and good humour at once.

'I do not know, master…'

'And the young lady? Will you see her again?'

'Who knows, master…?'

'You feel no jealousy, no possessiveness…?'

'No.'

'No desire?'

'Rather the reverse. Guilt…and dismay. Shame.'

'Ah Adam…'

'Women are faithless, are they not, master? They are deception itself, the devil's work. Women cause temptation, and men have no power of saying no…'

Geoffrey scratched his head: 'Well I am not so sure. Not always. Not always. My sister-in-law has been more faithful in her adultery than most women in their whole married lives.'

'But not Mrs Chaucer, master?…'

'No, Adam.' He paused. 'She made me jealous.' The dead man lay there, a witness to his words.

'You have said that jealousy is the raw material for wisdom.'

'I suppose that may be true,' said my master wearily. 'Jealousy contains the seeds – the germs – of both sex and intimacy. Philippa was envious. She failed to see the necessity and value in her own life, for her the value was the court. She took pleasure in her ugly feelings. She fed on her desire for what she did not have.'

'Yes, but you took pleasure in your suspicions about her. And used them in your work.'

'I am afraid this may have been so. When I was jealous all sorts of ideas, fantasies, memories, would swim in that sea of emotion. I wanted to know whom, exactly, in me it was that was jealous. I wanted to know more about my jealousy.'

'I understood Mrs Chaucer was to blame for your jealousy.'

He nodded. 'Jealousy draws out a strange list of characters. The sheriff, or seeker of the truth of a crime, the ill man, the insanely suspicious, the stern upholder of justice and order. We slip sideways into suspicions, in order that the dark can escape being honest.'

Oh he was off again on one of his flights. 'I think jealousy is just an ugly emotion, Mr Chaucer. But jealousy would seem to have fleshed out your characters and given them reality, I grant you that. As for me I feel ugly when I am jealous. Aphrodite was furious with Hippolytus for not responding to her attentions. As Aphrodite confessed, "I stir up trouble for anyone who ignores or belittles me, and if they do this out of pride they are worse." '

My master lifted his head in a gesture of supplication. 'My jealousy did at one time become so bad, Adam, that there came a day when I had only one chance of escape...'

'You were pushed too far?'

'I was beside myself. I was full of desire – and where there is desire there is pulse – lechery – and a need to stretch oneself...'

I was beginning to sweat. It had taken me so long once again to lead up to this, and not give myself away. 'So one day, master, your eyes fall upon this beautiful young wench, Cecilia Chaumpaigne...'

I had touched the spot. I was home. I waited silent in breathless expectation . His rapture quickened his words. 'Oh, Adam, I cannot describe what a dream, what an idyll Cecilia was! While Philippa was dark, powerful bluey-grey eyes, dark red hair, pale skin, this Cecilia was fair, a slightly delicate, retroussé nose, with smiling eyes! No grimness here, but alive like a dart or a lance, green and hazel, jumping and fluttering with bright-coloured streamers in the wind! Her skin and complexion were of a most perfect tint and transparency! Nothing was more exquisite than her whole head! Seeing her I could once again find adventure in the chase, even pleasure in the deceit.'

'The deceit? – she was not married?'

'She was a widow. Married at fourteen, widowed at sixteen. Her father and mother held her in a vice as strong as the most restrictive of marriages. I was not surprised, because if her pure oval face was perfect, her teeth brilliant, her figure, well Adam, I can't but wonder at her very delicate, creamy tint of smooth flesh; alabaster and ivory were not more delicate to touch than her flesh everywhere, from cheeks to her toes. Deportment good, carriage upright but easy, movement voluptuous and fascinating: everything she did, I tell you, was graceful, indeed as a whole she was one of the most exquisite creatures God ever created to give enjoyment to man.'

Wait a minute, wait a minute. Be careful, I thought. Had not he said that this was Lord John's sentiment about Katherine? Was my master now regaling me with fact, or fiction? Fact or fiction, Mr Chaucer?

255

'But if she was guarded by her mother and father, how did you find your way to her?'

He turned to me excitedly. 'Exactly, Adam! That's it, exactly. Her father was a saddler in London, but the family also held considerable property in Pembrokeshire, together with his wife Agnes. Now I told you the truth that first I was asked by John Grove, a friend, to woo her on his behalf. He was often away, so Lord John suggested I would be the suitable person to carry out the negotiations on his behalf. Grove was a man of about forty, but unlike me he had no wife. I was trusted by Cecilia's father, because Sir William Beauchamp, the king's chamberlain, had required me to act as surety for all matters relating to Pembroke Castle. We were friends and Sir William was, as "custos" of the Honour of Pembroke, lord of Alice, Cecilia's younger sister.

'Well at my first meeting I was, as I outlined, so struck with her physical beauty, and the first part I told you was true. She, rejecting my suit on behalf of Grove, turned on me, for what reason I cannot imagine, certainly not in response to my own portly presence and shortened perspective. By no stretch of the imagination was I handsome or debonair...'

'I think by now I have grasped this point, master...'

'Good. Unfortunately, however, there is no greater aphrodisiac, Adam, than being a poet.' My master sighed. 'She undressed. Philippa was away all the time and had found her own way of renewing her youth. As my great mentor, Signor Boccaccio, writes of the Lady Alatiel, "She, who had lain perhaps ten thousand times with eight different men, went to bed with him as if a virgin and made him think she was one." And after this she lived with him happily as queen. Hence the saying: "a kissed mouth loses no savour, but is renewed like the moon".'

'So this, you are saying, in so many words, master, is what happened?'

'There ought to have been a time of circumspection, a time of mutual self-awareness, a growing period of warmth, a period of courtship, several serious conversations, a step by step measured growing acquaintance with the physical side of it – so that we arrived at an adult, and thoroughly worked out, appreciation of the situation.'

'And was there?'

He hung his head with shame. 'No, Adam. We just went for it...' He lowered his eyes significantly, '...straight away.'

I wondered what he would say then. How far would he go to convince me?

'I will be brutal and not spare you. Perhaps now you will believe me. We went on without care, without a thought of the consequences. I sorely repent of it now. I lost my head. It was as simple as that. I failed lamentably, and overwhelmed by my incoherent feelings for her, I could dream only of one thing. I was physically infatuated, Adam.'

My mouth was open with disbelief, and I looked at his eyes. They met mine. They were much larger than usual. 'Oh come on, master,' I said to him. 'So this ends up with a charge of rape against you…?'

'I am coming to that –'

'How did it happen that you passed your sister-in-law and Lord John delicately through the stages of courtship, and even in their adulterous affair, yet with you, you ignored the preliminaries and just jumped on Cecilia? – '

He turned on me. 'Have you never noticed how absence intensifies the vision and needs of the heart? Of Cecilia, I couldn't have been fonder. Take off your shirt, she would say, and as I removed it she lay on the bed with her thighs apart.'

'We need to go into this?'

'Do we? I cannot say. Perhaps now I am old and this is but a vision and a dream. Once it was real. The thighs led to that exquisite temple of pleasure which was perfection itself.'

In spite of my wild gestures of protest he would stop at nothing. He began a torrent of concupiscence that would make me blush to set it down. Stop, stop, stop… . I burned red, blushed with overbrimming, molten shame as my master insisted on such careful and precise naming of parts, of bottom opening, of nether lips, of rifts and buttons, of delicate and youthful pink colouring which were degrading to the female sex. I could only be grateful that he had never gone so far – although sometimes nearly – in his pictures in the tales of such matters. I feared the books would have been seized by officers of the king and thrown on a pyre, and I cast in prison for copying them.

I gave in. I thought of last night and of my own trespass. To stop him I said, 'I have to admit, master, it doesn't sound like rape.'

'Rape?' He laughed. He began a new cycle. 'Never have I experienced such exquisite delight! Again and again I enjoyed her, kissed and smelt that divine body, and looked into those voluptuous eyes. I had for her at once a great love as well as lust…'

My master, transported in raptures of joyful memory, began once more to glorify Cecilia's skills. He shed the years as he claimed she shed his seed. He was in seventh heaven. He looked at me with disarming innocence.

'But had she no pleasure herself, and is that why she brought the charge?'

'No. She had few scruples in satisfying her desires. How we would eat and drink with joy and expectation – and she was pleased by my rapturous eulogiums of her loveliness – "You know a well-made woman when you see one." She would drop her chemise, while our fingers would play. She most loved me kissing her thighs, which while resting would be open and soft, and that which lay between. She was lovely and exquisite to the marrow, and mysterious though it was to me – indeed unbelievable – my body pleased her. Not that she said it then, she was too clever a Paphian. What a delicious spectacle in her room it was, through the windows of which both back and front were green trees and gardens. If I subtract myself, that is.'

I had my hands over my ears. 'Enough, now, please. Enough, master. Is not this lascivious gratification a revolt against women?'

He was enjoying the game. He continued in his delineation of passion till again I implored him to stop.

'No,' he wagged his finger, for then the *post coitum tristia* of his account fell on him like a stone, and his mood swiftly changed, 'all this is but the tired game of an old man, like the stimulant at bedtime with which my stepfather Bartholomew used to lace his claret: "Ypocras cordial and a vernage of hot spices." True love needs no potions, not even the posthumous potion of words. I regret it all. Even the nonsense I have just spoken.'

'What did Philippa think of this?'

'She was cold towards me and she turned me away. Yet in the very power of her rejection she still possessed me.'

My master was silent for some moments as he reflected and moistened his lips with his tongue. 'It's a paradox, Adam.'

'What is?' I asked sharply.

'The love of man and woman.'

'Why didn't you divorce Philippa?'

'Cecilia wanted this, and when I didn't, it also made her angry. Divorce is difficult, Adam. It is an offence against God.'

'Is it? But not the divine monarch. The arrogant, empty-headed Marquis de Vere, duke of Ireland – the king's favourite – divorced King Edward's grand-daughter, Philippa Coucy, and married his mistress Agnes Lacecrona, the Czech who waited on Anne of Bohemia. Richard favoured the divorce...'

'How well-informed you are, Adam. But then de Vere was murdered,' said my master thickly, as if a similar threat to him was only too real.

'No. He died in France in a hunting accident.'

'He was condemned to death by parliament and lived in exile!'

'This was nothing to do with his divorce and remarriage. You could have channelled John's patronage into freeing you from the chains of marriage.'

My master looked deflated, depleted, tired and no more the dazzling lover as depicted by himself.

'And lose all this?' he almost mumbled.

'All what?'

He turned on me, inflamed with sudden anger. 'All what, you ask!! The royal patronage, the princely connections, the sistership of Katherine, the public occasions where I read! This scarlet robe I wear given me by no less than Prince Henry of Bolingbroke! Do you believe that Philippa would not have wreaked her revenge on me for divorcing her, for I gave her above all what she desired. Do not forget, Adam, she was first in Queen Constanza's household, a position she could never, with that fanatically religious lady, have held as a divorced woman. This apart from the sense of rejection she would have felt which would have made her act, have no fear.

'No, Adam, as Mr Cecilia Chaumpaigne I would never have attended the reading of John's will. Nor would my poem of Griselda have been read aloud and thunderously applauded at the court of the king. I would have been an obscure, provincial figure. I probably even would have forfeited Lancaster's yearly stipend.'

It was then my turn to sigh. I could not but agree that it would have hit him where it hurt. 'Well, all matters in human life proceed by decay and corruption, master. And now before it's too late it is your turn to profess repentance and penance. Poor Cecilia became enraged and brought the charge of rape. Then she died.'

He raised a hand in a further plea for attention. 'It was by no means simple. Cecilia, poor deluded soul that she was, loved me to distraction. She had to be persuaded by her brother to accept the terms...'

'The terms?'

'Of my compensation. My worldly goods, or most of them. My house in London – remember Aldgate was but a grace and favour from John – while I had sold Thames Street to finance the bond that Mr Grove took up on my behalf.'

'Oh yes, what about this Mr Grove? He cannot have been too pleased when he lost his bride-to-be.'

'He had found another woman abroad, and married her. He was happy not to have to pay me the fee for the work I undertook on his behalf.'

'So the whole charge of rape, the arrest, the pleas for John to release you, it was all nothing but an elaborate charade? You expect me to believe this? Why didn't you keep the whole affair secret?'

'I was afraid you might ask, but the family, the father in particular, was outraged. They were after my blood. They wanted revenge for the stolen honour of their daughter. She was pregnant, I couldn't marry her, and then she had a child. She and I had to plot the whole subterfuge together, and as plots go wrong so did this one, for the plan was that I should not be arrested, but simply discovered. Unfortunately,' smiled my master, 'Cecilia was too good an actress.'

'You mean, unless I misunderstand, master, that she was truly aggrieved and the seduction of her by you was against her better judgment. She had second thoughts, and felt angry and full of recrimination.'

My master contemplated me fully in the face. He took hold of my hand. 'By all the friendship I have given you, Adam, I swear what I have told you is the whole truth.'

'But where is the proof?' I cried out. 'There has to be some, for think of all the sacrifices that have been made, the lives of Rachel Dempsey and Basil...'

'I swear.'

His eyes had not left mine, and I saw from his hard and incessant reading and writing how the flesh sagged above and below each, hiding its inner rings, but whether these, even if I saw them, were of truth or falsehood who could ever tell? I had read the confession that his wife made in her journal, but here she used the rape as a pretext for lewd thoughts and voluptuous sensations, wallowing in its aphrodisiacal power. And then she was fuelled by her own resentment. Surely the whole world at this century's end had gone mad with a concupiscent fever, with my master as its chief clerk.

'I can read your expression,' said my master. 'You still have doubts.'

'You make your pilgrims disclaim responsibility for their stories and actions. You disclaim responsibility for what you write and do. Your story tellers delineate their own responsibility to recite or rehearse the facts, but they insert fictions. I think – '

My master interrupted. 'Ah Adam, is it possible to separate fact and fiction? I think it is rather playing and telling. That is a better way of expressing it. Listen to my Miller:

"But first I make a protestation
That I am drunk, I know it by my sound – "

Swynford, imposing his will on Katherine on his wedding night, he well knew what he was doing...'

'What you told me does not tally with what Katherine said. Her account – '

'Her account? What is important to women is not male truth, but play and telling.'

'Are you saying women are liars?'

'Not exactly, Adam. But fabrication is a special female skill...'

'Then you are placing women on the side of madness and lies?'

'Not exactly, Adam... . Not exactly...'

Fury and indignation continued once again to mount inside me. 'Then you are saying you raped Cecilia Chaumpaigne, at the same time she agreed to it and enjoyed it, that both of you made up the story of the rape, and that she acted it so well you had to provide compensation! That she was angry that you would not leave your wife, and that the birth of an illegitimate child proves it was true love!'

My master heaved a great contented sigh, and then interlaced his fingers. 'That is about the sum of it. Yes, it is complicated. Well done, Adam. Love is *our* invention. And so is the rest of the world. But the reckoning must come, for God is there, inevitably, and the reckoning must be paid.'

'Let's just leave it, master, at this. Rape is rape. And if it wasn't true you could have sued her for perjury or defamation.'

'In English law there is one definite proof that an act of congress taking place against the will of the woman is not an act of rape.'

'And what is that, master?'

'No woman can conceive if she does not consent.'

'Are you saying that because Cecilia had your child, it could not have been rape?'

For a long time my master pondered the importance of this.

'Yes.'

This to me became as a ray of light, a blessing, a release.

'Then I, too, cannot be the issue of a rape?'

'You too, Adam, cannot be the issue of a rape.'

'So then your tale of my mother's wedding night is also a lie?'

'Was I there, Adam?'

Here some impulse of peace, unexpectedly, like a blessing, seized hold of both of us, so that we were disposed to silence and friendliness. After some minutes had passed, my master reflected, 'All this is beside the point. For the most solemn moment in the passage of a man's life approaches. I speak of John's requiem and his burial.'

Twenty-seven

Scriven

THAT NIGHT I COULD not settle. My master had cut off any further conversation on the matter, and sent me to rest. He had threatened me with dismissal. I was his servant still, and I obeyed.

Rest? What hope of this, for after the clash of swords in the court of Ely House my mind was feverishly active, and I continued to remain surprised, exhilarated, and even ecstatic at my own courage.

I could not claim that I had been the most skilled of swordsmen. Apart from the unknown young man who had joined us, then slipped away, none of us was highly trained. A little after the combat, if such you may call it, a heavily cloaked and hooded figure stole down the stairs behind me and slipped away unnoticed in the night. Katherine. She had taken refuge in a hidden recess off the stairway. My master believed she then took a quick route to the Carmelite monastery to be re-united for the last time with her dead husband. He reassured me that the danger from King Richard's followers was over; and now that he had finished with his play-acting and grand gestures, the Lancastrian guard over the hearse would be reinforced.

'We mustn't mistake his impulsiveness for violent and extreme action which is carried through,' observed my master. 'Vain, and ultimately angry men such as he react with impulsive cruelty, but then suffer a crisis of conscience and regret what they have done. He intends no harm to the duchess, although some of those who surround him have decidedly other thoughts.'

He could only mean Scrope. I did not agree. The king was not likely to forget a slight or failure. Look how he had taken his revenge against his uncle for standing up to him and curtailing the power of his favourites. Richard had commanded John Hall, a former valet of the Nottingham household, with half a dozen accomplices, in that back room of a Calais hostel, to suffocate Thomas of Woodstock under a feather bed. He had waited before he did this. This time he would not wait so long.

The rhythm of the bells was somewhat too violent to be an ordinary summons to early mass. I made my way towards them. In the pale lemon dawn I sought a barber to shave off the scrag of my beard for the ceremony of entombment. Of washing some of this filth from my person, I was constrained to forego.

The new light of this forty-second day cleansed and purified. There had been further riots and unrest during the night. Gangs of Lancastrians and supporters of the king had fought and fired houses, but the greater power of the city, the sheriff, his guard and armed deputies, had brought these incidents under control. The Cheshire men had been driven back to their pallets in Westminster, the Lancastrians had gathered at the Fleet Monastery, where, awake and fully armed, most of them stood ready for the day. They were all too keen for this to be over, so they could go back to their comfortable strongholds in the north.

I entered the vast nave, with its many shafted pillars, and gazed up at the high vaulted roof. The sheer size was breathtaking, and this morning it was clear of its pickpockets, and even of the scribes who wrote letters and legal documents. At the north end of the transept was the charnel house and sometimes, although not today, an awful burial smell spread outside Paul's Cross where sermons were preached.

Not many of us could read or write, but with the introduction of English more and more had become interested, especially among the noble class who formerly used to feel delight in their ignorance of the written word and employ many letter writers. Perhaps those who no longer wrote the nobles' letters were finding work in English to copy. More books were put on sale here, and I noticed the market of bookstalls against the precinct, and between the buttresses of the cathedral. Bibles, catechisms, medical books and treatises on the properties of herbs were on sale, and even one book, *The Birth of Mankind*, to describe gynaecology. There were prognostications and prophecies in cheaper copies and thinner shapes, but few books in Latin.

The hearse had not yet arrived, but around the temporary catafalque the candles were being lit again, the first time since John's body left the Collegiate Church of Our Lady in Leicester. Ten large tapers in the name of the Ten Commandments burned in atonement for his trespasses; the seven candles above in memory of the seven deadly sins. Higher yet, the five large tapers in honour of the five principal wounds of Our Lord Jesus, and for his five senses which John of Gaunt said he had expended negligently and for their misuse had prayed to God for mercy. And then, crowning all these, the three tapers in honour of the blessed Trinity to which he commended himself for all the wrongs he had done during his life.

Behind this, the tomb in which he was to be laid alongside his first wife. Henry Yevele, who was in his eightieth year, designed the alabaster effigy on it. Twenty-five years before, five years after her death, Yevele had designed Blanche's permanent tomb.

My master was already here. And with him someone else. He led me out into the yard. The poor were gathering in great numbers. Last night, from every part of London, the poor converged on the Fleet. The news had spread that for the salvation of his soul John had not only given the poor fifty marks of silver for each of the forty days of his lying-in state, but that on the eve of his entombment he was leaving three hundred marks of silver to them. But, afterwards, it would be said that the money distributed never reached the sum John promised, the excuse being that the disposal of the money had been at the discretion of the executors.

Katherine was also there, humble in expression, surrounded by the poor, receiving the thanks and pleas. Seeing her, a figure of such grace and beauty, so composed and so elegantly garbed in black, a crowd of frightful ideas rushed upon my mind and threatened to overwhelm it. I saw plainly into the recesses of my own soul, and I shuddered when I thought of the unhappy girl who had undone me, as I had undone her, and I confessed that for the first and only time in my life I was strongly in love… . Not with her, but with Susanna, the one I had taken her to be.

'Here is your proof, Adam, that my love for Cecilia was not rape.' It was my master's gentle, loving voice beside me. He laid hold of the arm of the blond young man who stood beside him and who smiled at me with an open, innocent spirit. It was no other than the skilled swordsman of the previous evening's engagement.

'This is Lewis. My son.'

My mind worked swiftly. 'Lewis to whom you dedicated the treatise on the astrolabe?'

'Lewis to whom I dedicated the treatise on the astrolabe. His mother, name of Cecilia Chaumpaigne, died shortly after his birth. After a few years with us but when Philippa died he was raised by an uncle, a man of law, in Barnet. When I left you in St Albans I stopped to collect him. And so he is here.'

The son. The epiphany. He had saved us all. Me included. We shook hands warmly. I was speechless.

As we stood there awaiting the full morning sunrise, it promised to be a warmer day, so different from the wretched ones of our journey. Leaving her entourage of the poor, the scabby, the homeless, Katherine glided over to me with open hands and greeted me.

She left my master and his son to minister to John's beneficiaries and led me a little apart where we could sit down on a bench of stone and not be interrupted. She seized me by the hand and pressed it close to her stomach, an intimacy which I found both flattering and embarrassing: close as I was to her, I looked into her bright and smiling blue-green eyes, which in spite of her grief were warm and comforting.

'You know, Adam, that they still say that I am a witch and an enchantress, and that I put a spell on John to entangle him with me in lechery. That I was the heart and cause of the hatred that men bore him, and were it not for me he would have been popular like his father and his brother.'

'Do you believe this?' I asked.

'God knows I never wanted to do him harm, but only to love him.'

I stared a second time into her eyes, and saw much beauty, as well as suffering, in her drawn and haggard face. I believed for a moment that I understood what it meant to look into the face of Our Saviour. It could be that the misfortunes she had suffered sprang from the essential goodness of her nature.

'Like many, I did not approve of what you did,' I began my answer. 'I can see you had good intentions. Your spirit shines through your face, and through your body. If you were crooked in thought and feeling, your body would be bent and twisted. If you were just a beautiful, empty vessel, you would ring with a false sound.'

'I have no sense of this,' she answered. 'I feel more than most women miserable and cut down. For years my sin with John mortified me. I was suspected of murdering my husband. Even though his death happened nearly thirty years ago, I still suffer the shame of accusation. Anyway' – she saw the nobles and ladies arriving for the funeral – 'I have little time now to speak.'

Unconvinced as I had been by my master's explanation, it was on the tip of my tongue to ask her why she thought John's corpse had turned from being so putrid and stinking into the odourless, even sweet-smelling, chestnut, or pressed orange of yesterday. But I stopped myself.

'Royal funerals are few,' I said. 'There will not have been such a magnificent one since the death of our royal Edward.'

She ignored my words.

'I had to wait,' she said rather breathlessly in that lovely voice of hers, which in our native tongue still retained some of its unfamiliar French accent. 'Until I conferred with Brother Thomas to tell you this. He explained what I did not know, namely why John before we married became so distant to me…on account of his confession and renunciation of venery…now I understand.'

She did not go on. I remained in the dark, but kept my silence and my place. Now she regarded me even more strangely.

'Until I arrived in St Albans the day before last I did not know how intimately connected we were, and that I was your stepmother. That Hugh was your father. You have so little of him in you.'

The spurt of emotion could not be contained. 'I don't know,' I replied. 'The anger is more hidden, that is all. Hidden venom.'

'Walsingham also told me you always believed that John and I plotted to have your father killed. It may certainly have seemed like this, for everyone assumes lovers want to remove all obstacles to their love.'

I just about refrained from placing my hands over my ears. I did not want to listen. 'Nothing you can say will make me change my mind. It's no good coming here offering excuses. John – my lord (I add hastily for I must not sound too rude) is dead and – well, you have to live your own life. You may make penance, you may confess, but nothing will change the nature of your crime, which will live on and on as the most hidden vicious action of this reign.'

'Nothing?' Her eyes, which were forgiving, were also inquiring. I had to admit that I could see no guilt in these eyes.

'It is supposed to be established upon good evidence that my father was poisoned by a cup brought to him by you. Now he may not have been the best of men, but his own nature did not justify the evil deed that was committed on him.'

'And so he was. Or this was part of it. He also choked on smoke.'

'Well, this may be claimed as an accident or fault of the house. But are you trying to tell me you did not know what was in the cup?'

'I swear I did not know.'

'Then who prepared it?'

Katherine caught my look of apprehension in those lovely candid eyes of hers, and held it as if she was trying to melt any accusation.

'You are not answering.' She made as if to move away. 'And now,' I pursued her angrily, 'you are about to make off! You don't want to hear the truth!'

She came back and began again, sweet and controlled in her mellifluous voice.

'Well last night, Adam Scriven or Swynford, or whatever... You shall listen. When the Cheshire men invaded Ely Palace, and I was with the nun. They took us, and would have killed or abducted both of us, had not the nun...'

'Yes?' The grey-haired biddy. She took Katherine's place. A look – a something – had passed between us, some flicker or shudder of recognition. Often I thought of her, and of the terrible, unknown end she might have suffered at the hands of those murderous bullies had they carried her off.

'This is awful for me, Adam Scriven. I had rather not say.'

I exploded with anger. 'For the love of God, Katherine! Forgive me, but what offal of rank, lying deception are you now trying to ram down my throat?'

'I grant you,' she answered, evidently spurred on by my hostility. 'You want the truth. You shall have it. The nun, Sister Pervil, was the one who killed Sir Hugh. I swore not to tell you until she was dead. It was she who used the fire, the cup which she poisoned, and with a mixture of poisoning and suffocation subdued that brute strength...'

I interrupted. 'Tell me another lie, Lady Katherine! It is all very well saying this now. She cannot answer for herself, or deny it. Trust a woman to pick on such a wily trick, it is worthy of Synon at Troy. What motive or reason could she possibly have had to kill my father? Tell me, and I might believe you. You never can, can you! You can't even face me with your eyes, can you? : you can't look at me straight.'

'The reason, Adam, Pervil killed Hugh, my husband and your father, was' – here she stopped, forestalling revenge by looking me in the eye. 'It was Hugh, many years before – how old are you, Adam?...'

'Forty-six, but what's my age got to do with it? Stop playing this game, my lady. You've changed the subject yet again.'

'No,' said Katherine very quickly, 'I want to be sure of my ground. Sister Pervil had only once before seen and met Hugh – forty-seven? forty-six? – years before, when he stopped by a lake, took her from the water while she was bathing there naked, and cruelly raped her. In other words...'

My hands went to my throat. The very stones of St Paul's, lime white-washed, blurred and dissolved before my eyes.

'Pervil was your...'

Mother, my mother. Now I know. Christ save me. Christ save me.

The words clanged in my mind like the deranged bells all over London, suddenly renewed and summoning us to the last rites for Lord John of Gaunt.

Then, quickly, Katherine told me the details as Pervil described them to her. When the nun was eighteen, a young novice in a convent near Lincoln, she was out alone one scorching summer's day walking in the middle of a forest. Coming to a lake she decided to swim and took off her clothes. She was discovered by a young knight riding nearby who had disguised himself as a wandering friar just for the purpose of seducing her. He found her clothes where she had hidden them, and teased her to leave the water holding the undergarments up as bait. She grew suspicious, telling him she feared he intended something bad towards her, and he answered that in this case he would have to withhold the clothes, which was a pity as she had such a beautiful body. At least, she begged him, would he respect her virtue when she left the water?

Covering herself as best she could she emerged from the lake dripping wet. He handed her the chemise, and helped her fasten her cloak. He implored her to accept him as her lover and then prevailed upon her to walk with him in the forest. Again and again she refused his advances, and then the wicked, false knight said he would not be able to get what he wanted without force. He led her further into the wood, laid her down on the ground, and ravished her.

'Soon after this,' Katherine concluded, 'she found that she was carrying a child. From that moment on she suffered an undying desire for vengeance, until she found the knight and settled the score. Then she felt only remorse.'

When Katherine began telling me this I was keeping an eye on arrivals for the entombment. But for the last part of her revelation I had forgotten there was anyone there except for her and myself. As swiftly as she had been here, now she had gone, and my master was beside me in her place, leading me away into some alleys and to a barber's shop hidden from sight of the cathedral, where I took refreshment while he settled in a chair to be razored. He looked well, refreshed and brimming with good intentions.

'I have now pieced together what has actually happened during these past few days, and why whose murders took place on the express orders of the king.' So he set out to recite once more the whole horrible history.

'I know all this, without you telling me again. I heard the very same words from the murderer's mouth. But one thing I would like to clear up is how and why, if, as Scrope said, Yole in Huntingdon ran away without those papers, he sent Scrope to – '

'Tut tut!' My master ignored what I said and went on. 'The king has always been like this, he lets minor henchmen do the job, and when they bungle it he sends in the more weighty disposers of life – and they have to stick near to the law and say they act like this because there is a plot against the king – when there is no such plot at all. The king is playing many, many people. He does not know which of those different people he is, or has, to play next...'

'You mean it comes back to your poem?'

'You cannot play an image, then change the image and play another image. In the final reckoning no one trusts you. John had never been an image, he had always been real, and he had always shown integrity. He had the solid following, Richard only the cheers from the play-watchers – a bit like his father and great-grandfather Edward II.'

'So why did the king want proof of John's adultery, and why did he think this was to be found in Philippa's papers, and so order his men to have them stolen?'

'He thought Philippa had continued as John's mistress, and he thought he would find references to John's liaison with Katherine.... Not only did he think this, he was sure he would find reference to Swynford's murder, and even reference to the plots John was supposed to have hatched to take the crown from him...'

Twenty-eight

Chaucer

IN THE FRONT ROW of the cathedral, to the left of the aisle, two places had been left empty. I told Scriven these were for Katherine and the king. Behind, in the second row, were already seated members of John's family, with them their royal or ducal spouses. The eldest, Henry Bolingbroke, was of course notably absent, for his arrival would have served only as the prelude to his execution. Neither was his wife, Mary de Bohun, here, for she – a captive John made to advance his son's fortunes – had died, while Henry in Paris was reputedly wooing another lady. His sister Philippa was present with her royal spouse, King João of Portugal, and several of their eight children. Next to them an usher was positioning Catherine of Castile, sole daughter of John and Constanza, with her husband Henry of Castile, and their son who was destined to become king of all Spain. Their presence provoked audible groans and hostile glances from the other side of the aisle.

Elizabeth of Huntingdon sat bolt upright in the pew behind, with John Holland, her husband, never much of a Lancastrian, but less even now, wanting to show himself firmly of the king's persuasion. She had seduced him, become pregnant by him, then John had forced them to marry. He looked most uncomfortable seated among his sworn, if secret enemies, and later was to die for plotting to restore Richard. But now Huntingdon was surrounded by the powerful, well-made Beauforts, John, Henry, and Thomas, all three, with Joan, the newly legitimized children of Lancaster and Katherine, and therefore, you might add, the issue of my own, carefully crafted love verses. Long before his death John manoeuvred the king's half-niece, Margaret Holland, into marriage with John Beaufort, who was now ennobled as earl of Somerset. Even more inevitably, Henry Beaufort had been consecrated bishop of Lincoln, for it lay in his father's gift. He had just reached the age of thirty, and for all his ecclesiastical finery hardly looked more than twenty. He must have taken after Katherine more than his father, for they say he was, if one might coin the phrase 'unimpeached by venereal leanings', and had no children. Then there was Thomas, or Tamkin, and his wife, finally Joan Beaufort, who in the year Katherine had married John, herself had married Ralph Neville, earl of Westmoreland, the greatest Lancastrian champion of all. He was here too. Behind them, among a greater mass of Lancastrian supporters, I could easily pick out my own son, Thomas, his wife Maud Burgesch, whom he married several years ago: Thomas was Richard's chief butler, and together with him I had taken out the lease on the house in Westminster. Next to him was Lewis; then Sir Thomas Swynford, with his second wife Margaret Darcy (I shuddered to remind myself what had happened to Jane Crophill, the first). Sir Thomas was due to be advanced next year, for he was destined to become the deposed king's jailer in the mighty Lancastrian fortress of Pontefract (and, by deliberately starving the king to death, some say his murderer).

The throng of Lancastrian mourners was thick and close; they were watchful of whether or not the king would attend; while most of their pursuivants waited outside, for there was no room for them, they wore swords under their cloaks, as did the nervous foreign envoys. The gracious women in black radiated calm and sorrow but were fearful of catastrophe. Five years ago when Queen Anne died and Richard gave her a magnificent funeral, with the greatest display of wax candles ever seen in England, there had been a considerable disaster. The earl of Arundel arrived late, and Richard was so incensed at the insult to his wife that he snatched a wand from a verger, and knocked Arundel to the ground. As Arundel's blood from his hurt was polluting the abbey, the ceremony was suspended and the abbey reconsecrated. So when the report reached us that Richard, sensing public outcry at the actions of his men the night before, and especially of his Cheshire archers' thwarted aim to abduct and detain Katherine, had left without warning early this morning for Canterbury, heads had turned and the whole cathedral became abuzz with uncertainty and tension.

I had elected to be seated humbly at the back, with the excuse that I was nervous that what had happened in the chapel of Leicester

Castle might be repeated on a much more magnified scale. And indeed it may well have been, for if the pews to the left of the aisle were filled with the might of the Lancastrian household, those to the right had been reserved for the king's host, and few on either side had left their swords behind, hidden though they tried to make them – and they were not ceremonial weapons, befitting the occasion, but ones for bloody conflict.

The sheriff of London, expecting trouble and disorder, had a company of deputies outside. Both sides had scores of men-at-arms in the guise of liveried servants and men-in-waiting camped on the slopes of St Paul's Hill. But there were also many richly attired city merchants there, with their buxom wives, and for them it was an occasion for peace and grateful mourning. No more would my brother-in-law be able to pillage their coffers and make war against France. As far as the king was concerned they had managed to make themselves untouchable, so they could afford to be generous with their floral wreaths and tributes. Their leader, the mercer Richard Whittington, who was Lord Mayor for the third time, bowed solemnly towards me as he passed to take up his place in the congregation.

Some rows ahead I noticed a gathering of chroniclers and poets, gossips and tittle-tattle merchants, come to record the funeral in their vain and boastful pages, bending interpretation to where their own self-interest lay. Most conspicuous among these was Jean Froissart, newly arrived from France, who had vividly although untruthfully recorded our world of chivalric conflict. He travelled everywhere, eager for further bloodshed and battles between Plantagenets and his native Valois. To seek matter for his histories he had even journeyed as far as Scotland, which showed his extremity of mind. But in general, ignorance was never a barrier to his invention, and no doubt he would adorn this funeral with the most lurid and unlikely details, such as were invariably supplied by those forced to rely, as he was, solely on the earnings of their quill.

But today he sat among his equals, and perhaps these would hasten and sharpen his tongue even further: John Gower was one, the Lancastrian panegyrist and my dear friend, to whom I had dedicated *Troilus and Criseyde*, and whom we all admire.

He wrote not from his own opinion, but spoke out what the voice of the people had reported to him. Like me he intended his words of good to bring evil to the light. He looked much older than his years and, half blind, had been led to his place by the self-opinionated

Welsh, or borderman, Thomas Usk, who, unlike Gower, was quite without tact, a sense of timing, discretion, or any judgement at all – and therefore well-equipped to be a chronicler. A little apart from these three, recoiling perhaps from the sense of his own repellence, crouched Thomas Hoccleve, not yet recovered from the excesses, as reported to me by Scriven, of the previous night's entertainments.

The uncertainty dissolved as word arrived that the king was on his way from Westminster. Trumpets blared, solemn music played, sad funeral dirges were sung as we waited. St Paul's was ablaze with every colour and sound. Richard Bruges, grizzled and stout, revered Lancastrian herald and king of arms to John, awaited him and Katherine at the head of the aisle before the altar. This was the forty-second day since John died, and so many tribulations had followed this prolonged presence of his on earth before the tomb. I prayed that the swift, changing events since his demise would not, at this final hour, overtake and overturn his funeral rites, for the path to this entombment had been littered with corpses: first with those of the two knights who had mistakenly squandered their lives to revenge Swynford. Then Rachel Dempsey, then Basil Worth. The attacks on my scrivener and I which failed, the arrest, then reappearance of Petronella Swynford; her deception of Scriven by pretending to be Susanna; the death of Sister Pervil, the deaths on the command of Scrope of Yole, Wade, and the others. The theft of the venereal ramblings of my wife (my own work). Then Richard's murderous and vacillating moods, his switches between great piety and spiteful homicide. The cathedral was supposed to be a sacred place, but would it be on this day of all others? Who knew or would say what could happen?…

The aisles which were not already filled with the blue and white men-at-arms and members of the cortège now suddenly became crammed to bursting with rough Cheshire bowmen in brown with white hart emblems, making sure their beloved 'Dickon' would not be seized by supporters of Bolingbroke. There was silence. Everyone turned to watch. Then, with multiple fanfares, Richard of England made his appearance. Like John when young, his hair was blond but not as tawny, more yellow, which he wore tightly coiffed, short and no doubt scented. He was dressed in black, black tunic and cloak, yet the brocaded black of his tunic sparkled with diamonds. The short goatee beard did not hide the softness of his chin. This morning with his large and heavy-lidded eyes, his pettish lips, he looked very boyish, in spite of his crown of mourning.

Everyone attended to the king as he sauntered down the aisle, glancing to one side, then to the other. Why had he changed his mind yet again: was it mere capriciousness which explained it? Or was it something deeper? The rows of Lancastrians gave one great collective shudder, as if they did not already feel jostled and threatened with the signs that their kingdom within the realm of England was to be broken up. Had the anointed king something deeper on his mind, such as God or salvation? A dark foreboding, perhaps, of his own fate?

In the short space of six months Richard was to lose his crown. Within a year his coffin, too, was to be brought in a hearse draped in black cloth, adorned with the arms of St George and St Edward, winding in solemn procession from Pontefract Castle to St Paul's where a requiem mass would be sung, attended like this one was supposed to be, by the king himself – only no longer him, but his usurper.

But this would be only the beginning of the fortunes of Richard's poor corpse.

Scrope, too, who would be left in charge of England while Richard invaded Ireland, was to die, caught and executed in Bristol, along with Sir John Bushy and Sir Henry Green. Chester, the inner citadel, the Troy of Richard's kingdom, was to fall without a fight.

One requiem at a time. Now it was John's turn. His good fortune, should it in the final reckoning work in his favour, would be to stay where he was put. And now quickly, almost apologetically, but as if she had been waiting at the back for the king to arrive first, Katherine walked swiftly down the aisle, unattended, alone, to take up her position at the side of the king, to whom she curtsied low. She looked round him anxiously, as if to ask where was the queen, but she was not present.

The long procession of black-robed celebrants, headed by the bishop of Winchester, William Wykeham, arrived at the high altar. Like Walsingham, the bishop had once been John's enemy, but in his last years had become his friend and supporter. At a signal the screens shielding the catafalque from public view were taken aside, and once again, and for the last time, surrounded by its blazing candles, we beheld our illustrious prince's body in sweet repose on the bier, re-embalmed and re-anointed, ready to be interred in the tomb alongside Blanche in compliance with his first marriage oath.

The sight was startling, and the congregation, united in awe for a moment, gasped at the splendour. He was to be placed there on his bed, which was now, from his will's express command, endowed with a priceless cloth of gold, with perse field powdered and with gold roses ordered along piping of gold. White ostrich feathers adorned the outer frame, and with them the bequest of perse taffeta batuz. Thirteen miraculously woven carpets surrounded it, with other luxurious gifts of cloth, and receptacles of gold and silver.

The solemn mass commenced. After a short time I felt my scrivener fidgeting by my side.

'Do you think,' he whispered close in my ear, 'that Henry will dare to take up arms against Richard? As a cousin he has no title to the crown.'

'Nor had Richard, in the eyes of many, since he lost most of France.'

'Yet he is sovereign. He is lawful king. It is his birthright.'

'I support Henry,' I told Scriven very quietly, but clearly not quietly enough for him. He looked around to see who might have heard.

'He has taken an oath of loyalty to Richard.'

'Early this morning the seizure of Lancastrian lands and goods began; pretending to act according to what is rightfully inherited by the king, the agents of the king deliberately exceed their bequests. Richard is breaking his oath to Lancaster.'

'Yet John would not break his oath for a kingdom; nor will his son. Bolingbroke may legitimately take back his lands.'

'Can he take them back without deposing Richard? By sending him into exile, Richard once and for all forfeited Bolingbroke's support.'

'Henry could still let Richard reign, and like his father rule as his protector.'

'Look how the king weeps.'

Just before the time due for his eulogistic address, Richard had mounted the altar steps, and fallen on John's open catafalque. He was shedding tears without restraint. He had to be lifted up by two of his gentlemen, who held him by the arms and led him to where, unaided, he mounted the pulpit.

'The the...the...' he began...'g-g-great duke is dead, long live the duke!'

He needed to find some fluency if not his reason:

'Lancaster was always my support, and do you know why? I saved his life many times. First it was my mother, Joan, who gave him refuge when the Londoners were after his blood, and would have caught him and strung him up had he not escaped on a Thames barge and been given protection in Kennington. Next the revolt of the Kentish churls, Tyler, Straw, and the evil and defrocked John Ball. It was not me they rebelled against, but my uncle John's poll tax. He wasn't here. Lucky him!

'We huddled in the Tower which became our vessel. The great storm raged, God's curse descended on the peasants, and turned them into beasts. Asses deciding they wanted to be horses and career bloodstained over the fields where they refused to do any more work. Oxen whose only thought was murder! Swine possessed of the devil! He wasn't going to have his head caught on their sickles and poles and mattocks, so he had flown to Scotland. It was me who put an end to their murderous insubordination. When my faithful knight struck down Tyler, I rode straight into the midst of those thousands of brutish slaves: 'I am your king!' I said. 'Would you have another?' 'No,' they answered back in one shout. 'I will redress your wrongs,' I told them, and they dispersed calmly and went back home. Here we could indeed redress their wrongs by having them arrested quickly, and their vicious ringleaders killed.

'So Lancaster basked in my protection. I let him pursue his continental ambitions, and when these failed I allowed him to serve me as my chief diplomat. He was better at peace than war. When his son Henry and Mowbray quarrelled, and Henry called Mowbray a liar and Mowbray called Henry a traitor, Lancaster pleaded with me to stop their duel so that Mowbray would not harm Henry. Then he persuaded me to limit Henry's exile to six years to allay the grief of an old man who could not bear to be separated from his son. He had plenty of others to support him in his old age – as we well know! And here was this son living a luxury exile in Paris. Why didn't he visit him there? I'd have gone with all speed!'

There was laughter from his Cheshire scum. Stony silence from the Lancastrians, although in some of them the temptation to unsheath their swords was strong.

'Oh he was a clever one, was my Uncle John… . We all owe him love and respect.'

He turned to the embalmed body. 'Oh uncle, how I loved you! Yes I loved you. And I loved Robert Vere, my friend whom you all, you lords and parliament, by sentencing him to death, took from me. Rumour has slandered me all my life, but I tell you that handsome though he was, better-looking even than I, I had no carnal love for Robert. The allegations that we enjoyed a base passion as my great grandfather did with Piers Gaveston were lies. Lies. He had my favour, he was my true friend – he made enemies because he left his royal wife for another woman…'

Richard rambled and stuttered on, stammering badly again once or twice, at other times taking out a pocket handkerchief and dabbing his eyes. And now it was the turn of his followers to sit in silence, chins jutting forward in defiance, hands on their hilts of their swords. Then he left the pulpit and sat down to the clear relief of the entire congregation, who had attended for the most part in bewildered silence.

'Well,' I sighed, because there was little else to say after such a performance, 'they are both Plantagenets.'

The mass picked up again. The body of John was raised from the catafalque and solemnly lowered into the open tomb. The bed was placed beside the tomb.

'Anything the matter?' I whispered to Scriven whose face had turned green.

'No, why?'

'Well you look – I can't quite explain it. Just a feeling. Apprehension. A premonition of evil?'

'Yes, if you like to put it that way. A feeling that something is going to happen.'

But he shook his head. For it seemed he had no definite apprehension of any particular thing. Perhaps it had only been a wave of depression and fear.

Katherine came forward to the chalice to take the host. Her head was held high; her lips pressed together, her face grave and beautiful. She looked like some young priestess. Like Judith before she cut the head off Holofernes. Turning back to take her stand beside the king she smiled and raised her eyebrows.

She had been the cause of so much in our kingdom. It seemed to me that in these two figures, the one still alive, the soul of beauty, a beauty that haunted men in their sleep so that they would undertake the death of all the world to live an hour in her bosom – the other now dead, a bloodless remnant of royal blood, although potent in influence, and magisterial beyond the grave – would one day to come to embody the very essence of passion, fidelity, and enduring love.

'There you are,' I concluded with a philosophical flourish for the benefit of Scriven, yet I knew him to be beyond being impressed by anything: 'John should have married Katherine much sooner. All along I had wanted him to.'

'Then no more Monsieur d'Espagne,' he whispered. 'It sounds faintly comic, like one of those half-mad fools you find at holiday feasts and fairs.'

Well he would say that, wouldn't he? 'John became destined to be the begetter of kings in Spain and Portugal, although never one himself.'

'Perhaps,' Scriven answered, 'it won't be long before his son and heir does fulfil Merlin's prophecy, that John's heirs will be kings of England!'

I heard this, but the surprise of his sudden volte-face robbed my response of much of its force. 'I shall always believe that John of Lancaster was the greatest prince this country ever had. Your opinion of him was always poor.' He was probably thinking, 'Is that why you thought fit to procure for him?'

'Yet I suppose it could be said that your true act of chivalry – indeed of charity, the greatest of the virtues – was to give away Katherine, the woman you loved most, to John. Then to marry, try to govern, the unruly sister, who caused you endless but ennobling pain. So while painting adultery and fornication, you hungered after loyalty and fidelity?'

'Ssshh, Adam!' I said, unable to believe that I had actually heard him say these words. 'Do you see what I see? I am afraid, Adam, you are about to see, for the first time in my life, your master's face turn to the jelly of fear itself.'

I believe I had begun, visibly, to shake.

I pointed to a tall lone figure who had edged himself forward to a position close to the aisle at the front with the mourners. He was dressed in a brown Capuchin cloak, and his hood remained drawn over his head.

The king stood up. He came forward to meet the figure face to face. He raised a hand. The ceremony suddenly halted. The cathedral became deathly silent. The king was alone, naked. An isolated figure. So was the other person. None dared move for the king gave no signal as they stared at one another. The king was driven to enjoy

279

such dramatic moments. But what of the other person? What if he drew a sword, or dagger?

I had another severe frisson. I smelled trouble. Would this intruder be another like that Carmelite friar who before the mass in Salisbury, and in the presence of Richard, had accused John of treason? It later had emerged that Robert de Vere, the favourite of the king, was behind this plot. Would there be further outrage against John? Or this time against Richard?

The intruder turned away. There was an audible rustle, a sigh of relief which rippled down the aisles. He went over to Katherine, inclined towards her, and whispered something in her ear: she turned to look at him full in the face, started up in fear, and then he took her hand as if he meant to console her. She anxiously stared towards the coffin of her husband.

'Who is it?'

I could claim that at this moment my eyes shone with an appearance of triumph.

'Remember my dream? Perhaps he is Death. This time the king's.'

'This is no occasion for levity,' Scriven snorted.

'Well,' I continued, 'I have a strong hunch.' I paused for a moment or two. 'The walk, the posture. Remember, Adam, who it was thirteen summers ago that arrived at the last moment to dine in Plymouth where John assembled his great host to recapture Spain? John on his flagship was ready to sail with Constanza, and he was not to see England again for three whole summers.'

'Oh go on, tell me,' whispered my scrivener in an anguish to know.

'He wanted then,' I went on, but more quietly, 'what he thought might be one last look, just as he wants it now...' as I said this, my voice broke with emotion, and tears flooded my eyes as I muttered, 'The son of the father...the son of the father...'

'You still haven't told me...'

'Hush, Adam. See, he cannot keep away.'

We watched. Swiftly the tall Capuchin broke away from Katherine, moving forward to kneel before the open tomb of John. A slight commotion in the crowd of mourners: they turned to one another, for no one quite knew what to do. He bent down his head, the heads touched, the live figure's head with the dead one. There was a gasp of horror and indignation.

Before any action could be taken by guards, the figure had left the altar and was walking quickly back down the central aisle. The funeral ceremony resumed. At the end of our pew I leant forward deliberately to jostle the hunched and round-shouldered monk when he would pass. I managed to catch him, and the face of the intruder turned briefly towards my scrivener and I. Adam responded with a look of horror because it was white, leprosy-ravaged, the nose eaten away, his two eyes little dark-bright, pin-holes in a puffed pastry of feature. It was a diabolical vision.

Scriven gave me a black look as if to say, 'Well now I know, and my master is once again in error. I am little surprised that lepers are considered such a curse. Yet this must be a receiver of charity, come to give his thanks and blessing, for John has given each lazar house in a radius of five miles around London five nobles in honour of the five wounds of Jesus.'

The afflicted creature rotated his lips, mumbled a few words in my ear, sucked, whistled, and passed swiftly out. I had known all along whom it was.

'What did he say?' Scriven asked breathlessly.

'*Cucullus no fecit monachum,*' I answered, unable to resist the opportunity.

He was silent.

'I see, Adam, you do not understand. It means the cowl does not make the monk.'

'I understand the Latin. I still do not follow, master.'

'Appearances generally lie.' I felt impatient with him. It was hard to forgive all that objectionable accusation.

'You mean it was no monk? Or...' he hesitated, 'no leper monk?'

'Did you see his hands? Were they mitten? Were his fingers clewed?'

'But there can be no doubt he was...'

I tried to look exasperated beyond belief.

'Neither a monk nor a leper. Henry of Bolingbroke, Adam. Henry of Bolingbroke. Come to say goodbye to his father.'

'Oh, I understand. So he wore a mask!'

'At last, Adam.'

'Well to think I could, if I had raised the hue and cry, have altered the whole course of England's history.'

'Yes, Adam,' I could hardly restrain my sarcasm, or shall we call it irony, 'and also caused an almighty bloodbath.'

I managed to breathe out with a gentle sigh, 'You, Adam, would then have earned your place in the chronicles!'

Sighs, like adultery and rape, were infectious. Mine no less than another's. Adam in turn sighed, but much more deeply. How would we ever understand? The obsequies of John drew to a close, for now, where he was placed for eternity in his tomb alongside the remains of Blanche, the lid descended a final time. The mourners left the cathedral, led by Katherine and Richard...

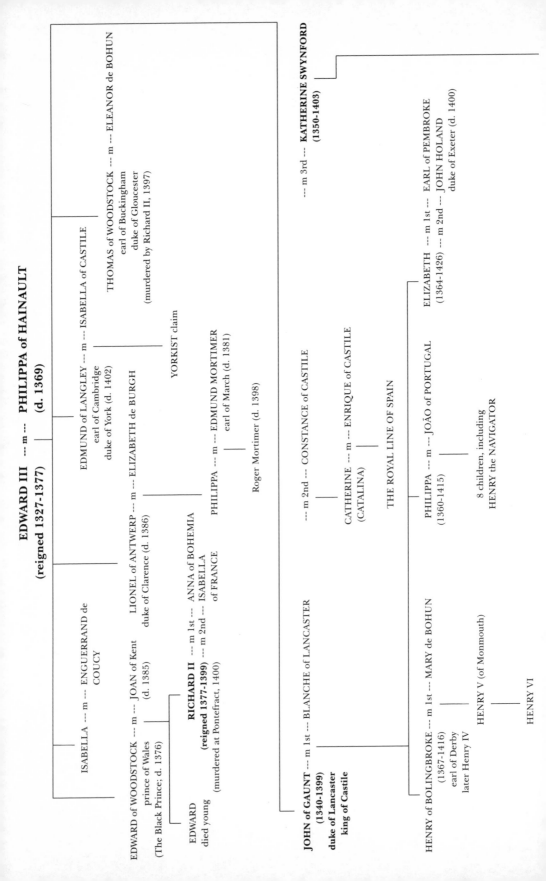

EDWARD III --- m --- PHILIPPA of HAINAULT
(reigned 1327-1377) (d. 1369)

ISABELLA --- m --- ENGUERRAND de COUCY

EDWARD of WOODSTOCK --- m --- JOAN of Kent (d. 1385)
prince of Wales
(The Black Prince; d. 1376)

EDWARD
died young

RICHARD II --- m 1st --- ANNA of BOHEMIA
(reigned 1377-1399) --- m 2nd --- ISABELLA of FRANCE
(murdered at Pontefract, 1400)

LIONEL of ANTWERP --- m --- ELIZABETH de BURGH
duke of Clarence (d. 1386)

PHILIPPA --- m --- EDMUND MORTIMER
earl of March (d. 1381)

Roger Mortimer (d. 1398)

EDMUND of LANGLEY --- m --- ISABELLA of CASTILE
earl of Cambridge
duke of York (d. 1402)

YORKIST claim

THOMAS of WOODSTOCK --- m --- ELEANOR de BOHUN
earl of Buckingham
duke of Gloucester
(murdered by Richard II, 1397)

--- m 3rd --- KATHERINE SWYNFORD
(1350-1403)

JOHN of GAUNT --- m 1st --- BLANCHE of LANCASTER
(1340-1399)
duke of Lancaster
king of Castile

--- m 2nd --- CONSTANCE of CASTILE

CATHERINE --- m --- ENRIQUE of CASTILE
(CATALINA)

THE ROYAL LINE OF SPAIN

ELIZABETH --- m 1st --- EARL of PEMBROKE
(1364-1426) --- m 2nd --- JOHN HOLAND
duke of Exeter (d. 1400)

HENRY of BOLINGBROKE --- m 1st --- MARY de BOHUN
(1367-1416)
earl of Derby
later Henry IV

PHILIPPA --- m --- JOÃO of PORTUGAL
(1360-1415)

8 children, including
HENRY the NAVIGATOR

HENRY V (of Monmouth)

HENRY VI

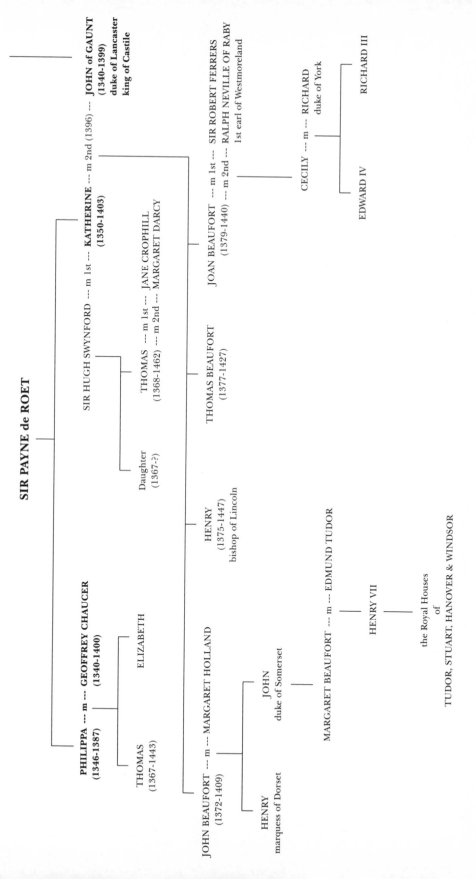

SIR PAYNE de ROET

PHILIPPA --- m --- GEOFFREY CHAUCER
(1346-1387)   (1340-1400)

THOMAS
(1367-1443)

ELIZABETH

SIR HUGH SWYNFORD --- m 1st --- KATHERINE --- m 2nd (1396) --- JOHN of GAUNT
                                 (1350-1403)   (1340-1399)
                                                                duke of Lancaster
                                                                king of Castile

Daughter
(1367-?)

THOMAS --- m 1st --- JANE CROPHILL
(1368-1462) --- m 2nd --- MARGARET DARCY

HENRY
(1375-1447)
bishop of Lincoln

THOMAS BEAUFORT
(1377-1427)

JOAN BEAUFORT --- m 1st --- SIR ROBERT FERRERS
(1379-1440) --- m 2nd --- RALPH NEVILLE OF RABY
                          1st earl of Westmoreland

CECILY --- m --- RICHARD
                 duke of York

EDWARD IV

RICHARD III

JOHN BEAUFORT --- m --- MARGARET HOLLAND
(1372-1409)

HENRY
marquess of Dorset

JOHN
duke of Somerset

MARGARET BEAUFORT --- m --- EDMUND TUDOR

HENRY VII

the Royal Houses
of
TUDOR, STUART, HANOVER & WINDSOR

Endnote

Eighteen months after Lord John's funeral, on 15th October 1400, Chaucer died suddenly. The cause was unknown. Thomas Chaucer died in 1434. Thomas, who like his father stayed an esquire and did not aspire to knighthood, led the life of a notable courtier, while by his death, according to a contemporary chronicler, 'There can have been few knights in England richer than he.'

Thomas's daughter, Alice, married first a baron, then one after another two earls, the first Thomas Montague, Earl of Salisbury (d. 1428), the second William de la Pole, Earl of Suffolk (d. 1428), which made her a countess. Rivalling Henry V as a commander, Alice's second husband, the renowned warrior Earl of Salisbury, featured in the king's battle cry in Shakespeare's play:

> Then shall our names,
> Familiar in his mouth as household words –
> Harry the King, Bedford and Exeter,
> Warwick and Talbot, Salisbury and Gloucester –
> Be in their flowing cups freshly remembered.

Suffolk was the hated favourite of Henry VI. He was murdered in 1450, the year England lost Normandy. John de la Pole, Alice's son by Suffolk, married Elizabeth Plantagenet, the sister of the Yorkist kings, Edward IV and Richard III. Their issue, three sons (Chaucer's great-great grandchildren), died fighting the Tudor monarchs who were the direct issue of Katherine and John of Gaunt.

Of Lewis Chaucer, we know no more than is shown in the dedication of the *A Treatise on the Astrolabe*.

Of Adam Scriven no more than Chaucer's lines to him:

Adam Scriven, if ever it falls to you
Boethius or Troilus to copy new
Under your long locks you must have scales
But under my correction you'll write more true...

So many times I must your work renew
Correcting it with many a rub and scrape
And all is through your negligence and rape.

It is not known that he did indeed have the last name Scriven, or where exactly he came from, although the names Stedeman and Pinchers have also been cited by scholars as alternatives; both these belonged to the Brotherhood of Writers of the Court Letter of the City of London between 1392 and 1404.

The reader can find a full discussion of Chaucer's alleged rape in *The Personality of Chaucer* by Edward Wagenknecht (Oklahoma Press, 1968). Here is a key passage:

> Apart from the alleged skeleton in the Geoffrey-Philippa family closet, one other sinister question mark has been set against Chaucer's name. On May 1 1380 Cecilia Chaumpaigne legally released him from any sort of action which might be taken against him '*tam de raptu meo tam de aliqua re vel causa*' [literally: 'to such a degree as concerning, or from, my *raptu* or from any other cause'] . Two months later she also released Richard Goodchild and John Grove, who, in turn, released Chaucer of all obligations to them, and Grove promised to pay Cecilia ten pounds at Michaelmas.
>
> In fourteenth-century Latin, '*raptu*' could mean either rape or abduction. That the second meaning could have applied in 1380 has been denied in two articles in *Law Quarterly Review*, P.R. Watts, 'The Strange Case of Geoffrey Chaucer and Cecilia Chaumpaigne' Vol. LXIII (1947), 491-515, and T.F.T. Plunkett, 'Chaucer's Escapade', Vol. LXIV (1948),

33-36. Watts does not actually pronounce Chaucer guilty, but he does interpret the evidence so as strongly to indicate guilt. He wonders, for example, 'Why Chaucer was not prosecuted at the suit of the King for the *raptus* of Cecilia Chaumpaigne. She must have made the incident the subject of open complaint; otherwise it could have been hushed up without the notoriety of a release under seal witnessed by the King's Chamberlain and other well-known persons and enrolled in Chancery...' He cites as 'one answer Chaucer's great influence at court...from which he goes on to speculate on the possibility of Cecilia having been a consenting party...'

Plunkett commits himself to another hypothesis – that Goodchild and Grove entered the case as sureties for Chaucer, to assist him in raising the money, which Cecilia demanded. He concludes: 'Finally, we must be fair to Chaucer. Rape is a brutal crime and implies a degree of depravity that should make us cautious in fixing such a charge. There is really no evidence for it. That he seduced Cecilia we may well believe; that she was angry with him, thought that because it all happened against her better judgement, that therefore it was without her consent... . But there is nothing to suggest that Cecilia could have convicted Chaucer of felony. The single word in the close roll is the only word anywhere suggesting crime of any sort in this affair, and we must bear in mind that no one incurred legal responsibility for its truth... . It was unlucky for Chaucer's memory that one of them was engrossed in chancery.' None of this is eminently unreasonable as hypothesis.

For a long time the possible explanation of 'raptus' as abduction as opposed to rape provided an alibi or escape from the charge. Today members of the Chaucer Society and traditional critics continue to defend their favourite. 'How could the man who wrote the poems we know,' asked one, 'have been guilty of committing rape under any circumstances?' Professor Stephen Knight, of Cardiff University, calls the case, 'Not proven' or 'doubtful', and pleads the humanity of the poet in his defence. The defenders of Chaucer's reputation, if admitting there must have been something there, in the words of one of them, 'dismiss it as a youthful escapade' (although Chaucer was nearly forty, beyond life expectancy in those days).

More recently too, with the rise of feminist critics, the '*raptus*' has become a hot issue among some Chaucer scholars, such as Professor Carolyn Dinshaw, Director of the New York Institute of Gender Sexuality, and Sheila Delany, of Vancouver's Simon Fraser University. When I spoke to Ms Delany she told me forcefully that, 'To ignore biographical probability in relation to an author's work is to commit an offence against history.' She went on, 'This is collective censorship – repression – such as several generations of Chaucerians have already committed, on behalf of posterity, in the interests of preserving this purified, moralistic view of a great English poet.' Adam Scriven would agree with her.

To add to the confusion, in the year following the alleged '*raptus*' or rape of Cecilia Chaumpaigne there appeared a Chaucer child, whose life is shrouded in mystery except that we know his name was Lewis. Was Lewis, Chaucer's lawful offspring (and remember Philippa and Geoffrey were much separated)? Or was he the child of the poet's one-off fling, or violent encounter, with Cecilia? The date of the birth of Lewis – and there appears little doubt among scholars that he was Chaucer's son – fits in with the idea he was conceived from a sexual union with Cecilia. Mediaeval medical and sexual theory – which go back to the Greek Galen – held the belief that a child could only be conceived if the woman had an orgasm. If Cecilia was made pregnant and conceived a son, ergo, she must have actively and pleasurably participated in her sexual congress with Chaucer. Therefore it could never have been rape. This, of course, might be the reason she never brought the accusation to trial, for a jury, had she been pregnant, would have decided in Chaucer's favour.

Whatever happened there was a heavy price for Chaucer to pay, which suggests it was truly a serious matter. To begin with, he had to sell his City of London house, inherited from his father who supplied wines to Edward III, to Herbert Herbery, a vintner. On top of this, he had to hand over a further sum of ten pounds (worth in comparative property values many hundreds of thousands today).

Here are some further considerations which might interest the reader.

From Michael A Calabrese, *Chaucer's Ovidian Arts of Love:*

> Modern scholars have celebrated Chaucer's distance from overt moralisation as a distinct virtue, and perhaps that is why Matthew Arnold complained that Chaucer lacked 'high seriousness'. In Arnold's famous evaluation we see the same type of criticism that Petrarch levels against the Ovid of exile. If Ovid had not had a lascivious spirit, says Petrarch, he would have earned a 'greater reputation among serious men'. Ovid's suffering for his banishment to the Black Sea is well known, but what price did Chaucer pay for his own lack of high seriousness and his addiction to amatory literature?

> …Caesar Augustus regarded the *Ars Amatoria* as antithetical to Roman moral laws because it encouraged adultery. …Thomas Gascoigne, fifteenth-century chancellor of Oxford University, under the topic '*Poenitentia*' in his *Dictionarium theologicum,* testifies to Chaucer's repentance. He says the poet regretted having written of base loves and was upset that he could not destroy his works. And Chaucer, at the point of death, cried out: 'Ah me, ah me, I cannot now revoke or destroy those base writings of mine about the foul and vile love of men for women, for already these words have passed from man to man.' (*Vae mihi, vae mihi quia revocare nec destruere iam potero illa quae male scripsi de malo et turpimmimo amore hominum ad mulieres sed iam de homini in hominem continuabuntur*). We recall that Venus's words to Chaucer in Gower's *Confessio Amantis* also depict Chaucer as a love poet who must come to reckoning and confession…Chaucer wrote ribald poetry, and now he, and perhaps posterity, will suffer the consequences.

> Chaucer, or at least the voice he creates to deliver *Parson's Tale* and the *Retraction,* offers his reader the stark image of a love poet confronting his work and his own death… . Before Chaucer commits his final act for his own soul's

nourishment, this prose tract tells how his readers can escape 'exile' from the heavenly kingdom and find salvation, the true goal of pilgrimage. *The Parson's Tale* offers a new kind of 'art', an art of Penance.

From F N Robinson, *Introduction to the Complete Works of Geoffrey Chaucer:*

> Chaucer's *Retracciouns. The Parson's Tale* is followed by the much discussed *Retracciouns*, or Retractations, of the author. In them Chaucer revokes all his 'translations and enditynges of worldly vanitees,' mentioning by name not only those Canterbury tales 'that sownen into synne' but also some works which seem quite inoffensive... . To Chaucer, in the mood in which he wrote the *Retracciouns*, nothing seemed worthy except works on philosophy and religion, and he specifically excepts from his condemnation only the translation of Boethius 'and other bookes of legends of seintes, and omelies, and moralitee, and devocion'...

> Literary history affords many examples, from St Augustine down to modern times, of similar changes of heart. In Chaucer's own century Boccaccio, who is so much like him in temperament, is reported, while still in middle life, to have undergone a religious experience which led him to renounce his frivolous and licentious writings in the vernacular and devote himself to learned treatises in Latin.

Posterity was kind to Chaucer. He was the first writer to be buried in the renowned poets' corner of Westminster Abbey, indisputably one of the three great poets, along with Shakespeare and Milton, of our cultural heritage.

Yet even here there is a further curiosity, if not a mystery. It seems he was never buried here as a poet, even less as someone closely connected to the Plantagenet family – although this might have had something to do with it – but simply because, at the end of his life, he lived right next to the Abbey, in Westminster Close, and had taken out a lease on a house there. The Abbey was therefore his local church. When John Dryden died, in May 1700, exactly three hundred years after Chaucer, the Abbey authorities decided he took up too much room and halved his grave to put Dryden in beside him. Samuel Pepys noted in a letter that Dryden was buried in Chaucer's grave. But Dryden had never thought much of Chaucer, considering his verse 'rude' (i.e. crude) and for some reason 'Scotch', and was indignant that it was unmetrical (he had no idea how to pronounce it).

What the prim and decent classicist poet would have done had he found out this charge against Chaucer, no one can say. Turned over in their shared grave? Or at least the other way? Perhaps both poets are even now locked in a heated discussion on the nature of...well, what, exactly? As Andrew Marvell wrote:

The grave's a fine and private place,
But none I think do there embrace.

It has often been said that the virtue of writing a historical novel is its vice, which is the flat-footed affirmation of possibility as fact. All the dates in this book are as accurate as I have been able to determine, while its cast of characters could have been, or were as far as I have been able to check, in the places and at the times I mention. These have been mainly sourced from the Oxford Histories of the Fourteenth and Fifteenth Centuries, from Nigel Saul's *Richard II,* and from the works listed below. As sources to a lesser or greater degree I acknowledge my debt with gratitude chiefly to the following:

Richard II	William Shakespeare
Chaucer	Emile Legouis (London, 1934)
The Allegory of Love	C S Lewis (London, 1936)
Geoffrey Chaucer of England	Marchette Chute (London, 1946)
John of Gaunt	Sydney Armitage-Smith (London, 1950)
The Poetical Works of Chaucer	Edited by F N Robinson (Oxford, 1952)
Passion and Society	Denis de Rougement (London, 1952)
The Age of Chaucer	Edited by Boris Ford (London, 1954)

Katherine	Anya Seton (London, 1954)
The Sicilian Vespers	Stephen Runciman (London, 1961)
The Black Death: A Chronicle of the Plague	
	Compiled by Johanes Miles (London, 1961)
The Personality of Chaucer	Edward Wagenknecht (Oklahoma, 1968)
The Black Death	Philip Ziegler (London, 1971)
The Family, Sex and Marriage in England 1500-1800	
	L Stone (London, 1977)
The Image of the Poet	David Piper (Oxford, 1982)
The Erotic Poems	Ovid (trs. Peter Green) (London, 1982)
The English Family 1450-1700	
	R Houlbrooke (London, 1984)
Marriage and Love in England: Modes of Reproduction, 1300-1840	
	A McFarlane (London, 1986)
A Theatre of Envy	René Girard (New York, 1991)
Richard II	Nigel Saul (New Haven, 1997)

I thank Samantha Hill for word processing various drafts, and Christopher Sinclair-Stevens, John Tydeman, Richard Cohen and Christina Mason for valuable advice, criticism and support.

My thanks also to Emilie O'Connor, Fred O'Connor, Richard Unthank (map and tables) and Jane Tatam.

London, October 2006